BLOSSOM LIKE THE ROSE

BLOSSOM LIKE
THE ROSE

by
NORAH LOFTS

HODDER AND STOUGHTON
LONDON SYDNEY AUCKLAND TORONTO

4 023663

ORMSKIRK

254150624

01762186

CONTENTS

AUTHOR'S NOTE

Because I have been accused of having an over-inventive mind I should like to say that Eli's feat of endurance on page 272 has been equalled in real life.

BOOK ONE

INITIATION

They hanged Shad Woodey on a September day, just when the year was on the turn. It was cold when I let myself out of the house and as I went across the fields the path ahead of me and behind was shrouded with blue mist. Underfoot the grass was as wet as if it had been raining; you could have traced my footsteps all the way from the Manor to the Ten Acre. But soon after that the sun rose redly over the massed trees and by the time that I reached Marshalsea the mist was shredding away like a torn veil and my hands and face, clammy from passage through it, were warmed by the autumn sun. The heavy headed knap-weeds and the blackberry bushes by the side of the path held the dampness longer and the drops sparkled in the light.

I had been walking swiftly, but as I neared the end of the field path and came near the public road I slackened pace and had time to note the shining of the new-ploughed stubble, the fresh bright green that had come upon the pastures with September's rain after the August drought, and the way the trees, particularly the elms, were already turning yellow at the edges. Far, far too lovely a day to die on, even if one were old and past all pleasure—and Shad wasn't that.

When I reached the end of the last field and stepped on to the rutted lane I was amazed. Except at Fair time I had never seen so many people. And all their faces were set towards Marshalsea and they moved and spoke with a kind of hidden excitement. Many were on horseback, but many more were stumbling along on foot, women holding their skirts on either side, men stepping out freely, and many children running at heel like young calves and colts. No one noticed me.

The lane opened out on to the green by the Church

corner and when we had rounded that we could see the gibbet rearing up gauntly against the pale clear sky. It had stood there for years: Bob Finch the footpad had swung from it, and so had Dave Parsons who had killed his master, not without provocation, they said. But despite this the gibbet had always been to me part of the scenery of the green and until Shad hung from it I had given it no more thought than I gave the Church, the Parsonage or the sign of the inn. Since that day, however, I have never willingly looked upon a gibbet; coming upon one inadvertently I have turned away my eyes; and sometimes a dead tree or the cross rafter of a tall barn will remind me and turn me sick to this day.

The Crier was out—we had heard him while we were still out of sight in the lane, but now we could both see and hear him and it was plain that he was enjoying himself. To cry a crime and a hanging was delightful to him after weeks and months with nothing more exciting than a stray horse in the pound to holler about. Not that anyone marked him much for what Shad had done and what he was to suffer had been familiar matters for a long time. But over that crowd of quietly excited people the loud deep voice sounded, rolling the unfamiliar 'Whereases' and 'aforesaids' with which the plain story had been decked for the occasion.

For it was a plain story. Shad Woodey was being hanged on this bright morning because he had, with his black-smith's hammer, struck and killed the Conventicle man who was arresting old Parson Jarvis for holding a service among his own people, not in his own church, for that was closed to him, but in Hunter's Wood. A few of the little congregation, scenting the Conventicle spy, had tried to hide the old man in the forge. The King's men (we called them King's men, or Conventicle men, or simply Claren-dons indifferently) had followed and were dragging the old man out forcibly when Shad entered the forge. He picked up his hammer and struck. That was all. And the irony of it all was that Shad was a good churchman who had never run after Parson Jarvis, but had accepted the new clergy-man as he accepted most things except injustice, with a shrug and a smile of cynical tolerance. But that availed him little. He had opposed a Clarendon in the performance of his duty, and he had committed murder. His crime was always given like that. Even today, upon the Crier's tongue the opposition was mentioned first as though that were the prior charge, as indeed we knew it was. To strike a man in anger and by accident to kill him is a thing that many a person has not paid for with his life.

There were soldiers at the foot of the gibbet, standing shoulder to shoulder, keeping back the people from the space where the cart would stand. I was in about the middle of the crowd on the left-hand side with my back to the Church. By this time the sun was warm. Women loosened the necks of their bodices with furtive, ineffectual fingers; men fidgeted and wiped their faces on the backs of their hands. An odour of crushed, warm, excited humanity rose upon the air. Just by my shoulder a big burly farmer said audibly, 'Well, 'tis a shame say I. Whatever he did he wuz the best smith for ten mile around. Who'll shoe that devil of a mare now?'

'Hush, somebody'll hear you, Alfred,' said a frightened voice. Turning, I saw a woman pluck at his sleeve, and seeing me turn she drove her elbow into his ribs and looked from his face to mine, significantly. She needn't have bothered: but in those days it was never safe to express an opinion within the hearing of a third person. When I looked again the farmer and his wife had gone, hidden in the crowd, hiding from me. But the old man's words were answered by another man who said with a ponderous, off-hand kind of pensiveness, 'Need a new plough shoe too, I do.' Shad would be missed—but not as I should miss him.

Suddenly over the waiting crowd something ran. I say 'something' because there is no word for it that I know. It was neither murmur nor movement. I could feel my part of it, a kind of shudder of the mind and I have no doubt that a similar shudder had run through every mind in that assembly, though in some the shudder of horror was replaced by one of excitement. The cart was coming!

For the first time I wondered why I had come. Not from curiosity, that was certain, for I had not attended the hangings of Dave Parsons or Bob Finch. And I hadn't come from love of Shad; one would scarcely walk five miles to see the object of one's affection dangling from a rope's end! I believe that at the back of my immature mind there was the ghost of a hope that a miracle might happen. It seemed impossible that Shad, so kind, so merry, so truly good a man should be hustled out of life like a felon. But it was the impossible, not the miracle, that I saw.

The cart came along slowly. Shad was in his best russet breeches and a white shirt with the collar open and laid back from his thick muscular neck. His hands were tied loosely behind his back. The hangman and a man whom I didn't know rode in the cart which had a rough piece of board laid from side to side across its top, making a kind of seat. The man who led the horse halted it so that the body of the cart was just beneath the arm of the gibbet. The soldiers fixed themselves more firmly shoulder to shoulder. The unknown man spoke to Shad who smiled at him. I could see the flash of his teeth, white in the dark of his beard. And then suddenly, as the moment of climax came a woman in the front of the crowd began to scream, the long shrilling screams of hysteria. I tried to see her. Was she somebody to whom Shad was dear? I could think of none such. He had neither mother, sister nor wife. Or was it just some overwrought woman who should have stayed at home? She caused some slight confusion, around her the crowd stirred and shifted, but I could not see her. By the time she was quieted the formalities, such as they were, were over. The strange man had got down from the cart, Shad and the hangman were standing on the board across its top, the rope was around Shad's neck and the other end was knotted in the groove worn by others of its kind. I could see, now that Shad was high on the board, that his ankles were tied together too. The hangman stepped down, the cart moved forward and Shad's weight pulled the short rope taut. A long 'Aaahh' went up.

I tried to take away my eyes, to look at the heads of the crowd, at the sky, at the trees beyond the green, but I could not move my gaze. I saw the heavy body spin quite quickly in one direction, pause, and begin to spin more slowly the other way as the rope twisted. The dark beard covered cheek and chin, but I watched with horror as the rest of his face, nose and forehead, turned dark too. The mouth

14

opened and the tongue lolled and the heavy body jerked and leaped in spasms. He wasn't dead. Oh God, you might have let him die.

I knew that my fingers were in my mouth, but I did not know that I was making noises like a frightened pup, or that I was elbowing my way to the front of the crowd. I found myself just behind the soldiers without having been conscious of any of the people I had passed. My eyes had never left the face of the man who was strangling by inches. And now that I was so near him I could feel the full impact of the horror that cruelty and violence pour out as though it were a tangible thing. I felt it first that day. I have felt it many times since. A cornered desperate rat pours out enough of it to make *me* feel its terror and desperation. And now it was as though *I* were strangling. A bloody mist obscured my sight, shutting out everything except that awful face, those jumping limbs. My heart pounded and I gasped for breath. It went through my mind that I was dying, and hard on that thought came a flash of conviction, so sure, so clear that in the relief of it I filled my labouring lungs with air and let my bitten fingers fall to my sides. I had come to the hanging for one reason. The miracle had not happened. God had neither saved Shad nor vouchsafed him an easy passing. I must be God's deputy. I crouched down. My head and shoulders, like the point of a human arrow parted the two soldiers immediately in front of me. I stood in the open space with Shad's fettered feet swinging above my head. I leapt, caught those feet in my hands and swung on them. I felt the downward 'give' as his neck broke.

One of the Justices, Sir Neville Stokes, roared out,

'Bring that boy here,' and the sergeant of the soldiers took me by the shoulder and hustled me across the space. I saw a red angry face glaring down at me, but I was not much frightened. The shattering emotions of the last fifteen minutes had left my mind numb, immune for the moment to anything but sorrow.

'What the devil do you mean by interfering with the course of justice, you young rapscallion?' he asked furiously. 'Speak up, or have you lost your tongue? What do you mean by it, eh?'

15

He had obviously been enjoying the spectacle of the King's Justice, which he represented, taking its horrid course, and to a man of that sort what explanation could I make? Tell him that I had only given Shad the *coup de grace* that I would have given a snared rabbit? Tell him that I had ended it in order to end my own pain? He would not understand. I said nothing. I suppose he read defiance in my silence, for when he spoke again his voice was softer but incisive with spite.

'A day or two in the Bridewell with bread and water would do him no harm. It might even teach him that interfering little busybodies are not to be allowed to thrust aside his Majesty's soldiers in order to interrupt the process of law. Take him away and lock him up.'

I steadied myself and managed to raise my head and look him in the face: and as I did so another man gave a start of surprise, leaned forward from his horse and said,

'Excuse me a moment, Sir Neville. What's your name, lad?'

'Philip Ollenshaw,' I said.

'I thought so,' said the man who had asked my name.

'Well, I'll be damned,' said Sir Neville. He raked over me with his prominent angry stare, from head to foot and back again. 'So that's poor Ollenshaw's skeleton, is it? All right, sergeant, let him go.'

I turned and limped away, holding myself stiffly. Behind me I heard them laughing.

It was, I reflected bitterly, the first time in twelve years that being my father's son had ever brought me any good.

I suppose that that sentence needs some explanation, and though I do not wish this chronicle to linger over my youth, or indeed over my own affairs at all, but rather to deal with the wider matters in which I played but a small part, some mention is needed of my home and childhood, since only so can I explain what I am, and why.

My father was Sir John Ollenshaw, and if the name means little now to the casual ear that is only another proof of Time's destructiveness. He was well known once. King Charles the Martyr is reputed to have said to him after the battle of Naseby, 'Had I but three more like you the day would have been mine.' I could believe it, for my father was the stuff of which leaders are made, single-minded, ruthless, brave; and as far as I could discover the Ollenshaws have always shown those characteristics; which makes it the more a matter for wonder that I should be born of their line.

But courage and ruthlessness, even single-mindedness are unavailing in the face of changing history, and my father, stripped of his lands, went into exile with his young king. In France he was fortunate, for his fame as a swordsman and a soldier had gone before him and while Charles Stuart came near to starvation and knew the bitterness of snubs and slights and hope deferred, John Ollenshaw held high and honourable office in the French army.

Two years before the Restoration he was well enough established to take himself a wife, no penniless exile either, but the daughter of a Suffolk squire who, although Royalist in sympathies had never been active enough to endanger his fortunes. She sailed for France, my mother, and married him in Paris, and I have often regarded with the backward-looking eye of imagination, those two years of her married life.

She was young and pretty, I understand, but she was country-bred, gauche and ill-trained in the mannerisms and subtleties of the society in which my father moved. She was appalled, I imagine, to discover that his marriage was no more than a momentary interruption of his *affaire* with his French mistress—the woman whom I always knew as Madame Louise. Unwilling, or unable to compete for the favours of her own husband she retired into the country and there waited, with who knows what bitterness and disillusion for my birth. It may have been mere carelessness, or ignorance, or an attempt to forget her rival that made her, in a state in which women lie on couches, surrounded by female friends and the odour of burnt feathers, take an unknown fence upon an untried horse. The horse came home alone, and when search was belatedly made, she was dead and I was lying beside her in the ditch, with the old French woman who had acted as midwife stripping off her petticoat to wrap me in. I had arrived in the world a good two months before my time and that was supposed to account for my youthful delicacy.

The mishap gave my father no grudge against Fate. He had his son and his wife's dowry, and very soon there was a prospect of regaining his lands as well. For England tired of Puritan rule, and the young king, lean and brown and shrewd returned to England determined to go on his travels no more, and not unmindful of those who had stood by him and by his father. Marshalsea Manor, with many acres added returned to my father's possession, and in addition he had a pension of five hundred pounds a year and the certainty of the King's ear at any time.

Madame Louise was soon installed at Marshalsea, mistress of the house as well as of the master. She was a thin blade of a woman who would have been a perfect mate for him had he met her earlier, or on a more equal footing. But by the time of their meeting she must have been hard on forty, past child-bearing age; and for all her airs and graces she was of humble stock—the kind from which the Ollenshaw men took their playthings, not their wives. When I knew her and was old enough to look at her appraisingly she had still a hard bright beauty, a savage temper and an overwhelming passion for my father which nothing could shake.

If I had been a normal boy my father would have been contented enough, and probably very happy in the looseness of his domestic ties. But alas, I, his only child and in any case his first-born, was maimed from the day of my birth. At first the damage was not obvious and I believe that my first tottering attempts at walking were ordinary enough. But by the time I was four or five the disparity between my legs had grown with me so that the left one lacked some three inches of the length of the right. Also it was small in girth and weak of muscle.

A physician from Colchester—surely more versed in mechanics than in medicine—advised the attachment of a weight to the faulty limb. This was calculated to 'draw it down' and for six months or more I limped round like a hobbled horse with first three, then four and finally six pounds of lead tied around my ankle. It was dreadfully difficult for me to walk at all, and the weight increased the difficulty, but my father was always willing to neglect his estate, sacrifice his shooting, riding or gambling in order to walk with me and exhort me to perseverance. Even in bed I knew no respite, for the weighted leg was supposed to hang over the bed's edge so that the 'drawing down' might go on while I slept. Small wonder that I was, what my father often called me in impatience, 'a miserable brat'. I was; thoroughly miserable, weary, fettered and aware with increasing force of awful inferiority.

Just at that time there began to be talk of 'circulation' of the blood, and one of my father's London friends advised him to take me to Doctor Forster who was performing wonderful cures in fashionable circles by nostrums calculated to increase or retard the blood's motion. So to London we went, I on my father's pillion, a groom following with baggage, presents for father's friends and an empty valise that was to return filled with fripperies for Madame Louise. We lodged at the *True Troubadour* in the Strand and there Doctor Forster visited us and kept me in bed with a ligature upon my right leg to retard circulation and bags of hot sand upon my left to encourage it. He succeeded marvellously well in the first design, my good right leg was soon cold and numb, but wherever the baffled blood flowed it did not reach the starveling left of me. That remained as it was, shrunken and short, though burning as though in Hell before its time. Meanwhile I was forced to swallow bitter and nauseating draughts, and also—curious tempering of trial—a quart of mulled ale a day. Every third day my leg was measured. Every evening the ligature was removed from my right leg and I endured agonies as feeling crept back into it. At times I wept and protested and then my father stormed, at me, at the stupidity of doctors and at the folly of my mother. Altogether it was a trying time for him and I was not surprised when, one evening as Doctor Forster tightened the string on my leg and I protested, father's patience gave way.

'I've had sufficient of this foolishness,' he shouted. 'Get out and take your —— nonsense with you.' Doctor Forster, a man of age and dignity, accustomed to respect, turned upon father and described his manners, his ignorance and, alas, his offspring in terms more concise than polite.

'You breed a pingling little weakling and come to me and ask a miracle,' he concluded, 'and because I cannot mend what you marred you insult my profession. Take your poor crooked crutcher and heal him yourself if you find you cannot breed a better.'

He snatched up his bandage, his sand bags and his potions and swept out of the room, his robe billowing behind him.

'Get up,' said my father, 'we're going home.'

So we made the first stage of our journey through the soft summer twilight and I thought of footpads and robbers on the road. Though God pity any whom we had met, for my father rode with a brow of thunder and would have welcomed a butt for his wrath. The meek groom and the willing horses and his crestfallen child offered none. Safely behind his back I cried quietly to myself, for I had set out with high hopes of returning sound, able to run and jump like other boys, eager to learn to ride and fence and shoot. And I was going back, crippled as I had come, with an added sorrow, that my protests in the face of pain had precipitated the return. A miserable brat indeed.

From that time my father ignored me. Whether I sat or stood, wept or smiled, was well or sick, became no more to him than doings of the lowest churl on his estate. The fact that I admired him with a frenzy near to worship, that I was teachable and eager to please meant nothing to him. I could almost count upon my fingers the times when he spoke to me, though I sometimes, lingering on the stairs or by a half-open door, heard him curse to other people the fact that he had sired a cripple and a poltroon. Like many men of war he became savage and moody as he grew older and Madame Louise, grown old for love's dalliance, lost power over him. When I was ten he went to London alone and was away for a long time. I know that the next incident concerns neither me nor my story, but it does show, past all mistaking, the kind of man my father was.

He came back, after a two months absence with a young girl in a grey cloak on the pillion behind him. Madame Louise and I were together on the terrace in front of the house. We had come to terms in our loneliness and she had been teaching me a few French words. She went to the top of the steps that led to the drive and I stayed where I was in a strategic but not obvious position. Father lifted down the young woman, the groom led away the horses, and holding her high, like a doll, father mounted the steps, crossed the threshold and set her down just inside the door. Madame Louise followed, demanding, 'Qui est cela?'

'My wife, Lady Ollenshaw,' said father. 'She's a leather-merchant's daughter and ignorant as a hind. You can take her in hand and do her hair and tell her what to wear.'

Madame Louise let out a few shrieks that reminded me of a cat I once heard screaming from a trap, turned on father in a fury and ripped her nails—they were long and pointed—down his cheek. Father laughed and took both her hands in his and slapped her hard with the free one. He slapped her where one slaps children and he slapped her until she stopped yelling and began to cry. Then he set her free.

'That's better,' he said. 'Now off you go and arrange to live in peace, otherwise one of you will have to go.'

He didn't say which. The little new bride had watched the scene with big startled eyes. As Madame Louise stumbled towards her with the tears streaming down her thin face the little thing plucked a handkerchief from her cuff and held it out towards her. Madame Louise took it and they went upstairs together. I had been holding my breath and now I let it out in a gusty sigh. Father turned and being in a good mood, addressed me. This is what he said,

'That's the way to deal with women, my boy. But there, what's the use of such a lesson to you?' His face darkened as he turned away.

The two women evidently did arrange 'to live in peace'. More, they became firm friends. I once heard father tell Agnes, my stepmother, that Louise had been a perfect mistress for twenty years and more and that she couldn't do better than model herself on her. But Agnes did do better. She presented father with three sons in as many years and they were all big and sturdy, beautiful children of whom any man would have been proud. With them and for them father did all the things he would have done for me had my legs been well matched. I suffered agonies of jealousy over Charles, the eldest of them, but by the time that he was a year old I had tapped a source of mighty consolation.

Which brings me back to Shad. Shad Woodey who was destined to hang on the gibbet at Marshalsea.

I was getting along towards my eleventh birthday, I suppose, and my already dreary life had become even more darkened by Charles' arrival. Nobody in the house seemed to have a thought that was not connected with the baby. I was hopelessly jealous. Even Madame Louise had no time for me and I spent longer and longer among the servants and the men in the yard. I was growing fast and since my lame leg failed to keep pace with the rest of me I was horribly crooked, even my head had a list to the left. I was supremely ignorant, unable to read or write, and frequently far from clean. An unprepossessing child indeed.

The morning came that was to change my life. It was summer. I remember how the hawthorn bushes that studded the park were all draped in white blossom and the pink ragged robins made beauty in the ditches. I had been in the yard, aimlessly wasting another hour of another day when Sam the groom came out of the stable leading two horses.

'Where're you going?' I asked.

'Down to the smithy,' he said, cuffing back the sniffing muzzle that nosed his shoulder.

'Can I come?' I asked suddenly.

'Aye,' he said, and set his foot on the mounting block.

'Lift me up, then,' I said sharply.

'Holy saints, I forgot.' He lifted me easily and I settled myself on the broad brown back.

We jogged along in single file by the field path, came out into the lane, rounded the church, crossed the green and pulled up at the smithy. Shad came to the door, a brown man, lean but muscular, like a good hound, in a sleeveless blue jerkin and with sweat on his forehead where his curly hair dangled.

'Morning, Sam, wholly hot,' he said and then he saw me. 'Your boy?'

"Smaster Philip,' said Sam shortly, and I realised with a pang that the groom resented the implication that he could have sired me. But Shad put one enormous hand up to the curls on his forehead and said, 'Good morning, sir,' and I almost fainted from surprise. Nobody ever called me 'sir'.

My father's contempt of me was so well known at the Manor and throughout our own village that scorn was my portion from all but the kindly-hearted in whom it was leavened by pity. Inspired, I now slipped to the ground unaided and went inside the smithy. Sam led the horses in after me and tied their halters to the rings in the wall. Then he eyed me uncertainly, fidgeted for a minute or two, and muttering something about another errand, set off across the green. I knew well what the errand was—a visit to the ale-house, and he needn't have waited a second for fear of me. I was well content to be alone with Shad. I watched him take the bar of iron, heat it, shape it with pincers and hammer, cool it a little and then apply it, still sizzling hot to the hoof that he lifted to his knee.

'Does it hurt?' I asked.

'No more than this,' he said, rubbing the end of one of my locks of hair between his fingers. 'Hoof is like hair.'

When he reached for the bellows I said, 'I can work them,' and limping forward I did so, resting my short leg on a pile of scrap to give me a level standing. I saw Shad eye me carefully. Finally, after a few casual remarks he said, 'Has ought ever been done to that leg of yours?'

I told him all about the weight that I had worn, and the visit to the London doctor. By that time the shoeing was finished and Shad after wiping his hands on his apron reached up to a shelf and took down a mug and some bread and cheese on a wooden platter.

'Care for a bite?' he asked. And I, who was at least as well fed as any boy could wish to be, nodded because I wanted to share something with him and to prolong the first real conversation that I had ever had with anybody.

'You can have first draw,' he said, pushing the mug along the bench towards me. To me the strong brown ale was like the wine of sacrament and I drank deeply. It was more potent than the homebrew served in the kitchen quarters at the Manor and I suppose that it loosened my tongue. Or it may have been the unusual sympathy. Anyhow I found myself telling him all about my bitterness and jealousy, about the way my father treated me and the emptiness of my life. Shad waited until I had finished and then he brushed the crumbs from his beard and drew it several times between

23

his fingers, thoughtfully. At last he said, 'Walk over to the door yonder.' I rose and crossed the floor.

'Ummm,' he murmured, not moving his lips. 'A short leg is a short leg and I see no cure for that. But I don't see why the whole of you should grow crooked because of it. Give me your shoe.'

I took off the rough leather shoe with the tarnished brass buckle and put it into his hand. The toe of it was worn bare where it touched the ground, the heel was as good as when it came from the cobbler. He turned it about in his big hands. Then he took another piece of iron, heated it, hammered it thin and turned up each end so that it was like the rocker of a cradle. In either end he pierced a hole and then dropped it into the water. Just then Sam returned.

'All ready,' Shad said. Sam unknotted the halters, led out the horses and then turned back, looking over his shoulder at me.

'Come on,' he said.

'I'm staying here.'

'How're you going to git home, then. I can't come back for you.'

'I'll get home,' I said.

'Aw right.' He hoisted himself upon one of the horses and clattered away. Shad fished out the piece of iron, laid one end to the toe of my shoe and one to the heel and hammered them home. He wriggled a finger inside the shoe, feeling for the nail points, reached for his file and levelled them off.

'Try that,' he said. 'To my mind it should be better.'

I buckled the shoe firmly and stood up. At first I couldn't manage at all because I still tried to walk in the old way, on the toe. But after a few assays I caught the knack and it was better, miraculously better. I went rocking round the smithy almost crazy with joy. The lurch and twist with which I had walked in the past and which had pulled my body awry was no longer necessary and when I stood still I could stand level, one foot on the sole of my shoe, the other on my sturdy iron.

'Oh, thank you, thank you,' I cried. 'It's the most wonderful thing that ever happened to me. Oh, it's wonderful. I do thank you. And my father will pay you. He gave a lot of

24

money to the Colchester man and to Doctor Forster, I know he did. And they didn't do anything. He'll pay you for this.'

Shad had been watching me with a bright pleased look, but a scowl came over his face when I mentioned my father.

'I don't want his money,' he said, quite fiercely. 'Anybody but the drunken whoremonger that he is could have thought of something like that years ago.'

'You don't like him?' I asked quickly.

'I shouldn't have said that,' Shad muttered.

'Oh, I don't like him either. But he'll be pleased about this.'

'Maybe,' said Shad.

I struggled home, two miles of lane between the hawthorn hedges, three over the fields along the edges of the baulks, further than I had ever walked in my life. The sweat poured off me. But I walked proudly, holding myself straightly, trying to undo in a single day the damage wrought in years.

I cannot, even now, remember with equanimity my arrival home. My father burst into a roar of laughter when he saw me. I understand now. I realise how deep a disappointment I must have been to him, proud as he was of his own strength and prowess and of that of those before him, and I ought, I suppose, through understanding to forgive him. But I don't. He stood there with his own great legs planted wide like towers and said, 'So it was a smith's job after all!' And he laughed.

Any love I had ever borne him had withered long since in the icy blast of his scorn, but I had, until that day a kind of sneaking admiration for the man who was all that I should have liked to be and could never hope to become. Now, as he stood there, his red face creased in laughter the last shred of admiration died away, leaving only hatred. I had learned that morning that it was not inevitable that the big and lusty should despise the small and maimed. Shad Woodey was as big and well-muscled as my father; I was sure, in my boy's heart, that he was as brave; given the opportunity he would, I guessed, have been as good a swordsman. Yet Shad

had been moved to help me, not to laugh. Drunken whore-monger, I thought, even the village smith knows you for what you are! A great wave of comfort rushed across my bitter little soul as I thought that. My scorn was like a tonic. No longer even did I think it wonderful of him to have compelled Madame Louise and Agnes to accept one another. Any bull in any field can do as much, I reflected.

From that day the Manor saw me little. Almost every morning I went rocking off over the field path to spend the day in the smithy where Shad did much to restore my self-respect by letting me be useful. 'Your arms are all right,' he would say, and I would swing the heavy hammers and lift logs for the fire, hoping that exercise would one day be rewarded by shoulders like Shad's. They were never so good, but they did develop. And so did I.

It was Shad who taught me to read. He was quite horrified to find that I was as ignorant as any boy in the village. We were sitting outside eating our noonings with our backs to the sun warmed wall of the forge and I re-member how Shad stopped in his eating and took up a twig and drew the letters of the alphabet in the dust of the path. He named them over, slowly, twice, and made me repeat them. Then he smoothed them out and scratched them again, odd and disconnected this time. I found—and I was quite as surprised as he was—that I could remember them perfectly. 'Ah, you're quick,' he said, drawing his hand over the dust. 'I dunno how long it was before I knew them off like so.' He filled his mouth and wrote 'Shadrach Woodey, Smith' in big sloping letters. 'See, that's my name and trade. What's yours?'

'Philip John Alexander Ollenshaw.'

Shad wrote it and added 'Gentleman'.

'What's that?' I asked, counting five words where I had looked for four. He told me. I dragged my ironed foot over it. 'Put smith for me too,' I told him. 'I'd rather be like you than like my father.'

'You are what you're born,' said Shad with complete conviction. 'And one day you'll be Sir Philip and own all this.' He waved his hand about him.

'No,' I said. Charles will do that. Father will see to it.'

'He can't help himself. You're the eldest son.'

'Then I shall have you to live at the Manor and we'll have baron of beef and red wine every day for dinner and figs and raisins and oranges and syllabub. And I hope,' I said in a rising voice, 'that all the servants are still alive. I'll show them something. They'll hustle for me then.'

'Can you spell out your name yet?' asked Shad mildly. I dropped my eyes to the scrawled dust for a moment then turned towards Shad and closed them. 'P-h-i-l-i-p J-o-h-n A-l-e-x-a-n-d-e-r O-l-l-e-n-s-h-a-w s-m-i-t-h.' I opened my eyes and was delighted to see an expression of amazed admiration on Shad's face.

'Learning comes easy to you, same as smith's work to me, I reckon. I'm not so sure I could tell the letters over with my eyes shut. Even when I read I kind of make the shapes with my hand all the time. Very slow I am at reading. But it seems to me that you should be a good scholar and ... and that might make up to you for ... for a lot of things.'

'Maybe it might,' I said. 'Show me how to read, Shad, will you?'

'You'll soon be teaching me by the looks of it.'

And that was true. My mind, empty so long and chained as it were to my lameness, seized eagerly upon something that was on a plane not bounded by infirmity or hatred or neglect. Long before the winter set in I could read far more fluently than Shad. I did not have to form the letters as I sounded them. I was soon reading avidly. There were plenty of books at home, mouldering in their leather covers in a damp room that no one ever entered. And when the wet windy weather came and the journey to Marshalsea could not be made every day I used to curl myself on the wide window seat with the heavy curtain wrapped round me against the cold and slip through doors that opened to the key of printed words and which led to countries, scenes and peoples of which I had never even dreamed.

Do you wonder that I loved Shad Woodey, the worker in iron who had freed both my body and my mind?

It was after I was able to take the Bible out of his large hands and read to him with ease and swiftness the story of the psalm that he was laboriously spelling out, that Shad stopped treating me as a child and very soon I was allowed to stay in the forge after nightfall, whereas before I had always been started off home as soon as the sun began to sink. And in Shad's forge after sunset I met men of the kind I was to know so very well, and heard for the first time the discussions of the problems that were to mould and alter all our lives.

We were backward at Marshalsea, and it had never struck me that it was old-fashioned and wasteful for most of the farmlands to be divided into portions with time-honoured boundaries and for men to take their chance in the yearly draw, accept their luck and till their lot. True, my father's lands lay all about the Manor, and there were four or five other little farms which were self-contained and the permanent property of the men who tilled them. There had been Hunts at Hunt's Farm and Chisnells at the Ten Acre since time immemorial. But I had never heard the word 'enclosure' until I heard it spoken as men might speak of Utopia or Paradise, after sunset in Shad's forge.

Nor had I given much thought to religion. That it was in some obscure way connected with politics I knew. That was why my father, to whom the name of God was merely an expletive, presented himself with unfailing regularity at his pew in the church every Sunday morning. His attend-ance there had as little religious meaning as his order to Madame Louise that her crucifix and candles, her rosary and her figure of the Virgin were never to be seen outside her own room. I went to church very seldom myself for that would have involved a public appearance of the Squire with his mis-begotten son. So it was with much surprise that I learned how large a part in some men's lives God, and the form that His worship should take, played.

Both over enclosures and religion Eli Makers, that quiet man, waxed voluble and I have sat for hours on end in some dim corner of the forge, listening to his views. He was not an old man, yet in a community where age was re-spected for itself alone, he was listened to and regarded. Even now, at the far end of the long road upon which he, more than any other, set our feet, I cannot deny that there was power in him and force and a certain integrity. Physic-ally he was a fine man, tall and upright with wide square shoulders and arms knotted with muscles. He was proud of his strength and at this time, when he was young, he was not above seizing an opportunity to display it. It was said in the village that he could carry a sack of grain up the granary steps by his teeth. I never saw him, or any man do it, but I did see him throw a steer by gripping its horns. That was at Marshalsea. Later on I saw him endure such things as would lead one to believe that either God or the devil must have been in him in no small measure. He had a stern, beautiful face, a mass of golden hair and a great yellow beard. When I was older and had read more I used to look at him and remember that Marshalsea had known the terror of the Norsemen and wonder whether they, who took away so much that was removable, hadn't left behind a permanent thing—a strain of men like Makers.

His first words to me were not kindly. I remember the evening well. It was summer, half an hour or so after sunset and the door at the back of the forge was open so that the scent of lilac from the great laden bushes in Shad's yard came in and mingled oddly with the odours of the smithy, scorched horse-hoof and hot iron plunged in water. Earlier in the evening I had enlivened Shad's labours as he fixed an iron rim round a wagon wheel by telling him the story of 'Othello' which I had read by rushlight far into the night before. When the story was finished and the hot iron was drawing in around the wood of the wheel I had gone into the garden and eaten far too many little green unripe gooseberries, fit only for pies and hardly that. When I came back I could hear voices in the forge and because I was so used to having conversations at home stop when I entered a room I waited, just outside in the yard, and listened. I was at that time an inveterate listener at doors and on stairs. I heard a strong voice say bitterly,

'Last year it was mine and may I be hanged if there were over a dozen weeds on it all told. This year it's all ablow with them. Wafting over on to mine, too, with every breeze that blows. It takes the heart out of a man.'

Shad was farthest from the door and all I caught of his speech was '. . . speak to him?'

'Speak to him! I spoke when the first thistle reared its ugly head. "You ill-judge me, Eli," he said, "I do my best. We can't all be hoeing the road you do. Haven't all got your

29

power," he says.'

'. . . word of truth there . . .' came Shad's voice.

'He has little power for labour, but he's powerful enough when it's a matter of rolling Seeley's Peg in the hedge. Aye, and I see little weakness about him when it comes to lifting a quart pot. But the sight of a hoe is enough to start the sweating sickness in him.'

'The vestrymen could order him to weed,' said Shad.

'So they could,' said Eli satirically. 'But would they? He's in good odour at the vestry, and I am not. Maybe you've forgotten what the vestrymen said when his pigs over-ran my rye. " 'Tis an accident the like of which might happen to any man, Eli Makers. 'Tis an ill thing when neighbours fall out over such a matter." No Shadrach, I'll get no good of the vestry in the matter of weeds, not when they're Jem Flower's weeds. Call to mind who sits in the vestry and directs the silly sheep that sit with him.'

'Squire do you mean?'

'Who else? And while Jem Flower tumbles his Peg how is Ellen Flower spending her time?'

'Sh . . .' said Shadrach, and then, raising his voice, 'Hi, Philip lad, where are you?'

I took three hasty steps away from the open doorway, put my hand over my mouth to muffle my voice and called back,

'With the gooseberries. Did you want me?'

'What lad is it?' I heard Eli ask, and Shad replied,

'Squire's.'

'Then I take it ill of you, Shad Woodey, to let my tongue run unchecked in such company.'

'He'd think nought of it,' said Shad easily. 'Besides he's but a lad.'

'I've known young dogs bring home big hares,' Elie retorted, and his bulk filled the doorway just as I deemed it time to present myself on the threshold.

'Get away home with you,' he said harshly. 'You're over young to hang about where men foregather.'

The scathing tone in his voice angered me, akin as it was to the scorn of which I had my daily fill.

'It's Shad's forge, Eli Makers,' I returned hotly. 'If you choose to speak your mind in it that is no business of mine.

And I shall go home when Shad tells me to, not before. Shad called my father a drunken whoremonger the first time I met him. There's nothing new that you can say about him.'

Eli wheeled round on Shad. 'You mind what I said about young dogs. There's a hare he's carried whole!'

'Philip is all right,' Shad said in that same easy way. 'He doesn't get on with the Squire and small wonder.'

There was a brief silence in the smithy. Eli stared at me, disapproval plainly written on his face. Shad looked at me with affection and confidence. He broke the silence to say calmly, 'I'd never thought to tell you, lad, that it's likely that you'll hear things within these walls that wouldn't sound well outside them. I didn't think we needed to say that.'

'And you didn't need to,' I cried. 'Who would I tell them to? The grooms or the serving women? Who else would listen to me?' I crossed the uneven floor with rapid stumbling steps, longing for dignity, burning with shame both for my infirmity and for something else, something bigger and deeper. I was an outcast, even my presence in the forge must be explained and condoned. I had been happy there, but I didn't fit or belong. I said 'Good night, Shad' over my shoulder and limped out into the summer dusk.

Something happened in me that evening. I was Saul. There were two Sauls, you remember. Saul the son of Kish who sought his father's asses and found a kingdom and upon whom the tongue of prophecy descended unaware. And there was Saul of Tarshish who was bent on another errand when the light blinded him on the Damascus road. Strange that they should bear the same name and both be men of destiny. I thought that as I dragged myself slowly along the baulks by the field path. Half my mind was remembering Eli Makers' talk of tillage and weeds and for the first time I looked intelligently at the portions of furrowland, lighted by the moon. But the other half was walking an unfamiliar road through a world of words. I saw the meadowsweet foaming in the ditches, unsubstantial, a froth of lace on the night's garment. I saw the tall trees, black against the moon. I thought, this is my home and my habitation, would I could remain here. And it was all entangled with things that I had read, stories and poetry in those neglected mouldering books, so that at that moment Héloïse and Abélard were more real to me than Shad and Eli, I was more likely to meet Juliet than Ellen Flower. And all the time I took no comfort from my state, for my thoughts escaped me even as I thought them. Just the act of thinking, of pinning a feeling down with words destroyed the essence of it. I sighed as I stumbled along and it seemed to me that the sweet breath of the meadowsweet had been borne to me upon a like sigh. And yet there was happiness in it too. I cannot explain any more and will desist from trying, for it seems to me now, that I, who all my life have hovered upon the brink of knowing something and of being able to put that knowing into words, have never succeeded. I hesitate to liken my mind to my body, it was less obviously disabled, but there was about it the same lack of perfection. I have never been able to walk as freely as I wished to do, and I have never caught, in a few clear vivid words the thoughts that have passed traceless through my mind. A bird leaves no track in the sky, a cloud casts a shadow over a pasture and is gone.

But on this evening I did not know my limitations. I was drunken with my own feelings and inexperienced in failure so it was with delight that I cut myself a new quill, got out my ink (made from an old recipe of oat galls and iron filings from the smithy) and upon the fly-leaf of a book penned my first verses. It was delight that I found the rhymes running easily. Only when I had finished did the inevitable discontent set in. Reading through the lines I was aware of the dearth of magic and knew that the moment had escaped me. What I did not know was that my mind was a universal discontent; that every word penned is but a blurred mirror of a thought.

> Outcast am I, without a home or place;
> Knowing no corner where I can abide
> With any surety. Not a friendly face
> Looks into mine without a thought to hide.

> Only the night is kind. The tall trees stand
> And do not judge, or mind that I am I.
> And the white meadowsweet on either hand
> Voices my sorrow with a scented sigh.

You see I was already wronging Shad who had looked upon me kindly and hidden nothing. And I was wrong to say 'tall trees'. The words went well together, but the very aptness of them should have warned me. The little trees, the slim young birches and the small round hawthorns were as unjudging as the great elms and thickset oaks. Still, it was my first effort at verse making and although I could see faults in it I was excited to see it and read it over again and again, with undiminished pleasure. Most people write their first verses I believe in praise of some fleshly beauty, 'a woeful ballad' to a mistress' eyebrow. I wrote mine because Eli Makers had invaded the little haven that I had made of the forge, and all my life I have found myself more easily moved by the less soft of the emotions.

However, the night's despair was not justified. By almost imperceptible stages I was admitted to the councils of the smithy and soon knew as much about enclosures and the danger of Popish practices in the church as any boy of twelve just growing into youth could hope to do. I believe that the men liked to meet at Shad's place because Shad possessed that rare thing, a balanced and tolerant mind, and they could measure their complaints and their enthusiasms against it, so that in some way a complaint that was still urgent after Shad's level eye had scanned it, an enthusiasm that endured after his cool judgement had weighed it, was a complaint, an enthusiasm indeed. Most of the men who gathered there were of Puritan mind, and when old Parson Jarvis was driven out their eyes were hard and their words bitter. Shad understood their feelings, but he went to church as usual and said openly that the candles and the altar cloths, the gilded cross and the white flowers made 'a pretty picture and did no harm'. And he took one view of the enclosures which Eli and several others advocated so heartily that made them pause to think.

'As things are now, you know, you get a chance of a fertile piece each year. Everybody hopes for some of the Layer Field and a bit of Sluice Meadow, and it's an ill draw that doesn't give you a bit of either. But if you get these permanent divisions that you want one man may have the whole of the Layer, and one the whole Sluice while the rest are saddled with Old Stony and Sweatmore.'

33

'That could be arranged,' said Eli.

'And who'd arrange it?'

'General meeting of the parish.'

'Where Jem Flower's word would weigh as much as yours, Eli.' But Eli was not easily discouraged.

'Give me Old Stony to myself, aye, if you like give me Sweatmore to do as I like with and I'll be hanged if I couldn't raise more on it than Jem Flower could do if he had all the Layer Field to himself.'

'Well, if you've heart stout enough to face Sweatmore on your own with never a share in the Layer, damn me if you shouldn't have it,' said Shad. And I felt the same.

Eli's golden beard bristled. 'Mersea's been enclosed and is doing well. There isn't an open field left in Ardley either. We're held back'—he paused and gave me a glance but decided to plunge ahead—'because Squire won't listen to reason and is set in his ways.'

'Mersea men appealed to Parliament,' said Eddie Lamb, another who was of Eli's way of thinking. I swallowed a lump in my throat and tried to keep the maddening break out of my unreliable voice as I said,

'My father has the ear of Parliament. He could have spoken for Parson Jarvis if he had cared to. And he's all against the enclosing. I know, because when first I understood about it I tried to talk it over with him. I—I thought perhaps he didn't understand.'

'And all ee got was a clipped lug, lad, likely?' asked Eddie. I was silent. The very memory of that day could make my face burn yet. My lugs had gone unclipped indeed, I never knew my father to touch me, but he had laughed and mocked me,

'Proper little chawbacon you're going to make. We'll get you a smock yet. . . .' There was a lot of that kind of thing, mingled with the assurance, which I might report to my friend of the dunghill, that while he lived Marshalsea might whistle for enclosures, it would go on exactly as it had done in the past. There was no mistaking that, and there was no chance of his changing his mind. The very thought of change was an abomination to him, and if he could have had his way he would have put everything back to where it was before the outbreak of the Civil War.

I did not recount the whole of his outburst to my 'friends of the dunghill' but I did try to show them that a petition would be useless, especially as the men of the parish, the very ones concerned were not all of the same mind. Men like Jem Flower gained by the system because there was hardly a chance that they would draw a worse cultivated strip than the one that they were leaving for some other poor wretch to deal with. And between idlers like him and ambitious men like Eli there was a mass of undecided men who dreaded change, who knew all the evils of the present system and preferred a familiar ill. Whenever enclosures were mentioned I used to look at Eli and think of that lead which had been fastened upon my leg.

But Eli himself did not consider the weight of prejudice and tradition which dragged on him. He continued to talk of a petition to Parliament and I continued to look upon him with pity, which was rather comic had I but known it. And so the year passed over, with Shad working at his iron and Eli delving in his strip and cursing Jem Flower, and Parson Jarvis stealing back to preach every now and then at the risk of his life, and my father continuing to maul Ellen Flower. The corn was losing its fresh green when Shad slew the Conventicle man and in September he was hanged.

I mourned Shad for a long time. The whole of life seemed different in the light of knowledge that never again would I hear that voice, bask in that smile, see those mighty shoulders rise and heave beneath the hammer. Here is proof, if any were needed, of the inadequacy of words. I have shown you—what? A man in a white shirt going to his hanging, a man in a blue jerkin shoeing a horse, a kindly man pitying a boy's lameness, a friendly man listening to the complaints of his friends. But what does that tell you of Shad, the life, the force, the personality which animated twelve stones or so of earthly substance, was wrenched out of it and left only a lump of carrion swinging at a rope's end? And if I cannot show you Shad who was a living man how can I hope to describe my sorrow for him, sorrow having no colour, shape or sound. Sometimes I caught myself thinking, 'I must tell Shad that' or 'I must ask Shad this', and then I would remember. Sometimes my feet set out for the field path and the lane to Marshalsea and as the church spire and the chimneys rose above the houses I would realise with a pang that the smithy was now the place where a new man plied his trade.

And then one day I had another visitation. It was full two months after Shad's death and the last torn yellow leaves were twisting down through the grey November weather, I walked in the park, alone, and thought of the buds from which those leaves had broken so joyously in the young month of April. And I realised that life and death are not two separate things, but as united as a man's right hand and his left. Every man born must die some time. The moment when the life quickens in the womb and the woman is aware of it and is glad, in that moment the death sentence is pronounced, and whether it comes soon or late is a matter of no importance. Shad had died oversoon, and violently, but that was no worse than dying overlate and dirtily, shivering and dribbling away the last cold dregs of life. Suppose Shad had lived until he could no longer swing his hammer or man his bellows, his voice become a whistling twitter, his strength a memory, his smile the betrayal of mumbling toothless gums. Why should gradual decay be preferred to sudden oblivion? And why should the sheep tethered at the door of the shambles waste pity and sorrow on the dead mutton just carried out? I should die some day too, I was the tethered sheep.

I looked round me at the hawthorn trees where the sparrows pecked off the crimson berries and I lifted my face to the lowering sky. I felt better, as though an obligation to sorrow had just been removed from me. I should still miss Shad and still pity myself for the loss of my friend, but I need not mourn the manner nor the time of his death again. Comfort flowed in upon me like a resurrection.

I gave myself up to my books. Looking back, although I can remember some winters of hard frost and snow and the merriment that was made for Charles and the succeeding children at Christmas time, I seem to see those years mostly in the sun. It seems to be summer when I remember finding my way into Colchester with the carrier and there buying with any coin I could get hold of, eked out with things I stole from larder and smoke house, the books that I wanted. It was summer I know, when I read 'Lycidas' in the orchard under the pink apple blossom, and heard the cuckoos calling in Hunter's Wood and thought of Shad with a poetry-drugged and not unpleasant pain. It seems to have been summer when I carried on the old talks with Eli Makers and Andy Seeley and young Joseph Steggles, as discontented with the old order of things as his father was contented.

Anyhow, summer or winter they sped past, those years, and I grew from a boy into a young man, lame of one leg and not overstrong, but active and capable of energy. Agnes, who never profited by Madame Louise's tuition in the arts of love, grew motherly, stout and dowdy: but she was fairly kind to me when such kindness did not demand support beneath my father's eye. She saw to it that I was tolerably clad and occasionally, with a furtive gesture, would slip a stray coin into my ready palm. I think she liked me because I had long ago found myself unable to resist the blandishments of Charles, who was indeed a taking and lovable little fellow, a proper Ollenshaw in appearance, and daring and pertinacious enough to satisfy even my father.

I was seventeen I suppose when I first set eyes on the man who, in two ways, was destined to shape my life for me. My father received a letter which he read with a great deal of eye-screwing and finger work. Then he bade Agnes open up a guest room, see that the best silver was polished and in use and that every resource of the household was in order because during the next week a London acquaintance of his, a Mr. Nathaniel Gore, was going to spend a night at the Manor.

I was in the room at the time and I broke my habitual silence towards him to ask, 'The Mr. Gore who wrote "A Year's Journal", sir?' My voice was incredulous, for what could a man of that stamp want with my father, a country squire who could just about sign his name on a document and with difficulty understand his agents' accounts and little more.

'How should I know what he wrote?' asked my father irritably. 'Thank God I've had something better to do with my time than to sit with my nose in a book and my arse in a chair.'

Usually that would have been more than enough to drive

me back into silence, but interest and curiosity gave me courage to persist.

'Has this Nathaniel Gore been to America?'

'Yes. He came back last year full of colonising ideas. I shall not put any money into them, however glibly he asks. He says he has a favour to ask me. It's either that or he wants land to experiment his crazy schemes for growing Indian corn over here as fodder.'

I had learned what I wanted to know. This was the Nathaniel Gore of 'A Year's Journal' and punctually on the day of his arrival I presented myself, washed and combed at the family dinner table.

He was a small man with a high wide forehead and a small chin that jutted forward in an aggressive manner. His wig was ill-kept and woolly looking but his linen was fine and snowy white. He had a small, quiet voice and a deprecating smile and it was hard—until you looked again at the chin and the bright lively eyes—to connect him with the 'I' of the journal who had dared such dangers and escaped out of so many perils.

He had spoken to me as though I were indeed the son of the house, and I had told him, shyly, for I was unused to the company of gentlemen, that I had read his book. He was pleased with that and would have talked to me at some length had not my father nipped off my budding eloquence with a sour look and a 'Dinner is on the board'. There was little conversation at the table and I was determined that after the meal I would not be banished. So I lowered myself into the settle at the distant end of the room and prepared to hear for what possible reason Nathaniel Gore had come to the Manor. The conversation came to me in a whisper and a roar as the soft voice of our guest and the loud one of my father alternated.

'It would give me great pleasure to be the means of finding them an asylum. Seabrook was of great help to me and gave me the advantage of his enormous scholarship many times. But of course he is eccentric and his known Catholic leanings makes it difficult. I thought the country—and then naturally I thought of you. Could you find some kind of shelter for them?'

'Them?'

38

'He has a daughter, quite young and very beautiful. That has caused trouble too. I'm afraid London morals have not improved since our young days, my friend, and the girl has come home several times in great distress. I should be most happy if I could see them both settled in your delightful, peaceful countryside, away from mass prejudice and amorous young gentlemen with too much time on their hands.'

'As lovely as that, is she?'

I could hear the interest in my father's voice and was not surprised to hear him say,

'It should be easy to find them a house, or for that matter to build one. Let me think. Why yes, there's nobody to my knowledge in old Madge's house at the top of the Layer Field in Hunter's Wood. That's remote enough even for an eccentric with a lovely daughter. I'll ask my steward to have the roof seen to and the doors renewed. They'd not be particular, I suppose.'

'Bless you, no. I knew you wouldn't fail me. And if ever there's anything I can do for you remember I'm your debtor over this.'

'I shan't remember it and I trust you won't,' said my father, in the hearty manner that endeared him to those he set himself out to charm. 'And now that that's settled, a glass of wine, Mr. Gore, and after that, it's a fine moonlit night, how about a walk to view the place?'

They drank their wine and left the house, both well pleased; my father calling up pleasant visions of a beautiful successor to Ellen Flower; his guest imagining that he had found a sanctuary for his protégées.

That night, after the house was sealed in slumber I stole along to the room where Nathaniel Gore was housed and knocked very softly on the door. After a pause, and just as I was preparing to tiptoe away again the door opened and Nathaniel, without his wig and with his bald head shining in the candle-light, quietly bade me enter. I saw that he had made no preparations for retiring, except to remove his wig. His greatcoat hung loose from his shoulders against the coldness of the room, and paper, ink and quill were laid in orderly fashion upon the table before the dying fire.

'I began to wonder, after I'd said "Come in" twice, whether it was the family ghost paying me a visit,' he said

39

with a smile, indicating a chair and seating himself by the table.

'No, I'm the family skeleton,' I said.

'Indeed. Why is that?'

I pointed to my leg, but hastened to say,

'I didn't come here to talk about that, Mr. Gore. I really wanted to see you properly and just hear you talk a little. I've never seen anyone who had written a book before.'

'We look much like other people though tradition has it that we are lean and pale—that is when we're not green with envy. What did you want to talk about?'

'America, Mr. Gore,' I said promptly. 'I told you I'd read the "Journal", didn't I? I lost myself in it, it was like being there. I . . .'

'Where did you learn to shape a pretty speech, lad?' he interrupted. 'Or didn't you know that that is the most gratifying thing you can tell a spinner of yarns?'

'But *were* they yarns?' I asked earnestly. 'That was what I wanted to know. You see, I read about so many places, Utopia, and the lost city of Atlantis, and the Islands of the Blest. I did wonder whether perhaps your Salem was like that?'

'Now, now,' he said reproachfully, 'what in my poor, accurate pages leads you to compare it to those others? Haven't they all one thing in common—perfection? And did I ever even hint that Salem was perfect?'

'No,' I said, 'but it might be.'

'Ah, there you've hit the nail right on the head, my boy. It might be. But it isn't. And why? Because laws must be made for the people, not the people for the laws. In other words, those who order Salem, well-intentioned men all of them, haven't allowed for the little peccadilloes to which even the best of us is prone. And if you stop up the spout the lid blows off as every housewife knows. But it is a land of boundless opportunity.'

He paused and looked at the bare wall ahead of him as though he were seeing the land and every opportunity that it offered. I hesitated to disturb him for a moment or two and then asked nervously, 'There's one thing I should like to know, Mr. Gore, if you don't mind telling me. The land there—is it free?—can any man own it and till it in his own fashion?'

'Any freeman can.'

'And what does a man do to become a freeman?'

'It varies. Roughly speaking I should say that any man who goes out unassisted is entitled to a grant of land. In Salem it's also a matter of church membership—I disapprove of that, but that doesn't matter. A man who goes there as another man's servant may have to wait some time before he gets a grant. But of course if land is all he wants and he doesn't mind what he does for it there's plenty there. You could drop down the whole of England into it and never even notice it.'

'Oh,' I said.

'Tell me, lad, why are you so eager to know about the land in the new world? You'll have all you can manage right here in Marshalsea, won't you?'

'Oh, it's not for myself,' I said quickly. 'I'd be no good there. I suppose I like reading about daring deeds and mighty efforts because I'm never likely to share any. It's for Eli Makers I'm asking.'

'And who may he be?'

So I settled down, forgetting the hour, forgetting to wonder what my father would say if he discovered me badgering his guest, and told all I knew about Eli; how bitterly he hated the open field system of farming; how he hated the candles and the altar in the church; how hard he worked and how well he could farm if he could have land of his own. I forgot myself utterly, but I came back with a start as my new friend said,

'Philip—that's your name isn't it? Philip Ollenshaw you say that I have shown you a land that you have never seen, allow me to return the compliment. You have made me see this Eli Makers, this tiller of the soil, dividing his soul between two stern gods, the Old Testament Jehovah and Mother Earth. I don't know anyone who could have done it better. I may be mistaken, but I think that your future lies with your pen, my boy.'

I smiled in an embarrassed fashion and hastened on to the other matter that I had come to discuss.

'Who are these people who are coming to Madge's cottage?'

'An old man whose life has been spent in researches for many things, all for the use of his fellows. Born out of his time he has met with opposition and criticism that have embittered his nature. Too late in life he married a young girl who excited his compassion. She used him and left him with an infant daughter. Her treatment of him helped to turn a brain already unsteady from too much study and too few human contacts. In London, where prejudice and hysteria are apt at any moment to rise up in search of a victim he has been mobbed in the streets, and now that this anti-Popery feeling runs so high he is no longer safe from his neighbours. Your father has kindly offered to give him an asylum here. In his more lucid moments, Philip, he is an interesting companion if you can break down his reticence. I hope that you will countenance him.'

I wanted to say that Marshalsea was no place for a pretty girl with a doddering old father, but somehow the words stuck. Not through loyalty to my father so much as consideration for the little man who seemed so pleased with his arrangements for his friend. His complete confidence in the safety of the country as a retreat seemed to me pathetic and rather unworthy of a man who had travelled so much and understood so many things so well. Prejudice and hysteria were just as likely to break out in Marshalsea as in London and in the darkness and quietude, in the remoteness and ignorance of the country places it was likely to take a more morbid form—or so it seemed to me.

However, here was a man of the world, a traveller and a writer well content with the result of his errand and I felt that it would ill become me to question his wisdom. So my protest died on my tongue. If I had been bold, if I had had the courage of my convictions I might have shown him one definite drawback to his plan and then perhaps the Seabrooks would never have come to the cottage in Hunter's Wood. And what a difference that would have made.

We talked for a little longer and Nathaniel Gore asked me whether I had ever been to the theatre. I told him no.

'You should,' he said. 'You should come to London and visit the playhouses. Who knows, you might have a playwright in you. You showed me your Eli Makers clearly enough. I shall never forget him. In any case you should make a stay in the city, great things are moving there, great minds are at work. And you'll be welcome, very welcome at my house, the Crooked Fleece, hard by Essex House in the Strand. Remember that.'

'Thank you,' I said heartily. 'I will remember. Why is it so oddly named?'

'It was the headquarters of hide smugglers in Elizabeth's time. It looks out on to the river.'

Nathaniel Gore rode away next morning and that very day the steward set off for Madge's cottage with men and straw for thatching and seasoned oak for doors. My father exerted himself mightily, and just before the Seabrooks were due to arrive on the coach at Colchester he had the shed at the back of the cottage filled with dry logs, the pantry stocked with salt meat and herrings, cheese and flour and a great barrel of ale. These preparations sickened me, for I knew that if old Seabrook had been coming alone, or with a plain woman, his woodshed and his pantry would have been as bare as old Madge's had always been. I saw all the preparations going forward but outwardly showed no interest and although I was in Colchester, swopping brawn and sausages for a copy of Browne's 'Urn Burial', on the very day when our groom had set off leading two horses for the Seabrooks' use, I did not trouble to stand in the crowd that gathered to watch the coach's arrival.

It was months later, after the days had lengthened, when the woods were full of oxslips and windflowers that I went to Hunter's Wood in search of a dog that I had lost. There were always at least a dozen dogs around the Manor but Quince belonged to me because as a puppy he had lost his mother and I had reared him on a rag soaked in goat's milk. He was an ugly little pup, which further endeared him to me and his temper was unreliable, though to me he was always affectionate and fawning. He grew into a leggy, loping creature addicted to stealing and snarling, but to me he was dear. I hadn't seen him for three days and I had searched in every likely place and was now trying the less promising. Hunter's Wood was among them, and on this sunny afternoon I pushed through the undergrowth calling him by name and whistling on my fingers. I expected that he was trapped. Even so he might still be alive and he might whimper.

Suddenly, as I came blundering out of the thicket on to the open ride I saw a woman walking towards me with a great basket that trailed roots and leaves weighing on her arm. She was unknown to me and although she might have been Mrs. Hunt, or one of the Chisnell girls whom I did not know by sight, there was something so completely strange about her that I knew at once that this was Linda Seabrook. It was too late to turn and plunge back into the wood, besides a kind of morbid curiosity held me to the spot.

She was finely clad in a gown of mulberry-coloured silk that rustled as she walked and it had little ruffles where the short tight sleeves ended at her elbows and where her throat rose from the moulded bodice. I saw the flash of silver buckles as her feet came out in turn from the full whispering skirt and there were purple stones in her ears. No Marshalsea woman would walk in the woods dressed that way.

I had drawn back, so that my body was pressed against the bushes and my feeling of meeting her unwillingly must have given me a skulking furtive look, but she came on without quickening or slackening her step and when she was level with me she paused and looked me in the face.

'I heard you calling,' she said. 'Is it possible that you have lost a dog?'

'Why—have you found one?'

'Father did. I thought I heard you call "Quince". Is that his name?'

'If he's the one I'm looking for it is.'

She gave a little laugh, 'That is funny. We thought he looked like Snout. He's in a rather poor case, I'm afraid. Some boys had got him. But father set to work on him and he'll recover.'

She took a step along the leaf-covered ride and the dress whispered and the buckle flashed. I became suddenly conscious of my rough, haphazardly acquired clothes, and knew that when I moved out of the bushes the iron on my shoe would show. So I stood still. She took another step, swung round and looked at me inquiringly.

'You'll walk back with me, won't you. He can't be moved of course, but he'd like to see you, I imagine. He

44

doesn't seem to take very kindly to us.'

'Yes, I'll come,' I said. 'Let me carry the basket.'

She slipped her arm from the handle and I could see the red weal where it had pressed into the white flesh.

'It's rather heavy. The earth was so damp that it clung to the roots,' she said, and then, glancing down at my foot and up again quickly into my face, she said,

'Why, you're Philip Ollenshaw, aren't you? I might have known before. You're so like your father.'

'I'm not, but it's kind of you to give that reason for your recognition. I suppose my father has mentioned his crippled son!'

'Indeed not, but Mr. Gore did. He said that you were the one person in these parts who was likely to be a friend. I thought that as we hadn't seen you before you might be away from home. All the same, you are like your father, you know. And I'm glad. He's been so good a friend to us.'

I never saw so straight a back, so small a waist in the tight embrace of her dress, I never saw a head put on so elegantly, a throat so smooth and long. I never saw hair so black and shiny growing back from the temples in so sweet a curve. And my father was her good friend. Such a bitter taste came into my mouth that I felt my lips twist and if I had been alone I should have spat.

'Father is so happy here,' she went on. 'And now that the spring has come, with all these flowers and the sweet birds, it really is like Paradise. Especially after London. Do you know London? We lived there at the top of a tall house full of people. There were always babies crying and women screaming on the stairway and the men seemed to be drunk most of the time.'

'You look,' I said slowly, 'as though you might have come straight from Whitehall Palace.'

'Oh,' she said, and the straight little shoulders rose and fell in a gesture of amusement. 'This, you mean, and this?' She touched a fold of her dress and one earring with a pointed, earth-stained finger. 'They were my mother's. I've only just grown big enough to wear them. Until then I wore fustian, and if they wear out before I die I suppose I shall wear fustian again. But it is nice, isn't it?'

45

She preened herself like a lovely bird. And there was something so simple in the gesture of pleasure and in the words that preceded it that I realised suddenly that she was young, not years older than I as I had at first imagined. That eased me a little and I walked along beside her to Madge's cottage in a more comfortable frame of mind.

If I had come upon the cottage suddenly I should not have recognised it. The plaster had all been washed white and the old beams and the new door had been oiled so that they shone richly dark. There was a chimney too over the hole from which old Madge's smoke had poured for so many years and all the little window panes were whole and glittering in the sun. A barrel, sawn across its middle had made two rubs, one on either side the doorstep and they were filled with oxslips and dark wall flowers. The new thatch was deep and even.

'Isn't it beautiful?' she asked, pausing half way up the path which had been laid with bricks that matched those of the chimney. 'And look, these are rosebushes, there're buds on them already and this lavender will be sweet in the summer. All those came from the Manor. I can't tell you how kind your father has been, especially since he knew how fond I am of flowers.' Her voice changed a little. 'Wait here just a moment, will you, I will prepare my father. This isn't one of his best days and he might be alarmed to see you. But when I explain that you are *his* son he'll understand and be delighted to see you.'

Nothing must spoil this. I repeated that to myself rapidly and firmly. To enter the cottage now and be welcomed and made much of because I was Sir John Ollenshaw's son would poison any friendship that might grow out of the meeting.

'Listen,' I said, and was surprised at the harshness of my own voice. 'I would like to see my dog and I would like to be friends with your father—and with you. But it mustn't be because of my being my father's son. Do you understand that? My father and I live in the same house and bear the same name, but actually we are much worse than strangers to one another.'

'Why, have you quarrelled?'

'No. We're not near enough to one another to quarrel. I

can't explain it, but we're just nothing to one another. And I don't want your father, or you, to look at me through a veil of vicarious gratitude. Is that clear?'

'Quite. You're just a young man who has called to see his dog and you happen to be Sir John's son.'

'Mention that if you have to, not otherwise.'

'Come along, then.'

She went up the rest of the path with her quick light step and pressed down the latch of the door. I followed her in, ducking my head beneath the lintel. Inside I could stand upright easily because the floor had sunk so that the room was a foot at least below the level of the path.

The walls within had been whitened too which made the room look lighter than it really was. The floor was of pale brick, what we called Suffolk brick, and much scrubbing had removed all old Madge's grime and left the original colours, primrose and cream and pale amber to glow underfoot. Bright rugs of darker colours lay in front of the hearth, the door and under the sturdy black table that stood in the centre of the room. There were two chairs and a stool and a settle by the fireside. A bowl of wildflowers stood in the middle of the table; a spray of wild plum blossom was poised as though for flight in a jar on the shelf over the fireplace; beside the hearth on either side roughly made shelves laden with books reached from floor to ceiling.

Linda had glanced round the room, seen that it was unoccupied and opened another door which led into the kitchen.

'Father,' she said. A snarl answered her and then I heard the frenzied flopping of a tail on the floor, sure sign to me that Quince had growled when he hadn't really intended to do so.

'Come through and see your dog,' Linda called. 'I'll have to step out and call father. Really, he'll wander out of Heaven's gate if he ever gets there.'

She opened the door that gave on to the back garden of the cottage and I could hear her voice ringing out over the Layer Field and echoing back from the wood. 'Father! Where are you? Josiah Seabrook! Come back home.'

I knelt down beside the sack stuffed with straw upon

47

which my dog was lying and fondled his head. He ran his pink tongue around my fingers and flopped his tail wildly, but made no attempt to rise. 'What is it?' I asked him. 'Did you walk into a trap?' I examined his paws one by one, but though he flinched as I touched him I could see no damage that might be ascribed to trapping. He was soaked in some evil-smelling lotion and his skin was broken in one or two places.

'Leave that dog alone,' said a voice behind me and I twisted round on my knees and looked up at the strangest figure I had ever beheld. Even the knowledge that this was Josiah Seabrook whose daughter was calling him vigorously at the back of the cottage while he entered by the front, even the knowledge that this was a scholar and a friend of Nathaniel Gore could not keep back the chill of horror that ran down my spine. The face might have been a skull for all the flesh there was on it, and the skin had a dusky look like old parchment. From purple pits, incredibly deep under white eyebrows, two burning black eyes looked out and as he repeated his order to leave the dog alone the thin purple lips moved over long yellow teeth. I stared at him for a moment, then clambered to my feet so clumsily that my iron rattled on the brick floor and I reached out my hand to the wall to steady myself.

'Your daughter asked me to come in. This is my dog, Quince. I lost him. I am very grateful to you for looking after him.'

Of it all only the words 'my daughter' made any impact.

'My daughter, where is she? Come away from that dog, young man. He has been ill used and is uncertain of temper.'

'I'll tell your daughter that you have come back,' I said, and going to the door I shouted the news. Linda came running back like a swallow swooping.

'You make me so anxious,' she said breathlessly. 'Why do you wander off like that if I leave you for an hour?'

'Who is this young man? One of the village bullies come for the dog again?'

'Oh no, father. He owns the dog but he lost it. He is Philip Ollenshaw, Sir John's son.'

'Sir John Talbot is a very able man,' said the old man,

looking at me earnestly. 'Very able indeed. But he can't persuade the people that the river water is a source of infection, and neither for that matter can I. And while they go on drinking it, with the filth from the drains and the burying places in it, they *will* have plagues. Commend me warmly to Sir John, young man, and tell him that I will send him a fresh supply of the salve as soon as bugloss blows. How are his eyes?'

I looked helplessly at Linda. She took the old man by his stick-like arm and turned him away. With her free hand she lifted the basket.

'Come to your room, father, and sort out the things that I have found for you,' she said in the voice that one uses to a child. She led him away and I turned back to Quince.

'I'm sorry,' she said presently appearing at the door, 'his wits are all astray today. I think finding your dog upset him a little. Any sight of violence unsettles him nowadays. *He* has been much persecuted in his time.'

'Where and how did he find him, then?'

'Some boys from the village were having sport with him. Father went to the rescue. Violence may upset him but it can't intimidate him. Poor Quince, he was hurt inside, the blood was pouring from his mouth, but father gave him white of egg and alum and it stopped. He'll be all right in a day or two.'

'I am most deeply grateful. I hope I shall be able to express my gratitude to your father on some future occasion. I'll call and see whether the dog can be taken away on the day after tomorrow.'

'Father will be quite all right by then. Perhaps you'll come to dinner and eat some of your own excellent beef.'

She walked as far as the gate with me and when I turned back just before the path dipped and hid the cottage from sight I saw her leaning over it, looking up at the sky. Lovely, rounded, delicately coloured thing, how long before the satyr's hoof shows from the hem of the cloak of Squire Bountiful? How long before you learn that all beef must be paid for in one coin or another?

For the next forty-eight hours I thought of little but the cottage on the edge of the wood and at the appointed hour, very clean and wearing my best clothes, I presented myself

49

at its door. Within I heard the scuffling of feet and as soon as the door opened Quince wriggled through the opening and threw himself upon me. Someone had washed off the lotion and his coat was all fluffy. He wound himself round my legs as I entered the room and when I was seated sat beside me with his muzzle on my knee.

'There's no doubt whose dog he is,' said Linda's father, 'and little doubt whose son you are, though I didn't realise it when I saw you the other day. You must forgive me for that. I have a great deal to think about.'

I endorsed that statement long before that first visit was ended. Never before had I been within hailing distance of anything like so well-informed a mind. His repulsive physical appearance was forgotten, more it ceased to be, as one listened to his conversation. And he had one rare virtue in a scholar, he was willing to believe that you were well-informed too. He did not instruct, at least not consciously, though the most ignorant person would have gained something from half an hour's conversation with him.

He told me on that first evening about the plague that had swept through London twelve years before and how he had been execrated because he had stated in a pamphlet— printed at his own expense—that the bodies of those who had died should have been burned, together with the filthy courts and alleys where the disease originated.

'Fresh air and good water and cleanliness in the streets, when we have those simple remedies there will be no more plagues. There should be strict supervision too on the vessels that sail up London river from the East, those lands where the plague is always lurking. Men shouldn't land without a bill of health from a doctor. Rats come ashore too, I've seen them swarming down the ropes. Rats have fleas,' he said dreamily, 'and the fleas bite men. There may be an idea there, who can say?'

Linda said. 'Get on with your dinner, father, and don't talk about plagues and rats and fleas at the table. It spoils the appetite.'

She had a way of speaking to him as though he were a child.

I was interested in all his talk, it was the kind of thing that had never come my way before; but I am not going to repeat it all; I should grow weary of remembering and others would weary of listening. Enough to say that he showed me a world that was neither Marshalsea nor the world of my book-led fancy. He showed me London, a three-sided city, the London of fashion and fine ladies and gentlemen, of intrigue and battle for influence, of plays and masques and amorous dalliance; the London of the slums and courts where the soil of filth and poverty brought forth the rank jungle of crime and cruelty and despair; the London of the scholars where eager minds questioned everything and found sometimes a startling answer to their questions. Of the king he spoke well, 'A many-sided man,' he said, 'wrapped up in his women, yet considerate and kind to his wife. A man of wit and humour and with a more enlightened mind than those surrounding him. Medicine and science owe him more than most men realise and his influence on the arts will provide a harvest for other generations to reap.'

Anyone but a dolt would have been proud of the right of entrance to the cottage on the edge of the wood, but I of course, went with special gladness because Linda was there. My first love. I run the years through my fingers as Madame Louise would run her rosary and for every year there are a hundred visions of Linda. Ah yes, my love, I have seen you proud and beautiful, ashamed and weary, soiled and sick. I have seen you with all your bright beauty blotted out. But I, who ever sought your presence, whose eyes were ever drawn you-wards as a needle to a magnet, am yet unable to name the charm that you bore for me. Not without faults, my dear, headstrong and vain, and over one thing at least incredibly foolish, weak where strength would have profited you and yet strong enough to kick against the pricks continually, fawning when you should have snarled and snarling at the one who ached to cherish you, and in all Linda, my love.

And now, of course, I have the threads of my story tangled. I am like an unskilful driver struggling to keep six horses running at even pace. I have Eli to consider and old Seabrook, myself and my father and Linda, and beside them all, hardest horse to coax along, the story of the times in which our life was set.

At first when I thought of Linda and my father and saw the joints and the honey and the sacks of flour smuggled from the Manor to Madge's cottage, my feelings were of pity for her and of scorn and hatred of him. But after I knew her and was struggling in the toils of love myself my pity became tinged with anger and my scorn and hatred took on the fatal hue of jealousy. He began to take her riding. In those summer evenings when the bees were drunk in the scented lime blossoms and the wild roses shone on the hedges and the whole world seemed aswoon with desire and tenderness, he would come out from his five o'clock dinner, mount one of the waiting horses and ride away towards Hunter's Wood. On such evenings I would shut myself withindoors trying to avoid the hurt of the heavenly weather, trying by concentration upon some heavy tome or stirring tale, not to see the pair of them jogging along the scented rides, not to imagine what feelings of lechery the sight of her body would stir in his.

But one evening I did not see the waiting horses so I set out on foot for the cottage. There were horses aplenty and so far as I knew I was welcome to them, but except to go to Colchester I seldom borrowed one. Mounting and dismounting was always a trial to me. Long ago Shad had made me a stirrup iron deep enough to take my shoe with its support, but if I tried to mount from that, the normal side, there was always a moment when the whole of my weight was supported on a weak limb which was supported in its turn by slippery iron on slippery iron. And if I mounted from the other side there arose the problem of swinging the weak, weighted leg across the horse's back. Actually I needed help to mount and was too proud to ask for it often. (And all this made the sight of my father's agility and competent horsemanship the more hurtful.)

So on this particular evening I walked to Madge's cottage and found old Seabrook alone. He was in a sensible mood to start with, insisted that I should enter and help him to taste some wine which had been sent him by a friend of his, a wine merchant in the city. It was ruby-red, sweet and heady, and certainly played its part in the scene that followed. The old man sipped daintily, but with appreciation and I copied him. Quite suddenly he set down his glass, looked at me with the queer shuttered look which I was now experienced enough to realise was a sign of his wits having wandered, and said,

'There were two men in one city; the one rich, and the other poor. The rich man had exceeding many flocks and herds but the poor man had nothing save one little ewe lamb which he had brought up and nourished; and it grew up together with him and with his children; it did eat of his own meat and drank of his own cup and lay in his bosom, and was unto him as daughter. But why "as"? She *is* my daughter. No matter what that mistress of Satan may have hinted, she is indeed my daughter. My mother was beautiful in just that way. Isn't that true?'

'Do you mean Linda, sir?'

'Aye. Of course you know it too. You can look upon her beauty without longing to spoil it, but the rich man baits the traps with gifts and will not rest until beauty lies snared for his pleasure. And David's anger was greatly kindled against the man and he said, "As the Lord liveth the man who hath done this thing shall surely die." But David was King of Israel, he had not eaten the rich man's salt.'

His thin claw-like fingers strayed to the bowl of roses that was in the centre of the table and he pulled off petal after petal from a fine dark red bloom that drooped over the side. I was silent for a little while and then I said, 'Do you mean Linda and my father?'

'They are out riding. Exercise is good for her. Bright birds that are kept in too small cages dash against the bars. I made that error with the mistress of Satan.'

Oh God! I thought. Stay sensible just long enough to let me know whether your suspicions run alongside mine and then perhaps we can do something.

'Listen,' I said, and he turned his eyes towards the window and set his head aslant.

'No, no,' I said impatiently, 'listen to *me*. My father, who is out in the woods with Linda at this moment, is wanton. Why do you think that he, who has little or no generosity in him, has been so overwhelmingly generous to you. The cottage was repaired, the woodshed filled and the pantry stocked for one reason only. Nathaniel Gore told him that your daughter was beautiful, and he had exhausted the

53

bucolic charms of the village girls and hoped for better things. There you have the plain truth. And if you have any friends who can help you the best thing you can do is to go away. At once, if you value your daughter's chastity.'

'And would you question it, young man?' he asked fiercely. 'Her mother was wanton, but if as the poet says "Good wombs have borne bad sons", may not the reverse be true? Never take any situation at its face value, young man. Even the humble pudding has more than one ingredient.'

'Did you *hear* what I just said about my father and Linda?' I tried to make my voice as incisive as possible. He looked me full in the face and I thought that some logical answer was forthcoming. He said, ' "And Nathan said unto David, Thou art the man." Ecce Homo. How frail a thing is virtue to be undermined by green cloth and a string of pearls!'

He rose to his feet and all his joints cracked like little pistol shots.

'You must excuse me, Barbara. I am not well. I cannot share your bed tonight. I will go to my own.' He opened the door at the foot of the scrubbed wooden stairs and went up them as though he were blind.

I poured myself some more wine and drank it quickly. It ran warmly round my veins and the fumes dazzled my brain, so that I thought it an easy thing to wait for Linda, repeat what I had said to her father and urge upon her the wisdom of going away. 'Green cloth and a string of pearls,' eh? So he was following up general generosity by personal gifts, the kind of thing that appeals to girls' hearts. I realised with a new pang of jealousy that he was enjoying the novel sensation of having to woo for a favour. His size and virility, his name, even his title, had made most of his conquests too easy. But Linda's innocence must be assaulted gently, her confidence gained. How sweet would be his victory—unless I took a hand. I drank more wine and was now so far under its influence that I did not know it. I didn't see myself any longer as a puling lame boy in love with the woman that his father coveted, about to lay himself open for God knew what rebuffs, fortifying himself with unfamiliar liquor. I was just Philip Ollenshaw about to

54

save the one ewe lamb from the rich man.

I heard the soft thud of hoofs on the woodland path and then voices. I pressed myself close to the side of the window and looked out cautiously. The horses came to a standstill by the gate at the end of the brick pathway and my father dismounted. Thick and heavy he was but nimble. He came round to Linda's side and as he came I saw his heavy-joweled red face lifted towards her and there was an expression on it that I had never thought to see there. He looked hungry, but there was tenderness and merriment there too. He held up his arms and lifted her down as though she were a doll. A stab of sharp agony went through me as I saw his big red hands, ungloved, close on her body, under the arms, close to the soft round breasts. I knew that he felt a stab, strangely similar, for I saw the tenderness and the merriment die out of his face, leaving only the hunger there, naked and hurting. Then he dropped his hands, swept off his wide hat—and devil take him there was grace in the gesture and a kind of worship. He lifted one of her small hands in the white glove, held it to his lips for a moment and let it go.

'Good-bye, and a thousand thanks,' she said.

'I'll take the thousand off the million I owe you,' he said. 'That leaves plenty, doesn't it?'

He mounted, reached down for the bridle of the horse that Linda had been riding, gave his hat a final flourish and trotted away. She leaned far over the gate. I saw her hand rise once and knew that he had waved just where the path dipped, where I had looked back on that first day. Then she turned and came tripping up the path. I saw both the green cloth and the pearls. The green cloth was a habit, made, I will swear, to her measure, and within its square cut neckline the pearls lay against her white throat. I knew the pearls. Both Madame Louise and Agnes had had their turn with them.

She unlatched the door and stepped into the room. Sparkling eyes and more often ascribed to beauty than possessed, but hers did actually sparkle as she turned them on me and said brightly, 'Good evening, Philip. Where's my father?'

'He wasn't very well. He went upstairs.'

She gathered the back of her long green skirt in her hand

55

and took the stairs two steep steps at a time but almost
noiselessly. She had the knack of moving like a bird. In a
moment or so she tiptoed down and said, 'He's asleep. Did
anything upset him?'

Here was my cue.

'He was anxious about you,' I said slowly. 'And so, to tell
you the truth, was I.'

'Anxious about me? But I was with your father.' She
eyed what was left of the wine and the two glasses, 'Have
you and father been drinking?'

'Your father drank very little. I rather more. But our
anxiety is not the outcome of that, Linda. Your father
wasn't very lucid, but I knew what was on his mind. He
quoted the story of the one ewe lamb, and said that virtue
could be undermined by green cloth and pearls. And,
Linda, it is true. Please don't have any more to do with my
father. I do implore you.'

Her face hardened. She began to strip off her gloves with
little plucking movements, and when her fingers were free
she tossed the gloves across the room on to the fireside
settle. They went through the air like doves. Then she came
close to me, so that I could smell the new cloth of her habit
and see that the green of it was echoed in her eyes. Usually
they were a curious mixture of green and brown, very
bright. I have seen just the combination on a hawthorn leaf
when it was changing colour at the turn of the year, and, I
think, nowhere else.

Accustomed to Madame Louise's tantrums I steeled myself against the shrill anger that I was expecting, but Linda's
voice was as smooth as silk as she said, 'Now, Philip, once
and for all have done with hints and half meanings. What
have you against your father that you should be *anxious*
because I go out with him?'

'I can tell you that, quite briefly, Linda, though it won't
be pleasant hearing. My father is a man without kindness.
Before his marriage to my mother was a year old, before I
was born, Madame Louise who had been his mistress before
his marriage, was installed in Paris, usurping my mother's
place, wearing those very pearls that are round your neck
at this moment. As soon as Madame Louise was no longer
sufficiently attractive he brought home a new wife, and he

56

struck his mistress, Linda, I saw him do it, because she protested. Since then every girl in the village who happens to
have some claim to comeliness and complaisant parents
(and most are complaisant where the Squire is concerned)
has had some sort of truck with him. You're new, you're
beautiful, and he wants you. And he'll have you, by force if
necessary, as sure as Heaven is above us, unless you go
away.' The long speech and my earnestness had taken all
my breath. I drew it in sharply and I heard her breathing
hard too. From that and the way that the colour was fading
from her cheeks I knew that I had shaken her.

'I shouldn't have told you all that so suddenly,' I said
with compunction. 'Sit down.' I pulled the chair that I had
been using earlier in the evening round the table a little and
she sat down.

'You're very handy with your tongue, Philip, very handy.
You almost make me believe that it's all true, that you
couldn't have made it up.'

'I didn't. Make it up! Why should I? My mother's story
is well known. Madame Louise and Lady Ollenshaw are at
the Manor. Ellen Flower might lie about who was the father
of the brat she has by the hand, Martha Baines might lie
about who got her in the state she is in ... but all the
village *knows*.'

She stretched out her fingers towards the petals that still
lay on the table, creased from her father's hand and
smoothed each out, spreading and pressing them with her
finger-tips as though her life depended upon their restoration. At last she raised her head.

'I believe you,' she said, 'but it doesn't make any difference. You see, Philip, I love him.'

'Oh God!' I cried. 'You don't know what you're saying.
He has dazzled you, just as he's dazzled all his other
women. He's big and active, and he can pick you up with
one hand; he's wooing you with presents and pretty
speeches. But they mean only one thing—the price he's
willing to pay for his pleasure. Don't be misled by him,
Linda. Don't deceive yourself. You can't *love* him. There's
nothing there *to* love.'

I knew the words were vain even as I uttered them.
There is so much of the Beggar-maid in every woman that a

man has only to adopt the Cophetua role in order to win her. I think women like presents, not so much from greed as from a queer streak of self-abasement in themselves. To Linda, who had been poor and scorned and unsafe there was, I can see it clearly, something almost irresistible in my father's wealth and power and patronage.

'Even if you love him, and even if he does feel differently about you from how he feels about the others,' I began again in a reasoning tone, 'what good can come of it? He is married. Agnes is young. You don't want to be his mistress and the mother of a bastard, do you? Don't be offended with me, Linda. You're so alone: you need somebody's guidance now.'

'I'm not offended. I believe you are my friend, Philip. And I believe you're right. I'll try to go away. Because if I stay here ... and he wants me ... he'll have his way. I haven't any resistance where he is concerned....'

I asked out of sheer brutal curiosity, 'Doesn't it make any difference, what I've told you about him, that he is unkind and unfaithful, wanton?'

She looked at me. 'I suppose you've never been in love. You're how old, twenty? Older than I am. But women grow up sooner, they say. If you'd ever been in love you'd know that what the person is has nothing at all to do with it. What you know with your mind hasn't any effect on what you feel. You love where you have to.'

Quite softly and very sadly she spoke my doom as well as hers, looking into my face.

I wished, harder than I had ever wished for anything, even a cure for my leg, that I were older and rich and powerful and knowledgeable, so that I could say, 'Come away with me now, tonight. I'll look after you.' I would have shortened my life by twenty years to have had the power to say those words. I looked down on the full red curve of her mouth, bitter-sweet at the moment with sorrow, and the white parting that ran from her forehead to the crown of her shapely head where the black coils lay knotted and I regretted with a bitterness past description that I was my father's dependant, that I had never earned anything, should not know how to start to earn. I looked on her beauty and saw how defenceless she was alone with her half-crazy father, in this lonely place, safe enough from all but her protector, like a lamb with a wolf for watchdog. Well, let him play at watchdog for just a little longer and she might be safe after all.

'Listen,' I said. 'Don't do anything reckless in connection with my father. If you really love him, remember that I tell you, I who know him, that rapid conquest means rapid satiety with him. And I will go to London and see Nathaniel Gore and try to make other arrangements for you and your father. You're young, amid new scenes and new faces you may overcome this infatuation.'

'Don't speak as though it were a sickness and you were prescribing a pill,' she said: but she smiled as she said it. I stood up and wished her good night.

It was dark by this time and all the night was full of the scent of hay from the Sluice Meadow. I walked slowly, going over the interview and feeling my bruises like a man who had been in a physical fight might do. She loved my father. I think that no young man has ever taken a shrewder blow. I could have bellowed loud in the night. Still, that made the situation call more loudly for action and I planned action in between my bouts of self pity all the way from the cottage to the little gate in the park wall. I latched it behind me and stepped out on to the turf which was grazed down by my father's animals and which was easier to walk on than the field path. I had taken perhaps a dozen steps and was noticing with the surface of my mind how the hawthorn petals had showered down and lay in pale pools around the trees, when a solid shadow barred my way and my father's voice said.

'Where have you been?' He had never in all my life since about my sixth year shown any interest in my whereabouts and the sudden question warned me to be careful.

'I've been walking. Why?'

'Been to Madge's cottage, haven't you? I saw the mark of that iron of yours all about the gate.'

'All right,' I said, 'why ask if you know where I've been?' I made to move on towards the house. He put a heavy hand on my shoulder. 'Not quite so fast, my lad. How often have you been there?'

'Almost every day since the time I lost Quince.'

59

'What do you go for?'

'I talk to old Seabrook,' I said, still being careful. 'I was with him this evening while Linda rode with you.'

'Oh. Well, in future you'll oblige me by keeping away from there, do you hear? Not that I mind your talking to Seabrook, if one of your ideas of how to spend time is to chatter with an addle-witted sorcerer. But I have interests at the cottage myself and I don't want you there, see?'

'I see,' I said. 'As a matter of fact I meant to ask you tomorrow to give me some money so that I could go to London.'

'And what do you aim to do there? Dance at the Assembly Rooms? And why should I give you money?'

'It would keep me away from Madge's cottage,' I said as casually as I could. 'It's rather awkward for me when the Seabrooks refer to Madame Louise as my aunt: and one day soon Agnes will miss the family pearls and I may not be able to keep a kind of knowing look out of my eyes.'

'You are the most ——ing little bastard,' said my father with a hiss in his voice. 'Don't think you can threaten me. I'll give you the money because I shall be glad to be shut of the sight of you. Lame leg, chawbacon friends, cheeky tongue and as much idea of how a gentleman should behave as a muck heap, that's you.'

'Then let me take myself out of your sight. I wonder you've never suggested it yourself.'

Next morning he handed me, without a word, a pigskin purse full of gold pieces. I muttered 'thank you' as I took it, but I thought, ha-ha, my lord, if you knew what I was going to do with this you'd take it back, double quick.

I had got my things together overnight and had a valise of clothes and books which explained my demand for a horse to ride and a groom on a second horse to bring back the one I rode. No difficulty was raised about that and the fact showed me how very glad my father was of my departure. I took Quince a little way into the woods and shot him as he sniffed at a rabbit hole; then I said good-bye to Agnes and Madame Louise, promised Charles a puppet show from London on my return—he would have forgotten before he realised that I was not coming back—mounted my horse and set out with the groom beside me. At Marshalsea Green I sent him into the ale-house, bidding him wait for me, and a nice long wait it would be too, and rode, leading the spare horse, to the cottage by Hunter's Wood.

The door was open and the sun streamed into the little room. I knocked, and after a time Linda came downstairs. Her hair, more simply arranged than usual, hung in a heavy knot at the back of her neck and her sleeves were turned up to her smooth white elbows.

I blurted out my errand at once.

'Linda, I want you to get ready and come away with me today. I've two horses and plenty of money. We'll go to London, and get Mr. Gore to advise us. Everything I told you last night is quite true. My father is even paying me to take myself out of the way. You can't stay here.'

'I should stay if the devil himself were at the Manor,' she said fiercely. 'My father is ill. He couldn't move today.'

'Too ill to sit a horse as far as Colchester? We'd stay there if we must.'

'He's *raving* ill, she said impatiently. 'You wouldn't make him understand why he had to go, or anything. Besides I wouldn't try. And, Philip, there's no cause for anxiety. I will be careful to let your father see that I am not another Ellen Flower. It'll be all right, I assure you.'

'Well,' I said heavily. 'I hope it may be. I shall go to Mr. Gore's as soon as I reach London. I'll write to you from there. Will Baines will bring you the letter. And if you have any message for me he'll put it on the coach for me. I'll ask at the *True Troubadour* every time the Colchester coach comes.'

'You're very good to me, Philip.' She looked at me confidingly, and once again I was stricken through with the knowledge that she was very young, very inexperienced, very trusting. Here was I playing almost the very same game as my father's and she was trusting me as she had trusted him.

'Be very, very careful,' I said. 'When your father is better keep near to him.'

'All right,' she said like a child being instructed by its elder. 'Thank you, Philip,' she said again. And although my name on her tongue sang out to me like music I did not

61

take courage enough from it to say, don't thank me, I'm only doing what every man must, take care of the interests of his own heart.

I mounted again, dismally conscious of the difference in my performance and the one my father had given on that very spot last evening.

'Good-bye,' I said. Then, remembering, called back, 'And give him back those pearls.'

A noise at the upper window made me look at it, there was hardly need for me to raise my head for my horse was tall and the window low. Josiah Seabrook's demented face looked through the opening. 'Pearls of great price,' said his purple lips, 'and all cast before swine, a procedure which, as the Bible warns us, is unseemly and unprofitable.'

'Out of bed again,' said Linda from the doorway. 'Good-bye, Philip,' and she vanished. I rode on to the tavern and was shouting to the groom within when Eli came past carrying a ploughshare to the smithy. I stopped him.

'Eli,' I said, 'I'm going to London. I shall see that Mr. Gore I told you of earlier in the year. Would you like me to ask him about the new settlement he mentioned?'

'Aye. I should take it very kindly. So would Steggles and one or two more I could name. We'll never get forward here that's a sure thing. Not till you sit in your father's place, lad. And he's a lusty man yet.'

'All right, Eli. I'll see what I can do.'

And so I came in time to Colchester and so to London where I lost no time in presenting myself at the *Crooked Fleece*, an imposing house in a lane that led from the Strand to the river.

Nathaniel welcomed me with great kindness, some surprise, and reproaches that I had not advised him of my visit.

'I should have liked to have taken you about London, myself. It would have been a privilege to have taken you to your first play. But I am leaving London this evening for Bristol where I have business that cannot wait. And that makes it awkward, too. I've let this house to a cousin of mine, who, after vainly trying to marry off six painfully plain daughters in the depths of Wiltshire, has suddenly decided to bring them up to London to display their charms. I hardly like to ask him to offer you hospitality—six women with their attendants take up a lot of room. And even if I did I'm afraid, as a personable and eligible young man, you'd find yourself torn into six roughly equal pieces.'

'Please don't suggest it,' I begged him. 'I shall find a lodging easily enough. And I shall enjoy being on my own.'

'I don't doubt. But we must dine together early before I set out, and you must tell me all your news.'

We dined at a house in Fleet Street where the benches were set back to back and each couple was shut in the privacy of a high church pew. And there, over excellent stewed beef with dumplings floating in the brown gravy I told him about Linda and my father, this time concealing nothing, for I had regretted my earlier silence every day since I set eyes on Linda.

'Dear, dear,' he exclaimed. 'What a bother these perpetual adolescents are. I should have thought your father far too old and settled for such things. Why, he was every day of thirty when I first met him and that's let me see, a full quarter century ago. Linda Seabrook indeed. A mere child. It's fantastic. It's horrible. Still you say you've warned ... what a sorry task for an eldest son indeed ... and old Seabrook is no fool. I don't think you need *worry*, Philip, though we'll get her away by all means. Listen, I'm going to Bristol. I can't do anything now. But I shall be back within a fortnight, if all goes well. If I am delayed I'll let you know. I'm very busy, you know. I've got a grant of land from the New England Company and I intend to take possession of it next year. I'm looking about for suitable people to take up the land. There're two men in Bristol who have taken interest and written to me, I shall see them while I'm there on this other business. Lomax is their name, good substantial people I believe. And there's a parson who has lost his living for some reason or another. I must see him too. People like a parson in the party, gives them the idea that at least they'll be buried properly. Very particular about the final rites, many people are.'

'Eli Makers would go, and another man called Joseph Steggles from Marshalsea. You know, earlier on we really did make an effort and got together a petition about the enclosures that I told you about, do you remember? We had it properly drawn up and everything. But my father laughed and said he hadn't served the king for nothing. And sure enough a Parliament man came down and looked at the village and went back and reported that Marshalsea was in perfect order, most people were contented and that it was one of the most prosperous villages in England. Father had just whispered his wish you see.'

'I'm learning more about your father in one meal time than I knew before. Well, Philip, I must leave you. I shall be at the *Crooked Fleece* a fortnight from today. Meet me there. And make the most of your first visit to London.'

I walked with him as far as the corner where he turned down to his house and then I said good-bye. After he had gone I was aware of a feeling of loneliness and desolation such as I had never experienced in all my life before. The streets full of busy people, all to my country eyes, hurrying about their business, all knowing where they were going, which turning to take, at what moment to cross the road under the very noses of the horses, amazed and frightened me. For a whole fortnight I must wait here, getting no more forward, speaking to no one. I must not even spend much money, for when Linda could move I must be ready to pay for a lodging for her and her father. That thought killed my first intention, which was to walk along to the *True Troubador*, the coaching place where I had left my valise, and hire a room there. I must find something cheaper. And then I remembered Linda's mention of one of the cheap and horrible places in which she and her father had once lodged. The New Cut. That was it. I walked a little farther, mustering courage to ask a passer-by for direction. This one looked hurried, this one cross, these were engaged in such earnest conversation that it seemed a pity to disturb them. At last a porter trundling a barrow stopped near me and sat down on the handle of it to draw breath. I asked him if he could tell me the way to the New Cut, and with a curious glance at my shoes and my clothes, he told me.

When I reached the place I could hardly believe my eyes, and I understood why the porter had looked at me so oddly. It was a narrow street of houses whose overjutting top storeys seemed to lean together as though they were confiding some filthy secret to one another. The space between the houses was set with cobbles and the spaces between *them* were filled with every kind of filth imaginable. The houses themselves reeked of dirt and decay and the people who sat on the steps or leaned in the doorways were like caricatures of human beings. I walked up slowly, seeking a house less repulsive than the others, and when I had found one which I thought was so, I strengthened myself with the idea that Linda, so delicate and dainty, and old Seabrook, so learned and wise, had managed to live in such surroundings. And by doing the same I should be saving money to spend upon Linda's comfort when she came. In better heart from these reflections I knocked on the greasy door.

A woman, so fat that she was a collection of globes in shape, waddled at length to the door and opened it. Like the house she was slightly more clean and prosperous looking than her neighbours, but it was very slightly. Also she had a sly eye and a wheedling way of speaking which I did not like. But having climbed her steps and brought her to the door I felt impelled to state my errand, and she seized on me at once. Yes, she had a nice empty room right at the top of the house. Yes, it was clean, but if I was a particular sort she'd give it another clean before I moved in. I said I would fetch my bag. Immediately she said that her terms were payment in advance. No, she never let a room for a day. It must be a week or nothing. I daresay my inexperience was patent. Anyway I paid her for a week—and it was cheap, that I must admit. So I moved in at Mrs. Craske's.

I began a letter to Linda, I meant to write a little of it every day, though I could not send it until the following Monday when the coach left for Colchester. I told her about the New Cut, described Mrs. Craske's wheezing bulk in as amusing a way as I could, and promised her that when she arrived she should not join me there. I urged her again to be careful and to come to me as soon as her father could possibly move.

Day by day, for a week I added to the letter. Telling her of the plays which I had seen from the Pit, of the books that I had read, standing in book-shops and pretending to be casually considering a purchase, of the strange and sorry meals that I had eaten in cheap eating houses. That last was as much an experience to me as the other things. For the first time I realised that whatever else I had lacked in life I had enjoyed a good home. The tough grey meat I ate, the anonymous dishes I swallowed to sate my hunger would have been thrown out of the Manor kitchens into the pigs' troughs. I carried my letter down to the *True Troubadour* early on Monday, paid the fee, watched it into the coachman's pocket and received his assurance that Will Baines, the carrier, known to him by sight, should have it handed to him in the Goat yard at Colchester. I then waited about, impatient and hopeful, until the coach from Colchester arrived, which it did on Wednesday morning. There had been no time for Linda to receive mine and answer it, I knew that, but I did hope that she would have written to me. There was no letter, however, and I comforted myself with the reflection that if her father were still unwell she would be tied to the cottage and unable to reach the village to see Will Baines even if she had thought of and written to me. But soon Will Baines would make his way to Hunter's Wood, bearing my epistle and then she could give him hers, and next Wednesday for certain I should hear how her father was and when I might expect them. No child, awaiting a long-promised treat, could have been more impatient.

I wrote again so that the coach that went on Monday should carry the letter to her, and on the Tuesday of that week the fortnight that Nathaniel had set as the limit of his absence was up; in the evening I presented myself at the *Crooked Fleece* quite excited at the prospect of seeing him again.

Another disappointment awaited me. Nathaniel had sent me a message in a letter to his cousin. The cousin, like Nathaniel in size and shape, even in voice, but without his humour or good-fellowship, read me the paragraph. 'A Mr. Philip Ollenshaw will inquire for me, I flatter myself, on Tuesday next. Tell him please about my enforced journey to Plymouth and say that if he is still concerned about his friends, Sir John Talbot would and should be able to help him. Give the boy directions to the house and tell him to mention me. . . .'

With the way to Sir John's house roughly drawn on a

scrap of paper I left the *Crooked Fleece*, more depressed than ever. No letter from Linda and Nathaniel still away. I might as well have stayed at home! Still there was the coach tomorrow to await and hope for, and leaning upon this thought I made my way to Sir John Talbot's. He was the physical replica of Mrs. Craske, unwieldily fat and wheezy. Also his eyes were afflicted in some way. Their lashless lids were red and swollen, and little blobs of yellow matter hung on their edges. He was a repulsive old man, and although he offered me a meal incomparably superior to any I had partaken of in London, I did not really enjoy the food.

He remembered Josiah Seabrook, however, and swore that it was to his credit that he was not already as blind as his father had been before him. 'It's a curse on us,' he said solemnly. 'My great grandfather had a roving eye, and it roved once too often. An old woman whose daughter had been the subject of much lustful looking—and something more, ha! ha! ha! said, "You Chelliston Talbots would stand a better chance at the Day of Judgement if your sight wasn't so good." And believe it or not we've all had this trouble ever since. I never have been able to see whether a wench was comely or not. But that isn't a disadvantage, it's a great blessing. They all look the same to me, ha! ha! ha! But old Seabrook made a lotion of some sort of wild plant which really did relieve me. I wish you'd remind him of that, young man. You are young, aren't you? You sound young.'

'Josiah Seabrook isn't very well himself,' I said, seizing my opportunity. And not mentioning my father or anything about the Seabrooks' present plight I asked him whether he knew anyone who could offer them a safe asylum.

Yes, he had friends in Buckinghamshire who would, he thought, oblige him. He would have a letter written to them. But anything he did for Seabrook was on the clear understanding that a constant supply of the lotion was forthcoming. I promised that in Josiah's name.

As I left the house, resolutely repressing the gulps of the flatulence engendered by the rich meal taken without appetite, I thought, what is the use of this? It may just be my father over again, this time in Buckinghamshire. I will have no more of it. I will ask her to marry me forthwith, and as my father's eldest son I will demand a suitable home and establishment for my bride. But even as I thought of it I could imagine my father's fury. If I snatched Linda from him we might both die in the gutter for all he would care. On every side I was fettered and helpless. Perhaps Nathaniel could find me a job. I might be a clerk in a warehouse. My writing and figures were good. I imagined myself working at some humble but honourable task all day and returning to a little cottage and Linda every evening.

Dreams of this nature occupied me on my way back to Mrs. Craske's. But even they could not blind me to the fact that I was not feeling at all well. I attributed the feeling to the heavy meal I had eaten out of politeness with those suppurating eyelids turning my stomach the wrong way all the time. Or perhaps something I had eaten earlier in the day at the eating house just beyond the New Cut had disagreed with me. I felt sick and my head swam. Once or twice on the journey home I stopped in a dark doorway and tried to be sick, but my stomach seemed to have receded into a leaden lump, far far down. Once in my room I looked in my ewer, hoping that it had been filled, but it was empty, so I carried it down the two flights of twisting stairs and filled it at the well in the yard which served Mrs. Craske's and three other houses. Returning I found that I had to pause at every sixth step or so, my heart was going at such a rate that I could barely breathe. I hauled myself up by the railing and once within my room I drank about half the water and tumbled on to my bed. It was very hot and I threw off the covers until I lay, naked except for my shirt, upon the naked bed. Even so it seemed that a great weight lay upon my limbs and my head was so heavy that I could not turn it upon the soiled pillow. And presently it became imperative for me to move because Linda was in danger. What it was I could not see, but I heard her screaming and calling upon me to save her. It was fire, it must be fire, for I could feel the heat scorching my flesh. I made one last convulsive effort to leap from the bed, to push aside the weight that held me, and then Linda's voice and the heat of the fire faded away.

Now and again something stabbed momentarily through the darkness, but never long enough to give me any clue as to what was happening to me. Sometimes a light struck painfully on my eyeballs, sometimes a voice sounded harshly on my ears, but my mind was like a tiny piece of timber tossed on an incoming tide. It came to the surface for an instant and was submerged again.

But after a long time there came a light that did not vanish as soon as I looked at it and I heard a sound of feet moving and the sound was not silenced as soon as I listened. So I looked and listened and realised that the light was from a lantern which was coming towards me and the sound was the movement of the feet of him who carried it. I stretched out my hands on either side of me and wondered what had happened to my bed, for my narrow pallet was laid on the floor and the floor was of stone, damp and cold. And as soon as I had learned that I became conscious of the awful stench of the place wherein I lay, and of the terrific thirst that was consuming me.

The lantern came close, and by screwing my eyelids against what seemed to my unaccustomed eyes the intolerable blaze of light, I could see the long white beard and stooping body of the old man who stood looking down upon me.

'Where am I?'

'In lazar house,' he said laconically.

'Why?'

'Brought here to die, young sir. So be quick about it and don't be troublesome.'

'But I'm not going to die. I'm better. Will you give me some water?'

'I said, don't be troublesome. I ain't here to tend you. I'm here to see that you're properly dead before I puts you in the hole I got dug for you. So lay down and keep quiet.'

He passed on, and as the light moved I saw that he was bent over the floor a foot or two from me. I stretched out my hand and felt another pallet there.

'This one's stiff, Tom. Give me a hand with 'un,' said the ancient, and another man came out of the darkness. The lantern bearer shifted the lantern to his wrist and bending down stiffly took up the feet of the corpse while the other man lifted the head. They passed me slowly and I could see the stiff body with the grotesquely projecting feet and trailing arms as they carried it by.

Twice the dismal procession passed me, and on their next return they paused again at the foot of my pallet.

'Bury this 'un too an' make a clean sweep of it, shall us?' asked the ancient.

'Ah!' said his companion.

I dragged myself into a sitting position, and from that got on to my knees. I was still in my shirt which was stiff with excreta. Below that my legs were bare. My shoe was in the house in the New Cut where I had taken off my clothes on the night that I was taken ill. Last night? How long ago? There was no means of knowing. Without that shoe I could hardly walk, far less run!

I faced the pair of ghouls with the desperation of a cornered animal.

'You can't bury me alive,' I exclaimed in the strongest voice I could muster. 'I'm better, I tell you. I want to go from here. Get me some clothes—I'll pay you.'

'Us gets,' said the old man with a kind of poisonous patience, 'a shilling for every burial. Us gets no penny for them as walks away. Ain't that right, Tom?'

'Ah,' said Tom.

The old man turned and addressed his companion privately, but after the long silence in which I had lain my hearing was painfully acute and I heard every word.

'Knew this was going to be troublesome, Tom lad,' he said. 'Called out too lusty like all along. Anybody asked for 'un?'

'No,' said Tom.

'Where'd he come from. Do you mind?'

'New Cut. Just as he be now.'

'We'll have a shilling on 'un, then. Nobuddy'll be a mite wiser tomorrow morning.'

'You make a mistake there,' I said. 'I may come from New Cut and I may look penniless, but I'm not a beggar. I'm quite well known, and if one of you will run to Sir John Talbot's house and say that Philip Ollenshaw is here he'll send me some clothes and a carriage.'

'Raving again,' said the old man, touching his head with a

filthy finger in significant mumming.

' 'Sides, even if 'twere true we can't let 'un go now, Tom. He'd spread story of shilling all over Lonnon. No, it's under the ground he'll have to go.'

'Ah!' said Tom.

I struggled up, weaker than water, but alive and intending to remain so. I set my short leg on the pillow and so gaining a precarious balance prepared to do battle for my life. Fortunately the old man was senile and Tom without intelligence or enterprise. I thrust my fist feebly into the bearded face and with the other hand wrenched the lantern from his wrist. I swung wildly. The iron rim caught Tom on the bridge of his nose and as he put his fingers to the wound the candle fell out and was extinguished on the damp stones of the floor. I saw the old man recover from the push and come towards me and then it was quite dark in the lazar house and I dropped to my knees and started crawling along the wall. I could go silently, and their boots rattled on the stones, there was my only advantage. But I was crawling round a room that I had never seen, while they were on familiar ground. I heard the old man say,

'Make light, Tom. Where be tinder box?' and then a second afterwards there was a crash and a curse.

'That were my head you dunted, blast you for a fool, Tom. Which way were I going?'

While they untangled themselves I was going like a cat over the pallets and the spaces between them, feeling the wall with my hands. It opened into space at last and I could feel the sharp edge of a step. It was the bottom one of a twisting flight. It turned twice before it reached the top and there was still no sound of pursuit behind me. Crawling blindly I crashed my head against a door that stood at the top of the stairway and the bolts rattled in their sockets. Down in the pest house I heard the old man shout and knew that in a minute they would be on me. I rose on my good leg, fumbled frantically for the bolts and drew them back with raucous shrieks of iron on iron. The door gave outwards mercifully and I tumbled out into the summer night which seemed grey after the Stygian darkness there below. The door through which I had tumbled was fronted by a porch, like a church, and I crawled round it, and

71

stopped in the corner of shadow that it made as it joined the building. If only a watchman would pass with his lantern and his stave! Though even so he might be more disposed to side with the keepers of the lazar house than with me. There was so little to commend me to either a watchman or any other passer-by. I was filthy, I stank abominably. I was almost naked. I heard the clatter of boots on the stone stairs and then there were voices in the porch.

'You go left, I'll go right,' said the old man. 'We've got to catch 'un afore he see anybody. An' he can't of gone far, looked lame like to me.'

'Ah!' said Tom. I saw the light run out in a fan of yellow over the cobbles in front of the porch and then there was another crash.

'Blast you, Tom lad,' said the wheezy old voice again. 'I telled you go left. Don't you know your left hand, you clumsy mortal?'

Now I had turned instinctively to the right, as they say every man does, running blindly, so I should have the old man to deal with. I heard Tom's feet clatter off to leftwards and then I saw the old fellow walk straight out of the porch and raise the lantern, peering into the darkness that seemed the deeper by contrast with the light. He seemed in no hurry, or perhaps he was incapable of more rapid movement. He came round the porch, swinging his lantern and I leaned forward and caught him round the knees. He came down with a crash, rolled over and lay still, but whether he was really stunned or simply foxing in order to avoid further punishment I did not know. He was breathing steadily enough. I slipped off his canvas breeches and drew them over my own legs, tugged his smock over his head, tied his feet together with his own neckerchief and took the candle out of the lantern. Then I went on crawling away to the right. Whenever I came to a corner I crawled round it. I stopped once to drink from a puddle that lay in a hollow of the cobbles and it was the sweetest drink that I had ever taken. Soon my hands and knees were skinned and my heart pounded so that it shook my whole body. Presently I saw a deep porch in front of a doorway. There were oak benches inside it and I crept under the shadow of one of

72

them and lay still. I didn't sleep and I didn't think. I was not even much impressed by the narrowness of my escape or the villainy of the keepers of the lazar house. I just lay there, content to cease from the effort to escape and after a long time I saw the faint grey over the housetops opposite change to gold and rose colour.

It was still very early, though quite light when I was startled by the sound of a bolt withdrawing on the other side of the imposing front door against which I lay. I had just drawn myself up and stood supported by the side of the porch when the door opened and a pretty girl in a mob cap appeared with a broom in her hand. She gave a little squeal at the sight of me and I said quickly, 'Don't be frightened. I won't hurt you.' She stood dubious, one hand on the door, ready to bolt inside and slam it after her. Then I saw her eye rest on my shrunken leg, the foot hanging four inches from the floor.

'I'm a cripple,' I said, 'and someone has taken my crutch. I can't walk without it.'

'Well, I haven't a crutch to give you,' she said pertly, certain now that I was harmless.

'I could manage with a broom,' I said, eyeing hers.

'But this broom was new not a fortnight since,' she protested.

'And the old one?'

'You could have that.' She went inside, and bolted the door after her. I thought perhaps that she would not emerge again, but after some time she opened the door and showed herself with an old broom in one hand and little pie in the other.

'My master is charitable to beggars and cripples,' she said, rather piously. 'He would wish you to have this.'

She placed the pie in my hand and then stepped back sharply as the reek of my body reached her nostrils.

'The weather is warm enough for you to take a wash,' she said sharply, and handed me the broom at arm's length. I set it under my armpit, thanked her and hobbled away.

If everything else fails me I shall go to London and discard my boot and walk about on a broom! Long before I had taken my bearings and discovered whereabouts in London I was, a lady—going I imagine to early service at her church

—beckoned me across the road and gave me a silver piece. I took it too, for my own money had been in the house in New Cut, with my clothes and I hadn't any hope of finding it there. Soon after a gentleman, out for an early ride threw me two copper coins. And this charity was not because beggars and cripples and blind men were rare in London at the time, on the contrary the city swarmed with them, but many were impostors, many of their disabilities went no deeper than the rag that drew attention to them, whereas mine was patently genuine. I did not scorn to pick the coppers out of the kennel where they lay: they meant a meal and no amount of pride would feed me.

At last I met a waterman going his round and asked him to direct me to New Cut. After I had followed his intricate instructions for a time the streets began to look familiar and just as I thought that my last grain of strength was exhausted I came to the mouth of the alley and by a mighty effort reached the steps that led to the door. I sat down on the last one. There was no real need to knock on the door: upwards of twenty people lived in the house and sooner or later one of them was bound to come down the steps. Very soon indeed Mother Craske herself opened the door and flung some rubbish into the mouldering heap that lay in the middle of the road. 'Off you go,' she cried, spying me.

'Mrs. Craske,' I said, 'help me into the house. Strange things have happened to me and I'm at the end of my tether.' She made no movement but stood there at the top of the steps as though the sight of me had turned her into stone. Her broad purple face had changed to lilac colour and her eyelids fluttered up and down.

'You've nothing against me,' she said at last. 'I did what I could for you. You've no call to come back here and abuse me.'

'Am I abusing you? I'm asking you to help me into the house and give me a bed until I can get about again.'

'There's nothing of yours here,' she said irrelevantly and still speaking from the top of the steps.

'If I can get back my own shoes...' The humility of the request brought home to me the acute misery of my plight. I was ill and filthy and my money was gone and my hope

74

of helping Linda had gone with it. I didn't even know how long I had been ill. I had dropped my head into my hands as I asked for my shoes, and without looking up I said,

'What day is this?'

'The twelfth of July.'

'What?'

'You were ill here for a fortnight, and you've been gone four days,' she said, almost meekly.

'I've got such a lot to see to,' I said, truckling to her in my despair. 'Help me into the house, there's a good soul and get me my writing materials. And some brandy with an egg in it,' I added as an after-thought.

'But I told them you were dead,' and by this time the woman's rough voice was really frightened.

'Told whom?'

'The people who came asking for you. And you were dead for all I knew.'

I crept up the steps, on my hands and knees again.

'When did they come? And what were they like?'

'The day they took you away. A young woman and a man, not so young. Very pretty the young woman was, and the man had a big yellow beard. She cried.'

'Linda!' I cried. 'Quick, Mrs. Craske, find me a shirt and my own shoes, or I'll scream that I've been robbed, and your reputation won't help you with the magistrate.' I crawled past her and made for the stairs to my room. 'Bring me hot water and a razor. AND FIND THOSE SHOES!'

The room that had been mine contained none of my belongings and from the state of the bed and the dirty water in the basin I gathered that it was already occupied by someone else. I cared nothing for that. Mrs. Craske, on the move at last, soon followed me up with the water, the razor, the brandy and the egg, and glory upon glory, my own shoes. Even in my present state of mind I could not refrain from asking her why, having disposed of all my other things, she had preserved them.

'I thought I might find another gentleman with a short leg,' she said frankly. 'Nobody else would want them as they are?' She began to retreat from the room, but I said,

'Wait a minute, Mrs. Craske. It won't do you any harm to see a man without a shirt.' I wrenched it off as I spoke

75

and flung it into the farthest corner. 'Tell me about my illness. I can't remember anything after coming downstairs for the water that evening.'

'Well,' she began, rather unwillingly, 'you didn't come down all the next day and I came up in the evening. You lay on the bed there and kept calling me that name you said just now—Linda—and begging me not to be led astray. I brought you milk and water, sometimes you took it and sometimes you didn't and then it was rent day. So I hunted about and found your money. I'm a poor woman, Mr. Ollenshaw, and have my living to consider. When I found the money I thought you could pay a doctor, so I called one in. He said you had a fever and he took a handful of the money and sent a draught which you wouldn't take. You raved something awful,' she scratched her scalp through her scanty hair, 'went on about your dad something shameful. I used to come up and look you in the face and say, "Look here, you must keep quiet, you disturb all the house," and you used to look straight at me and say, "So you thought you were going to have her, did you, you old whore-monger? Wait and see, the crippled chawbacon will cheat you yet." At the end of the week the doctor came again and said it was plague, that you'd got the constitution of an ox to have stood it so long, but that you'd die that night and must be got out to the pest house or he'd have the authorities after him for not recognising it before. So we sent for the cart. And the men or the doctor took your money and it was rent time again so I sold the books and the things to pay myself. And you can't blame me for anything. Your own mother couldn't have done more for you.'

I accepted the tale with reservations.

'Get out, now,' I said, 'I want to wash.' So she went away and, piece by piece, sitting down when I felt too weak to stand, I got myself washed and dressed. The clothes she had brought me were not my own, neither were they clean, but at least they were free of the pest-house odour and I was in no position to be particular.

Clinging to the filthy black stair rail I reached the ground floor of the house and said, 'Call me a chair.'

When it came I directed the men to Sir John Talbot's house and then drew the curtains and leaned back. They carried me swiftly—their scorn of the New Cut neutralised by the address that I had given them—and in a short time we were at Sir John's door. 'Wait,' I said, 'I may need you.'

Sir John was in his study with a decanter of port wine and a dish of biscuits on the desk before him.

'Oh yes,' he said, squinting a recognition at me. 'You've called about the Seabrooks. You must be quite mad, young man. I made inquiries about them the very day after you came to see me, and learned that they were in very good hands, very good hands indeed, none other than your own father's. Why didn't you tell me that? Eh? I might have written to my friends in Buckinghamshire and set all kinds of plans working. You told me that it was essential to find them a home and all the time they had it! Really.'

'Forget all that,' I said, not bothering to justify myself—it was true that I said that they were in danger, but not from whom—'tell me, has Linda Seabrook been here?'

'Not since she came with her father to say good-bye, some time before last Christmas.'

'I won't trouble you any further, then. If she should come, tell her that I am in the third house in the New Cut. Good day to you, sir.'

I hurried out to the chair-men, who were sitting on the shafts, dozing in the sun. I realised that my letter to Linda in which I mentioned Sir John Talbot, had never been dispatched, she would not think that the chance name mentioned by her babbling father would have been remembered by me. She would never think of tracing me through him. God's curse upon that sickness, well was it named the Plague. But they would have come by coach! My circling mind presented me with that fact like a good dog retrieving a partridge. The Colchester coach.

'Run,' I said to the chair-men, 'to the *True Troubadour* in the Strand.'

And there I was lucky. The innkeeper remembered the young pretty lady who had arrived with an older man, because she had suggested lodging there and the man had called taverns 'the haunt of Satan'. So she had left her boxes there and had called the next day for one of them and man had carried it to the house on Ludgate Hill, the first one past Spindler's Green.

77

The chair-men, rather sick of me by this time, carried me to a prim house set back from the road and enclosed by iron rails. I offered them the silver piece that the lady had given me.

'But this is not enough for running about half the day,' said one of them. 'And kicking our heels in one place and then the other.'

'Enough or not it is all I have,' I said. 'It gives me little pleasure, I assure you, to rob you of what you think your dues, but everything I have has been filched from me and what I cannot pay for must be given me.'

They grumbled on, but I was already raising the knocker of the prim front door.

A tall gaunt woman with loops of lank black hair framing her sallow face opened to me.

'I believe you have living here a Miss Linda Seabrook. Take me to her, please.' By this time my impatience was such that I was tempted to thrust her out of my way and rush into the house crying 'Linda' at the top of my voice.

'There's no such person here,' said the woman. 'I've only my brother, Eli Makers and his wife. Why what's wrong with you, man?'

The next thing I knew I was in a high-backed chair and the scent of burnt feathers was strong in my nostrils. I looked up and saw Linda's face above me. I looked down and saw her hand waving the smouldering feathers close to my nose.

'I've been very ill, Linda,' I said. That was my first thought—she must never know. I must blame my swooning upon my illness.

'I know. The woman in New Cut said that you were dead,' she said. Her voice was very quiet.

I pressed my fingers to my eyes.

'So you married Eli, Linda. Whatever made you do it?'

I saw her finger go to her lip and her eyes take on that backward look that I was to know so well, so very well. Eli's voice came from a part of the room outside my range of vision.

'You'd best tell Master Philip about your father, wife.'

Her eyes filled with tears, but she blinked them back and said, 'He's dead, Philip.'

'Oh, he didn't recover, then?'

'He got better of that. He was killed at the Summer Fair.'

'Killed!' I cried. 'Why, who would kill him?'

'I'll tell him, wife, and get it over. You go help Keziah prepare the meal and bid her lay an extra place at the table.' Without a word Linda left me and walked towards the door. The spring had gone from her step and there were no rings in her ears, and her gown was black, with linen bands where the ruffles used to lie.

'Lad,' said Eli, looking down upon me from his great height, 'there is that in this story that I would not tell you, were your feelings for your father other than I have been led to think they are. . . .'

'Never mind that,' I said. 'Tell me quickly, for God's sake, what has happened to Linda's father, and what made Linda marry you.' The misery in my voice rang out so unmistakably that I tried to cover it by adding, 'So suddenly.'

Eli put out his big chipped hand and laid it awkwardly on my shoulder for a second. I started, both from surprise and from the horrid fear that he had guessed my state, knew how I felt towards Linda, and was sorry for me. But as he drew away his hand and lowered himself carefully into the high chair with fine needlework upon its back and seat, I saw by his face that the fear was unfounded. Eli was sorry because he was about to decry my father to me.

'Go on, man,' I said harshly. 'Out with it. God knows I shed all fancies about my father years ago. Tell me what happened at the Summer Fair.'

The clean, polished room and the view of the street through the little leaded panes faded as Eli began his tale. If I had once drawn Eli's portrait in words that impressed Nathaniel Gore I don't know what that worthy man would have thought of Eli's picture. Or was it my imagination that filled out the tale, stark and bare as it was, and made me see the dark places in Hunter's Wood and the cloud of superstition gathering in them, made me see the corn ripening and smell the thyme as the fair people crushed it, hammering home the uprights of their booths? I saw the whole thing happen.

Josiah Seabrook was old and strange and had mad ways. He had come from who knew where to live in the cottage

79

where old Madge, an acknowledged witch, had lived and died. Country people, in the days of my youth recognised two kinds of witches, harmless and vicious and Madge was one of the former kind. People were careful not to offend her, and few cared to pass the cottage by night, but in illness and misfortune they would turn to her, swallow the potions she gave them, repeat what she told them, make her a present and hope for relief. And perhaps through her luck, or perhaps by virtue of her wisdom her clients were satisfied and she was tolerated. She had been invited to the Manor to look at me. I could not remember the occasion, being very young at the time, but I had heard it spoken of. She had given the maid who had charge of me a bottle of pungent oil with which to rub my leg. It hadn't worked, but it had done no apparent harm, and I suppose the same might truthfully be said of most of her prescriptions.

But Linda's father, with his queerness and his living in Madge's cottage, was almost inevitably bound to inherit her reputation. He gathered—or had gathered for him—plants and herbs from the woods and the wayside. Apparently long before I had left Marshalsea he was receiving requests from afflicted people in search of pills and potions. Foolishly as it turned out, but innocently enough, he had, when a remedy was obvious, given the applicant a supply of his infusions and cordials. Nobody complained of that, indeed he might have continued for years, building up for himself a reputation not unenviable in its way, as old Madge had done, but something very unfortunate occurred. Shortly after my leaving, as soon as the old man was about again after his attack, a woman called at the cottage requesting a dose for her son who was taken with a terrible cough. 'Lung rot' as the country people called it when the sufferer coughed and spat blood. Josiah had looked at the boy, 'pulled down his eyelids, tapped his chest and held his wrist', said Eli, and then, sending the boy out into the garden to wait, had told the mother straightly that no mixture of horehound and liquorice and honey could do anything for him. 'He has little time to live,' he had said gravely, and the mother, very discontented had gone away. But here was the rub. The boy was one of those from whom Josiah had rescued my dog, Quince, and during the rescue he had said some hard things to the boys in question. Add to this his refusal to give a potion and the fact that the boy did indeed die in a fit of lung bleeding within two weeks of his visit to the old man and you have as pretty a little story as the most confirmed witch-hunter could desire to uncover. From then on Josiah was suspect.

Summer Fair time came and the Green at Marshalsea was crowded with booths and people. The pen for the greasy-tailed pig was roped off, the horse collars were laid out for the grinning competition. The hasty pudding was heated for the scalding of the competitors' mouths. Much strong ale was brewed. From far and near afoot, on horseback or riding in farm carts beribboned and beboughed the people came eagerly for the great merrymaking of the year. Linda and her father made their first excursion to view the booths. If they noticed them they were undeterred by the black looks that followed them, by the whispers and the pointed fingers. But I think they did not notice. The old man was interested in the people, the apothecary's stall, the bookman's pack, and Linda was looking—I swear—at the ribbons and the laces, the lengths of muslin and brocaded stuff that the chapman had unfolded. Anyhow they came at last to the stall of the man who sold pills. A man dressed in sailor's clothes paraded up and down before the booth, and there was a parrot on his shoulder, a bright gaudy bird who shouted at monotonous intervals, 'Why suffer? Why suffer?' And people, attracted by the strange swarthy face of the sailor and the novelty of the talking bird, listened to the vendor's patter and repeated to themselves the parrot cry, 'Why suffer?'

Why indeed when there was no ill of all those that flesh is heir to that this man could not remedy? Joint evil, lung rot, palsy, boils, scab and itch, he had remedies for them all. And he sold them as fast as he could hand them out once the people had overcome their shyness. And then he said, 'And now here's something specially for the ladies. Stand back there, you stout fellows, unless of course you know someone who needs this remedy and you'll know why, you rogues! Now all ladies have their little troubles . . .' He pattered on. I knew it all, and though Eli, naturally did not give me these details there was no need for him to do so. I had visited the Fair every Midsummer since Shad put the iron on my boot. I knew the sly, indefinite way in which the salesman vaunted the wonder of those pills and how he always ended with, 'Now, I know ladies are shy, so I'm not asking you to step up my beauties, you go your ways and enjoy yourselves and presently my man and I will be among you. Look at us well so you'll know us again, and a word in the ear, a coin in the hand and the remedy's yours and who's the wiser. Now is there anybody here with a toothache? You look solemn, my good fellow, is it your tooth or your heart that's aching ...' And right there Josiah Seabrook lifted up his voice and said, 'Any woman who takes rubbish in such a cause runs a danger greater than any known in childbed.' The medicine man was indescribably angry, and for this reason; cures for toothache or joint evil changed hands openly and might be had for a few pence. But the cures which he promised for the ills of womanhood were purchased secretly and, like all contraband, cost many times their value. A woman sliding up on the outskirts of the crowd would slip a shilling, or even two into the discreet hand and demand no change. His best market was attacked. He stepped off his little platform and began to berate Josiah. A few Marshalsea people joined in and very soon there was a riot. It remained for somebody to shout 'Drown the wizard' and the damage was done.

'I wasn't there, lad, fairs have no appeal for me. Linda told me this, and though there is great vanity in her there is no falsehood. And Squire was there, because Jem Flower told me, and so far from stopping the rabble, lad, he egged them on. They never got the old man to the water because with the frailty of him and the age of the rough handling he was dead before they got him off the Fair ground. And that groom of your father's, Jim, was foremost in the pushing and kicking. And at the end of the day, so the Marshalsea folks say, he had more money than he would have come by in any lawful way.'

Easy, all too easy to believe.

'Go on,' I said. So Eli's deep voice, with its old, surprising mellowness, its old surprising aptness of phrase went on. 'The lass was almost demented and when old Chopstick Cullum took the order from your father to make the old man a grand coffin she went down to the shop and ordered a plain one, swearing she'd pay with everything in the cottage. Mrs. Hunt, up at Hunt's Farm, she's a kind motherly sort, she went down and tried to comfort the girl and asked her to go there to sleep, but she just cried and carried on, and wouldn't move.

'By the funeral day all the folks were a bit sorry and turned out very sober and quiet for the burying. Your father wasn't there, but Jim the groom hung about until somebody who'd seen his knee in the old man's kidneys said he thought he'd do as well to take himself off.

'That night I was at work late on my strip in the Layer Field. It's before the cottage, you'll mind. And suddenly I hear the wench yelling. I think that perhaps the horrors are on her and she all alone there, so I step up, and there is your father, tearing at the girl's night rail and she screaming her head off. He's a stout man, your father, yet, but my blood was up and I slung him out on the path. And then the girl clung to me and cried and said that she'd trusted him and he'd helped kill her father. The story of Jim was all over the village, you see. And she said, over and over again, "Take me away, take me away," and she mentioned you. You'd gone to find a place for her, she said, and she knew your address in London.

'I knew that there'd be short shrift for me in Marshalsea after hitting Squire the way I did, and I was hopeful of what you'd said about Mr. Gore. So I sold my stock and took seats for us both on the coach and came to London. We found the place in the New Cut—and what possessed you, Mr. Philip to dwell in such a Sodom of unrighteousness I shall never understand—and there the fat woman said that you were dead. "Taken away this very morning," were her words. Well, then the woman was stricken indeed. Her last friend, her only friend, was gone she said. And at that the hand of the Lord came upon me strongly and His will was made plain to me in the matter. A vain, pretty girl in a great city, without protection with a nature trustful of any stranger, as I had proved. I could see little but a life of evil and peril before her. Moreover, though I did not mention this, I had seen her nakedness, that night, for the night rail was rent asunder. So I did what I thought was my bounden duty. I married her this morning. She was startled and stunned like when I first mentioned it to her, but this is the Lord's doing and He's a mighty worker.'

With that pious sentence he finished the story and the hope of my life at the same time. I sat in silence and drove home into my deepest consciousness the implication of that awful, monstrous sentence.

Oh, Linda, I know how you looked that night in your bedgown. Sweet, sweet, and above all things desirable. I know how the sudden lust leaped in this big slow man as you clung to him, helpless and tearful, with your black hair streaming and your face like the white briar rose from your terror. This was the Lord's doing! Oh, Linda, frightened and helpless and aghast at Mrs. Craske's news you might have been ... but if you had only waited, waited until you were sure, waited until you were at least in love again.

But nothing of this must show. Not a suspicious word or glance must escape me. Because wherever you go, Linda, my love, I must follow. I must be acceptable to Eli. I must swallow the gall of this, the bitterest draught I have been faced with since they found my leg incurable. I must grind my teeth upon my hasty tongue, drive my nails into my palms, control the impulse that impels me to drop my head on to the arm of this chair and sob and sob and sob.

'I spoke to Mr. Gore about America in connection with you, Eli. He is on the look out for men. But I suppose this alters things a bit, doesn't it? Though you can't go back to Marshalsea. It would hardly hold you and my father after this.'

'Why should anything be altered?' asked Eli. 'Ever since the moment that I wrestled with your father and had the victory of him, I have been turning towards Mr. Gore. If he will take us we will go. Keziah my sister has money a-plenty and I will borrow from her for gear and anything we need. I look for a country where men shall be free and equal as they are in the sight of God. A land where each man tills his lot and sits at peace under his own vine as is foretold in Holy Writ. We'll have done with taverns and bawdy behaviour, with hotbeds of Popery and Squires and bound acres.' He rose suddenly and went to the window, so that the whole room was darkened by his shadow. His voice rose into an organ note of ecstasy and promise as he slightly misquoted in a manner all his own, 'The wilderness and the solitary place shall be glad of us; the desert shall rejoice and blossom like the rose.'

As he spoke Linda opened the door and peeped around it. Oh, Linda, my throat aches with my longing for you. I couldn't help it that I caught the plague, or lodged in a filthy alley where no one cared whether I was quick or dead. It was for your comfort that I did it, and this is my guerdon.

'Blossom like the rose,' my bruised mind repeated the last lovely words of Eli's peroration : for me that did not mean the desert, or the distance, or the future. Here and now it blossomed, but not for me.

BOOK TWO

BOOK TWO

PREPARATION

It would make tedious reading were I to set down step by step our movements and arrangements, our discussions, our hopes and disappointments between the time when the deicision to go to America was made and the actual departure. But there is one matter which interests everybody and which isn't always as fully dealt with in journals or in history books as it ought to be, and that is the matter of money. I have been, in my time, a great reader and I must confess that in many accounts of campaigns and voyages I have been puzzled and rather angry because insufficient mention, or indeed no mention at all has been made of how funds for the ventures were raised. Here was I, for instance, with my fifty pounds all gone, my sole possessions the sorry clothes I stood up in. It would be easy to say, 'And so we went to America.' And if I found that in a book I should immediately question, 'But how?' So I will explain about those I know.

Linda was penniless and Eli, of course, had little. He had worked all his life and had supported himself, but had never had anything to save. Keziah however was rich. She had been housekeeper to a wealthy and eccentric city merchant who had never given her anything but an order in all her years with him. After his death it was discovered that some ten years before he had willed her the house on Ludgate Hill, his business premises in Bread Street and some two thousand pounds. The Bread Street property she had sold immediately and as soon as she decided to throw in her lot with Eli she disposed of the Ludgate Hill house to a printer who had coveted it for some time. She was responsible for her own expenses, Eli's and Linda's and for a little while she was deluded enough to reckon that this gave her a power over her brother. But Eli was versed in the writings of St. Paul and knew that man was made in God's image and that woman was an afterthought upon the part

89

of the Almighty who had designed her for helpmeet, not master and Keziah took out the bitterness of her discovery of importance upon any other woman who happened to be handy. That of course came later. Until all the business was finished Keziah had a very happy time talking of deeds and money and pretending to the printer that she wasn't certain about selling the house and even less certain about letting him buy it.

Nathaniel Gore, of course, had no lack of money, and he was responsible for the dispossessed parson, and two young workmen, Harry Wright and Tim Dendy. Oliver Lomax was a substantial leather merchant attracted by the Puritanic nature of the new colony—though it was a mystery to me how it was given that character in advance, it was none of Gore's doing, of that I am sure. With Lomax, a widower with one daughter, came his brother, a master baker by trade, the brother's wife and daughter, all very subservient to Oliver who obviously held the purse strings.

I got my money from my father. I drove a better bargain than Essau who gave his birthright for a paltry mess of pottage. I got a thousand pounds for mine.

Nathaniel, back from his prolonged journey, and full of his darling project, was astounded when I announced my decision to join in it. I could see the curiosity, which was one of his strongest characteristics, worrying the problem like a dog a bone.

'But, Philip, there's a Marshalsea to consider. Badly as you get on with your father the lands and the Manor will be yours in course of time. If you don't want to spend all your time there you can let one of those young brothers run it and you can take a house in London and live in it for the best part of each year.'

'I'm coming to America,' I said.

'So you said before. But I can't see *why*. It's not just a jaunt, you know. It's a serious undertaking and you seem to have come to such a sudden decision. You weren't in this mind when we were discussing the settlement over our dinner that day.'

'A lot has happened since then.'

He gave a little chuckle and his small shrewd eyes darted a glance at me.

'Pair of bright eyes, is it, Philip? Ah, I'm not old to remember the havoc they can cause. But you mustn't alter the whole shape of your life on such an account, you know. There are dozens of bright eyes about, and kind hearts with some of them, bless them all.'

Conscious of my youth, my gaucherie, my thinness and most of all my hateful affliction, I loathed that he should think of me as a lovesick youth. I said priggishly,

'My decision has nothing to do with eyes, bright or otherwise. Can't you understand that I want something of my own, something for myself, something I have made and have a share in. Any land that came to me from my father would be tainted for me, by his hatred, by memories.' And what memories! Small enjoyment for me in owning the Layer Field where Eli had laid down his tools to rescue a screaming girl.

'Well, yes. I can understand that,' said Nathaniel. 'But you should give this a little thought. Life in a new country isn't very easy. For a time, at least, there will be no room for gentlemen there. Your life, unsatisfactory in many ways as it may have been, has been spent in peace and plenty, you have had a wealthy home behind you, servants...'

'I am a moderate carpenter and handy at smith's work,' I said. 'I'm stronger than I look. And though I may not be able to plough like Eli does, I intend to take enough substance with me to carry another man or two as well. Andy Seeley, after Eli, is the best man in Marshalsea. He'll come with me.'

'And where will you get your substance?'

'From my father, where else?'

'He may object.'

'Not he. You see I have a bargain to make with him. Essau sold his birthright for a mess of pottage. I intend to do better than that. I mean to have a thousand pounds and Charles can have father's blessing!' Nathaniel laughed and argued no more. So I borrowed my coach fare to Colchester and was lucky enough to fall in with a man who was driving a cart out Marshalsea way. I rode with him until the main road ran into the four ways of the Green and there I alighted, paid him and set off on my walk. My last walk along the lane and the field path to the Manor.

It was a lovely evening with the lingering warm twilight of September. The hawthorn trees in the park were covered with pale orange berries and some of the leaves had the touch of brown that made them so like Linda's eyes. Behind me the sunset stained the clouds with rose and amethyst and daffodil: in front of me loomed the house of my fathers and within it somewhere was the man who had lost me Linda. My hatred of him, never for years allayed or appeased but always blown upon and smouldering, rose in me so strongly that when at last I came upon him, seated in the hall with a dog at his feet and a bottle on the table at his elbow, and he raised his eyes and said, 'Aha, so the prodigal has spent his portion and returned?' I did not feel like a beggar, or a returned prodigal or a crippled youth confronted by arrogant maturity. I was facing a man who had wronged me so much that he could never make amends, but a certain palliative was in his power and that I was determined to have.

'I have something to talk over with you,' I said, 'I won't take long about it.' My eyes were so blind with hatred that I did not notice for some time that he was not completely sober.

I plunged straight into my business. 'I know full well that you hate the sight of me, that you're ashamed of me and wish I'd never been born. There was a time when your feelings towards me hurt me deeply, but now I am quite indifferent to them; only I want to turn them to account. I want to go right away, to America. I won't come back, I won't claim a penny of the estate and I won't have the title. So far as you, and anybody else is concerned I shall be dead. But in order to do that I must have some money and that you must give me.'

'A little less free with those musts, my boy. Remember who you're talking to.'

'I'm talking to the one person who can give me the money,' I said hardily. 'Well, what's your answer?'

'It needs thinking over. For Charles' sake—now there's a likely lad, hardly out of petticoats before he knew one end of a gun from the other and sits his horse like a jockey—for Charles' sake, I say I'd give you what you ask. But how can

I tell. The money gone you'd as likely as not come limping back and setting up a claim. Your mother was a shifty piece and . . .' He looked at me with the narrow fixed stare of the drinker who has not yet reached the expansive stage, moistened his lips as though he would have said more, but I broke in,

'It's hardly a matter that can be taken to the lawyers is it? I'm afraid you must trust me. At least I can assure you of this, that I'm going to America, where dangers, they say, are many. And I never desire to see Marshalsea again as long as I live. Give me a thousand pounds and you've paid my funeral expenses for all you know. That ought to give you pleasure.'

'And Charles succeeds me?'

'Charles succeeds you.'

'You'll put that in writing?'

'Certainly.'

I wrote out, in the most pompous language at my command a promise to refrain from making any claim upon my father's estate in return for a thousand pounds paid on the twelfth of September 1678, that I would never dispute my brother's right to the property and the title and that I would never trouble him with my presence.

Then I wrote at my father's dictation, letters to two London trading houses with whom he had money deposited, bidding each pay to Philip Ollenshaw the sum of five hundred pounds with the most convenient speed. He signed and addressed them himself, handling the pen as though it were a red-hot fowling piece.

'Cheap at the price,' I remarked, folding the letters to the size of my pocket and flipping the other document across the table to him. He drank again—he had been doing so pretty steadily throughout the interview—and looked at me blearily.

' 'Sfirst time I've ever looked at you with any pleasure,' he said with almost a kindly note in his voice. 'Let's see, we parted bad friends last time, didn't we? What about? Oh, I remember, that pretty little piece up at Madge's cottage. Well, believe me, as man to man, we neither of us lost anything there. All the fire on the surface, cold slab inside. Screamed murder as soon as you laid a finger on her and then took off with that Roundhead chawbacon, Makers. I only hope she marries him. She'd get a surprise! Those fellows look as though they're content with one kiss a month and a —— once a twelvemonth, but I know different. He'll ride her like . . .'

I never heard the end of the sentence for I turned and left him without a word. I had not mentioned the affair of Linda and her father, for abuse, unless the recipient is of an extraordinarily sensitive nature, is merely ridiculous when unbacked by force. Nothing I could have said would have touched him, it would only have laid my own wound open to his scornful eye. I did muse, as I limped back to Marshal-sea village, upon the fact that he seemed even to have forgotten her name. He had offered the pair an asylum, he had repaired the cottage and wooed her with more patience than one would have expected from him, he had egged on the crowd against her father and bribed Jim to manhandle him all to one purpose. And that being defeated he dismissed the whole affair. I was prepared to follow her to the ends of the earth, to stand, if God permitted me, between her and the consequences of her folly, to serve her till I died. Did the difference between my father and me amount simply to the difference between being twenty and being over fifty? And would my desire weaken and dissipate itself over the years? I swore that it should not, and stepped out heartily. Going back to London, going to America, going to Linda.

We reckoned to sail in March when the winter storms would be lessened. I spent the winter in Gore's house, sharing his plans and helping him with the immense amount of buying that was to be done. Early in March he turned over his house to his cousin and we rode down to Plymouth to supervise the loading of the cargo and to await the assembly of our fellow travellers. Throughout that winter, which was hard and cold, so cold that there was a great deal of skating in London and the King gained great popularity by showing his skill in public, I saw Linda only once. Inaction was irksome to Eli and he sought a job in a livery stable, and came to Gore for a reference. While they were concocting it in the study Linda and I sat in the parlour. I was horribly ill at ease and could feel my unspoken questions and reproaches heavy as smoke on the air; but Linda seemed to have recaptured the old easy friendship which had been ours in the fields and woods at home, and chatted about Eli's projected occupation and about the exodus in the Spring, while I sat and made short answers as I looked at her.

She was wearing a cloak and hood, made in one piece, plain, slate-coloured and ugly. The hood hid her shining hair and cast its dull shadow over her face; the cloak hid every line of the slender rounded body. Only at the shoulder could it follow her figure and the lines of it there, straight and slim and squarish reminded me intolerably of the time when she walked beside me for the first time, preening herself in her gown of mulberry-coloured silk. I wanted to cry 'Why did you do it, Linda? Why did you throw yourself away?' But the urgent words were not spoken.

'I'm glad you're coming with us, Philip,' she said. 'It makes it seem a little less strange.' She paused for a moment and then asked. 'Have you seen Edith Lomax?'

'Yes. All the Lomaxes were here not a week ago, talking to Nathaniel.'

'What is she like?'

I struggled with my memory, for William Lomax's daughter had made so slight an impact upon my mind that I could not remember very well. 'She's young, of course,' I said, 'and pale. Rather delicate looking. Quiet and serious. I did not note her much.'

'At least she is young, and you are, Philip. There seems to be rather a dearth of young people . . .' Her voice trailed off in a breath that might have been a sigh.

'Mr. Gore's six recruits are youngish, and four of them, am I right? yes, four of them are married. Two of the couples have children. I don't think you'll lack for company.'

'Keziah . . .' Linda began, and I could hear the distaste in that one word and awaited the confidence to follow. It never came. She broke off and began again, 'Eli can think of little else but the fact that the land is free. The thought intoxicates him, and he seems to get confused with the Israelites being given Canaan. When he heard from Mr.

95

Gore about the grant of land being made for as much as we could handle, he went into a kind of frenzy.'

'Yes,' I said dully, remembering those faraway conversations by the dying fire of Shad's forge, 'it means a lot to him.'

'I think of you quite often when he is talking about the mighty ploughings and plantings. How shall you manage, Philip?'

'As well as the rest,' I said shortly. 'Actually when I went home to settle things with my father I spent the night in the village and got talking to Andy Seeley. He wants to come with me, as my man. He'll plough, maybe, while I do the smith's work.'

'The smith's work! How ridiculous, Philip. You're a gentleman.'

'No,' I said, 'there'll be none of those where we're going. I shall be an emigrant—and so will you.'

Just then the door opened and Nathaniel and Eli entered. Eli was storing a paper away in his pocket. He looked pleased.

'Good evening, Mr. Philip,' he said, nodding towards me. 'Well, wife, I am ready.'

Linda rose meekly and drew her hood farther forward over her face. I said discreetly. 'Good-bye, Mrs. Makers. Good night, Eli.'

I did not see her again until we all met at Plymouth.

Nathaniel who had attended to all the business side of our departure, had chartered a vessel with the strange name of *Westering Wing* and immediately upon our arrival we began packing into it the miscellaneous proceeds of our buying. It seemed impossible to me, as I viewed our stores, that so small and frail a ship could carry all our goods and all our hopes safely across that tumbling grey sea. There were casks of nails, bars of iron, ploughshares, window panes packed in sawdust, tools. There were dozens of barrels of provender, salt meat, salt herrings, biscuits, flour and sugar. There were our personal belongings, clothes, linen, crockery and books. There were bags of seed corn and stacks of fodder for our animals—ten horses, three cows and a bull, as well as goats and poultry. And then there were ourselves, and I will name the travellers now. First, of course, Nathaniel Gore, head of the party, leading spirit and for a time controller. Then Oliver Lomax, William his brother, Anne, William's wife and Edith their daughter. Keziah, Eli and Linda Makers. Joseph Steggles, his wife Lucy and Betsy their three-year-old child. Isaac Carter, Mary, his wife and Jacob their infant son. Two couples, Amos and Christina Beeton; Mathew and Dinah Thomas. Two young men, Harry Wright and Tim Dendy. There was my man, Andy Seeley, and myself. Twenty-two souls in all. But more than this number set sail, and over the newcomers Nathaniel and Eli first came to cross purposes. Even though it keeps us in England a little longer I must tell this story at length because, although it was simple enough at the time it concerned people who played no small part in the story of our venture.

Nathaniel and I had taken a lodging in a tavern on the waterfront—I forget its name—no, *The Sailor's Return* it was. Aptly named. The bar was always full of men just back from the Guinea trade, from the West Indies, from the East. A motley, colourful, interesting company, though I had no time to spend in it. One evening, when tired from our labours and falling heartily upon our victuals we were seated in our small room when the serving woman came in briskly and said, 'Mr. Gore, sir, there's a person insists on seeing you. I said you were at supper, but he won't take no for an answer.'

Nathaniel raised his pointed chin, 'What's his name? What does he want? Is it about the ship?'

'He don't give no name. But it's something about the ship, sir, I think.'

'Show him in then,' said Nathaniel and began hastily making the best speed he might with what food remained on his plate. After a moment a tall swarthy man appeared in the doorway, stooping his head at the lintel. He had no cap, but as his eyes lit upon Nathaniel he lifted one hand to his curly hair in a salute that was too jaunty to be servile. He wore a sleeveless leather jerkin over a ragged shirt whose sleeves ended at the elbow, a pair of tattered breeches thrust into coarse white stockings and a pair of heavy home-made shoes. All the same he was one of the most handsome and imposing-looking men I had ever seen.

'Good evening, gentlemen,' he said, and his voice was as strange as his clothing—soft, but strong and with a kind of lisp about it. 'You're Mr. Gore, I take it,' he looked at Nathaniel.

'I am. What can I do for you?'

'More than a little if you're so minded, sir.'

'Let's hear it,' said Nathaniel, leaving his place and coming round the table to the settle beside the fire. His smallness made him look like a child against the other's great height and I think he was conscious of it, for he said briskly, 'sit down, my good fellow, you're over tall for this room.' The man laughed, 'Or for any, sir, but then I don't use them much.' He sat down and clasped his brown hands between his knees.

'You're fitting out the *Westering Wing* to go to Ameriky they tell me, sir. . . .'

'Well, what of it?'

'I wondered whether your outfit was completed, or whether you'd have room for . . .' the smile broke out again . . . 'for three little ones like me?'

'A literal tall order,' said Nathaniel with an answering smile. 'First tell me what makes you anxious to join us?'

'The itching foot I reckon. We aren't cut out for staying in one place long. I never could see a road but I wanted to know what was at the end of it, nor a ship but I longed to sail in her. And I'm handy and willing, Mr. Gore, there's little I can't turn a hand to. I can sail, I've been before the mast to Guinea and Calicut and Amboyna, in a modest way I can work in metal and wood. I'd not be a drag on you and I can say the same for the others.'

'Who are the others?'

'My brother and sister, sir.'

'And what would you say your trade was—as apart from the things you're handy at?'

'What we're handy at is our trade. We're gypsies.'

Nathaniel turned to me. 'What do you think, Philip? We've the butcher and the baker and the candlestick maker, not to mention the amateur smith' (that was a good-natured poke at me), 'we've a leather merchant and several farmers, a saddler and a dispossessed parson. But no gypsies. Would

98

you call a party complete without gypsies, Philip?'

Now I had fallen victim to the man's personality as well as to his physical charm. Reviewing our party rapidly in my mind's eye I could see how different, how delightfully different, this man was from Eli and his kind. The dispossessed parson—Mathew Thomas—who had arrived on the previous day came into my mind and I turned with relief from that memory to the big smiling man who could ask a favour without cringing or beating about the bush.

'If there is room, and you know best about that, Nathaniel, I should say that the more man power we carry the better,' I said.

'Where're the brother and sister?'

'Out in the yard.'

'Fetch them in.'

As soon as the man had stooped under the lintel and disappeared Nathaniel darted up, snatched a crust from the table and crammed it into his mouth.

'Well,' he said through it, whirling on me, 'what do you make of that?'

'I liked him,' I said incautiously. 'He looked strong and healthy, and he was . . . merry.'

'And merriment is a quality that our party conspicuously lacks. I'll tell you one thing, Eli won't like it.'

'It's not his party,' I said.

'No, that's true.' He pulled his beard and looked at me with his bright eyes twinkling a little. 'But that is one thing which Eli finds hard to comprehend. He sees himself as Moses, leading the people to the Promised Land. To him I am a rather incompetent Aaron, useful but not very important.'

'And Keziah is Miriam I suppose?' And as Nathaniel laughed steps sounded outside. In a second the gypsy with his brother and sister were inside the room which was immediately very overcrowded. The brother was slightly shorter than the one who had come first, but a big man for all that and the girl was beautiful.

'My sister Judith and my brother Simon. My name is Ralph.'

'And your other name?'

There was a moment's silence; the three looked at one

another and the tawny heads leaned together. Then Ralph said, 'They call us Whistlecraft. If we must have names we'll stick to that.'

'Very well,' said Nathaniel. 'Now will you all sit down?' He sat himself at the table again in a high chair. The brothers took the settles on either side the hearth and the girl dropped naturally to the floor. The firelight touched one side of her head with rosy light, leaving untouched the hollows below her strong high cheekbones and in the deep eyesockets.

'Now listen,' said Nathaniel. 'It's perfectly true that I am in charge of this expedition. I have surveyed the country to which we go and the grant was made to me. But I cannot accept you without consulting some of my people; and before we go any farther in the matter it would be well if I made some things clear to you. We do not travel for adventure alone, nor for profit alone. We travel in search of peace and justice, for freedom to employ our labours for our own service and to worship in our own way. Those who come with us must be prepared to be industrious, orderly, law-abiding, God-fearing members of our new community. Idleness and drunkenness, loose living of every kind will be offensive to our standards. Naturally I know nothing of you, but the word "gypsy" calls to mind many things which will not be acceptable among my people—or to me. If I speak for you I shall expect not to have cause to regret it. Is that understood?'

'You shall never regret it, master,' said the girl in the same soft voice with the trace of a lisp that Ralph had used.

'Very well. If after more thought you are still of the same mind, call here tomorrow at about this time.' They filed out, each one saying a soft good night, each one ducking at the doorsill. Nathaniel closed the door and turned to me.

'It won't do, Philip. As soon as I began to outline our ideas I knew that they would never fit. They'll be a bone of contention every day and the girl will cause trouble. She dropped to the hearth like a dog, not a human being : and a female dog, loose . . . no. I'll tell them tomorrow that the ship will carry no more.' He sighed as he said it and I knew that despite his reasoning—and that was sound enough I admitted—his heart had gone out to the strange trio.

He took up one of his many lists and sharpened his quill.

'Tomorrow we'll load this and this and this . . .' he began ticking off items. 'And remind me, Philip that Mrs. Adams' brass lamp has not arrived yet. I promised it to her faithfully when I left Salem last and I do not wish to offend her. I have hopes of her husband's help in several things when we arrive.' For a little while there was only the squeaking of his quill to break the silence and then there came a heavy tap upon the door. 'Come in,' shouted Nathaniel without looking up from his list, and the door opened to show Eli Makers on the threshold.

'Good evening, Eli, anything wrong?' asked Nathaniel, removing the quill from between his teeth and laying it carefully on the table.

' 'Tis for you to judge that, Mr. Gore. To my mind yes, there is.'

'And what is that, Eli? Sit down and tell me.'

Eli remained standing.

'There be three gypsies that have been hanging about the harbour, Mr. Gore, this last two days. I've bid 'em begone a number of times. Just a minute since I met them in the road and since they were going towards the shipping I turned and followed them. I heard their talk, sir, and judged from it that you had promised them a passage and a share in our venture. Is that true?'

'In part,' said Nathaniel, getting to his feet and facing Eli across the table. 'I promised that I would discuss the matter with those of my company whose opinion I value—you and Mr. Oliver Lomax, and Philip here. Since you are here I may as well have your opinion now.'

'And here it is,' said Eli speaking slowly through his teeth. 'I turned from my homegoing to follow them because I mistrust their designs on the cargo. That's what I think of them. And you consider their coming I'm surprised at you, Mr. Gore, surprised and disappointed.'

'Now listen, Eli.' Nathaniel rounded the table and put his hand on Eli's arm for a moment. 'There are several things to consider. First, their interest in the ship—that was only natural seeing that they were hoping to sail in her. Secondly, in the place where we are going there will be hardships and possibly dangers. There are two strong, hardy fellows, not to be lightly despised upon a venture such as ours. There is also this to be considered. There is great shortage of women in New England, whatever recruits we might pick up in Salem and the surrounding districts we'll find few spare women among them. That gypsy girl is, like her brothers, strong and healthy looking. We carry five unmated men—I discount myself—who will want wives. Want? *Need* them, Eli, if our little colony is not to die with us. If I could ship five such as that wench I'd be inclined to do it, my friend, even if it meant sleeping on deck myself for the whole of the journey.'

'God,' said Eli solemnly, 'has never failed to provide fitting mates for the chosen. Yon raggle-taggle wench is none such and it's a rare mistake you'll be making if you take her, or any one of them aboard.'

'Very well. I'll take it that you are against it, Eli?'

'I'm more than that. Mr. Gore, if you start shipping those dishonest, ungodly, idle, worthless gypsies you'll be going against all that we have hoped and planned, and I for one shall never trust your judgement again.'

'Now wait a minute.' I saw the little man bristle and seem to grow bigger, as a dog with rising hackles seems to increase in size. I saw, in fact, the author of 'A Year's Journal' in action. 'My judgement, Eli, faulty as you may deem it, has made this expedition possible. Preparations have been made by me, the grant is made to me. I know the country. I know the conditions. I leave you to judge whether I can do better without you or you without me. Go down to the ship my good man, take out what you reckon belongs to you and sit on the wharf on Wednesday next while I and my raggle-taggle put to sea. The gypsies go with me and that's my last word.'

I saw Eli's mouth open. A choking sound came from it. He clenched his hands and swallowed. Then he said, and his slow country voice had a queer ring of doom about it.

'You have me in a cleft stick. The power is with you Mr. Gore, but that doesn't prove that the right is. The power often lies in the wrong places and that is one of the reasons that we seek a new country. It was, if you remember, in the power of that other ship-owner to take Jonah aboard. He was glad enough to be rid of him I reckon. Good night to you. Good night, Mr. Philip.'

He went out heavily and closed the door behind him. Nathaniel began to fill a pipe with nervous hasty fingers.

'A thousand curses,' he said suddenly. 'My infernal temper again! Hadn't I just said to you that I wouldn't take them? I meant not to. And now I am committed. Confusion take Eli Makers and his Jeremiads.'

'You haven't given them an answer yet...' I said diffidently.

'No, but I've given Eli one. And that I stand by.' He tapped home each word with a long thin finger. 'I cannot be ruled by Eli Makers, sound man as I know him to be. And after all, everything that I said in favour of the Whistlecrafts is true. His disapproval does not alter that. Say no more about it, Philip. They go with us.'

Five more days of intensive preparation, discoveries of things forgotten, delayed or lost; or being stopped in the road by strangers who looked wistfully westwards while they wished us Godspeed and then on Wednesday, the twelfth day of March in the year 1679 at eleven o'clock in the morning the sails filled gently, the *Westering Wing* slewed round, set her head for the open sea and England sank away behind us.

The voyage was singularly uneventful. Nathaniel who had made the voyage twice before had reckoned that we should reach our destination by the third week in May; actually, owing to a long calm when the sails hung empty for the greater part of a fortnight, it was the second of June when we put into Salem Harbour. But the delay caused us no suffering because Nathaniel in shipping food and water, had allowed generously. Three things stand out in my mind about the voyage; the first concerns the Whistlecrafts, the second, Eli, and the third, Linda.

Within twelve hours of embarking practically everyone on board was sick. Even Nathaniel, that seasoned traveller, lay on the bunk in the cabin that we shared and groaned that death itself would be a relief. I was horribly sick myself, and the sound and scent of his sickness increased my nausea tenfold so that even in my misery I was forced to spare a pitying thought for the women who were crowded together in the larger cabins. No ministering angel could have been more welcome than Ralph Whistlecraft when he appeared, to empty, unmoved, the brimming bowls of our humiliation, and to give us clean water and slices of fresh lemon to suck. He and Simon, he reported, were being wet nurses to the men, while Judith tended the women. I struggled up out of my wretchedness to ask whether Eli Makers were sick too. Ralph's answering yes and the thought of Eli being ministered to by Simon made me smile —with disastrous results. But I was certain that the Whistlecrafts' tough stomachs would have made them many friends—impossible, I thought, to despise or dislike anyone who had placed his physical superiority at your service. In that I was wrong. When our stomach muscles had regained their balance and one by one the pale travellers, heavy-eyed, appeared in the clean air on the deck, the three gypsies walked and stood alone.

Shortly after this wholesale recovery Nathaniel was waited upon by a deputation, Eli, Oliver Lomax, and Mathew Thomas who were, in the reverend gentleman's words, 'perturbed' by the rowdy behaviour of the sailors. Strong liquor, apparently was part of their regular allowance and in the evenings when this had taken its course the fo'castle was loud with songs of a bawdy character, unfit for Godly ears.

'In the stern cabins you may not be able to hear them,' said Oliver Lomax. 'But I assure you, Mr. Gore, that it is a matter requiring attention. Here on the bosom of the great deep floats our little vessel. From it, like the savoury smoke of the burnt offering goes up every evening to Heaven our prayer of thankfulness for another day's preservation. Is that to be mingled with and besmirched by the songs of these ungodly fellows. It is an insult to God.'

Now, Nathaniel and I had regularly attended the nightly service, held by Mr. Thomas in the men's quarters, and often we had caught some snatches of song, tantalising in their incompleteness, and had lingered on the way back to our cabin and even left the door open while we undressed for bed, in order to fill in gaps. Sometimes we had heard only too well, and once, after a particularly lascivious chorus, Nathaniel had said, as though in apology, 'We must remember that sailors' songs are the result of long years of loneliness and separation, of desire that they have no means of appeasing. To me, as a student of words and of human nature, they are interesting. But shut the door if you are offended, Philip.'

Nothing had been farther from my mind than offence. Everyone of those rough fellows, lustily roaring out the song about 'Mary's snow white breast' had in mind some woman, actual, ideal or composite, after whom he hungered as I hungered for Linda. I could have joined in the vocal manifestation of frustrate longing with every sincerity. I caught Nathaniel's eye as Lomax finished his indictment and saw an expression of comic shame shine in it before he turned hastily away.

'And what would you have me do?' he asked.

'Speak to the master,' said Eli promptly. 'Request him that no more ale or rum be given out until the journey's end. Ask him to order that every voice upraised shall be in praise or supplication to Him who rules the winds and the waves and orders the safety of them who go down to the sea in ships.'

'I could do that,' said Nathaniel, thoughtfully, 'but you must understand, my friends, that it can only be a request, not an order. The master is hired, with his ship and his crew, to carry us and our gear with all possible dispatch and to set us down at Salem Harbour. What his men drink and what they sing is no concern of ours.'

'Would it be no concern of a soldier's,' burst out Mr. Thomas in his sing-song Welsh voice, 'if he could hear treason to his king being shouted aloud. Are we, God's soldiers, vowed to His cause, to be less loyal to our Heavenly sovereign I ask you? No, indeed! And if you doubt your power Mr. Gore will you not send for the master here, now, this minute, and let us repeat in his hearing what we have said to you?'

Nathaniel pondered. 'I will speak with him first and if that has no effect I will turn him over to you.'

When they had gone Nathaniel turned to me and with as unhappy a look as I had ever seen upon his face said gravely,

'I begin, most unwillingly to perceive, Philip, that I am unsuited to my company. Because I have endeavoured to follow tolerance, because I believe that a man should reap that he sows and worship God as seems good to him, I have put myself in a false position. I cannot lead a second band of Pilgrim Fathers. I . . .' He came with his rapid step to the bunk where he slept, rooted under the blanket and brought out a small book stitched into a brown cover and turned the manuscript pages rapidly. 'Listen to this . . . it was written by a friend of mine who died, God rest him, last year. . . .'

Quickly and with a kind of passion he began to read, 'Had we but world enough and time . . .' laying emphasis on

> '*Two hundred to adore each breast,*
> *But thirty thousand to the rest.*'

And on

> '*. . . then worms shall try*
> *That long preserved virginity,*
> *And your quaint honour turn to dust*
> *And into ashes all my lust.*
> *The grave's a fine and private place*
> *But none methinks, do there embrace.*'

He finished,

> '*Thus, though we cannot make our sun*
> *Stand still, yet we will make him run. . . .*

Note the play on "sun", Philip. Now I admire that, I think it a fine poem. But allowing for the fact that this man was a poet which fo'castle hands seldom are, is there any difference between that and "Mary's snow white breast" or "The Month of May" or "Come give me your lips"? Not a scrap, and knowing that and liking this, how can I grumble about those poor fellows' version of a universal theme. If I speak I belie my beliefs; if I don't I offend my company. Help me, Philip. What would you advise?'

'They feel very strongly in the matter,' I said. 'Men always do when they talk of their duty to God. Perhaps you could suggest that the men sing softly . . .'

'In fact bow down twice in the house of Rimmon. Very well, that's what I'll do.'

He twitched down his coat and set off with his quick nervous step.

Left alone I picked up the book of verses. They were all written in his neat black script and they were almost all tinged with eroticism. Set out upon a page by themselves I found the following lines

> *'Oh western wind, when wilt thou blow,*
> *That the small rain down may rain.*
> *Christ that my love were in my arms*
> *And I in my bed again!'*

That set the tone for the whole of the little volume, and by the time I had read half a dozen or so of the verses I was wild with pain. Turning up the collar of my coat I made my way to the deck and stood leaning on the rail, looking at the night.

The western wind for which the lover plained in winter was blowing and the ship was tacking but making little headway. The soft gusts hit my cheek damply; overhead the thin dark clouds blew across the sky, obscuring the moon. Thinking of Linda and torturing myself with the thought of her in Eli's embrace I was hardly aware even of the singing of Milton's hymn, 'For His mercies aye endure, ever faithful, ever sure', the sound of which came up from the men's cabin below. When a shape came up noiselessly and leaned over the rail by my side I gave a great start of surprise. Turning just at the moment when the rack left the moon clear I saw Linda with her hood thrown back on her shoulders and the wind stirring her hair. The clouds blinded the moon again instantly and I was glad, for seeing her so suddenly, hard upon my thoughts of her, I was afraid that my face would betray me.

She set her elbows on the rail and put her chin in her hands. It was a moment before I could trust myself to speak. Then I said, 'What are you doing here, Linda?'

'I had to come out of the meeting,' she said. 'Praying seems to exhaust the air and I felt faint.'

'Shall I get you something to sit on?'

'No thank you, Philip. I'm all right now. The wind has changed, hasn't it? There's almost the feeling of spring in the air tonight.'

'It's not so good for progress,' I pointed out.

'Shall you be glad when the voyage is gone?'

'Most heartily. And you?'

'Not really. This is unreal, like a dream. When we land everything will begin again.'

And instantly I thought—she sleeps now in the women's common cabin and is free of Eli. There was so much unspoken between us, so many things that I longed to say and to ask that I turned aside again and looked into the darkness over the waters. Down below the hymn ceased and in the sudden silence there came the high merry, yet wailing notes of the fiddle and the voices of the sailor men, lifted in 'Come give me your lips'.

I could feel Linda draw herself together. She said in a muted voice, 'I thought they weren't to sing any more.'

'Mr. Gore is seeing about it at this moment,' I said. 'For myself I shall miss it.'

'And the meeting will be in its final stages,' Linda murmured irrelevantly. 'I must go. Good night, Philip.'

That was my rendezvous with love on the night when the west wind blew.

I stood there for a little longer and when at last I turned to go below three tall figures emerged from the fo'castle hatchway. They linked arms as they gained the deck and came towards me, whistling clear as throstles in the darkness. 'Come give me your lips,' the crazy catching tunes rose and fell, until they saw me standing there. Then it broke off, 'Good night, master,' they said, almost in unison. I said 'Good night', and left the rail. Behind me I heard the sound of laughter, and after a second the whistling broke out again,

'In the pleasant month of May, if you should go a'wooing,
The wench will hardly say you nay, which may prove
    your undoing . . .'

I went below to await Nathaniel and hear the result of his mission.

The captain had promised to speak to the men about the matter, but he had pointed out to Nathaniel that they would consider it, as he did, an unjustifiable interference with their liberty. So long as they did their work properly and moved sharply when given an order and didn't complain about their quarters or their food, they should be allowed to occupy their scanty leisure as they chose. I could well imagine that Nathaniel had not forced home his point with any great assurance and was not at all surprised to hear the same old songs being roared out the following evening.

On the second evening I went to the service because I had not managed to catch sight of Linda all day long. At least I could sit there, while Mr. Thomas' sing-song voice with all the v's turned into f's and all the s's trebled, fell on my unheeding ears, and watch Linda sitting among the other women with their meekly-covered heads. The hymns, the psalms and the preaching made a background for the things I was thinking, for the wordless poetry that ran through my head as I looked at her. The parts of the Bible that I liked were never read at the meeting. I would have given all the fiery denunciations of the prophets, all the pallid exhortations of St. Paul for a simple sentence such as 'A bundle of myrrh is my beloved unto me'. Stooping my head now and then so that my prolonged staring should not attract attention, I still kept my mind on her and my heart cried 'Linda, Linda, Linda' with so insistent a cry that I sometimes wondered why she did not hear it and turn.

In every lull of our praying and singing there sounded the faint singing, the wail of the fiddle from the fo'castle, and the distance made it sound plaintive, as though the lusty hearty singing were the keening of the lost.

When the final 'Amen' had come to its long-drawn-out close I rose from my back seat and limped out of the cabin. I lingered for a little while, thinking that Nathaniel would overtake me, but as he didn't come I went to my own cabin, undressed and lay down reading by the light of the lamp on my locker. It was some time before Nathaniel returned and when I craned my neck to greet him I was interested to see the conflicting expressions on his face. He looked at once amused and grave, puzzled and impressed.

'Philip, lad,' he said, before I could speak, 'when you described yon Eli to me you didn't do him justice.'

'Oh,' I said, in an uninterested voice. 'What has he done now?'

'He's had every sailor in this ship, save the captain and the watch on their kneebones.'

'Battered unconscious?' I asked flippantly.

'Don't mock,' said Nathaniel gravely. 'I'm no ignorant sailor, Philip, but he had my bowels all a-quiver with the picture of Hell he held before them. Before God there's a strange power in the fellow. It wasn't easy, they laughed and jeered and shouted. One actually called out, "You're Makers aren't you? Well, if I had a wife as comely as yours it wouldn't be men's souls I'd be bothering about at this hour."'

'I hope Eli felled him,' I said viciously.

'No. He drew a deep breath and roared out, "In the hour of death and at the Day of Judgement, it'll be men's souls, not women's bodies that will matter, my friend." I'd sneaked down after him, lad, wondering what he'd do and say. But by the time he'd got silence and was talking about this little cockleshell boat tossed on the surface of great waters, which great as they were and dark were no more than a drop in the palm of God's hand; and how death waited for everyone, maybe tomorrow for some of us; and had quoted that bit about the wages of sin in a way that made the words come to life—well, there was I kneeling down when he said, "Let us pray for God's forgiveness and the mecy of Christ". And he's a younger man than me, less seasoned and neither priest nor parson. What do you make of that?'

'He always had that way,' I said grudgingly, remembering the days when I too had fallen under the spell of that voice and eye. 'He used to talk to the men in the forge until they were willing to face my father. You see Nathaniel, he's only got two ideas in his head, one is how men should farm and the other is how men should worship. All the power in him goes to them.'

'While mine is frittered away, I suppose. I'm interested in

so many things ... and I don't suppose there's anything I'd
be martyred for. Would you?'

'One ... I hope. But it's nothing to do with God.'

'You're young, Philip. Death is a long way from you—
though Eli made it sound imminent tonight. But when the
better half of your life is over—then God is the antidote of
death.'

He had taken off his coat and loosened his collar as he
spoke. Now he dropped his breeches to the floor and
stepped out of them. As he lifted and folded them with his
usual care I saw his thin legs, old man's legs, the 'shrunk
shanks' that Shakespeare spoke of. Suddenly, with his shirt
flapping, he dived under his pillow and brought out the little
book of manuscript poems.

'Only one,' he said quietly, 'only one has any rightful
bearing.' He read out in a voice that I can hear to this
day,

> 'O mortal folk, you may behold and see
> How I lie here, sometime a mighty knight;
> The end of joy and all prosperitie
> Is death at last, thorough his course and might;
> After the day there cometh the dark night,
> And though the day be never so long,
> At last the bell ringeth to evensong.'

He closed the little book and stood weighing it in his hand.

'The rest of them are all vanity,' he said sadly, and
moved as he spoke to the open porthole.

As soon as I saw what he intended to do I gave a great
scream which arrested him and made him turn, thinking no
doubt that I had taken a fit. That gave me time to scramble
from my bunk, hop across and snatch the book from him.

'You fool,' I said, forgetting his age and all I owed him.
'Would you be one with those who smashed the church
windows and cut down the market crosses at Cromwell's
bidding? What harm has the book done? In it lie the
thoughts of men whose horses Eli is not fitted to hold. Give
it to me if you would be rid of it. I'd sooner risk Hell in
company with Raleigh and Wyatt and Marvell than go to
Heaven with Eli.'

The night air was cold on my legs and I scuttled back under the blanket with my prize.

'You didn't hear him,' was all Nathaniel would say.

'I've been hearing him ever since I was ten,' I said scornfully. 'Forgive me, sir, for miscalling you. It was said in haste. But frankly, I am surprised that you, who have faced death—if your journal is to be believed—many a time, and bravely, should be so moved by his ranting.'

And then he said something else that I remembered later and knew for very truth.

'Faced with the danger of it, Philip, you're so busy thinking of ways to avoid it that you don't recognise the dread face. But tonight, when Eli was speaking, I knew what it feels like to turn your face to the darkness and draw the last breath. And every man in that stinking Bedlam knew it too....'

Looking back later on I wondered whether on that very night he had felt the icy hand on his shoulder and knew that this time there was no way to avoid the sight of what he called the dread face. But at the time I was occupied in fanning my distaste for Eli who had stopped the singing and made a handful of verses, lovingly culled, seem a sin: Eli, who, with Heaven to his hand, could only think of Hell. To watch Nathaniel's new way of treating Eli with respect, almost with reverence, was as hurtful as biting on a hollow tooth.

After that there came the calm. Day after day the sun shone from a sky that was like a blue platter, and yet was no more calm, no less rippled than the oily sea upon which we lay. We were, thanks to Nathaniel's foresight, well found for food and water, but in that fantastic weather all things seemed possible, and with an eye to the possibility of the strange hot calm lasting for a month or more, strict rationing was introduced. Nerves, already tested by close quarters, anxiety for the future and—I believe—the unremitting religious atmosphere aboard the *Westering Wing*, now became frayed. It was such an anti-climax, after all our preparations and our brave departure, to lie here becalmed, watching the idle sails, hoping against hope to see one flutter and fill. The women quarrelled shrilly, the men prayed with a fervour that was almost threatening.

Eli made no secret of the fact that Jonah, in his opinion was aboard, and that Jonah, in this case was incorporated in the three Whistlecrafts. They were irregular in their attendance at the meetings. They still sang and whistled, breaking into the forbidden tunes, unconsciously, I believe, and falling silent when one of the elders passed them. They did not reckon me as an elder and in consequence I was privileged to witness a strange thing.

On the last night of the calm I did not go to evening meeting. I had wearied of the monotony of Mr. Thomas's hissing requests for a wind to the Almighty and I had seen Linda during the day in far more happy circumstances. In the cool of early evening she and Judith Whistlecraft had played with little Betsy Steggles on a corner of the deck where I could sit on a coiled rope and watch them. Linda had abandoned her cloak and though the silly little cap which all the women wore after marriage, marred the beauty of her hair, and though her gown was plain and drab, she looked more like the Linda of Hunter's Wood than she had done for a long time.

So when the members of the community were crowded in the stuffy cabin, praying for the fourteenth night that God who ruled the waves and the winds would see fit to fill their sails and carry them to the new land of promise, I went on deck and sat down again on the coil of rope in the corner. Presently the three gypsies came along and stood at the rail within earshot of me.

'Well, do you still feel like whistling for it?' asked Simon. 'You know what it means, a year off your latter end.'

'That'll be three of mine gone,' said Ralph with a laugh that sounded a little uneasy. 'I've paid once off the Bermudas and once off Guinea. But, God's eyeballs, I'll do it again. Nothing to drink, nobody to tumble. If the latter end is like this I'll be glad to have it shortened.'

'I'll give two of mine, then,' said Judith solemnly. 'That'll spare yours.'

'No. If I don't give a year I can't whistle. And I'm practised. Those other times I mentioned, sink me if the sails weren't filling before the echoes had died down. All right, we each give a year. Now slew round a bit, Judy, your face isn't due East yet. That's better.'

113

Then, with complete gravity he proceeded to ask questions and at the same time to lead the responses in which the other two joined.

'What do we whistle for?'

'We whistle for a wind.'

'Feather breeze or hurricane?'

'No breeze or hurricane, a good following wind.'

'And what do we give?'

'A year from our latter end, and we are young.'

And then, clear and shrill as a nest of throstles they began to whistle. There was no tune, just the long pealing calls which men use when a dog has strayed. At first I had been amused, interested but amused. Now, as the calling notes rang out towards the East I had a moment of aberration in which their gravity and conviction touched me and for just that moment I could imagine, in some far corner of the sky the recalcitrant wind lifting its head, listening, remembering and obeying. I half expected it to come running, leaping with breathy cries of pleasure upon the *Westering Wing*, setting the shrouds bellying, making the rigging quiver. But nothing happened. The last shrill peal fell into silence and as it died I heard the solemn measures of the Pilgrim hymn,

> '*Thy Will our law, Thy Love our light,*
> *The cloud by day, the flame by night*
> *Lead on Thy people.*'

At two o'clock in the morning the sudden motion of the ship after the long stillness awakened us. Nathaniel and I turned over and stirred and muttered to one another that the wind had come. The elders called a special meeting at mid-day and rendered humble thanks to God for the answering of their prayers. Ralph Whistlecraft listed a third success in his beckoning of the wind and swaggered about, looking knowing and proud, but too wise to say anything.

And so we came on a fair June day, safely into Salem Harbour.

We had arrived in Salem at an interesting time, and although to us it was merely a place of call as it were, the prevailing atmosphere may be worth of mention. The great war with the Indians, called King Philip's War, from the name of the Indian chief who was most active in it, was over. It had cost the settlers dearly, both in men and money. Six hundred men of the New England colonies had died, and there were unreckoned numbers of women and children slain as well. The houses and barns that had been burned were numbered at twelve hundred and thirteen little settlements had been wiped away as though they had never been.

But for the Indians the war had been, not merely a matter of loss of life and property, but of complete annihilation—at least so we were told. (Later on we had proof that the wounded serpent can still strike.) Upon the face of it certainly the colonists had reason for self-congratulation. Whole tribes had been wiped out, and they the most warlike. I have heard the figures given as thirty-five hundred of braves killed in the war, and those left were mostly domesticated ones who had been softened by civilisation and a touch of Christianity. There were Indians in Salem, but the friendliness with which they had been treated—I was told —before the war, was now tinged with half-suspicious patronage, and at nightfall they were compelled to retire to their own quarters and stay there. The bell-men who roamed the streets in the hours of darkness were bidden watch out for any Indian disobeying the order.

But it was not in the numbers of dead, or in the subjugation of the nations that the influence of the war was most felt: it was in the reaction of the people who were left, victors in the field. They regarded the war, as in fact Puritanically minded people were apt to regard any untoward happening, as a judgement on them, sent directly from God to draw attention to the fact that they were not serving Him with sufficient single-mindedness. Salem, when we landed was in the throes of a religious revival, in which gratitude and placation were about evenly mingled. An attractive way of dressing the hair, a dress with short sleeves, an unexplained absence from meeting was likely to be met with a rebuke or a fine. Even the children were to be whipped for the second offence of fidgeting during the service. On the first Sunday after our arrival I was amazed to see all the solemn little creatures gathered together in one corner of the church, under the supervision of a female, well chosen, I felt, whose demeanour would have awed the most riotous.

All this, of course, was meat and drink to Eli, Oliver Lomax and Mathew Thomas. In fact, so delighted were they with Salem that I rather hoped they would decide to stay there, where the roads were at least well trodden, where there were shops, and people and an occasional tavern. Sometimes in the night, before sleep took me, I had time and opportunity to dread the long marches we must take, the streams we must ford and the hills we must cross before we reached the spot that Nathaniel had noted upon his journey of exploration as 'a fine and fruitful spot, well watered, sheltered from the North wind by a range of hills, open towards the South; the soil rich and black, the grass plentiful, timber in abundance and in all a place well-favoured and promising reward for labour'.

But Eli, at least, and after all it was Eli I must follow, although he thought well of many of the institutions in Salem, had no intention of stopping there. The fields were in strips! Poor Eli, when he saw the neat fields carved out of one great one, and heard the land referred to by the communal names of 'North Fields' and 'South Fields', his reaction was amusing. Eli's notion of a farm was a square with a house in the centre of it and if any labelling were to be done it was to announce, 'Eli's wheat field,' 'Eli's meadow', 'The place for Eli's kine'. Also there were, oddly enough, taverns in Salem. They were recognised, there was even a law that Indians were not to obtain liquor elsewhere. To Eli a tavern was an abomination and in Zion, as he persistently called the place to which we were by stages making our way, there would be no liquor sold, or drunk, or brewed. It became a thorn in his flesh that the wagons for which we were waiting, were being built in a workyard near Beadle's Tavern, and that during the hot days of July Steggles and Carter, my man Andy, Tim Dendy and myself were often known to down tools and slip into the shady cool taproom. Impossible to make Eli believe that a pint of ale in a pewter mug was not a surety of drunkenness, or that we were capable of merely standing or sitting in the wicked place talking over what we had done and what was still to do. The word 'tavern' called up into Eli's mind all the fine biblical attributes of the whore of Babylon.

Fortunately for us, perhaps, Nathaniel had, since that night aboard the *Westering Wing*, regarded Eli as his second in command, and kept him fairly busy showing him the things he thought he should know ... how the frame houses were made, how food was stored and preserved, how virgin land was cleared. And fortunately too, Mathew Thomas had been taken straight to the bosom of one, Alfred Bradstreet, another expelled clergyman who kindly arranged that Mathew should conduct a service and christen a child or two and in other ways, including the exhortation of sinners, preserve touch with his spiritual office. So Steggles and Carter, Andy and I were left to help the local carpenters and wheelwrights and make our wagons in comparative peace.

Perhaps most fortunate thing of all was that the Whistle-crafts, almost delirious with the grand weather and at being loosed from the ship's confinement, took themselves joy-fully to the Common Pasture that lay under Gallows Hill and camped there with the horses that we had brought and the rest of the cattle that we were acquiring as opportunity arose.

Hospitality had been offered us with an amazing free-dom. Mr. Adams, he whose wife had desired a brass lamp, (now cold and burnished in her small parlour, awaiting the dark evenings of winter) had taken in Nathaniel, myself, Andy and the Beetons. I suppose that we were the most comfortably lodged of the party, for the Adams' had reared a large family, mostly boys now engaged in the fishing grounds, and they had room to spare, but on the whole space was scarce in the township, which made it all the more honourable of the people to have taken us in; at the same time it made us speed our departure. That and the idea that the dry bright weather would not last for ever and that we must reach our Zion and have houses reared before the winter came.

I saw Linda only at meeting, and didn't miss a service once while we were there. The second Sunday of our stay was a day so hot that even in the church one longed to throw off one's coat and sit in shirt-sleeves. That was im-possible, of course, but I sat and sweated and wondered what made Linda cling to her cloak. True the hood had been taken off, but why wear it at all? All the other women were wearing gowns of print or muslin, dolefully coloured most of them, but some almost gay. I didn't hear a word of the sermon. I just sat there and told myself a fairy-story. Eli was dead—unborn—anything, he didn't exist any more, and I went to Linda and ripped off the horrible slate-coloured cloak and the drab gown beneath it. I helped her into the mulberry coloured silk, buttoning it for her and pulling out the folds, and I set the wine-coloured stones in her ears again, and watched while she arranged the loops and curls of soft hair on the top of her little crown. And when that was done I took her away, far far away to a land where the people were all beautiful and kind and generous and had never heard of original sin and the need to eradicate it, a land where the people were poets and musicians, a land that was full of flowers, where the almond trees dropped their pink petals on paths that even scents and stars, were made for lovers.

The church faced North and South, with windows on the East and West, so that no sun came in at morning service time. The air, though hot was grey and flat feeling, as though many congregations had breathed it over many times. And there, ahead of me in an ugly yellow pew Linda sat beside Eli, with the slatey cloak blotting her out from everything except my imagination. Here was where dreams ended.

As we came out into the hot sunshine and people gathered in the little yard before the church door to meet, in some cases, for the first time in a week, to talk over crops, and ailments and recipes, Linda passed me closely so that I could smile and speak to her without anything being made of it. But my smile and my greeting were wiped away as I saw the reason for the cloak. A new piece of stuff, darker than the faded drab of the gown had been let into the front of her dress, but even then it was strained in ungracious fashion over her swelling body. Linda was going to have a baby! More handicapped than I was she going to ford streams and climb hills and foot the weary miles. My heart turned over with pity and compassion, and also with a dreadful raging jealousy. Eli's baby, another squareheaded squarehanded farmer, who would call Sunday the Sabbath and taverns sinks of iniquity, another Eli who would disarm your hatred by his honesty and singleness of purpose, by his bullish courage. And this was to be born of Linda's sweet flesh.

Linda herself touched me gently on the arm and said quietly, but with a touch of something that was almost malice,

'Eli spoke to you, Philip.' At the same time, as though to rebuke my staring she drew the cloak across her body, holding it with little dry hands which work might roughen but never redden.

'What did you say?' I asked, lifting my head and staring unseeingly at Eli.

'I asked you how the wagons were going on?'

'Very well. Yours awaits its second coat of paint. If you've finished inspecting houses and cesspools you might give it that yourself and set Steggles free.' I was surprised to hear my voice so bitter.

But next morning Eli, with the two Lomax's like faithful shadows behind him, turned up at the yard and set to work. In the course of a morning he had laid twice the amount of paint than the other two combined had managed, smoothly and well upon the wagons. I watched him out of the corner of my eye, hating and admiring him at the same time. Stripped to his shirt he might have been the model for one of those old Greek sculptors. I thought, if only he's tolerably kind to her Linda will come to worship him, she can't help it, no woman could. And in the life to which we are going physical power will count so much! Oh, damn Eli Makers, and with him damn John Ollenshaw. Between them they have taken my love from me.

About midday I downed tools, wiped my face and hands on a towel that I kept for the purpose, and slung my coat over my arm. Slowly and deliberately I crossed the yard aware of Eli's disapproving eye following me, and made my way to the back entrance of Beadle's Tavern. Sooner or later the man I wanted would appear there, and my recent thoughts about Eli made me glad that if he had physical power, I at least had a certain amount of money and a perception that he lacked.

For once I was in luck. Mike was sitting on the settle beside the empty hearth, he was tapping out his pipe on his heel, and the house cat was curled up on his knees. There was a tankard beside him on the end of the settle, but it was empty and I carried it to be refilled before I said anything to him.

Mike was one of our finds. Andy had one day gashed his wrist with a chisel, and the red blood spurting, the power of it, and the way he was paling turned me sick. I had dashed across to the tavern, yelling for help, and Mike, with his pipe in his mouth and a tankard in his hand had wandered out casually, raising his eyebrows at the uproar.

I had gasped a few words about a chisel, wrist, blood. Mike, without haste as without delay, had gone up to Andy raised the cut wrist well above his head and snatching up a loose end of twine tied it tightly round the wrist above—or below, since Andy's arm was in the air—the wound. The dreadful spurting stopped and I was able to breathe again. The queer little man had since become a source of interest to me, and I had often paid for his drinks. In Beadle's he was a matter for scorn, none the less definite for being seasoned with good nature and one or two men had laughed at my continued interest in him. 'Must be something about that Andy,' they gibed. 'Bet you've saved lots of women, Mike and not got this much ale outa their husbands.' Since I could not adequately resent these quips I had ignored them and gradually they had ceased.

Mike gazed at his refilled tankard and grinned at me.

'Good day, your honour,' he said. 'And how's the carpentering? Will you get away this fall?'

'The beginning of September should see us on our way,' I said, taking a seat opposite him.

'Going up to the Nawkatcha country, I hear. Fine pretty country it is too.' I was quick to hear and assess the little sigh that accompanied the words. He lifted the replenished tankard and drank. I looked at him.

He was not over-clean. There was a good deal of pepper and salt stubble on his cheeks and chin. The whites of his eyes were yellow. But there was about that odd, knobbly face something kindly, and human, and to me, attractive.

'I've never been inside it, mind you,' he continued, ruminatively, 'but I've looked down on it from the Burnt Hills. 'Twasn't safe country then, but of course that's all over and done with. Indians don't amount to a row of beans these days. But they did, mind you, they did. I recall it though, a fine pretty country. Could almost find it in my heart to wish I was going with you.'

'Why not?' I asked. 'We're open to recruits, you know.'

For answer he put his hands in his breeches pockets, turning them inside out, one after the other, lugubriously demonstrating their emptiness. The cat, disturbed, stretched and sneezed.

'That's why, your honour. Old as I am I could go as an indentured servant, devil a doubt of that, skilled in livestock as I am. But so could I cut my throat, or dive into the harbour with my boots on. And to tell you the truth I'd as soon do one as the other. A penniless man is a slave anytime, but mostly he can move away if he doesn't care for his master. If I was to let an idle fancy lead me into the Nawkatcha country with another man's bread in my belly I might slave for years before I gathered enough gear to get myself out again. Besides, I hear that it's going to be a place where a man is grudged his pipe and his glass. No thank'ee. I'm right here at this minute to await the blessed arrival of Hick Maguire, of the Newfoundland fishing fleet, who, I hear, has had to drop his surgeon overboard with roundshot on his toes. Not before time either with him nearly blind this fifteen years. I somehow feel that with winter coming on and the slippery decks making men fall down, and the frozen hands on them making them clumsy. Hick'll be glad to hire me. Not that the fishing fleet's any heaven.'

'Been with it before?' I asked.

'Yeah. 'Bout four years ago. Lookit me ears.'

He pushed back his decrepit hat and his hair and showed me his ears, mere ragged, fringed holes in his skull.

'Frostbite,' he said. 'Your ears and your fingers and your toes break off like brittle candy. It's no treat I can assure you. Also I had a mighty row with Hick once. He's an obstropulous fellow. But I can't pick my job any more. And I guess Hick won't have a whole string of proper trained medicine men pleading with him for a job.'

'Listen,' I said, having finished my ale and being unwilling to waste any more time. 'If you like to come with us, I'll stand for you. I'll buy stores for you. You can travel in my wagon. When I get a house built there'll be room in it for you, or if you like you can have a house of your own. After about ... about next New Year I guess ... you can come back here at my expense if you like. What do you say? Will you come?'

For a moment his face was a mask of amazement. Then it narrowed into one of caution and suspicion.

'What do you want me for? You ain't sick, are you?' His eyes dropped, rested on my ironed leg and then rose again to my face. 'I tell you straight, your honour, me and you being mess-mates like. There's nothing I can do for that. Lame since birth, I reckon. Ain't that so?'

'It's nothing to do with that.' My voice betrayed my irritation. 'I reckon that you're clever, but I don't think you're a miracle man. You ask me no questions or I shall start inquiring how you come to be in a place where you haven't a penny and 'll think yourself lucky to go freezing again with Maguire's fishing outfit. See?'

'And easily can I answer you that,' he said, unabashed. 'Drunk on duty. There's my story in three words. Kicked out of His Majesty's navy I was, in the year of grace sixteen forty-nine, for sawing the wrong leg off a fellow. So what with my ministrations and the rot that set in the one I should have hacked off he had never a leg to stand on. That's my story. Downhill from that day to this. And now I have this lordly offer. Well, accepted with thanks, your honour.'

'My name's Ollenshaw,' I said. 'Here's some money. Get yourself tidied up. And remember, I don't travel alone and the less you say of drunkenness or anything like that the better my company will like it, though I'll see that your pipe and your glass aren't interfered with, so long as you do what I ask. It isn't much.' I went happily back to the wagons.

Oddly enough, while I was buying Mike's company, Nathaniel was also adding to our party. Two families of Quakers from Essex Street had approached our leader, requesting permission to join us. For some time Quakers had been half-tolerated in Salem, but they never quite belonged there, and with this new searching out for offences several people suggested that the tolerance of Quakerism might be reckoned with gaudy apparel and immodest bearing as a cause for God's displeasure. I think myself that the Quaker religion was not sufficiently belligerent to suit the taste of such powers in Salem as Alfred Bradstreet. Whether Eli wrestled with Nathaniel over their inclusion as he had done over the Whistlecrafts I do not know, for I was extremely busy at the yard and saw him little. All I know is that the Cranes and the Pikles, twelve persons in all, came with us on our journey, and that I liked them as well as I could ever like people so radically different from myself. Phineas Pikle, a widower with six children, had taken a whim to name every one with a name beginning with M. Mahitabel, Mary, Martha were the girls, Mark, Matthew, Moses, the boys. Jacob Crane had a wife, Deborah, a daughter, Hannah, and two sons, one christened Jacob but called Jake to distinguish him from his father and the other Thomas. The two families were slightly related and all had a look of one another, having, without exception, long thin bodies, frail looking but tough as whalebone, fair thin hair, large noses and blue eyes. To see them together was rather like seeing a flock of sheep; like sheep too, they were placid and amiable.

We were now thirty-eight in number and we had in all twelve wagons, a fact which allowed Nathaniel to put into practice for the first time his budding ideas about having all things in common. And since most of the shared things were his own, even Eli with his almost fanatical notions about independence and self-sufficiency could not grumble. It was obvious that some things must be shared—some of the cows were in milk, some dry. Some of the horses were larger than the others and could pull bigger loads. There were two to a wagon, but the Pikles and the Cranes who owned four wagons between them, had ox teams instead of horses on two of them.

We carried stores to last us for a year besides the supplies of corn, peas, and beans and potatoes which were to be saved for spring planting. We took also sacks of a seed that we had met for the first time in Salem, Indian corn, a seed shaped like a horse's tooth, which grew into a plant with many uses. The seed head, like an ear of corn, but smoother and twenty times the size and packed with the green seeds, could be cut young and made a sweet vegetable when cooked in salt water. The tall green plant itself, the height of a man, could also be eaten young by the cattle. Full grown and ripened the yellow seeds could be used for fodder or for flour.

I think that no journey ever began more joyfully or auspiciously. It was beautiful weather, clear and dry and golden. Most of our people, after the cramped quarters that had been their lot in Salem, knew the uprising, the spreading of the spirit that comes from sudden freedom and an abundance of sweet fresh air. Maybe there is a trace of the gypsy in every man, perhaps that is why we were happy, gay even when we were weary. I know that the evenings, when we made camp, and the hobbled horses hovered munching just out of reach and the fires were lighted and the smoke went up straight into the calm evening sky, and there came sounds and scents of cooking that set the mouth watering, were among the happiest of my life. I liked the mornings too, when the cows came lowing to be milked and a few handfuls of dry grass and sticks that could be easily stamped out afterwards were sufficient to boil a kettle and the horses were called up and harnessed and we could look back presently at the black spots where the fires had been and think that another day's journey had begun. Eli, with his team and his wagon to mind, and the wide open country to watch and gloat over, was a different person from the man he had been on board the *Westering Wing*. The singing and whistling of the Whistlecrafts, away back with the cattle, was either unnoticed or unheard by him, and often enough he himself would break into the Pilgrim's hymn. He was at his best then, ingenious and busy and careful for the teams, going to endless trouble when the trail was steep, to combine forces so that often four and sometimes six horses went up and down again until all the wagons had been taken, without strain or misery, to the top of the incline.

We passed several small settlements, Neathead, Columbine and Sanctuary, groups of squat strong little houses clustered around wooden churches, in the midst of well-tilled fields. In every one of them the people gave us warm

124

welcome and offered little gifts, pots of the honey just lifted from the hives, baskets of plums or apples, little new potatoes, loaves of sweet bread. They would tell us, too, of any dangers or difficulties on the road ahead, and Nathaniel would whip out his map and make alterations. As I look back on that time it seems as though it were enchanted, enshrined and wrapped in a golden light of sunshine and friendliness and happy labour.

We travelled slowly—cow's pace we called it on account of the animals that brought up the rear under the Whistle-crafts' care and which must be kept in sight and it was the beginning of the second week of September when we saw the last settlement that we expected to pass. It was marked on Nathaniel's map as Fort Outpost and was one of the places which had been razed to the ground and deserted during King Philip's War. On account of the fact that the land around it had been tilled it had been occupied again in the spring of this year. It lay in the valley and as we mounted the hill and reached the top and sent the teams down again to bring up the other wagons while we waited, we could see the roofs of the houses and the yellow of the corn fields standing out against the encircling greeny-grey of the summer-bleached grass. For several days it had been growing colder, the wind had changed and had come whis-tling down from the north, chilling our faces and hands. As I drew up my wagon alongside Nathaniel's and unharnessed my team for Andy to lead down again to help up Lomax's wagon I turned up the collar of my coat and shuddered. Nathaniel said suddenly, 'It looks to me as though they're very late with the harvest. I can't see anyone working either. We haven't missed a day and this is Sunday by any chance?' As though in answer Eli brought his wagon into line behind mine, unhitched his traces and going to the heads of his horses to turn them about called over his shoulder, 'Mr. Gore, tomorrow being Lord's Day, what do you think of camping at the foot of the hill and having service in the church yonder?'

'It's a good idea, Eli, and the last chance we shall get. I should like too . . .' He broke off and screwed up his eyes. 'Philip, your eyes are younger than mine, look yonder and tell me what you see.' I looked along the line of his pointing finger and said after a moment's pause,

'It looks like a man coming towards us, stumbling ... Yes, there he goes again. He was flat almost a minute then. What can be wrong with him?'

'We'll soon see,' said Nathaniel and set off briskly down the hill. I followed him, taking a hopping kind of running step every time I fell behind. The man regained his feet and came on to meet us, stopping and stumbling so frequently that it looked as though he had risen from his death-bed in order to make the journey. When there were only about twenty yards between us, and we could see the pallor of his face and the glitter of the sweat on it he stopped and held up his hand. We could hear the croaking of his voice but not the words, so we went nearer and a second time he flung up his hand, which fell down again as though his arm were stuffed with sawdust, and he repeated his croaking. This time I caught the sense of it. 'I ought to warn you. There's a sore sickness.'

Nathaniel's eyes met mine. As though pulled by the same string we took a simultaneous step backwards and then several forward, as though to deny that the recoil had ever-been. 'I can see that, my poor fellow,' said Nathaniel. 'What is it? Are many sick?'

The man put one hand to his throat, 'It's the throats' he said speaking with difficulty, 'I was taken this morning. It's been with us all summer.' And then, as if the effort had been too much for him, he reeled and fell full length to the ground where he lay. I took another step towards him, but Nathaniel clutched my sleeve. 'Wait,' he said. 'There are others to be considered. This must be talked over.' We took another look at the supine figure, and then, again moved by common impulse, began to strip off our coats. Nathaniel threw them over the body, going no nearer than he could help, and then we turned and as far as a cripple and an elderly man can be said to run up a steep incline, we ran back to the others. Two more wagons had reached the top and two more were creaking their way up.

'Give the order to camp, here on the hill-top, Eli, and then come to me. You, Philip, get Lomax and Pikle and I'll collect Crane and Thomas. We'll have a meeting over there by that red bush. And get yourself another coat.'

126

Within a quarter of an hour the seven of us were crouching on the sheltered side of the bushes and Nathaniel was speaking gravely.

'The first thing to decide,' he said, 'is whether we are in a position to decide. In a sense we are responsible for the others, and I have no doubt that what we decide will be accepted by them. But should we take the responsibility or should we put the matter before all the men?'

'You haven't told us yet what the matter is,' said Crane quietly.

'Fort Outpost has a grave sickness. Philip and I have just talked with one man, in sore enough case himself. We didn't go very near him, or touch him. But the matter for decision is this, do we—some of us, that is, go down into the valley and render what assistance is in our power to give, or do we leave them to struggle on as though our trail had not led us past their doors? And do we, as elders and freeholders, make the decision or do we ask the opinion of every male in the company?'

It was a pretty problem. Sitting there, crouched in an inadequate shelter against the wind that grew in fury with every minute of the dwindling afternoon, we faced the question which has faced mankind ever since the beginning of history. Shall age and property qualify a man to rule his fellows, or is each voice to be counted in every matter of the common weal? The small number of rulers makes for swiftness in decision, the large is cumbersome and slow ... but we had come thus far to escape from tyranny, and though I was ready to swear that among the seven of us there were few tyrants, and at the moment we were trying to do the best thing for us all ... I wondered. Why should Mathew Thomas count for more than my man Andy, for example? He had brought nothing but himself to the venture, just as Andy had. Thomas was as much Nathaniel's pensioner as Andy was mine.

I suppose everyone was thinking in the same way. Perhaps I thought more quickly, had a mind more shallow and reached a more hasty decision. Anyway I spoke first.

'Every man,' I said, somewhat startled to hear my own voice break the silence, 'has a life to lose. Every man should therefore have a share in the decision.' Mathew Thomas

127

turned on me as though I had spoken blasphemy.

'Why not effery woman, then, and effery child too, maybe. We are the elders, responsible to God. What we decide should be good enough for them, why not?' His eye lighted on me with no great favour and I read his mind. I was not an elder. I should be one of 'them'.

'Who made us responsible?' I asked, and regretted, though I did not abate, the warmth in my voice. 'Mr. Gore is undisputed head of the party. He got us together and did all the business. *Some* people put in money and some labour and that makes one man's word as good as another's. And anyway it's not a matter for us to decide, Mr. Thomas. What Mr. Gore says is what matters.'

'Then why, may I ask, did you speak at all?'

'Thinking aloud,' I said, and waited for somebody else to take up the matter.

'We've come to the turning point,' said Nathaniel quietly. 'What Philip said about who gave us the responsibility is a question that every man should ask and answer faithfully. And the answer is "nobody". But we'll ask for the responsibility and waste no more time. People are dying down yonder.'

So all the men were called together and the question of leadership, responsibility and power to make decisions was gone into thoroughly and in about as primitive a manner as it has ever been. For some reason, possibly because there were seven of us at the first meeting under the bushes, seven was the number of elders decided upon. So each man was given seven pieces of twig and requested to lay them at the feet or in the hand of the seven elders that he had chosen. Their decisions in all matters were to be final, to have the power of law among us who had left all law behind : but it was agreed that in questions like the one now confronting us the others were to have some say.

I stepped away from the self-appointed elders as soon as the voting began, I didn't want anyone to feel that I was soliciting his vote. But Andy came and tried to thrust all his seven sticks into my hand.

'Fool,' I said. 'You can't do that. You must give one to each of seven elderly men. Go on, start with Mr. Gore.'

'You take one first—don't I shan't bother,' he said stubbornly. So I slipped his stick into my pocket. Immediately afterwards Ralph and Simon Whistlecraft each thrust a stick at me, and after that I abandoned my undignified protests and gravely accepted a vote from Mike, Isaac Carter, Tim Dendy and Harry Wright, William Lomax, each of the male Pikles, young Jake Crane and Amos Beeton. Thirteen votes in all and most of them from young men. Then to my intense surprise Eli came thrusting his way towards me and gave me the last of his twigs, and Nathaniel, with those that had been given him bristling from his hat, dived in his pocket and gave me one of his own. I knew at that moment that he wanted me. I was pleased beyond measure.

Every one of the twenty-two men had voted for Nathaniel, who was as touched and delighted by this inevitable happening as if he had expected otherwise, twenty had voted for Eli, fifteen each for Oliver Lomax and myself, Phineas Pikle had fourteen, Mathew Thomas twelve, and Jacob Crane ten. In fact the elected Council consisted of the seven people who had sat down behind the bushes and decided to hold an election! It looked as though the best part of an hour had been wasted.

As soon as the results were known Nathaniel clambered up on to the tail-board of the last wagon and stood there with the cooking pots swinging at his feet and a muslin wrapped ham on one side of his head and a bunch of dry herbs on the other. The men gathered around and listened to one of the most moving speeches I should think ever made. He described the sickness as he had seen it in the person of the man whom we had met: he mentioned the untouched harvest fields. The question was, should we go down into what might prove a place of pestilence, or should we pass by and leave the people to their fate?

'Far be it for me to persuade you into a course of action that will cost you time, certainly, and possibly life: on the other hand I should be failing in my duty if I did not point out to you that as these people are today, you may be tomorrow. At the moment they are at the farthest end of the road that we with our feet are making. Next year, if God wills it, we shall be in the place that we already call Zion, and we may be smitten with sickness and there may come other men on their way to the West who will stop and ponder as we do now, whether to help or to pass by. Do you wish to vote separately upon this matter, or will you leave it to the Council of your own choosing? That is the first question.'

Now this is strange, but it is also true. All the while that the voting had been going forward the women had been lighting the fires and setting the pots over them. There was a smell of cooking in the air, bacon frying, frumity bubbling, salt herring grilling on pointed sticks. And as Nathaniel spoke I saw men's attention waver. It was almost twilight, they had worked and walked all day and were hungry. What was a council for, if not to make decisions and leave other men to go to their food? The cry, 'Leave it to the Council' was unanimous, and within a few moments of Nathaniel's nodding and stepping down the only men left at the tail of the wagon were the Councillors. The decision that we made might mean life or death to them ... but supper was ready!

'Well,' said Nathaniel, 'what is it to be?'

I knew what Nathaniel wished to do, that had shone clearly enough through his speech; but he made doubt impossible by saying at once, 'I think we should go down and do what we can. I am willing to go myself.'

'Could'st thou not let one younger and less needed go?' asked Phineas Pikle. I had seen both his face and Crane's go greyish when Nathaniel mentioned the throat sickness. 'There is a chance that this may be another case of the evil that swept Salem two years since. It is no light thing. Twenty people were dead before we had it in hand and set up a pest house on one of the islands in the harbour. Every sufferer and every person who had been in contact with him was sent there. Not many came back, Mr. Gore.'

'Well, if no one else goes, I shall. After all I went close enough to the man before I knew.'

There was nothing after that for me to say but, 'So did I. I'll go.' And having said that I felt I might as well add, 'Let me go by myself and see how things are.'

'We'll go together,' said Nathaniel.

'But we depend upon thee, Mr. Gore,' Pikle persisted. 'If a life is to be risked let it not be thine. Also, for all we know the man thou sawest may be the last one left alive. In that case thy risk would have been taken for no purpose.'

'It may be a punishment for their sins, see you.' Mathew Thomas took up the tale. 'And those who would have saved Sodom and Gomorrha would have met with the same fate as the cities of the plain, through their own choice. Better not meddle, I think.'

I said, 'If we're going to quote Scripture remember that the Good Samaritan didn't stop to ask *why* the man was naked and wounded....'

'We'll say no more,' said Eli. 'Those who vote for going down to the valley hold up their hands.' He shot his own high above his head as he spoke. I put up mine, Nathaniel raised his shoulder high, and Crane and Pikle, after a moment's hesitation during which they again looked at one another sickly, raised theirs as though the effort cost them dear.

Nathaniel wasted no more time.

'Philip, are you willing to come with me? Good. We'll go down and investigate. Eli, stay here and explain that we may need volunteers. Pick out three after supper, come to the top of the hill and if we want them we'll wave a lantern like this.' He waved his arm from left to right, slowly, three times. 'It may be that there is nothing that we can do to help. In that case we shall wait there for a few days until risk of infection has passed. It will do the beasts no harm to have a rest.'

'But I'm coming,' said Eli. 'Mr. Thomas and Mr. Lomax can carry out those orders.'

'I want you to stay, Eli. At least until the camp has settled, do you understand? One disaffected word might start a panic.'

By this time it was dusk and when we had collected two well-filled lanterns, and some vinegar for disinfectant and a few other things that we thought might be useful it was almost dark. Eli came to the top of the hill with us and gripped our hands, 'God have you in His keeping,' he said simply.

When we were half way down the hillside and were beginning to walk carefully, looking for the man who had fallen, we heard a step behind us, and turning saw the tall Quaker, Crane, take form against the night.

'I could not let thee take the risk alone,' he said, falling into step beside us, and in half a minute there came a clumping noise to the right of us, 'Hi there, hi, your honour, what are you thinking of? Have you no use for a doctor the same as myself?'

Now it had gone through my head, as Nathaniel and I set out, that Mike ought to have been included. But by that time the pity that had impelled me to volunteer had turned into the most frantic error that I had ever known. Pikle's expression when he had looked at Crane, and his memories of the outbreak at Salem had reduced me to a quaking jelly of fear. I was sure that Nathaniel and I were going straight to our deaths, and the one comfort that I could clutch to myself was the thought that Linda would be all right. Her husband was with her and Mike was still there. My death— for by that time my cursed imagination was offering me a picture of my own death from closed throat—would mean no more to her than the falling of a leaf.

I said, 'I meant you to wait, Mike. We don't know yet what is the matter.'

'And who's the more likely to know, tell me that?' And as he spoke we came upon the man whom we had talked with some two hours ago. He had rolled over once so that our coats were huddled half underneath him and his fevered body was exposed to the icy evening wind. But he was still breathing. Mike stooped over him quickly, and after that there could be no question of sending him back.

Crane bent his tall slender body and with a surprising power and skill slung the body across his shoulders. Half way towards the houses Mike took a turn, stumbling along like a bear on his little bow legs and breathing hard. I offered to help but Mike snapped, 'I can manage.' At the foot of the hill a little stream was spanned by a bridge, just wide enough for two men to walk abreast, with a slender handrail along one side of it. We crossed this and a few steps more took us into the village. We stopped at the first house. There was no need to open the door, it stood ajar already, and as I pushed it open there came a squeal and a scuffle and two half half-grown pigs shot out, colliding with our legs and almost knocking us down.

Nathaniel took out his tinder box and lighted one

lantern and then the other. Mike laid down his burden along the wall that ran to the left of the door and we stood still for just as long as it took the flame to catch hold of the wicks of the lanterns and throw a light. There was a stink in the room that boded no good.

I suppose that in every man's mind there is a dungeon, where the banished things, the things he tries not to remember or think of, lie in all their horror, locked in by the man's will, but still vital and ready to stir. Mine is a full and horrible dungeon, for my observation is keen and my memory uncommonly good. But few of the things that haunt me are so vivid or distressing as the memory of the first sight of that room, where, on blankets hastily thrown down over the bare floor, there lay what remained of three bodies after disease and swine had done with them. An angry Indian can make a mess of God's image, but a hungry pig can make a worse one.

When we had opened both doors and looked into the lean-to cabin at the back of the room and in the little upper chamber at the head of the stairs and found no other body alive or dead Nathaniel spoke the first words.

'We can do nothing here.'

Crane lifted the man again and we went out, being careful to close the door.

Two more houses were mere tombs. In one a body was wrapped in a sheet and made ready for the burial that had never taken place, and across the sheeted feet lay the woman who had tended the corpse. She had been dead only a day, or two at the most. The bowl of water, the comb, the sprigs of rosemary that lay on the table gave evidence of what her last sorrowful task had been.

The fourth house was clean and empty and there were a few logs, smouldering dully, on the hearth. It suggested itself as the house of the man who had come to warn us, and there we left Mike to put the man to bed and tend him as well as he could while we went on.

This sickness had struck most severely along the riverside. House after house there held only emptiness or death, but when we reached the shelf of land that lay between the river and the tilled land we found people who had been stricken later or more lightly and were still alive. In one we saw a light and made haste towards it. A woman with a starved white face and the fixed tranced look of a sleep-walker was making bread-and-water-sop in a yellow basin. Along the wall of the cabin, on blankets and pillows arranged with some degree of order lay a man and two little children, their sunken, fever-bright eyes turned upon us without curiosity or surprise.

The woman spoke, and her voice, though weak and hoarse had a triumphant ring in it. 'We're getting better,' she said.

Nathaniel looked at the water sop and said, 'You shall have milk in the morning. Lie down now, we'll serve them.' We could see the fourth pillow and the turned back blanket that was the bed she had crept from to serve her family.

'We shall do. There are many who cannot stir.' She knelt by the bed of the smaller of the children and held a spoon-ful of the warm wet mash to the white lips.

'Her task is keeping her alive,' Nathaniel whispered and we went into the night again.

We found twenty others living. In one house in which both upper and lower rooms were full of beds we found eight people being cared for by an old blind man who turned to us as we entered and looking full at us, said,

'I knew you'd come back, Walter. Did you find the cow?'

At first we thought that he spoke in delirium but when we spoke he said, 'I don't know your voices. I am blind, you see. What do you want here?'

'We've come to help you . . . do anything we can.'

'We want milk. Have you seen a boy with a cow? Walter, my grandson, the young rapscallion. It shouldn't take him so long to find the cow and milk her.'

Some of the old man's charges were raving, some lay in coma, but at least none were crying for water, begging for help like some of those we had found. I asked curiously,

'Have you been sick at all?'

'Not this time. There was an outbreak like this at this very spot two years before the Indian raid. It's a cursed spot. That's what it is. I was sick that time. You never have it again.'

We promised him milk and all else that he needed in the

134

morning, and went on.

In most cases all we could do was to give water to the parched sufferers who had had no one to tend them for days on end. Nathaniel made me boil and cool every drop before we offered it. 'The water is to blame, I suspect,' he said. 'The stream was low, did you notice, and the water stank. They probably throw their rubbish and let their privies drain into it. We'll manage better in Zion.'

Yes, I thought, if ever we live to see it.

But I only said, 'What about the volunteers. Shall we signal for them?'

The night was far spent by this time, but Eli had kept a faithful watch and replied when I waved the lantern from the bridge. Before it was light Andy, Ralph Whistlecraft and Tim Dendy, Thomas Crane and Moses Pikle came down the hillside bringing breakfast for all of us. When we had eaten Nathaniel drew out paper and pencil. He wrote a note to Eli, telling him to get the cows milked and to stand pails of milk half way down the hillside, where we would collect it. He tied the paper to a stone and then Tim after waving to attract attention threw the message as far up the hill as he could manage. Within half an hour the milk buckets stood there and we fetched them down.

That day we got the sick together under two roofs, leaving the two families who had survived under the care of the woman and the blind man where they were. We made certain that we had missed no one, and being uneasy about the boy Walter whom the blind man had mentioned I made it my business to search for him. It was mid-afternoon before I found him, lying in the most distant corner of a meadow, the bucket clasped in one cold hand. But he was still alive, and I stumbled back with him to our temporary hospital. I wished for a sound leg that afternoon as much as I have ever done, but I managed.

Tim and Ralph set about digging graves, and later in the day, when our simple ministrations were finished we helped them, and began to carry out the dead. The bodies were thin and light, but they had stiffened as they lay, and some had been dead for days, so it was not an easy task.

'They should have a service held for them,' said Nathaniel. 'I've a good mind to tell Eli to send Mr. Thomas

135

down.'

'A service held by a conscript wouldn't have much value, would it?' I asked. 'We'll have a proper service for the poor souls when this is over.'

Perhaps because of Mike's ministrations, perhaps because they were better tended, perhaps because they were naturally the strongest of the little community, only five of our patients died. The evening came when we could reckon three days without a death. Mike finished his round at the house where the blind man was still in charge and returned to the room that we had made our headquarters, the kitchen of one of the houses that we had made into an hospital. Andy was frying eggs and bacon over the fire and Moses Pikle was making coffee. Mike came in carefully carrying a quart jug in both hands. He set it down in the middle of the table and grinned his cheerful twisted grin.

'All those still living are on the mend, I'm thankful to say. And I've managed to have talk with one or two. Not that it helps to know how a thing starts if you can't stop it.' He sighed, then brightened as his glance fell on the jug. 'But look what the old blind fellow, bless his heart, thrust on me just as I was leaving. Jamaica rum of the best, and if anyone says we haven't earned a swig of it I'll smash the jug over his head—after it's empty that is.'

'I wouldn't say had'st not earned it,' said Jacob Crane. 'I'd say it was a poor reward. Thee won't think us churlish I hope, that we stick to the coffee pot.' His 'us' included his son and young Pikle.

'Each to his taste. Mr. Gore, sir?'

Nathaniel was bent over his paper. He was writing to Eli, I knew, telling him to move the camp on the next day to a spot about half a mile to the East of the village. 'Camp ground gets stale and poisoned,' he had said to me earlier in the day. He was doubtless writing the same thing to Eli now. He looked up as Mike addressed him, hesitated for a moment and then said, 'That'll be grand, Mike, with hot water and sugar, if that's not troubling you too much. It's turned very cold tonight.'

Why we didn't take more notice of that I can't think, for during the afternoon the wind had dropped and the almost wintry weather of the past ten days or more had given way to a pleasant calm. Nathaniel sprinkled the folded letter with vinegar and laid it aside. We took our places at the table.

'How long do you think before it'll be safe to go back to camp?' I asked Mike.

'Ah, that's what I've been talking to the people about. There's not much likeness in some of their stories, but everybody agrees that the first funeral took place on June the twelfth and the second a fortnight after. And those deaths are registered in the book in the church. After that it seems to have gone through like wildfire. But—and this does give us something to go on—one of the folks who is in the blind man's house had been down to Sanctuary to help a brother of his to get in his harvest because the brother had broken a leg. That man came back expecting to find his own harvest got in by his sons and he got back on the tenth day of August. That means that he came into contact with the disease on the tenth day of August and he was taken ill a fortnight later to the day. He remembers because he travelled on the Sabbath and he was taken ill on the Sabbath. He sees some sinister connection between the two. I ain't complaining about that, it gives me something to reckon by.'

'I see.' Nathaniel rested his little pointed chin on one hand and moved a crumb or two about with the fingers of the other. 'That means that we must stay here another fortnight at least. Well, that will give us time to get their corn in. A pleasant change of occupation!'

The rum was running warmly round our veins or I think we should have groaned at the prospect of any further occupation, however pleasant. Lifting, washing and feeding the sick, carrying out and burning bedding that was beyond all hope of cleaning, keeping fires going and water boiled, sitting up with those who struggled in delirium to throw off their wrappings, composing the dead limbs, carrying out the corpses and digging graves for them ... ten days on end of that was hardly a fit preparation for harvesting.

However, since we must stay we might as well be useful and next day there was great searching out of scythes and honing stones, the cheerful sound of sharpening blades rose on the air which was warm and mellow again and all through the bright shortening day those of us who were not on hospital work went up and down the little fields cutting the brittle dry cornstalks and gathering the heavy ears.

I called in at the house of the blind man to report to him how Walter, his grandson, was progressing down at the hospital and so was behind the others in arriving home to supper. I knew the moment I turned the bend in the street that something was amiss. Andy and the Cranes and Moses Pikle stood talking before the door in subdued whispers and there was consternation plainly written on their faces.

'Mr. Gore's sick,' said Andy. 'Croaking he is, and the fever on him.'

'Oh God!' I said. 'Why did it have to be him? Why couldn't it be one of the young ones . . . strong?'

'There's time for that yet,' said Jacob Crane solemnly. Something in his voice sent a shudder through my very soul.

I had come to take an impersonal view of the sickness; assuaging my coward's fears by attributing it to the water that the people of Fort Outpost had been drinking, when I had time to remember that I was frightened, which was not very often. We had come to think ourselves immune . . . and now one of us was stricken. I ducked my head at the lintel of the door of the hospital and came to the side of the bed where Nathaniel lay. His cheerful canary-coloured breeches and his russet coat lay on the floor at the foot of the bed. At the sight of them lying there, despite the fact that every night on the voyage out I had seen them thrown down in just that way on the floor of our cabin, something struck through me and I knew that he was going to die. Some feeling in me, regardless of time leapt straight back to the night when Eli's sermon to the sailors had found an unexpected target in Nathaniel's heart. It was as though the days between had never been real at all. Nathaniel had received warning of death that night and this night was the sequel. Through the bluish smoke of the smouldering vinegar rags and the burning herbs I saw Nathaniel's face, sunken and wasted suddenly as though the fever burned like consuming fire. But he was conscious and he knew me. He moved one hand a little and smiled, and then he said, in the strangled choking voice that we had grown to know so

138

well as a sign of the disease,

'Well, lad, it's got me.'

In the inconsequent way that the mind does choose to throw up thought at the most unlikely moment I remembered Antony's dreadful simple statement, 'I'm dying, Egypt, dying,' and I felt the wetness come into my eyes. Tears for Antony, for Egypt, mere figures on a tapestry, for Nathaniel who was my friend, for every one of us who, having drawn a first breath must needs draw a last. I swallowed hard and tasted the tears salt in my throat, and said with what cheer I could muster, 'Mike has pulled twenty people through, he won't fail you.' He croaked on, as though I had not spoken, 'Everything will be in order, Philip. I leave you with my plans ... my dreams. Remember what I said to you, years ago at Marshalsea ... about stopping up the kettle's spout. Eli will try, with the best of intentions. The others ... but I look to you, Philip. Tolerance in Zion, the gentle curb....'

His voice failed and for a moment I saw his eyes fly wide open, fearful, surprised, appealing, then with a little peaceful sigh he rested back against his pillows and seemed to sleep. For two days Mike stayed beside him, but there was nothing that anyone could do and just as the third dawn was breaking and I was quietly laying a fresh billet of wood on the fire, Mike went to the bed, looked down as he had done a thousand times, at the unconscious figure, and then drew the blanket over the face.

We went out and stood just before the doorway. The world was grey and cold and more quiet than anyone could imagine. To the East, from behind the hill where our camp had been there came a clear lemon-tinted light. At our feet the wasted stream moved sluggishly, leaden of pace and colour and around it clustered the little houses, some empty, some sheltering the people whose lives we had saved, whose harvest we had gathered—at what cost! The windless chill of the morning touched our hands and cheeks as we stood there in the queer enchanted light; the intense silence was like a thin cord, stretched and stretched until it must break. Mike broke it. Shrugging his shoulders as though he moved beneath a burden he said, 'Moses died before he got there, didn't he?'

When I did not answer he looked at me, half anxious and half truculent, like a rough dog uncertain whether to bite or fawn upon the man who has chidden it.

'I did what I could,' he said.

'I know that,' I said. 'He died before he ever saw you, Mike.'

The truculence faded, leaving plain anxiety.

'You ain't sickening yourself, are you?'

'I'm all right. We'd better tell the others.' We went into the sleeping house and told our heavy news.

We buried Nathaniel a little apart from the others whom we had lain in the burying ground beside the wooden church. I chose the spot, a grassy slope at the foot of a clump of beech trees. The smooth grey trunks rose like the pillars of a cathedral and against the dull sky the leaves, already turning, burned like a funeral pyre. Light and small, a frail lantern whose candle was extinguished, we laid him there in the strange earth. Over the grave we made a pile of the biggest stones we could find, mortared together into a solid mound that neither wind nor cattle rubbing their itching hides upon it could soon destroy. And in the centre of the top of the cairn we set a copper plate, made by me from a tray offered by one of the Fort Outpost women. With heat and hammer and a sturdy nail I raised upon it his name, the date of his death and—all that there was space for, the letters 'R.I.P.'

No one else had sickened, and after we had buried Nathaniel we met to discuss our plans. The work at the settlement seemed to be completed. The grain was stored, what wandering animals had been recovered from the woods and the wastelands were fenced and stalled again. The sorry remnant of the people were once more upon their feet. It was time for us to press on, The sudden cold, the steadily darkening mornings and evenings, the changing colour of the trees, the wild geese honking overhead on the way to the South, all these warned us that winter was not far away and that we had a journey to finish and walls to rear against the cold. Yet we dare not go back to the wagons for a time, there was still time for one of us to fall sick. What to do?

I realised at that first meeting, with Nathaniel barely an hour in his grave, how concrete and real a thing is leadership. I realised too, with a nervous quickening of my pulses, that questioning glances and words of tentative suggestion were directed at me. But could I, could any man, by one decision, both arrange for the journey to go forward and wait to see whether the sickness still lurked within this little group? My mind spun ... and then suddenly it was easy.

'Listen,' I began. 'I will write to Eli and send him a copy of this.' I tapped the map over which Nathaniel had pored so often, 'and ask him to start, leaving two wagons well supplied and the horses tethered. We'll wait a day, so that they are a clear day's journey ahead of us. We cannot harm them then. He could start tomorrow. Does that solve it?'

I made a careful copy of Nathaniel's map and wrote my letter to Eli. I carried a flask of vinegar with me, and when I came in sight of the new camp I sprinkled the papers well, shouted and waved to draw attention and threw the packet along the ground.

Next morning, from the hilltop from which we had first viewed Fort Outpost we looked out across the little valley and saw the fires stamped out and the wagons move off in a line as soon as it was light. We could see the wagons that awaited us, lonely upon the hillside.

It was a day of biting wind with now and then a flurry of rain that stung the bare flesh like splinters. Through it we did the last offices that we could for the weakened people of the village, ploughing brown furrows across the bleached stubble and threshing out a further supply of corn. In the morning we breakfasted in the windy darkness and reached the wagons in the red dawn.

We were surprised, as we struggled uphill against the wind to see, first the glow of a dying fire and then figures moving, laying the harness upon the horses and leading them towards the wagons.

'My folks,' said Ralph Whistlecraft, calmly. 'They would be concerned for me, knowing that one has died.' He was right in both his statements. Judith and her brother ran downhill to meet us and their greeting of Ralph showed how deep their concern had been.

In their soft gabbling speech they told us the news. Eli had lost a horse with colic and had had to lighten his wagon. Harry Wright and Hannah Crane had taken advantage of the prolonged leisure to fall in love and had been married by Mr. Thomas about four days ago. The child Betsy Steggles had crawled down the hillside and fallen into the stream, luckily it wasn't very deep and she had escaped with only a wetting and a few slaps from her mother who was weeping with relief and delight even as she slapped her. Oliver Lomax's mastiff bitch had had two pups, result of some mesalliance in Salem. They were mustard coloured and fluffy and were both spoken for when they were weaned.

We went down the far side of the hill and Fort Outpost was lost in the valley. The marks of Eli's wagon wheels were plain in the rough grass. The track that we had followed as far as the last village was ended now and the caravan that had gone before us had made its own road, here swerving aside to avoid a boulder, here turning at right angles along a clump of trees and creeping along until an open space offered a passage. Nathaniel, in that last prospecting journey, had ridden horseback, with spare horses for supplies and it was likely that the front wheels of Eli's wagon were the first to grind down the grass and the little bushes that now lay flattened for our passage. We had done a mile or more when Judith Whistlecraft, walking just ahead of me with her shawl over her head and her skirts flapping like loose sails in the wind, suddenly brought her hand down on her thigh and swore.

'God rot it,' she said, 'I've forgotten something. Head like a leaky bucket, that's what I've got.'

Before we could ask her what it was, whether it was worth going back for, or anything about it, she gathered her fluttering petticoats in her hand and went speeding back running like a lapwing.

'Some women's gear,' said Ralph easily. 'There's no call for us to wait, she'll catch up by the noon spell.'

'If she goes at that gait we'll hardly have time to miss her,' I said and laughed, though the old familiar pang had gone through me, as it always did and would ever do, at the sight of some unwontedly agile and untrammelled movement. And the lifted, kilted skirts had shown a pair of admirable legs, long and slim with well-muscled calves within the coarse white stockings.

Several times I looked back that morning, half uneasy that she should have gone back alone, half curious to know what it was that was so easily forgotten, yet worth a journey of two miles to recover. When we stopped at midday and fed the horses and crept into the shelter of the wagons to eat our own noon pieces I said to Ralph who was near me, 'Your sister isn't back. Running like that she might have twisted an ankle. If she isn't back pretty soon we'd better go to see.'

'She's all right,' he said again, but he stood up and went a step or two back along the trail, screwing up his eyes against the wind. 'Here she is now,' he said after a moment, and standing myself and rounding the wagon tail I saw her struggling along, a bundle swinging from one hand and poised on the other shoulder what looked like part of a tree or an uprooted bush. As soon as he saw her burdens Ralph stepped out to meet her and in a few minutes he was back, flinging down the bush and the bundle and setting straight to work upon the food he had left. Judith followed him, her arms raised, pinning up her hair and setting her shawl straight again. She breathed deeply, but evenly and there was a fine scarlet colour on her wind-whipped cheeks and little drops of moisture in the corners of her eyes.

'What is it?' I asked, jerking my elbow at the bundle as I sawed a slice off the loaf.

'Some things of Mrs. Makers'. *He* tossed them out last night when he was lightening his wagon—you know, because of the horse. Most of the things went in the other wagons but he said this was rubbish,' she indicated the bushy thing with her toe, 'and this,' she laid one hand on the bundle and with the other raised the bread to her mouth, 'was vanity as well,' she said through the mouthful.

I looked at the bundle more closely. It was tied in a striped cloth, the four corners brought to the top and knotted; through the gaping edges I caught a glimpse of something familiar. I widened the gap with my fingers and knew that my memory hadn't tricked me. Inside, together with some other clothing, was the mulberry-coloured dress in which Linda had walked among the oxslips in Hunter's Wood!

Throw it away, out with it. It is useless weight and vanity as well ... what will the wife of Eli Makers ever again want with a thing like this? My dear you might as well have had my father for a season, if he threw away a woman's gown he did it for one reason only, and Marshalsea Manor would have housed you like a queen!

Lest my face should betray me I looked past the gypsy girl munching her crust to the bushy thing that Ralph had dropped by the wagon tail. 'And that?'

'Oh, just some plants and things, a lavender bush and a root of rosemary, and several roses, damned scratchy things to carry in a wind.' She rubbed her cheek with one brown hand. 'I came on her, crying about them,' she said, with a certain scornful pity in her voice, 'and I said she could trust me to tend them. If I can't find a cranny for them I'll carry the truck—she's the only one of the whey-faced hags that ever has a civil word to spare.' She bit fiercely on the crust. The whole of the little scene came before me like a picture, Linda crying over her rose bushes and her mulberry gown.

'Bless you,' I said, overwarmly, crammed the last piece into my mouth and picking up the bundle and the bushes I mounted my own wagon, dived under the hood and dealt fiercely with the things within it so that Linda's treasures might ride in triumph into Zion. Damn Eli, I thought, couldn't he have done the same? So small they were, so light. I knew, and Linda must have known with equal bitterness, that had the gown been a print one and the bushes gooseberry or currant, they would not have been left to the gypsy's care.

All that day and all the next we watched one another for any signs of sickness. None appeared and I agreed with Mike that the cold weather had dealt with it as it had dealt with the plague in London. It was colder than any weather I had ever known, even in January, when in our East of England the wind blows icily off the sea. Our lips cracked until smiling was a thing to be avoided at all costs, and the skin of our faces and hands was marked into rough squares, like a field in a drought, and the edges of the squares would bleed like little scratches when the skin touched gear or clothing. It was, I know, a trivial affliction, but because it was trivial and always there it was annoying. Even the weatherbeaten gypsies suffered and kept saying that if only they could find a hedgehog to boil for its fat, we'd have done with cracks and chapping. Nothing, they said, nothing on earth was so good as hedgehog fat, it made the hair glossy and plentiful and the skin supple. It softened leather and cured sand crack in horses. If only they could find a hedgehog. But they didn't and the wind went on blowing and we all looked and felt as though we had pushed our way through a quickset hedge.

But as we went on, camping each night somewhere near the black fire patches made by Eli's company, there grew a holiday feeling in the air. We had divided by common consent into two parties, mine and Crane's. Mike, Andy, and the Whistlecrafts sat around one fire and cooked supper over it, Jacob and Thomas Crane, Moses Pikle and Tim shared another. Ever since Tim had heard of Harry Wright's marriage to Hannah Crane he had been making himself agreeable to the Quakers, especially Moses Pikle who had three eligible sisters. If one young Quaker girl could marry a young man with nothing but his hands to offer, why not two? His thoughts were quite plain to me, and the Quakers may have seen through him with equal ease. But when, on the first night, around the one common fire, Mike brought out the rum that the blind man at Fort Outpost had given him as a parting gift (the only one accepted of a score of pathetic offerings) and Tim refused his portion, when his pipe stayed unlighted, and he took no share in the merry chatter that went forward, then I knew what ailed him. And on the second night, without a word being spoken, there were two fires.

I went and sat by the second one for a little while because, looking out of our firelit circle where Mike was telling some tale of the seven seas, or Simon was giving away poaching secrets, or some homely jest had set the laughter bubbling, I thought that the four others sitting there looked so lonely, out of things. There is a tendency, I find, for rather selfish natures like mine, to imagine that those who are not with them are out of things. Yet when I sat with the four for a while, listening to their grave talk and exchanging remarks about the weather and the country, then I realised that their fire was just as much a centre and that although the other party was bigger and noisier it was no more important. And soon I rose and went back, dropped into my seat between Mike and Judith, took a swig of the rum and felt no need to be apologetic if Mike's seafaring stories sometimes dropped below the line of decency.

Nobody minded about Judith. One of the things that set us laughing one night was her story of how benighted she had slept in a barn and stayed too long in the morning and was caught by the farmer, who, taken with her face, or her manner, or simply her womanhood asked her to lie down again and permit him to lie with her. She didn't care for him, so she refused. As she brushed the hay off her clothes he said, 'Lassie I'll give ye a good fat goose.' A flock of them, waking and squawking in the yard put the thought into his head. But she still said no, idly picking a handful of grain from a sack as she repeated the refusal.

'Then get out o' my barn, hussy,' he said angrily, 'don't I'll have constable after ye for a vagrant.' So she went, leaving a trail of the corn behind her. Three geese in anxious competition followed the trail and she picked out the best of them and had it for nothing.

A story like that would start one or another with, 'And that reminds me . . .' and almost before we knew it it was time to roll into our blankets and sleep to be ready for the early morning's start.

Happy days which even the wind could not mar. But just before our inadvertent joining up with the main party something did happen which disturbed me. No, I have timed it wrongly, it started earlier than that, but I only admitted it to myself on the first night of the snow. It began, I think, at the moment when Judith kilted her skirts and started to run back for Linda's bundle.

The snow began suddenly one afternoon. All morning that same tearing wind had been blowing, hard on our right as we made our slow way westward. The ground rose and fell almost evenly, as though someone had pushed the surface of the earth into folds as one may push a tablecloth. But each rise was a little longer than the corresponding fall, so that we were rising slightly all the time, and, of course, since the folds ran roughly North and South they lay across our path. Uphill we sometimes made little more than a mile in an hour

On this particular day the wind had brought the usual hasty flurries of stinging rain with it, and the horses had to be held firmly on their course to overcome their tendency to turn their backs to the blast. We stopped at the foot of a rise in the land to eat our noonings and about two hours later came out on the brow of the hill. I was driving and Judith was riding beside me. Ralph and Simon Whistlecraft were walking ahead and as they reached the top I saw them stop and point. I leaned forward from under the wagon cover and saw that all the land before us was white. And at the same moment I knew that the wind had dropped so suddenly that Simon's exclamation, 'Damned early for snow,' a sentence pitched to carry on a tearing wind, came so roaring loud that I laughed. There was that momentary hush and then with a whisper the snow began, great white flakes as wide as a shilling falling dead straight from the clouds that the wind had piled above us. It was as swift and sudden as the dropping of a curtain, one moment the valley lay there before us and the next moment it was blotted out. I could hardly see the Whistlecrafts who stood by my horses' heads. Ralph came back and shouted. 'I saw trees in the valley, before this started. I'll lead you.' He went forward again, lost in a horse's length of snow curtain and then the horses went onward, the tilt of the wagon changed and we went slipping and slithering down the hill.

The trees, which we reached safely, would have been an excellent protection from the wind which had troubled us for days, but against the straight falling snow nothing but a roof could shelter us. However, we backed the wagons up to the edge of the thicket and tethered the horses within it, where the branches and what leaves remained upon them offered a little delay rather than any barrier, to the soft insidious flakes. The gypsies, with a skill all their own, got going a fire on which the snow fell hissing and we boiled water for coffee. The herrings that were to be grilled we abandoned because while one side toasted the other collected moisture, so we ate cold bacon and bread and raw onions. By the time we had finished it was dark, and even

147

the good fire was having a struggle against the flakes that hissed upon it, so we were all ready to go to bed. But sleeping arrangements offered a certain problem.

The wagons had never been intended for sleeping in. Normally we should have reached our destination long before such a procedure was necessary. But we had been delayed and the snow was extraordinarily early. Everything that we needed for a year at least was packed and repacked to get the most possible into them.

Hitherto, though the nights had been cold, we had been content to roll ourselves in rugs and sleep under the wagons, between the wheels, while the gypsies would take themselves off and sleep under a bush, or an overhanging ledge of rock or anything that offered itself to their undemanding eyes.

But the prospect of sleeping out in the snow was not attractive and directly we had finished our food we started dragging barrels and boxes out of the wagons, storing them underneath with more fragile things on top of them and preparing beds on the wagon floors. Although laborious that was not the trouble, the trouble was that there were eight men and one woman and though they be never so chivalrous it is impossible for eight men to lie upon one wagon floor unless they are prepared to lie on top of one another.

'We'd better split up,' said Simon, 'I'll go back with the others. Two of our size is too much when you're sleeping four abreast. Good night.' He took himself off and climbed in with the four men in the second wagon. Andy and Mike, both little men, curled up in the front of my wagon. Ralph, Judith and I were left by the fire. I looked at Ralph, calmly loosening his shoes and was shaken with a sudden irritation. Judith might have been his dog, not his sister. My irritation found vent in the sharpness with which I turned to the girl herself and said, 'And where do you think *you're* going to sleep?' It might have been the deceptive light of the spluttering fire, but it seemed to me that a gleam, oddly mingled of mockery and defiance and surprise, came over her face, and then in the whining gypsy voice that she used to such good effect in telling her stories, she said, 'In your wagon, if you please, master.'

Even more irritably I said, 'I can't understand why you and Simon had to wait. It was downright disobedience to start with. I sent word that everyone was to go with Makers. Now you see it's devilish awkward.'

Not looking at me she shook the snow off her shawl and wrapped it more closely round her head. Her full red lips stuck out poutingly. Ralph stood up and reached for a rug.

'We'll sleep out here, lass.'

'Don't talk nonsense,' I said to him. And then to Judith, 'Of course you'll sleep in the wagon. And another time you might consider such things before you interfere with other people's well-thought-out arrangements.'

'We wanted to travel with you,' she said, with surprising meekness. 'We wanted to be merry. You don't know what it was like. Why, even at Hannah Crane's wedding service we had the pestilence that walketh by night. We had it every *day*! As for me,' and the pout was suddenly gone; she snatched the rug from her brother and with a twist and a turn wrapped herself in it so that she looked like a carpet on end, 'what difference is there now?'

Her way of asking the question was deliberately provocative. There was all the difference. Ralph knew it.

'Shut your mouth,' he said shortly and taking her by the elbow hustled her into the back of the wagon, half lifting her because her legs were wrapped so closely in the rug that she could not lift them. He hoisted her by the side of the wagon and threw himself down next her. There was just room for me on his other side.

Sleep would not come to me. I lay there in the silence which the hiss of the snow intensified rather than broke and thought of many things. The white-stockinged legs, nimble as a boy's flashing back along the track: the way the tawny hair grew from the forehead and lifted the shawl's edge by the thick vigour of its growth; that pouting mouth; the inch of white skin that had shown at the base of her brown neck once when the top of her bodice had been unbuttoned; that last 'what difference is there now?' A difference that I wanted to explore.

It was impossible, in those close quarters, to toss and turn about freely, seeking another attitude that might woo sleep. Nathaniel's words in the parlour of the *Crooked Fleece* came

149

back to me. 'There are dozens of bright eyes about, and kind hearts with some of them, bless them all.' It was as though he were warning me that this might happen. I remembered the night, a few days after Linda's appearance in London, when I had looked into the future and seen the loneliness of a life of devotion unrequited. The words that I had scribbled in my little book came back to me.

> 'Lovely thou art, but being not for me
> Loosen this spell and set thy bondsman free
>
> Since in my loving thou can'st bear no part
> Renounce thy claim upon this heavy heart.
>
> Elsewhere bid me seek favour. Let me live
> To taste the joy that is not thine to give.
>
> Lovely thou art, but being not for me
> Deprive me not of all felicity.'

Stumbling and weak as all my verses were, holding but little of the emotion that begat them, yet they held something of what I felt. Linda was Eli's wife. The child that she carried was Eli's. Must I, because of her, go virgin to my grave?

There had been street women in London who had glanced back at me, sometimes spoken, with a tarnished, worn out endearment on their tongues. They were willing to overlook my infirmity—for money. Would any woman ever be equally blind, for love? Reminded of it I stirred the limb that was at once so small and so heavy. Not Eli, Not Linda, not my fruitless love deprived me of all felicity! The fault lay with this frame of mine. With two stout legs I should have been my father's equal. I could have wooed Linda from the first. I could have wrested her away as Eli did.

All foolish suppositions. And even now, with desire for Judith Whistlecraft sticking burr-like in my mind how could I be sure that I was not making a fool of myself. What use could she have for the maimed and halt thing that was I?

Annoyed with myself, and tired of thinking I rolled over once again and into the arms of sleep. The wildest dreams came to me. There was a woman in them, neither Linda nor Judith but one I had never seen. Nor could I see her now for her face was for ever turned from me and veiled by hair that blew out before her on a shouting wind. And then, just as the wind had dropped this afternoon the dream wind ceased to blow and I caught the figure that had eluded me and the curtain of hair hung motionless and I could not summon the courage to lift it, dreading to see what I had so eagerly pursued. I woke, shuddering in the darkness and there was a heavy weight on my shoulder and across my body. I moved, and the heavy thing stirred and sighed, then snuggled closer. Returning awareness told me that some- how during the night Judith had wriggled out from be- tween her brother and the wagon wall and was sleeping with her head on my shoulder and her arm around me.

Battling against temptation that was, at that moment and in that place, ludicrous, I lay for a moment and then wriggled out. I got the lantern going, and sitting on the tail of the wagon, thrust my feet into my shoes. No snow was falling but among the trees it lay a foot thick and twice that depth in the open. I went to the horses and shook the rugs that covered them, it was half melted, caked from the warmth of their bodies. Having wakened them I carried them their corn and water. Then I pulled out two casks, set the lantern on one and myself on the other and with my collar turned high and my hands thrust into my cuffs for warmth, I read in Nathaniel's little brown book until the tops of the hills that we had crossed were touched with the light that heralded the dawn.

All through breakfast, the reloading of the wagons and the business of getting under way again, my mind was vaguely troubled. The girl's non-committal manner puzzled me. Perhaps she had moved in her sleep and did not even know that I had wakened in her embrace. I wondered whether Ralph, finding her there and me gone had come to any conclusions of his own. Bother the pair of them I thought. Why should I care what they did or what they thought. But I did care. I knew, too, that the task with which Nathaniel had entrusted me, difficult enough at best, would be impossible if I let Judith make any kind of a fool of me.

Fortunately the morning was not conducive to much thought. After we had at length stored everything away and got started we found that heavy wagons on trackless country under more than a foot of snow demanded alert and whole-hearted attention. Boulders and fallen branches, dips and bumps in the ground all lay smoothly and deceptively covered. We tilted and lurched, we stuck fast. We went on ahead with shovels, we stood behind ready, with billets of woods, to steady the slithering wheels.

In the late afternoon, far far behind our day's stint of travelling, we rounded the edge of a forest and could see for a good way ahead of us. And there, in the middle distance was a slight hollow, and in it were Eli's wagons, people and and cattle all jumbled as though at a fair.

We halted our own and hesitated. There had been no sign, no suggestion of sickness among us, but I remembered Mike's mention of the man known to have sickened after a fortnight. Still, that didn't prove that he had been infected on the first day of his return. I said as much to Mike who gnawed his finger and grunted.

'Let them make the first move,' was his verdict. And very soon we saw Eli's huge form separate itself from the others and come striding back.

'Are you all right?' he bellowed.

'Yes. Are you?'

'In health we are. But just after we broke camp this morning we came to grief. The wagons had to fan out because the front one churned the snow so the horses behind couldn't get a foothold. So there were three front ones and at about the same moment all three went into a gully that was full of snow. The horses went kind of mad and dragged them in still farther. One overturned and stove a side in and smashed a wheel. We're in a proper muddle.'

'Shall we come down?'

'Eight men'd be mighty useful,' said Eli dubiously. 'You see Moses Pikle put his shoulder out when the wagon went over. Isaac Carter most cut his hand off back at Fort Outpost and of the others Mr. Thomas' hands blister worse than a woman's and Mr. Will Lomax coughs himself half to death directly he heaves on anything.'

'And what have you done?' I asked, pointing to a large purple crescent on the brawny forearm that the rolled back shirt sleeve left bare.

'Oh, that's nothing. One of the horses kicked out when I was cutting the traces.' He wiped away the sweat from his forehead with the back of his hand. 'It's a sorry state of affairs. Mr. Gore dead, and then this snow so soon. Still, with patience we'll manage. The thing is that the drift is wide as well as deep and there's a lot of digging to be done.'

'We'll come down,' I said. 'Young Pikle and Carter could do with a little of Mike's attention, and I think the cold has finished the disease.'

Truth to tell I was longing for a sight of Linda as a man in a desert longs for the sight of water. Already I was straining my eyes in an attempt to distinguish, among the many dark figures hurrying to and fro in the white space, the one that I loved.

So we went down to the others.

A very different feeling pervaded this company. The death of Nathaniel, the unusual weather, the disaster to the wagons and the accidents that had befallen the two men had cast a sort of gloom over everybody.

Mr. Thomas' prayer after supper did nothing to dissipate it. Apparently the same obvious thought that had struck Mike had occurred to him—that our Moses was dead. He elaborated it at great length, rambling on beseeching God not to repeat the forty years' wandering in the wilderness, and the discomfort of our sodden feet we were all ready to weep.

As soon as he had finished I said in a loud voice, cutting in on the last Amen so that I had a silence to speak into, 'Directly we're over this next hill we turn South and are there. The children of Israel didn't know where they were going, and probably didn't have a map, either.'

Mr. Thomas' eyes, still reverently closed, snapped open and darted a glare at me.

'That's blasphemy young man! The will of the Lord is more than a paltry map and the ways of the Lord are beyond man's understanding.'

'Then why always impute bad motives to Him?' I asked

mildly. To my astonishment Eli spoke up in the same strain.

'His promises are as sure as His punishments. And we have no golden calves hereabouts.'

I skirted round the crowd until I reached Linda with whom, thanks to Eli's dragooning in the afternoon, I had not yet had speech.

'Hullo,' I said softly. She turned swiftly.

'Hullo, Philip. How are you?'

'Very well. And you?'

'Very well too.'

'Look,' I said, 'I could get along with mending the side of that wagon if I had someone to hold the lantern. Would you hold it?'

Her eyes slid about. 'If Eli doesn't mind?'

Eli didn't mind anything that would contribute to an early start next day, and soon I had Linda comfortably ensconced in the empty wagon, with a rug round her legs, the lantern in one hand and a few nails in the other. I had cut the wood into the lengths that I needed before supper, so I had only to hammer them into place and could talk as I did so.

'I've got your bushes and your bundle,' I said and was glad to see her face lighten. Stupid loyalty to Eli, stupid because with me it was so wasted, made her say, 'It was because of the horse. He had to lighten his wagon, you know.'

'Yes,' I said, 'I know.'

I tapped away, conscious of the old lack of things to say. Linda spoke first. 'I wonder sometimes why we came, don't you?'

'No. I know exactly why I came.'

'Are you glad?'

'Just at this moment, yes. Do you regret it?'

'Sometimes I wonder whether . . . if I hadn't been in such a hurry . . .' I knew she was referring to the marriage, not to the journey, and waited, avid for some betraying word. It didn't come.

'It's just that I'm tired of living this way. And I'm going to have a baby—but I suppose you can see that—and I get sick and miserable. And Keziah is very difficult to get on with.'

'I do believe you,' I said heartily.

'She has the most nagging tongue I ever knew. Eli doesn't take any notice of her and thinks I'm silly when I do. I do wish somebody'd marry her!'

I laughed. 'I'll do anything I can to oblige you, Linda, but that I cannot do. And I'm dreadfully afraid that no one else will.'

'If I were a man in this company I should marry Judith Whistlecraft. She's pretty and good-natured. Philip why don't you?'

'Nail please,' I said, keeping my face out of the lantern's light.

'Why don't you?'

'Why don't I what?'

'Marry Judith?'

'Because I have no desire to do so,' I said stiffly. 'Marriage isn't simply a matter of expediency.'

'Are you suggesting that mine was?' There was a nasty note in her voice. Greatly daring I asked,

'Well, wasn't it?'

For answer she started to cry. 'Here, take the lantern,' she said, sobbing, 'I'm going to bed.' She started to get down, stumbled over the rug which I had so carefully wrapped round her legs, and as I went round to hand her down she fell into my arms. I stood there for one giddy moment pressed close to her. Then I took out my handkerchief and wiped her face.

'Don't be silly,' I said. 'I wasn't meaning anything. Don't go crying back to Keziah. God knows what she'd suspect.'

'I'm like this nowadays,' she said fiercely, snatching away the handkerchief and blowing her nose into it. 'I cry for nothing. You mustn't mind me.'

She put the handkerchief back into my hand and plodded away through the churned up snow. I went back and finished the job; rounded up the Whistlecrafts and told them they could use my wagon and then went along to Nathaniel's where I spent a mournful hour looking through his papers.

The map he had always carried with him to consult or alter as occasion demanded, but in a little leather bag fastened with a strap I found the grant with the seal of the

New England company on it, some lists of expenditure, the rough notes of his last journey, his will and a letter addressed to me.

I looked at the date on it, and reckoned backwards. It was the day after that night on board the *Westering Wing* when he had read aloud, 'Oh mortal folk'. I knew that what I had always dimly suspected was the truth. Down there in that stuffy fo'castle, reeking of liquor and tobacco, with the echoes of the bawdy singing that Eli had interrupted, still hanging about its beams, Nathaniel had felt Death's icy finger upon his shoulder and known that his time was short. And now, months later I stopped to pay a tribute to the energy and interest with which he had filled the interval. I remembered his busy dealings with salted cod fish and seed potatoes in Salem and realised how near his heart welfare of Zion had been.

The angular black letters drove straight across the page.

'My dear Philip,

'Last night you called me a fool; and if ever I get to Nawkatcha and set foot in the valley I shall call myself a fool as I tear up this sheet. But something tells me that I shall never again see that break in the hills and the silver stream dividing the daisied meadowlands. I feel that I have left the venture too late. But many a man has started what he has not finished and I am not sad on that account nor should I wish you to be. Who knows, I may be in Heaven, leading out a troop of cherubims and seraphims to some colony beyond the stars—or does that sound too much like Lucifer's fatal exploit.

'This will was drawn up in London and is quite in order. I made it on the day that you decided to come with us. You will see that I have left you my goods and my lands, my flocks and my herds. That sounds very patriarchal and only lacks that I should leave you my wives and my concubines, or like Elijah, my hairy mantle! In a way, Philip, I do leave you that, for I leave you my project, my darling dream of a land built by men's hands for men's enjoyment. A land where men are free and equal and have at least a chance of being happy. I didn't like Salem. I couldn't have been happy there: I am not looking forward to the stay that we must make in Alfred Bradstreet's holy land. There must be some mean between licentiousness and dreariness: between the worship of vice and the tyranny of virtue. If I do not live to find it, do you.

'I have confidence in you, Philip, because, although you may be handicapped for the life of a frontiersman, I who have always been undersized and unimpressive myself, have lived long enough to see that intelligence is often of more use than brawn, and that there are many kinds of courage. The kind that you think you lack may come. The kind you have already will increase. So with the very best wishes for your success and eventual happiness and that when your dream is saddled it may prove worth the pursuit, I leave you. If you ever read this you will know that I regard you with loving esteem, and am now, and forever,

'Your sincere friend,
'NATHANIEL G. M. GORE.'

A sensible and unsentimental letter from the best man I ever knew except Shad. It laid a heavy burden on me: it promised me that courage would come. But whence? Already the thought of all that must happen, the arguments, the labour, the endurance that would be needed before Nathaniel's dream came into being, appalled me. I did not want to be a founder of Zion. That was what Eli was born for. I wanted to take Linda and go away. But Eli and Linda and I had Nathaniel's trust. It was all the wrong way round.

In the morning, with the combined labour of everyone, we got the gully cleared, the wagons reloaded and the horses harnessed. In the cold, snow-reflected light I saw Linda standing idle for a moment, her face drawn and yellow, her eyes sunken and shadowy. I was going to approach her but at that moment Keziah's saw-shrill voice called out, 'Linda, Linda, you wash this pot before you pack it.' Linda's hands flew breast high in one of her funny little gestures and she called back meekly. 'I'll do it now, Keziah. I forgot.'

I remembered how sick Agnes had been in the mornings before her last baby was born and imagined the effect of the thick rim of grease, the slimy shreds of vegetable in the pot, upon a queasy stomach. I limped towards Linda and said, 'I'll do it.' But she looked half scared and said, 'Oh no, Philip, *please*.' And at that moment Judith Whistlecraft who had been harnessing a horse nearby, thrust home the last strap, strode over to us and said, 'Give it to me. Why won't you tell the old hag to do it herself?' She looked at me with almost equal scorn and said in a lower tone, not meant, as the other was, for Keziah's ear, 'Do you *want* to make yourself a laughing stock?'

She took a wisp of hay and a handful of snow and gave the pot as hasty, thorough, and angry a cleansing as ever a pot received, rinsed it out, clapped on its lid and heaved it into the back of the wagon. Linda and I with a childishly conspiratorial glance at one another went our separate ways.

Soon the track turned South and we were wallowing through melting snow, then mud, and then through water. Back on the hills to the North-East, no doubt, the snow was still falling, but here it rained as though the heavens wished to wash us from the face of the earth. That day and the next were the most wretched of the whole journey. The horses stuck, the wagons stuck, men digging and pulling and straining and sweating to free them stuck, our feet squelched in and plopped out with sounds like boiling glue. Every thread of clothing was soaked; it was impossible to make a fire; and although we halted when darkness set in we were too drenched and miserable to sleep.

Next day—the last—saw precious things discarded all along the way. Every sheltered place, the hollow under a stony outcrop, the lee side of a bush, the mouth of some beast's warren in the hillside, became the hiding place of something jettisoned to lighten the wagons. Even so they only just moved. Even when tools and ploughshares, casks of food, chests of clothing, cooking pots were sacrificed the heavy wheels were often axle deep in the sticky mire.

Everybody walked except the babies, stumbling along through the mud and the slashing rain, wrapped in cloaks and sacks and rugs that in their turn became burdens as the rain soaked into them.

But there came a moment when, raising my eyes as I plodded along at my horses' heads, I saw what Nathaniel had so often and so vividly described, the mile wide break in the hills which he had marked on the map as 'The Gap' I stared at it for a moment and then let my glance travel over the company and rest upon Linda, battling along with her wet skirts plastered to her limbs, the bulge of her body distinct in the wind flattened cloak, her head bent against the blast. I shouted to Andy who was trudging alongside the wagon wheels with a shovel in his hand.

'Run on,' I said, 'tell Mr. Makers, tell everybody that we're there. Just through that gap is the Nawkatcha valley.'

Andy shifted his grip on the shovel so that he was holding it half way down and ran on, kicking up a shower of mud at every step and brandishing his tool. Eli had had a map, and apart from that everyone in the company knew what we were looking for, but the rain and the mud and the difficulty of keeping the wagons on the move had so battered down our minds that I think we should have gone doggedly on past our destination had I not looked up when I did.

Eli was holding one shaft with both hands and had his great shoulder pressed against the corner of his wagon. He did not stop or shift his hold, but he raised his head and then nodded his head. A shout to his docile team leader changed the course of the wagon a little and there he was, headed for the promised land. A kind of new vigour spread over the bedraggled little band as though at each step they sank a little less heavily into the clay. Andy waited for me to catch up with him.

'Now,' I said, 'get hold of Mrs. Makers and tell her I want to speak to her.'

Linda was about half way along the line, walking beside Mrs. Will Lomax. They both waited for me.

'In you get,' I said, 'if they can't pull you on this last lap I'll take a turn in the shafts myself.'

Linda shook the water out of her eyes, stared at me for a moment and then without a word climbed in under the cover. Mrs. Lomax stood a little uncertain.

'You too, of course, Mrs. Lomax.'

'Oh, thank you, Mr. Ollenshaw. It's very kind of you, I'm sure.'

So after all it was in my wagon, with the bundle of

clothes and the cherished plants beside her that Linda first rolled into the valley that was to be our inheritance and our home.

Just beyond the Gap the land sloped gently down to the Nawkatcha. It was a long valley, shaped like a dish, about twice as wide from East to West as it was from North to South. The range of hills to the North, which was broken by the Gap was much steeper than the swelling ridges that closed in its other boundaries. Today there were no daisied meadows. The full brown stream raced between the stretches of autumn-bleached, rain-flattened grass: but as we steadied the teams down the slope between the Gap and the river I could imagine how lovely it must have been on the summer day when Nathaniel had looked down on it, written that description in his notebook and determined to have it for his own.

At last Eli stopped his wagon, took off his hat, shook it, sluiced the water from his head and looked round. Then he came towards where I, too, had drawn to a standstill and though his eyes were shining and I knew that inexpressible thoughts about the goodness of God and the goodness of the soil were chasing one another through his mind, his usual eloquence had forsaken him. He said simply, 'Well, we're here.' And I could only repeat, 'We're here.'

The way had been found, and the wayfaring men, though fools, had not erred therein. Now it remained for the wilderness and the solitary place to be glad of us, as we set about making the desert blossom as the rose.

BOOK THREE

CONSUMMATION

At first the solitary place seemed anything but glad. It rained for ten days without ceasing, damping very effectually the joy that our safe arrival would otherwise have caused. The rain did one good thing, it showed us just how high the waters of the Nawkatcha could rise and saved us from building houses where they could be flooded.

It also led to the common building. Eli was against it, as he was always, fundamentally and wholeheartedly against anything of a communal nature. He would have liked to have taken his axe and gone into the dripping woods, cut what wood he wanted for his own house and seen everyone else do the same. But in that weather it was necessary to get an immediate shelter and as I pointed out to him, a communal hut meant one lot of digging for the main posts and four corners to shelter the lot of us instead of four corners for each family, altogether a quicker and more sensible business. So Eli conceded and laboured mightily at the large wooden shelter that we made, with an inner division that made two sleeping apartments, one for men and one for women.

With every man working—except Isaac Carter and Mathew Thomas, whose hands were quite useless, like little pink cushions that rose in satiny blisters every time he handled a tool—and even the women dragging planks as they were sawn and handing nails and hammers, we soon had a more or less water-tight dwelling. The wood was unseasoned and warped as soon as it dried and gave me something else to point out to Eli, that we ought to content ourselves with the one hut until we had let the wood dry out first and could build our own houses at leisure. Eli nodded and said, 'Aye, you're right,' but all the time he was aching to start upon his own and it was indeed the first house to go up.

We settled the partition of the land without dispute.

There was more than we could handle, anyway, and there was nothing to choose between one portion and another. Here were no Layer Fields, no Old Stoneys. You chose to be near the river, or near the woods, facing East or South according to your fancy. Or you chose to be near a person. For myself I waited until Eli had broken his first furrow and then I took thought.

I wanted to be near Linda, but not so near that every detail of her life with Eli was visible before my eyes, an ever-turning knife. So when Eli had chosen his ground I took up my position just on the other side of the stream. No house could be built between us and one of the first things I did was to make a stout bridge over the water. Eli cut down the trees between his house and the river. I left mine. The trees made a screen and Linda would probably walk in the little coppice.

As soon as the rain stopped and he had chosen his ground and the young men who had been sent back for the jettisoned gear had returned, Eli started ploughing, and as soon as he started ploughing he decided that it was too far for him to walk back to the common dwelling at night. If one house could be reared so quickly, so could another and forthwith he set about rearing it.

I helped him because of Linda. Andy and Mike helped because I did; but the Whistlecrafts, who had done good work on the main hut were unaccountably elsewhere while Eli's house was building.

It was a miserable shack enough, two rooms, both at ground level, with a lean-to at one side for the cows and another at the back for horses; but I made the window of the front room bigger than usual, taking some of the glass which Nathaniel had intended for *his* house, for the purpose, making a deep window seat where Linda could sit and look out at my trees, and I also added a little trellis-work porch up which she could train her climbing rose. As far as the raw wood and Eli's impatience and my own physical limitations allowed I built that house with love.

We finished it on a bright sunny day and Linda and Keziah walked down to see it. Eli was lighting the first fire to see if the chimney 'drew' satisfactorily and the smoke from the green twigs was filling the room with blue haze. I was planing the doorsill because already, two days after its hanging, the door had warped and dropped and would not close securely.

Keziah lifted her black skirt and stepped over the shavings. Linda, moving with that heaviness which I found so pathetic, followed and they looked about the bare square room. Linda noticed the window seat at once.

'Oh, lovely,' she said, sinking down upon it. 'I'll have a tall jar of cherry blossom or something in the middle of it and a cushion on either side. I am glad you put that in.'

'You've Mr. Philip to thank for that,' said Eli with his usual regard for truth. 'This hearth has been my concern and a very bad job I seem to have made of it,' he added as another gust of acrid smoke set us all coughing and blinking.

Meantime Keziah had opened the door into the back room which was a slightly smaller edition of the one in which we stood, but lacking hearth and window seat. Then she stepped out and regarded the lean-tos on which Mike and Andy were trying their prentice hands. Finally she came back, went over to Eli where he was trying to look up his baulky chimney and rapped him on the shoulder with her long knuckly fingers.

'Eli,' she said ominously, 'where's my room?'

Eli stood up and wiped his streaming eyes on his wrists the only part of his hands not blackened from the fire. It was the first even remotely childish gesture I had ever seen him use.

'Why, here,' he said simply.

'Then where's the kitchen?'

'Here too. I am to make you a bed alongside the wall there.'

'So.' Keziah's stony eyes flashed and the first red colour I had ever seen on her sallow face sprang suddenly into her cheeks and rushed up until her very nose was scarlet. 'There's a stable for the horses, a byre for the cows, but I, I who brought you here, am to sleep in the kitchen! And I was fool enough to listen to your lying tales and give up my fine house in Ludgate Hill. Well, understand this, Eli Makers, I will not sleep in the kitchen, so you can lay your hand to your heart about that. Either you build me another

165

room or I take myself elsewhere.'

Eli rubbed his hands on his breeches' seat and spoke slowly.

'What lie did I ever tell you, woman? Answer that first. Not a soul lives on this earth who can rightly say that Eli Makers ever told him, or her, a lie. Come on, what lie did I tell you?'

'You promised me a better house.'

'And you shall have it. But for the moment you must be patient. As for the other other room I have no time to cut timber. As for taking yourself elsewhere where could you go? Without a man to fend for you you'd starve.'

He had touched Keziah's tenderest spot. The scarlet colour turned purple.

'I can find a man,' she said. 'And you'll build me a decent room to sleep in, or I'll find the man that will.'

Mike, who could never resist a row, had stepped up behind me as the sound of the bickering reached him, and I now saw Eli look our way. His glance had an uncertainty that sat ill on him. I knew the next thing. He would build her a room if we would help him. For he was mad to get to the ploughing, and although he had great strength and willingness he was not a gifted worker in wood. I reached out, gave Linda's cloak a pluck and behind the backs of Eli and Keziah who were glaring at one another like fighting cocks newly spurred, I mouthed, 'DO YOU WANT KEZIAH?' She caught the meaning with a swiftness that confirmed my belief in her unique intelligence and violently shook her head.

'... till the ploughing is done,' I attended to Eli once more. 'But if Mr. Philip and his men will help me I'll build you the room if it's to be the price of peace.'

'I'm sorry,' I said, not looking up and working my plane up and down some inch or so from the floor, 'but you can't count on me, Eli. We're starting another job tomorrow. I think myself that we've done a good job for you.'

'I'm not saying otherwise,' said Eli, reasonably, 'and I'm grateful. You see, Keziah, they've done what they can for us. And the room will wait, while the ploughing won't. You can stay down at the dwelling-house till the room is built.'

'That I will not do,' said Keziah shrilly. 'She,' she indicated Linda with one pointed finger, 'can get out of the riffraff. A room can be built for her, aye and a window seat to put her bow-pot on. And what did *she* bring you? Nothing but a pretty face that you were fool enough to be dazzled by. All right, keep it, live with it. See what sort of home you have with pretty face for breakfast and pretty face for dinner and little else beside. You'll be lucky if you're not poisoned—the way she keeps her pots, when I'm not there to tell her.'

'Oh,' cried Linda, jumping from the window-seat with the ghost of her old grace. 'That was only just the once when I had forgotten.'

The memory of the little cottage in Hunter's Wood with every surface bespeaking in its polish the care lavished upon it, thrust me into the quarrel.

'Linda kept house before ever she saw you,' I said hotly.

'A lot of cat-lappy young fools like you did the work for her, I shouldn't wonder, the same as you're doing now,' cried Keziah, kicking my plane as she made for the door.

There was spite in her voice, so vicious that it must have been long a-brewing. Linda shrank back against the bare wooden wall as she would have shrunk from a blow. I rose up to let the angry woman pass, and I looked at Eli. It was his wife who had been insulted, not mine, ah God, not mine. If anything were to be said he must say it. I had no right.

Eli spoke two sentences. One to Keziah, 'After that you will not be welcome in my house.'

One to Linda, 'Heed her not, wife. The chatter of fools is the crackling of thorns under the pot.'

He knelt again by his hearth. I tested the door and finding that it swung easily, gathered my tools and prepared to leave.

Eli looked round. 'I'm much obliged to you, lad. If there's ought I can ever do for you I'll be obliged to you for the chance to set myself right with you.'

'When I start farming,' I said lightly 'I shall live on your doorstep.'

Linda followed me outside.

'Thank you, Philip,' she said, 'for what you have done— and for not doing any more.' Her voice and her smile were so sweet that like the young fool I was I treasured them, hugging my chains, laying myself open to her charms. I went back to the village behind Keziah's upright angular figure with my heart singing like a blackbird. I was glad that I had come to Zion.

Sometime during the following week we heard that the widower, Phineas Pikle, was going to marry Keziah. The next day came the news that Martha Pikle had told her father that she must marry Tim Dendy or die of a broken heart. How far the one thing was responsible for the other it is difficult to say, but I should reckon that Mary and Mahitabel Pikle would also have snatched at a chance to escape from a home where Keziah was going to rule. She had got herself well hated in the communal dwelling by that time.

Before Christmas Phineas Pikle was busy on a house up by the Gap, and the Cranes were building opposite him. Then the whole settlement was startled by the news that Keziah was suing Eli for all the gear that had been bought with her money.

Mike was the newsmonger. He had shown that he had a certain skill in dealing with sick beasts as well as people and had gone over to Eli's place to give a horse a medicine ball and been there when Keziah arrived to make her formal demand. He reported that the Scripture had been so much quoted that you'd thought two Bishops were having a meeting, not a mere brother and sister quarrel.

Keziah and Eli both agreed to lay the matter before the elders. First a new member had to be elected to fill Nathaniel's place, and to Mike's amazement and my delight, the choice fell upon him. It was not really a surprising choice. From the moment when, after joining the main body in the snow he had put his stockinged foot into Moses Pikle's armpit and jerked his shoulder back into place with a noise like a pistol shot, his position in the community had been assured. And as time went on, and we were all busy and prone to have minor accidents with axes and hammers, his reputation had increased.

Phineas Pikle and Eli as interested parties were not allowed to sit in judgement, so the five of us, Oliver Lomax, Crane, Mathew Thomas, Mike and I, met in Eli's inner room by candle-light to consider the matter.

168

Keziah claimed that Eli, when he left Marshalsea, had exactly thirty pounds of his own, the savings of a lifetime. She looked towards Eli as she made this statement, and Eli confirmed it with a nod. She had lent him the money with which he had bought his wagon, his horses, his cow, his swine, his poultry and his gear. The blankets and mattresses and the crockery had come from her house on Ludgate Hill. And now he had ungratefully turned her out.

Oh no, she replied in answer to a question, she was *not* bringing this claim from spite, but simply from a desire to have what was her own so that she might go to her husband with a dowry as a woman should.

Eli spoke in his usual forthright manner. He admitted that he had borrowed from his sister, that he intended to pay her back, but that to do so now and all at once would ruin him, spoil the plans that he had come all this way to put into action.

'If you decide against me I shall have nought. I shall have no choice but to hire myself out as a field labourer and be worse off than I was back at home. And I've started my ploughing, too.' Even if I had hated Eli more than I felt I did those six simple words would have moved me. Oh, well might every spiritual teacher, from the old prophets to Christ Himself extol the merits of the single mind. To Eli the memory of his broken ploughlands, his straight brown furrows on the virgin soil gave justice to his cause, and you must have been blind and deaf indeed not to have seen and heard that justice.

When Eli and Keziah had finished they went into the outer room and left us to argue it out and decide.

'Property,' said Oliver Lomax, who was supposed to be Eli's friend, but was also a man of property, 'will not be safe if that which is lent may not be demanded with some expectation of repayment. There is no date in writing for the paying back and if Keziah wants her gear she must have it. Pikle can use it.'

'There is nothing in writing either about the lending. I doubt, whether, in a court of law, Keziah has a valid claim at all,' I said.

'This is a council of justice, not a court of law,' said Crane, mildly, but firmly. 'Eli admitted the borrowing.'

'He admitted it, yes,' I said. 'But ask yourselves, is it likely that a man would borrow in such circumstances and in such a cause on the understanding that the moment Keziah cared to choose he must pay her back in full? Eli is no fool. Think of this too. When Pikle set out from Salem he had no thought of ever counting on Keziah's property. He has now what he then considered sufficient. Eli is the best farmer of us all. It'll be a sorry thing if he is to be stripped and degraded because a spiteful woman is bearing a grudge that he didn't build a special room for her. He didn't turn her out. She left him. She's broken her bargain once and now she asks our sanction to do it again.'

'We must be *very* careful,' said Mr. Thomas, placing his finger-tips together and looking at them with what he considered a judicial expression. 'Far are we from the sources of law-giving and of order. No pressident haf we to go upon. See you, if we let Eli keep what he borrowed and what iss now demanded, no man will lend again because it will be known that in Zion to borrow iss to keep. Eli must give back the goods.'

So, I thought. You are supposed to be Eli's friend too. Hand in glove you've been over many things, but now that you see that Eli has nothing and Keziah much you're changing your coat with the wind.

'At least,' said Mike, 'she should wait until he has harvested. . . .' But Oliver Lomax with a glance that told that he was taking no counsel from a new member, cut in on upon the sensible suggestion.

'Argument is getting us nowhere. Call for the vote, Mr. Ollenshaw.' I knew then that Oliver Lomax was not sorry to take a hand in the stripping and downcasting of Eli. With all his faults he was a better man than Oliver and the knowledge irked.

Three against two the council decided that Keziah must have her goods. We called back the disputants. They both looked confident. I saw that the task of telling the verdict was being left to me. I pushed back my stool and stood apart.

'You tell him,' I said, looking at Mr. Thomas, 'or you.' I shifted my glance to Oliver Lomax. 'I dissociate myself entirely from your verdict. But I will say this. If Keziah

Makers is so blind to all decency as to continue with her claim, if a blood relationship means less to her than her miserable goods I hope that Eli will do me the honour of taking some of the superfluous goods which Mr. Gore bequeathed to me. And I still think that it is an unfair decision.'

Eli stood unmoved while they ordered him to pay back to Keziah everything that had been bought with her money, and named the morrow as the day of reckoning. But the golden beard twitched and I knew that under cover of it he was biting a trembling lip.

He stood there, a mighty man, a gifted farmer, his golden beard bright in the candle-light, and he owned nothing except some unbroken acres that he could not till without my help, and a wife whom I bitterly envied him. When he thanked me later on I wanted to cry in his face, 'Do you think I care for you? I do it for Linda's sake!' But even as I thought it I knew that it wasn't wholly true. Eli was pious, strait-laced, self-righteous. He annoyed me fifty times a day. He had married the woman I wanted and he treated her as though she were a squaw. But there was something about him that the frustrated man in me could not help but see and admire. He was a whole simple, straightforward male creature and to have him in my power increased my self-esteem in a way that momentarily endeared him to me.

In the morning I went over my stock carefully. Some choices were easy to make. For instance I liked my own horses better than those which Nathaniel had chosen. I don't know why. They were all good willing beasts, but I did prefer my own, just as I had preferred them on the day I chose them. And I liked my sheep, which were the kind I was used to, the Suffolk sheep of my childhood. Nathaniel had bought the kind that roam the South downs in England. I made careful selection of the cow, she must be in milk when Linda was brought to bed. Over tools and seed there was little choice. I loaded the wagon and with Mike and Andy bringing up the rear with the livestock I drove to the little house where Linda lived.

She met me. Every time I had seen her of late she seemed thinner of face, more bulky of body, more shadowy about the eyes. The sight of her hurt me and I looked at her unwillingly and helplessly, building up from this ruin of beauty the loveliness that had smitten and taken me long ago in the woods at home.

'Something terrible has happened,' she said. 'Both the horses have gone.'

'Gone!' I echoed. 'Well, perhaps Keziah couldn't wait until the morning. I should think she came straight here from the meeting and clawed them away in the night.'

'The stable door was open this morning. And the hoof marks led to the wood. Eli's out there now, searching. He didn't say much but I know he's upset. He thinks that Keziah will say that he's hidden them.'

'Small blame to him if he had. I tell you what. I should think that the idea of belonging to that bitch is so revolting to any right minded horse that they've run away.'

Linda laughed. 'Martha Pikle means to,' she said, giving her shoulders a childish hunch of delight that accorded ill with the maturity of her figure. 'She told me so. She said she'd never understood before how one man's meat could be another man's poison. She said too that the noise Tim Dendy makes when he eats makes her blood run cold, but anything was better than having Keziah prying round your saucepans. It was all lies you know, what Keziah said about my pans. I'm as good in the house as she is.'

'That was the trouble,' I said.

She looked beyond me. 'I suppose those are all the things you're lending us. You're so good, Philip. I don't know what we should do without you. Sometimes I think. . . . But come in, won't you?'

I went into the bare square room. I should have known it for Linda's because a bowl, an ordinary brown baking bowl, stood in one corner holding sprays of red berries against the raw wooden wall that sweated in the heat of the fire.

'Pretty, aren't they? I gathered them yesterday.' She followed my glance. 'I wanted to put my bushes in today. But the ground is so hard and I . . . well, you see.'

It would have been easy to have delegated the job to Mike or Andy, but I said eagerly, 'I'll put them in. I'd like to. I take quite a paternal interest in those bushes.'

'But you can't dig, Philip,' she said quickly.

'How do you know what I can do? Where's the spade?'

True enough, digging was one thing that I found impossible. I couldn't drive the spade home with my weak leg, nor could I balance on the iron while I drove the spade home with the other. But with my knife and my hands and the edge of the spade I could make a hole deep enough to take a rose bush. She came and stood beside me, telling me where to put them, and I grovelled and grubbed and patted all firm with my hands.

We were pretending that we were burying Keziah and laughing together, and I was thinking that they would bloom and she would take pleasure in them and that would be my doing too, when Eli was suddenly there by the house corner, sweating and breathing hard.

I jumped up and brushed the soil from the knees of my breeches.

'You haven't found them?' I asked, knowing the answer.

He shook his head and said despondently, 'I couldn't follow the trail once it was in the wood. Too many fallen leaves. I've hunted about though and whistled. They were good horses, especially Meggie. Always came to a whistle. You wouldn't think Keziah was playing a trick on me, would you? Leading them up to the wood's edge and then out again, just to worry me.'

'I wouldn't put it past her. But we'll soon see. Help me unload this stuff and then we'll go and find her.'

She wasn't at the dwelling-house, but every woman there was ready with the information that she spent the best part of the day up at the Gap. We drove there, following the trail that we had made on arrival and which was one day to be the main road through Zion. Phineas and his sons were labouring on the half built house and behind it, in the space that was to be the yard, Mahitabel Pikle was washing clothes in a tub and Keziah was berating her because the things were not white enough. Eli asked whether she knew anything about the horses.

'Why,' she inquired with poisonous reasonableness, 'should I trouble to steal what is my own?' Then from that attitude she flew into a mere vulgar rage and accused Eli of trying to cheat her of her dues. 'Very crafty,' she said spitefully. 'And I'm sorry to see, Mr. Ollenshaw, that though you dissociate yourself from a just verdict you are able to associate yourself with a low-down trick like this. Have I removed my own horses in the night indeed. What next?'

Her voice was like the creaking of an unoiled hinge, a shrieking assault to the senses. God pity Phineas Pikle, the meek simple old soul, and God pity those poor girls. I drove my elbow into Eli's ribs as he sat beside me on the seat of the wagon, looking bewildered and unhappy. Speaking out of the corner of my mouth I said, 'For God's sake, Eli, what did you spend your own thirty pounds on? You had thirty, didn't you?'

A great light dawned on the bearded face; beneath the tufted golden eyebrows the grey eyes twinkled for a moment before taking on their habitual gravity again.

'I was accusing you of stealing *my* horses,' he said slowly. 'Thirty pounds worth of that outfit was my own and I'll take it out in the horses. The rest of the stuff awaits your collection. Good day to you, Keziah.'

I gathered up the reins and the horses moved forward. Keziah took a step alongside us and said spitefully, 'Well you lost them, anyway, didn't you?' Then with a cackle of laughter she turned back into the yard and we heard the bawling begin again, 'More elbow grease, Mahitabel, my girl. More elbow grease and less soap.'

'That was a good idea of yours,' said Eli thoughtfully. 'But it doesn't bring back the horses. And it doesn't justify taking the name of the Almighty in vain.'

On the very verge of saying, 'Oh God!' again I changed it into 'Oh get up,' and flapped a rein. Linda, poor darling, had lived with the pair of them for months on end.

Days sped past. I had the wood for my house cut and sawn and laid out to weather. Various other little homes were set up. Pikle married Keziah and Tim Dendy married Martha. In the very darkest days of December Linda was brought to bed and with Mike's aid and the kind attention of various women was safely delivered of twins, both boys. There was a good deal of excitement about the birth, the first in Zion, and a good deal of talk about the sons of Boanerges, which inspired Eli to name them James and

John. Quite a number of people quoted the bit about the blessedness of the quiverful. I shut my eyes to it all, and when in the Spring Ralph shot a fine bear I bought the skin from him and had him dress it. I took the rug to Linda.

'For your brats to roll on,' I said offhandedly.

'Oh, Philip, they're not brats, they're delightful. You've never seen them or you'd know how lovely they are. Come in and see them now.'

'I've no time for baby worship,' I said gruffly.

'All right,' she said, as she gathered the great glossy skin in her arms and smiled at me over the top of it. It gave her a rich cherished look that sent a sudden stab to my heart.

'I wish I could do something for you, Philip.'

'You could,' I answered, speaking without consideration. 'You could wear that purple gown of yours to meeting one Sunday. I am so sick of drab and duffle grey, like a perpetual funeral. If you'll wear it, Linda, I'll get you a fur cloak to wear over it. Ralph has some grand skins.'

Her face took on a look of delight that lasted barely a minute. 'Would you really? How lovely. Oh, but I daren't. The wheat would rot in the ground, or the swine fever would break out if I did.'

'Yes,' I said savagely. 'There are so many kinds of swine fever aren't there?'

She never wore the purple frock. Nobody wore a purple frock, and largely on that account no doubt, the harvest was excellent and the pigs, instead of swine fever, had large squealing litters of piglets. Harry Wright, the landless lad who had married Hannah Crane, left his father-in-law and set up a mill just where the stream ran strongly as it entered the valley. And although the place was lonely throughout much of the year, after harvest Hannah had as much company and more than the other women for every day a wagon load of grain came in and another was carted away as flour.

The Whistlecrafts, Mike, Andy and I were the only people left in the old common building, most of which was now used as a meeting place. After harvest I built my house. The Whistlecrafts had tacitly attached themselves to me. Jake Crane, eldest of the Quaker youths, had shown a tendency to hang about Judith, and I half hoped that she would marry him. When she had made it perfectly clear to everybody, including the poor diffident boy himself, that nothing was farther from her thought I had suggested that the three of them should set up on their own. I offered to lend them what was needed, but neither Ralph nor Simon took kindly to the idea. They assured me that they knew nothing of husbandry, that the notion of being completely responsible, even to themselves, for the well-being of a piece of ground distressed and depressed them. If they could live in my kitchen and help me when they felt inclined and be free to have a day in the woods when they had a fit of wandering fever they would be much happier. Judith just calmly and silently assumed that I should need someone to look after my house when it was built. And since I had plenty of stores, and was fond of company and the six of us always got on excellently together I left off trying to inspire them with ambition and as soon as the harvest was over we began to build the house.

I was a little fussy about my house, that I will admit. I did not want a shack which would warp and gape in six months' time. I had had the wood cut in the previous autumn and it had laid out in the winter rains and then the long hot summer days had dried it.

I had a stairway and upper rooms, for there were six of us to be housed and it was necessary, I thought, for us to be able to escape from one another sometimes. I wanted spare rooms, too, for although we were now at the very edge of the inhabited country the day would come when people would pass through Zion as we had passed through Salem and some of them would need hospitality.

In the darkening evenings of that, our second winter, Ralph and Simon and I expended a good deal of care and effort on little finishing touches. Panelling for the parlour, a carved chimney breast, strong Suffolk latches for the doors, a wrought iron handle—and, rather ironic in that small and informal society—a great knocker for the front door which was itself a good solid piece of work in timber four inches thick.

When it was finished the house looked as sound and solid as though it had grown there. And that was not strange really, for the timber had grown within call of the place and the reed thatch had been taken from the river when Harry cleared it before making his mill.

As soon as we had moved in, and while we were still busy with little things, stools, chests and chairs, Ralph came to me with a request. Could he borrow a horse or two and make a trip to Salem. There were several things that the settlement needed; and he had skins for sale.

'Itching foot again?' I asked.

'It's that with me,' he said, grinning, 'and there'll be profit in it too. But it'll help Simon to get his mind off his trouble. He's not been like himself since the Pikles warned him off.'

'Warned him off? Off what?'

'Off Mahitabel, master. He's very taken with her, but her folks won't stomach a gypsy. Don't say anything about it to Simon. It went very deep with him.'

'I can't understand it. The Cranes were willing for Jake to marry Judith and Martha Pikle and Hannah Crane married their young men, who hadn't any more worldly goods and are no better, if as good, at turning their hands to anything than Simon is. Shall I have a talk with Mr. Crane?'

'For the Lord's sake, master, no!' His face showed real concern. 'You see, once or twice she slipped out of the house and met him. We don't do our lovemaking in the corner of the kitchen like most of these folks. And only a little while ago young Mark Pikle caught them. They made an awful fuss, the Pikles I mean, and said that if he ever told anybody how weak their sister was in the face of his wiles they'd make him sorry. I don't think Simon minded that, he and I could deal with any number of Pikles, but he didn't want to make it harder for the girl. So he sheered off and didn't say anything except to me. But he's eating his heart out, that I do know. So I thought a trip to Salem ...'

'All right,' I said. 'You may have the horses. But I expect you to bring them back. I don't want you to see another ship in Salem harbour and be taken with an itch to know where *she's* going.'

'You don't forget much, do you, master?' He laughed unabashed. 'But even if I wanted to cut my cable Simon wouldn't. He's absolutely set on the girl. He's going to let this blow over so they leave off watching her and then if she's willing he's going to get her to break out and marry him.'

'Oh,' I said. 'Mr. Thomas might have something to say to that.'

'That wouldn't matter. *I* could marry them. I'm head of the gypsies hereabout, I guess.' There was an assurance too deep to be arrogance in his voice.

'Ah well,' I said, 'perhaps it won't come to that. When the Pikles see that both Simon and the girl are serious there may be no need for a further call upon your versatility.'

'What's that?'

'Being able to raise a wind, and put a charm on a house and act proxy for the parson.'

'You may laugh,' said Ralph seriously. 'But the wind did come. And as for the house charm, why everybody knows about that. I've been called in lots of times to cut that first sod. And you'll see that it'll stand foursquare and you'll be happy in it. A house can't give you more.'

The charm to which I referred was another bit of gypsy superstition to which I had, half unwillingly, subscribed. When we had measured out the ground plan for the house and were beginning to dig the foundations Andy had just been about to drive his spade into the corner when Ralph had seized his arm, snatched the spade from him and with careful, measuring steps walked into the centre of the plot. He smote home with the spade four times and then lifted out the four-sided clod of turf.

'As this sod is foursquare, so may the house stand. As this sod is whole, so may the welfare of the building be. May health, happiness, prosperity and long-life be the portion of all within this dwelling.'

Remembering that, I said, 'You ought to make a charm for the softening of the Pikles' hearts.'

'Mahitabel is too good a worker, within doors and without. Charms don't work on people's fixed ideas,' he said in a matter-of-fact voice.

'Well,' I said, 'take the horses and go round and see what commissions you can take for people. For me you might look out for a decent quiet riding horse, not too tall a one.'

'You shall have the best there is for sale, and I'll buy it out of my skin money too.'

'Don't be silly,' I said. 'Save your money for such time as you're very taken by somebody's daughter.'

His white teeth flashed. 'I left all that behind me long before I was Simon's age. What's one wench more than another? They're all alike in the dark.'

With that piece of homely wisdom he left me. During the next few days he went around collecting orders for salt and cloth, gunpowder and needles, together with letters and messages for friends in Salem and some for passage overseas if he could find a calling ship willing to take them.

Simon, very dour and silent, saw to the packing of the skins and the food that they would need on the way, and on a bright autumn morning with a taste of frost in the air they set off, passing through the Gap and out of our sight. Already the outer world seemed very remote to us in Zion, and this renewal of contact gave our minds a jolt. It was strange to think that there were people in Fort Outpost and Sanctuary, in Neatshead, Columbine and Salem who regarded their own small settlements as the centre of the world, to whom Ralph and Simon would seem like strangers from the edge of that world. Strange, too, to reflect upon the power of the blood. Of all the people in Zion it was the gypsies alone who did not wish to own land, who were going wandering again.

I thought of that when I saw Judith watching her brothers clattering away over the bridge.

'Do you wish that you were going with them?' I asked. She went on following them with her eyes until they were lost to sight. Then without turning she said, 'You know the answer to that, don't you, *master*?'

On the lips of Ralph and Simon, and of Andy who had caught it from them, the word meant nothing, no more than Philip, or Ollenshaw meant on the lips of other men. But Judith only used it occasionally and always jibingly. I said in a sudden burst of irritation,

'I know I've asked you a hundred times not to call me by that stupid name.'

She twisted round without moving her feet so that her body, half turned, was balanced and pivoted on the slim round waist.

'Why should you mind?' she asked. 'You may call me

mistress any time you've a mind to.' And with that she strolled back into the kitchen, leaving me speechless.

Four nights later I took her to my bed. It was a damnable thing to do, I suppose, and only I know how stupid. I did not love the girl, and I did love Linda. I never for a moment stopped loving Linda, that was as much a part of me as my lame leg was. I could, and did, make a number of excuses for my folly, but I never deceived myself for a moment. There was the season of the year for one thing, dangerous as Spring is that wild glory, that blaze of colour soon to be quenched but capable while it lasts of breeding in the veriest clown a sense of time's passage through the promise of youth to the winter of the grave. There was the girl herself always about me, always ready to drop into my hand. There was the memory of that night when she had slept with her head on my heart, and the memory of a hundred other little incidents since.

What does it matter now? Now when it is all merely a memory; a tale that is told. Had I known what I know now and a thousand gypsy girls had waited for me in a thousand dark passages I would have led each one to the waiting bed and never felt, never allowed myself to feel the tearing, conflicting, humiliating remorse that I felt on that night so long ago when I felt that my treachery to myself was only equalled by my treason to Linda.

To begin with I was not exactly sober. There may be more than prejudice in Eli's frequently quoted dogma, 'Wine is a mocker, strong drink is raging.' Mike had ordered a fresh supply of spirits from Ralph and as soon as the gypsy had left Zion he had broken into his hoarded store. And I, an elder and a member of the council, had drunken with him, idling away an evening in the half finished parlour whose panelling called loudly for my attention. And as I drank and the grey bounds of everyday existence widened and fell away I thought again of Ralph's scornful philosophy. 'They're all alike in the dark.' Could I question the truth of that? I who knew nothing of what darkness brought. It might be true. Then was I wasting my life and spending my force in a vain hankering for the very thing which, under another name, was ensconced on my very hearth? How could I tell? I thought of my father, did he care what the girl's name was? Not he, six weeks after losing Linda whom he had winked at murder to possess he had forgotten what her name was. And he was experienced enough, God knew.

The spirits mounted to my brain, and sitting there I began to doubt whether I was not in truth the young fool that he had often called me. Hankering after another man's wife, and she the mother of twins. Seeing all beauty, all delight in the woman who was nursing another man's twins. Twins . . . somehow that made it worse. The sons of Boanerges mocked me with their toothless gums, white with the milk that flowed from the breast of her whom I loved.

I emptied my glass again and looked at Mike with eyes that did not see the shrewd grizzled kindly face, listened with unhearing ears to the trickle of talk that ran his rum-loosened lips. And I thought, I will know what it is that every man save I seems to share. Lame leg or no I am otherwise whole and I will have my share in this thing. Every poet, every clown, every lecher like my father, pious men like Eli and wandering rogues like Ralph are all bound with the same string. And I will not live like a eunuch simply because a girl walked in a mulberry gown through the oxlips in Hunter's Wood. Oxlips and mulberry gown I may never see again, the love that that day promised may never be mine. But this which is within my grasp I will take.

In that mood I mounted the stairs and stood with the smooth globe of the newel post beneath my hand wondering whether to call her or to seek her out. There was a window space at the far end of the passage and as the supply of glass had given out I had wrought an iron grill for it, a daisy centre with petals that radiated outwards and joined the edges to the middle. It had a shutter to close it in at night. Judith Whistlecraft stood at the window, dragging at the shutter.

'It's stuck,' she said, without turning her head. I limped over the dividing space and stood beside her for a moment looking through the iron daisy petals into the night sky, thick with stars. I put my arm round that supple waist and the dry hay-like scent of her tawny hair was in my nostrils.

'Leave it,' I said, and drew her towards my room.

Like the flat calm after a high fever sanity returned to me. You were sweet, Judith; sweet and kind, and any man might have been glad of you. But I was not any man. I was a man with one clear course to steer and any divergence from it demands the sorrowful retracing of steps, the shameful return from the pleasant pathways that are not his way.

For all it taught me, for all the relief it brought I might as well have spat. With Linda it might have been a sacrament. With Judith, for all she was sweet and kind and patient with my clumsiness, it was meaningless, mechanical, a succumbing to earth-driven instinct like the mating of the beasts that perish. Tears shed for sorrow and tears shed in a biting wind have everything in common save the feeling that makes the one significant. What is one liquid more than another if the feeling that gives the outpour meaning is lacking? Without the feeling I might as well have spat.

The failure would not be hidden. Judith knew it. She sighed once or twice and then stole away in silence. I thought, that is one good thing about it. Her queer fancy for me will change to scorn now, and she will marry Jake, or another, and fulfil her proper destiny. I thought of my father's outgrown fancies, the village girls who had been married off to complaisant yokels to whom a gold coin or two was compensation for their mates' lost virginity. I must see that Judith, when her choice was made, had something in her hand.

At last I slept. When I woke in the wide bed the morning sun was already spilling about the floor. From the kitchen came the clatter of dishes and I could hear the voices of Andy and Mike as they went about their morning tasks. I must go down and take from the hand of the woman who had been willing to share the most secret thing in life with me, a platterful of bacon rashers and fried potatoes. This was a day in a lifetime, just an ordinary day.

I washed and dressed slowly with the deliberate and futile intention of delaying as long as possible the moment when I must go down and face Judith. But at last I was ready. Still I hesitated and throwing my window wide I dragged up the one chair in the room and set it close to the sill so that I could lean forward on my elbows and breathe in the sweet sharp autumn air. I knew myself for a fool: and when I looked out across the trees by the river and thought of Linda, rising and going about her tasks in the little hidden house, and then was drawn back by the clatter of dishes to the thought of the woman in my own kitchen, then I felt a knave as well. The wrongs of the whole world could be laid at the doors of the knaves and the fools, and I sighed as I numbered myself in their company.

Still, there was no point in lingering here, with a sigh on my lips; I must go down to the sunny kitchen and face the breakfast table. Judith was stooping over the stove, but at the sound of my iron on the floor she straightened herself and brushed back a strand of tawny hair. I braced myself to face her—and then felt a fool for doing so, for with exactly the same expression, in the very same voice as usual she said, 'Your rashers are crisp as a biscuit. I thought I heard you stirring some time ago. Shall I cook some others?'

'I like them that way,' I said, and gave my attention to my ruined breakfast.

I was glad when Mike came in. 'It's a grand morning,' he said cheerily. 'We'd better get some corn up to Harry's, don't you think, while the trail's good.'

'We'll do that directly after breakfast,' I agreed. 'Where's Andy?'

The scraping of dirty boots on the scraper that I had planted outside the back door answered me, and Andy, who had copied the Whistlecrafts' method of address, came in with glum face, saying, 'Master, we're short of a couple of pigs. Them two that was in a pen, fatting. They're gone.'

'Did you shut the door last time you went in?'

'I did so. And what's more it's still shut. They didn't break out, they was took. And not by no wild creature neither. Somebody with hands took them pigs.'

I laid down my knife. 'It looks like it certainly. But who? I hate to think that anyone would just steal them. And I can't see how we're to find out. Pigs are so much alike.'

'Not Fatty ain't. I'd know that pig anywhere. Why if I went within sight of that pig with a stick in my hand she'd come up, grunting and arching her back to be rubbed. To tell you the truth I didn't like the notion of shutting her up to kill, for all she was sich a bad breeder. All the same if she's to be et she's going to be et by us. And as soon's I've had my food I'm gonna take a stick and go to every pigsty in this blessed place and call her by name and show the stick. And any pig that comes to be rubbed I shall bring home with its neighbour.'

'You can't do that, Andy,' I said, biting my thumb—a bad childish habit which often overtook me when I was thinking. 'You'd cause no end of bad feeling, suspecting everybody wholesale, like that.'

'I'll be crafty,' said Andy, unshaken. 'I'll just be paying a call, casual like, and singing, "Come Fatty, my dear one." '

We all laughed; his concern was so genuine, and the idea of his doing anything casually was funny. All the same the loss of the pigs was serious, not so much from the value of the beasts, though there were few enough yet in the valley, but because the loss pointed to the presence of a thief among us.

'We ought to find out whether anyone else has lost anything. Mike and I are going up to the Mill this morning and we'll call in at every thouse on the way.'

We loaded the wagon and set out. I found myself watching the faces of those to whom I said, 'Two pigs were taken from my place in the night,' and I hated myself for expecting to see a change of countenance take place. None did, I mean no one looked guilty though several looked concerned. When we called at Carter's we found Mary Carter trying to soothe young Johnny whose pup was missing. 'I tell him it'll come back,' she said, raising a harassed face. 'It's only just a year old, you know, a wild little thing, it often runs off.'

'I want it. I want my Fluffy,' repeated the child with the reasonlessness of the very young.

'When did you miss it?' I asked Mary.

'This morning. It always slept in the yard. I guess something disturbed it and it just broke its string and went off.' Johnny wailed louder. 'But it'll come back. Listen, Mummy'll call again. Fluffy, Fluffee, Fluff.'

There was no answer except the echo of her voice from the woods at the back of the house.

'Has anything else gone?' I asked.

'No.' She looked startled. 'Why?'

'We're short of a couple of pigs.'

'My husband didn't mention anything else when he came in for breakfast,' she said. And then, as the child tugged at her skirt again she dismissed us and the lost pigs from her mind and said, 'All right, love. We'll go a walk and hunt for Fluffy.'

I did not like the thought which my mind presented to me. Two pigs missing—a young undisciplined male dog gone astray—why connect them? But I slapped the reins on my horses' backs and hurried along to the Lomax place. At the sound of the wheels the two women's faces appeared at the kitchen window and they were both swollen with tears. Perhaps neither of them cared to appear before us so and argued about it, for it was quite an appreciable time before Edith, the girl, opened the door and said thickly, 'Good morning.'

'Good morning,' I said, 'Is your uncle—or your father about, Edith?'

'Didn't you meet them? They've gone your way. Uncle Oliver's nearly mad. Adam's been killed. Her throat was cut!' Her voice went up and up until it ended in a bellow and she put her apron over her face and began to sob.

'Adam?' I said, puzzled. 'Who's that?'

She took down her apron and gave me a look of something that was very like hatred. 'Adam's our dog.... I know it's a silly name for a female dog but she had that name before ... before she had the pups. And now she's dead.'

The little frightened thing in my mind popped up and said, 'I told you so.'

'I'm very sorry about the dog,' I said, unhelpfully.

'Somebody else will be sorry too,' she said fiercely. 'Uncle Oliver took his gun ... if he finds who did it ...' I turned the wagon round.

'Now we've come so far we'll just go up and leave this at Harry's, and then I'll get hold of Eli. I don't like this at all, Mike.'

'You know what I think?' asked Mike, tugging at a remnant of his ear.

'Indians?'

'Um-m. Nice thought, ain't it?'

Harry's Mill was the last place along the river to the West. Just beyond it the high land began and the river there ran swiftly, with power enough to turn the big wheel. Leaving the Lomax place we followed the river bank where the laden wagons that had gone on up the same errand as ours had made a well-worn track. We were still out of sight of the mill and not far from Lomax's when a woman ran full tilt at us, coming round the bend so swiftly that only the violent shying of my horses avoided a collision. She fell down on her knees less than a foot from the front wheel and even as I steadied the horses Mike jumped down and raised her up. It was Hannah Wright—the Quaker girl who had married Harry on the hill-top outside Fort Outpost. She fought against Mike's hands and from her horribly open mouth there came cries and screams that took my mind straight back to the morning when Shad was hanged and the unknown woman in the crowd had screamed as the rope went round his neck. There was the same abandon, the same terror, the same madness.

I sat there, unable to do anything but hang on to the reins, for the horses were almost crazy from the dreadful screaming just under their noses and were plunging about wildly.

'Hold her a moment. I'll drive around the bend and come back,' I shouted to Mike. Freedom to move, the fact that they had left the noise behind and the weight of the loaded wagon calmed the horses and as soon as I could I pulled up, climbed to the ground and wound the reins round the branch of a willow tree. Then as quickly as I could I ran back. Mike was still holding her with all his strength and she was still screaming and struggling.

'She's mad. She don't say no sensible word,' he gasped.

'Well,' I said, 'you're a doctor. What shall we do?'

'A good dash of cold water might help.

So I filled my hat from the river and threw it in her face. She stiffened, stopped screaming, looked at us both wildly and said, 'Harry's dead.'

'Drowned?' I asked that thinking of the mill and that perhaps it might be possible even yet to rescue him.

'No. Cut up. Carved like a pig. Oh God! Oh God!'

The terrible desolation of that cry was worse than the screaming. She put her hands to her poor ravaged face and the tears poured through her fingers.

'That's right,' said Mike, slipping his arm around her shoulder. 'You cry, my dear. It'll do you good.'

She cried on for a long time; cried until it seemed that her tears were exhausted, and then with Mike on one side of her and me on the other we set out to walk to the Lomax's.

'It was last night,' she said. 'The little dog kept barking and Harry thought it might be a fox or something after the fowls. So he got up and went out. He didn't come back to breakfast and I waited and waited and then I started out to look for him.' Dry sobs shook her again, but after a time she went on. 'Thou knowest how hard it is to find aught in the woods. I found the little dog first, his throat was slit . . . and then I found Harry. There wasn't . . . there wasn't any top . . . to his head . . . and there wasn't any . . . not much left of Harry at all.' She broke down again and we stood still in the road for a while. There isn't much that one can do for or say to a woman bereaved as she had been. We patted and held her and made vague kind noises. At last we came in sight of the Lomax place and met the two brothers just returning home. William looked weakly unhappy, Oliver furious. He had, as Edith had said, his gun in his hand.

I said, 'We know who killed your dog, Oliver. Call your women, will you?' The two came out of the house and after I had hastily whispered to them about Hannah's trouble they put their arms about her and took her away with them.

Then I said to Oliver, 'Have you got any spare guns?' He nodded and went into the house, returning with them and more shot and powder. We set off almost in silence for Harry's Mill, passing my wagon on the way. There seemed no sense in taking it along now. We went through the yard and through the open kitchen door I could see the remains of the fire and the breakfast table, set with Hannah's Quaker neatness, the corners of the blue and white checked cloth just moving in the morning breeze. Twenty yards from the house the wood began, thin larch and birch at first and then thickening with undergrowth and brambles. There was no question of following in the distracted woman's steps for she had gone this way and that—calling I thought, calling and calling. I could almost feel the impact of her anxiety: the place seemed saturated with her fear. At last we came on the little yellow dog, the mongrel, one of those whose birth had caused such excitement in the dull days of waiting above the stricken village. The blood from his throat dabbled the yellow coat.

'That's how Adam was,' said Oliver, breathing hard through pinched nostrils. 'The best dog ever I had and the truest.'

We pushed on, bracing ourselves for the sight of the dog's master. We walked warily, though there was little need. The Indians would surely know that such a thing would not pass unpunished, and would hardly linger about the scene of the crime. But back in Salem the people, although they seemed to be describing a peril of the past—as in England one might talk of the danger of the Danes—had yet told us such hair-raising stories of what the peril was like while it was existent, that we walked delicately, starting at every snapping twig, whirling round at a shadow or the passage of a bird from bough to bough.

And soon we came on Harry, the stalwart young man who had seen his ambition fulfilled when his own mill-wheel started turning, who had built with his own hands the little house back yonder and cleared the patch of soil behind it, who had sung hymns and psalms as he ground the good corn, and had risen up in the darkness to meet death in this shape. The knife that had slit the throats of the mastiff bitch and the little mongrel had not been content with such a performance here. There was almost an artistry about the devilish work. As Hannah had said, there wasn't much of Harry left, and what there was was no sight to dwell upon. It was almost like a symbol, a crudely written warning—see what happens to those who value a pig or a fowl overhighly—keep to your beds if you would keep your skins.

Shuddering I took off my coat and threw it over what had yesterday been a comely young fellow. I said, 'There's no purpose to be served in taking him back. Mike, fetch a spade from the house, there's a good fellow. I'm tired.' I sat down suddenly, as much through faintness as weariness.

When Mike returned, bearing a pick and a shovel, we made a hole, and then, after a moment's hesitation, approached what we had to bury. Soon it was hidden; and as we shovelled the soft loamy mould over it I thought how kind is the earth, bearing and tolerating and producing all things, and in the end covering them all. One minute Harry was a sight to scarify the shrinking sight, and the next it was all hidden away and one might pass over the spot and never know. Oliver Lomax picked up his gun, and as though inspired by the cold touch of it, said, 'May God accept your soul, Harry Wright, we will avenge your body.' I had always thought Oliver fish-blooded and in-human : I liked him better at that moment than I had ever done.

We went back to the Mill House and I closed the door upon the simple pathos of that breakfast table, made ready for the man who had never come back to the homely com-fort of food. We looked about to see what live-stock might need attention, but there was nothing left. Small wonder the little dog had barked !

'It's not just one lurking thief,' I said, putting my thoughts into words as we went back. 'The Mill and my place are opposite ends of the valley, and yours, Lomax, is in the middle. It's no very cheering thought to think that we were all in our beds last night while this raid went on just under our windows. And we've spread ourselves about so much. We ought to have copied Fort Outpost more, built the houses within reach of one another. Why, for all we know the Pikles and the Cranes up at the Gap may have been wiped out entirely.'

'We'll soon find out,' said Oliver Lomax. 'And then we'll call a meeting and talk over what's best to do.'

The general feeling at the meeting—which was a full one, attended by all the men—was that there was nothing much to fear, that the attacks had been merely pilfering raids and Harry's mongrel, the unfortunate Adam and the venturesome Harry himself, had been slain because they had interfered with the thieves' activities. Nevertheless it was agreed that a sharp look-out must be kept; live-stock

must be brought in at night and access to it made as difficult as possible. We must sleep lightly and keep our guns
near at hand.

But Eli voiced my own sneaking dissatisfaction.

'These measures are too mild,' he said. 'If we admit that
it isn't safe to leave a cow in a shed or a pig in a pen, or
when summer comes again, a horse loose in a meadow,
well then we've got to make it safe. That's what we're here
for. Once we begin locking ourselves in we've taken the
first step towards being afraid ever to put our noses out of
doors. They know we're here, and we've got to make them
know that we're not to be played with.'

'And how would you do that, Mr. Makers?' A respectful
voice, Carter or Dendy or Steggles.

'Rake through the woods,' said Eli. 'Sit up o' nights and
watch. Winter's coming on, we can sleep by day if we
must.'

'Harry Wright woke up,' I said cautiously. 'We kept to
our beds and lost only our beasts, he lost his life. If we're
going to take the offensive we've got to organise something
sensible and as safe as possible.'

'Well, go on then, Mr. Ollenshaw. Organise it and we'll
do it.'

'Mr. Ollenshaw' was beginning to sound to me like a
challenge. It was the badge of responsibility. What 'Philip'
or even 'Mr. Philip' might shuffle out of and evade 'Mr.
Ollenshaw' must face and solve. I thought wildly.

'Well, it's a big problem,' I said at last, after I had seen
the woods and the slopes of the hills crawling with furtive
prowlers and ourselves, a mere handful wildly shooting
separate shots into the darkness. 'The best thing I can suggest is that for quite a long period the women and children
are brought back to sleep in the common hall where we
were last winter. Then we should pool the beasts and house
them at one or two salient places with four or five men at
each place, one at least always awake. Then we might give
the thieves a welcome that at least they don't expect. It'll
be troublesome and upsetting, and if anyone has a better
suggestion I shall be very pleased to hear it.'

There was a long silence.

At the end of it it was agreed that no better suggestion

was forthcoming. So we made the chief points Eli's, Harry's Mill, the Gap and the Carters' place, that being nearest the centre of the village where the common hall stood. We divided out the beasts and the man power as well as we could.

Eli brought his things across to my side of the river and he, Andy, Mike and I composed the watch there. The Pikles and the Cranes, with the exception of Mathew and Moses who went to Harry's Mill, manned the Gap. Joseph Steggles, Amos Beeton and Tim Dendy joined the Pikles at the Mill, and the others took up a position at Isaac Carter's which was within reach of the place where the women slept.

It was, in a way, a state of war, and as such profoundly uncomfortable. The horses were always where they weren't wanted, the cows had to be milked where they had slept and the milk slopped in barrels and buckets all over the settlement each morning when the women went back to their houses. At each post half the men slept half the night, were wakened by the others and watched for the remainder. And nothing happened. Not a chicken squawked, not a pig squealed for the whole of a long fortnight during which the nights grew steadily longer and darker.

We were beginning to think that the animals had been taken and Harry killed by a passing band of Indians who had happened by chance to notice the new settlement, or perhaps had gone this way twice, taken the horses the first time and remembered that it was an easy place to steal from. In that case we might sit up for a year of nights, awaiting their annual visit. The muddle and the lack of sleep was beginning to tell upon our tempers. Even the women grew touchy and there was one enormous row between Keziah and Mary Carter over the milk. Keziah, as usual the aggressor, accused Mary of skimming off the cream for her child, so that when Keziah received her share it was nothing more than skim. The cows, as beasts easily moved and needing only bi-daily attention, had been chosen as a bait for the deserted Mill, and the milk supply on its way from the Mill to the Gap, reached Mary first.

During the second fortnight Christina Beeton was

brought to bed with her first baby. She was no longer a young woman and the labour was long and hard. They moved her out of the common hall into Mary Carter's house and Carter himself went up to Harry's Mill at night so that Beeton might be near Christina. Mike spent his time at the Carters' house and since I was not a ploughman by day I arranged to double my watch at night, sharing it with Andy first and then with Eli.

Judith, who had refused from the first to go back to the common sleeping room, used to sit up late and before retiring would bank up the kitchen fire and leave coffee simmering. In that way we were probably the most fortunate watchers of them all. We used to sit in the kitchen with the door wide open and every ten minutes or so walk around to the animals in order to keep ourselves awake. Two nights before Christina was taken I suddenly had an idea.

'It's the kitchen,' I said. 'With that fire going and the door wide open no doubt there's a glow that can be seen by Indian eyes for miles. It wouldn't look like a sleeping house, would it? We've got to let the fire out and sit in the dark like the rest of them do.'

And two nights after, on a whole night watch I was bitterly regretting the doused fire.

I stayed up for two whole nights and slept very indifferently by day. By the third night I was quite irritable as anyone in Zion, though I tried to rebuke myself with the thought that it was Christina's third night too, poor woman.

I sent Andy to bed. He waked Eli who came down yawning and stretching his great limbs in the darkness.

'It's a fine night,' I said, 'quite bright with stars.'

'I believe you were right in what you said the other day,' he said after a pause. 'They go past here once a year and we'd better remember the time next year and be ready for them sooner. This is a waste of time.'

I knew by the sound of his voice that he was as sick of the uneventful vigils as I was myself, and no doubt in the morning he would decide to go back home and stay there to sleep out his nights properly. And because it was night and I was tired and alone with Eli and must keep wakeful, the thought ended 'with Linda beside him'. Immediately my imagination was off down the well-trodden track and there I was picturing their whole relationship. That unhappy night with Judith had given shape to my formless thoughts and the inward sight of Eli's great limbs entwined with Linda's supple ones was the right and exquisite punishment for my evil thinking. I could hear his quiet breathing close beside me, I could almost hear his heart. Once when he turned to me with some quiet comment the great golden beard, brushed up during his sleep and not smoothed down again, touched my cheek as he spoke. I was even conscious of his personal odour, a mixture of homespun, farmyard, sawdust and sheer masculine humanity. I got up quickly and limped on my watchman's round. I could sit beside him no longer. As Eli Makers I could contradict him, respect him, accept and even admire him, but as Linda's bed-fellow he was loathsome to me. It would be just my fate to have to spend the long dark hours with him, with nothing to say, nothing to read, nothing to do but *think*.

I stopped in the dark angle of the outhouses and leaning back against the support of the wall, lifted my face to the sky. The stars, some twinkling some steady, were sown all over the sky, like seed on a dark field. Their number, their distance and the immense silence that seemed to link me to them had a calming effect upon me. Each one of those little points of light was as much a part of the created universe as I or any man. It was only man's colossal conceit that made him imagine that the sun was sent to warm him, the moon and the stars to cheer the darkness of his night. My own little life, my efforts, my fears, my love for Linda filled my mind, bounded my consciousness only because my mind was small. If I cultivated a wider outlook I should suffer less. I must proceed to do so, remind myself that there had been many frustrated lovers in the past. There were men in Babylon and Rome, men in Egypt and Jerusalem who had been crippled, dumb, blind, unloved. It was only my small personal tragedy that the scrap of consciousness which was I, Philip Ollenshaw, the spark of life that made me what I was, that did my thinking and my loving, should be housed in a body which had, after all, only two troubles, a short leg and no union with Linda. I must cultivate a sense of proportion. I must not hate Eli, who was only another pilgrim between the womb and the grave, who was not a being specially created to be the instrument of my discomfort.

I straightened myself and took the first step of my way back to Eli in this more reasonable frame of mind, and as I did so I heard, from the other side of the building, the shrill squealing of my pigs. I went, hop and run, hop and run, towards the pigsty and could just see in the starlight three dark figures bounding away with pigs slung sack-wise over their shoulders. Other pigs streamed out through the open door and even as I took aim one, running wildly, caught me across the knees so that I stumbled and fired into the air. Almost simultaneously I heard Eli fire and the hindmost Indian dropped with a scream, the pig got up and made off. The other two dropped their burdens and bounded off into the shelter of the trees.

Far off across the valley I heard other shots, muted by distance. Eli, running hard, his fingers busy with his gun as he ran, was in pursuit and I stumbled after him. Within the shadows of the trees it was dark, but I could hear the crashing of undergrowth and small low-growing branches ahead of me. Then there was a shot and a cry, and running on, with my whole skin crawling with terror at the feeling— not the thought, there was no time for thought—of what might be beside, ahead or behind me, I came upon Eli, astride a great fallen trunk one Indian on this side of it, grovelling on the ground, and the snapping of twigs on the far side of the barrier announcing the other's whereabouts.

'Got clean away,' said Eli, ruefully dropping to the ground on my side of the tree-trunk. 'Bounded over that like a hunting dog.' Turning he clubbed the fallen Indian with the butt of his gun.

Both Eli's shots had found their mark. I felt impelled to say, as we turned back, 'One of the pigs ran into me just as I took aim, otherwise we might have got all three.'

'We shall have a nice lot of trouble getting the pigs in again tomorrow. The woods and the acorns will tempt them finely,' was Eli's reply to that piece of childishness. Before we were out of the trees again we could hear Andy shouting, 'Hi! Hi! where are you? Answer me!'

We answered him, and he fairly danced with rage and

disappointment.

'That would happen to me,' he said. (That was one of his favourite expressions, and Mike had once sworn that if Andy predeceased him he would carve the words on his tombstone.) 'Sit up night arter night and the only minnit there's anything to show for it I'm rolling asleep like a hog.'

In the morning we examined the Indian who had fallen in the yard; he was rather pitiable. So thin and so dirty. His long black hair was all dabbled with blood for Eli's shot had shattered the back of his head. Yet when we turned him over there was an expression of peace upon his brown thin face that went straight to my heart. He had been a man who doubtless took some pleasure in his life. Somewhere perhaps a woman would mourn him, little children miss him. And then I thought of Harry, so fiendishly cut about. It was a pity. There was room here in this vast new land for all of us. Yet we could not leave one another in peace—except the peace of death. True, I thought, we have taken their land—but they weren't really using it. And they lived somehow before our pigs came. But the thinness of him, and the peace on his face, and the fact that he was armed only with a knife softened me towards him somehow, and I saw him buried, together with the other man whom Eli had killed in the woods, with no very great pleasure. The other had a far more brutal face, and I thought, they differ as we do. To us they are just Indians, but they have distinct personalities, are known by their characteristics among their fellows, just as we are.

The other shots that we had heard had come from Harry's Mill. No shot had got home, but Isaac Carter who was there because he had changed places with Amos Beeton, had got close enough to slay one with an axe, at the cost of a knife wound in the neck; and Tim Dendy had laid hold of one, 'slippery as an eel' he described him, and choked him after a struggle. In both places the raiders had outnumbered the defenders, but they had taken little advantage of the fact and we happily concluded that theft, not attack, was their motive. With four dead and no spoils we hoped that they would be discouraged. And it seemed so, for we had no more trouble in that way.

Christina's baby had come in the night. The shooting did

it,' said Mike, hastily gulping coffee before he went up to the Mill to see to Isaac's knife wound. 'With shooting to right of her and shooting to left she just couldn't hold on to it any longer. Great fat lump it is too.'

He went off to attend to Isaac and Andy busied himself about the yard until Eli and I called him to help us round up the pigs. Every one of them was loose and in the woods and if we didn't get them back that day they would have wandered in search of acorns and beech mast and we should never recover them. We took our guns as a matter of course. Every man in Zion had ploughed, even, since Harry's death, with his gun slung across his handles. And I had come to think of the two things as the badge of the settler. If this country ever is settled, a land like England with streets and roads and houses, it will be due to those two things, the plough and the gun.

Naturally, we separated in the big drive, casting wide circles and urging the straying swine within each circle in the direction of home. And so it is that I can, to this day, point to the spot where the greatest temptation of my life beset me.

I had just hobbled round a couple of pigs, stirred them from their gobbling and started them for home when I heard a shot from deeper in the wood. It shattered the morning quiet and set my heart racing. Then I heard a shout. I was moving towards the spot with all the speed I could muster already, and I doubled my efforts when I heard the cry.

A great bramble twined itself round my legs. I gave a hard jerk and as it gave tumbled into the trunk of a tree. I blinked and swore and made my way around it, and there I saw Eli, whiter than death, the stock of his gun raised like a club, face to face with an enormous bear. He had fired and wounded, but not killed the beast and had no time to re-load. The bear, reared on its hind legs overtopped Eli by some feet, and his chance of smiting it anything like an effective blow was out of the question. I saw the glitter of the little piggy eyes, saw the long claws of the fore-paws curved like sharp knives.

They say that drowning men, at the moment of the final immersion see all their lives in one instantaneous flash. For that I *cannot* vouch, for I have never been in any danger of drowning, but I *do* know that as I stood there with Eli and the bear face to face before me, in less than a moment of time I saw both the actions possible to me, and all their results. I might shoot, and Eli would go back to Linda and very probably outlive me. I might turn and steal away, escaping while the bear rent or hugged him—or whatever bears do to their prey. And within a week I might have Linda for my own. Nobody would blame a lone widow for linking her life with any man. Linda would lie in my bosom, be mine to tend and care for. There was no one in Zion to offer any competition. She liked me. Without a doubt she would be mine.

I had loved her for a long time, and because I loved her I raised my gun, took careful aim and shot straight at one of those glittering eyes. A bit of bloody fur hit me on the forehead and no baptism was ever more cleansing. I'll go to her clean, I thought.

Eli wiped the sweat of mortal fear from his face. He was shaking like a leaf.

'Thank God,' he said unsteadily, 'no pig bumped your knees that time lad. After the Almighty, I thank *you*.'

'I wonder,' I gasped flippantly, 'exactly what the Almighty would have done if I hadn't been there.' I giggled feebly as I spoke.

'Mr. Philip,' said Eli, gravely, wiping his face again, 'there's a lot about you that needs understanding.'

We left it at that.

The next thing of the moment was Ralph Whistlecraft's return. He brought all that had been ordered, even Mr. Thomas' letter from Alfred Bradstreet. He brought salt and needles and gunpowder and shot. He brought me Bluey, my beloved mare, and some plants for Linda's garden and my orchard. But he came alone. Simon had apparently got drunk in Beadle's Tavern, completely and wildly drunk after his long abstention, and been involved in some quarrel, the reasons and off-shoots of which were more than I could thoroughly master from Ralph's fury-distorted tale. Anyhow blows had been struck and a man had fallen into the hearth, cracked his skull on the irons and been taken up dead. Simon, the stranger, the gypsy had been accused and it was only by the exercise of craft—which included Simon's feigning death and being taken up by the weeping Ralph and carried out—that prevented his arrest by the constables. Once outside Ralph had hurried to the harbour and given half his fur money to the captain of a ship to take Simon away.

Ralph returned on Thursday. By Saturday it was common knowledge that when Phineas Pikle, going in to his meal, had said that the gypsy had come back without his brother Mahitabel had fainted across the supper table, and on Sunday it was quite clear to everyone that Mahitabel was going to have a baby.

She was not at the meeting—which was held in the old communal building—but everybody else in the settlement was, and Mr. Thomas prayed long and lustily for 'our young sister who has fallen into grievous sin, sin which will be visited, according to Thy promise, upon the head of the soul yet unborn.' Being in the household of the co-sinner's brother, I was naturally in ignorance and looked round to wonder to whom the man could possibly be referring. I caught Ralph's uneasy eye, noted Mahitabel's absence and drew my own conclusions. I waited impatiently until the meeting was over and then, hurried out after Ralph. 'You double-dyed fool,' I said hotly, 'what is all this about? Why didn't you tell me?' Ralph drew a deep noisy breath through his nose, opened his mouth and let it all out in a gusty impatient sigh.

'You're an elder, master, and so is Pikle. I didn't want to make ill blood between you, you being my master and Simon's and him being the wench's father. I did what I could. I offered to stand up in church with her—what more could I do? But she's crazy, and so are they all. So there you are.'

'You just answer questions,' I said. 'Now. Mahitabel Pikle is going to have Simon's baby?'

He nodded.

'Where is she?'

'Mrs. Pikle turned her out. She's up at the Mill House. I took her.'

'When?'

'Last night. When Mrs. Pikle turned her out.'

'Who else knows?'

'Why, everybody.'

'Then why the hell didn't I know?'

'I told you,' said Ralph with another impatient outlet of breath. 'Nobody wanted you to know.'

'Why not?'

'Well. . . . I sorta thought you might want to do something silly like and Pikle was afraid you would go after him, knowing that you didn't care for Keziah, Mrs. Pikle I should say. And Mr. Makers said your ideas were all wrong . . . so you see . . .'

'You're a great stupid fool,' I said again. 'How long did you think I'd stay in ignorance? And I credited you with more decent feeling than to leave the poor girl up there in that dreadful place alone.'

'I offered to marry her, master. More than that no man could do. And I couldn't stay with her without getting her a worse name, could I?'

'You could have come straight to me! But then you great lolloping things never do have any sense. Stand there until I want you and don't shift,' I said crossly.

Eli, who had halted by the door to speak to Mr. Thomas drew level with me and I put a hand on his arm to halt him. Linda peeped round his bulk to give me good day, but somehow this morning even Linda's smile was a secondary consideration.

'Eli,' I said, 'have you heard about Mahitabel Pikle? Where she is, I mean. Did you know he'd turned her out?'

'Yes,' said Eli, who had been so considerate to the horses when the trail led uphill. 'Quite right too. I wouldn't have a harlot under my roof.'

'But she isn't. Have you ever *seen* a harlot I wonder. If you had you'd know that that kind of thing doesn't happen to them. She's just a poor simple girl who was in love with a man her parents didn't approve of. She can't be up there in that awful place alone.'

'She shouldn't be anywhere in Zion at all,' was Eli's rebuttal of that. 'I agree with Pikle, she should be sent clean out of Zion. She should be like Hagar.'

'God supported her,' I parried. 'And this lass shall have support too. I'll speak to Pikle. I'll call a meeting.'

'You'll just make a fool of yourself, lad,' said Eli in kindly warning. 'This is a Christian community and that girl has committed a deadly sin.'

'She didn't commit it alone,' I began, but Eli set his jaw. 'Come along, wife, such talk isn't for your ears.'

I saw Linda's lips move at me, and her eyes met mine. I mistook their message, I thought that they were begging me to desist. But as she turned away in Eli's shadow she gripped her hands together and said, in a clear, desperate voice, 'I think Philip is right, Eli, Nobody should be up at the Mill alone.'

'Come home, you don't know what you're saying,' he replied, and with a motion more forceful than any I had seen him use towards her he took her by the wrist and hurried her away.

Since taking up dwelling at the Gap Phineas Pikle had driven in to meeting in a wagon from which the rear had been sawn. It just seated four people back to back. He and Keziah sat in front and Mahitabel and Mary usually sat at the back. This morning Mary was climbing into the back alone when I reached them and Keziah was arranging a rug across her bony knees.

'Pikle,' I said, 'I want a word with you.'

'Well,' he said, with an air of knowing only too well what it was about.

Standing on the ground I was hatefully conscious of having to look up at him.

'It's about Mahitabel ... you know that I expect. I guess you were shocked and angry, but it isn't so grave you know. They were just young and in love. Don't add to her burden. She's lost the man she loves and she's going to have a baby. Let her at least have the comfort of her own home and the backing of her own folk.'

Of course I was a fool to start pleading in Keziah's presence. Phineas, never a very powerful man, was completely under her thumb. Now he said nothing, just looked miserable, fiddled with the reins and left Keziah to answer.

'It's easy to see, Mr. Ollenshaw, why you plead for her. Her fellow sinner is your man and they say, like master like man you know. But Christian people don't tolerate fornication even when it's dressed up in pretty speeches. Drive on,

200

Phineas.'

'No, wait,' I said and limped swiftly round to the horse's head so that to drive on he must needs drive over me. Ignoring Keziah I fixed my eye on Pikle's pale sheeplike countenance and made one last appeal.

'Stepmothers are notorious,' I said. 'Don't listen to her. Think of her own mother. What would she have said? Even if the girl has done wrong, sending her up there alone to that dreadful place won't right it. Ralph Whistlecraft says he's willing to marry her and I think that wouldn't be a bad thing. I seem to remember something of the kind being advised in the Bible. Drive up there now and take her home to dinner and talk the whole thing over. Will you do that, Pikle?'

A thin pink flush spread glaze-like over his prominent cheek bones. Then he tightened his hands on the reins till the knuckles gleamed and said,

'Thou makest a good advocate, Mr. Ollenshaw, but good pleading is the devil's weapon in such a cause. Thou seem'st familiar with thy Bible, thou had'st better read the law as laid down with regards to whores and fornicators and remember that they who tolerate sin are in equal case with the sinners, or worse, not having the temptation. As for the lass's mother she was an honest woman, not to be mentioned in the same breath. I give thanks to God that she does not live to see the day. She would say as I do, as she has made her bed she must lie on it. Get up, Brownie.'

I loosened my hold on the horse's head and stood back. Ralph remained where I had left him. 'Take my mare,' I said, 'and get along to the Mill. Bring the girl back with you. We'll wait dinner until you come.'

Judith set an extra place at the table and I laid out a dish of apples and another of raisins which Ralph had brought back from Salem. But my hopes of solacing Mahitabel's grief with any creature comforts were quelled as soon as I saw her. Always, in my opinion, a pale and colourless creature she now resembled nothing so much as a sodden dish towel. Her eyelids were quite transparent and so swollen that she could hardly see and her nose seemed to stretch half across her face which was ashen in hue.

Apart from the wreckage wrought by tears there was

nothing at all wrong with her appearance and I found myself wondering why she had betrayed her secret at this stage. Was it panic? Or had women some special way of ferreting out such things.

She sat down in the chair that I pulled out for her, accepted a plateful of food which she cut into pieces and then ignored, said, 'Oh no, thankee' when I asked whether there was anything she preferred and for the rest was silent. On the company at the table a dreadful constraint fell, so that any remark tendered to relieve the silence and promote a natural atmosphere sounded strained and tinny and made the situation worse.

Poor old Mike, with a sympathetic look on his funny monkeyish face refilled with water the beaker that she had emptied thirstily and said 'There, there' when the tears began to stream again over her ghastly cheeks. But that didn't stop them and in a minute or two we had all ceased to ply our knives and just sat there, helplessly looking at one another. Presently I signalled with my eyes to Judith who rose and led her away to the room that she was to share with her.

Andy, always hungry and avid for food reached out and helped himself heavily to vegetables. We took up our knives again, relieved against our wills.

'Poor young devil,' said Mike, 'women do get a damn twisted deal and no mistake. If that young brother of yours was here I'd go for'm old man as I am.'

'It wasn't Simon's fault,' said Ralph, shifting uneasily in his chair. 'He loved her all right, though by God it makes you wonder what he could have seen in her. But he did, always hanging about the Gap, he was, with a bunch of posies. Took her the very best skin he ever shot too. And he'd never have set out if the Pikles hadn't treated him so bad, damn 'em all to hell. I'd never seen Simon cry since he was just a little chap, but one night he howled like a baby. Quakers are all very well and godly men are all very well, but give me a heathen to deal with.'

'Heathen can hurt you too,' I said, remembering my father and thinking suddenly that the most godly man and the least that I had ever known had united to hurt me more than anyone else. 'These people have got God all muddled up with ther own ideas, and so they get Him all wrong.'

'They'll get you all wrong, too, master,' said Andy. 'You're an elder don't forget. They'll take it very hard that what one elder turned out you took in. You'll have Mr. Thomas on your trail iss it not? And he will tell you that he who harbourss a ssinner iss ass bad ass the ssinner maybe.'

Andy's homely Essex drawl imitating Mr. Thomas was a thing to smile at, but nobody did smile.

'I built this house both broad and long and I shall fill it how I will without Mr. Thomas' leave,' I said. 'He'd be only doing his duty if he made Pikle take her back.'

'Oh God forbid,' cried Mike feelingly. 'Remember Keziah. Why, a galley slave'd have a better time than she would in that house after this.'

'You're right there. I suppose the best thing would be that she should marry Ralph—if she can face the prospect!'

'Or even me,' said Mike with an answering twinkle. 'I could bear the prospect of a nice strong boy to work for me in my old age. And ten to one it will be a boy, love children almost always are.'

'I'd be kind to her,' said Ralph simply, ignoring the interruption.

Andy's prediction was not long in being fulfilled. In the evening Pikle and Mr. Thomas arrived, without Keziah, I was glad to see. I welcomed them ceremoniously, striving to create a good atmosphere. Andy took the horses and I led the men into the parlour where I offered refreshments that were refused.

They seemed to be waiting for something. Pikle certainly said, 'I hear thou hast the girl here, Mr. Ollenshaw,' but when I nodded he merely grunted and relapsed into silence. After a few moments however, Judith showed in Eli and then I understood the delay in broaching the business.

'Now,' I said, making it easy for them, 'you've called about Mahitabel, I take it. Called to take her home I hope.'

'Indeed no,' said Mr. Thomas with a glance that was almost coy in its sidelong significance. 'Indeed no. As the elder who has known you from childhood, as the father of the offender and as your minister we have come to tell you that you have done a very foolish thing. And a very wrong thing. Young you are yourself and a single man. Your own reputation will be ruined. Maybe perhaps you will think of that even if justice means nothing to you.'

Before I could reply Eli weighted in with that dangerous eloquence of his, ready to exhort as to persuade, powerful alike in reason and in bigotry.

'You're young, lad, as Mr. Thomas has said. We are all older men, men of experience. This kind of thing has got to be stopped at the beginning. We must punish the first offender so that offences may cease. We have other young women here and the devil is ever ready to lead the poor young things astray. Only by making the consequences painful enough can we keep them from sinning. Mahitabel Pikle, disowned by her family, exiled to the Mill to ponder her folly and wait her time is not an enviable creature nor one to be lightly imitated. Mahitabel Pikle, riding back in triumph on Mr. Philip's own mare, with one man to lead her in, another to make her welcome and two more to pity her and think her hardly done by, that, you will agree, is another matter. If she'd done something fine and noble you could hardly have treated her better.

'Can't you *see*, lad, this is a new place, this is the first downright sin we've had to deal with. We *must* make the result of sin so horrible that every other light-minded girl in the moment of temptation shall pause and say, "What happened to Mahitabel Pikle?" and put temptation behind her. Isn't that worth the tears of one woman? Women are weak things, they've got to be guarded and fenced round and made so that they dare not transgress.'

Speaking so emphatically he failed for breath and before he could speak again I said,

'Unlike most sins, Eli, this is one that hurts only the sinner and hurts her most of all. Nothing that you can do, no punishment that you can devise will be worse than the pangs of birth, which a woman can hardly ignore even in the moment of temptation. A girl willing to risk that wouldn't hesitate to remember Mahitabel Pikle. There's another aspect too. Ask yourselves this, all of you, of what value is virtue which only resists temptation because of the memory of another's punishment? It seems to me a sorry thing; so does putting down one wrong by means of another. This isn't like theft or murder. And it isn't as though the girl were merely wanton. If her father hadn't rejected Simon Whistlecraft's suit with scorn that he ought to remember with shame, the girl would now be as respected a matron, as happy a prospective mother as any in Zion....'

I looked at my hearers. The three faces were like three masks of indifference, Eli's carved in stone, Mr. Thomas' in suet, Pikle's in chalk. I could see that my words were carrying no weight at all. Desperately I turned to Eli, exerting so much personal force that I tired myself.

'Eli, do you remember Marshalsea, and the days when we were all begging my father to be tolerant, to listen to us and modify his point of view. Today *you* are in his place and I am begging you to be tolerant, to modify your view....'

Eli tweaked his beard and I thought for one moment that I had him.

'I can't see what call you have to excite yourself about the wench. It's none of your business at all.'

'It's as much my business as the way Marshalsea was farmed. *I* wasn't trying to wring a living out of Sweatmore, was I?'

I had overshot my mark.

'I'm beginning to think, Mr. Philip, that you like being on the opposite side, whichever that may be. Either you have an argumentative mind simply, or maybe you have a grudge against one of us as you had against your father and that always makes you disagree with what we try to do for the common good. If you hadn't so girded against the setting up of stocks we'd have them at this minute for Mahitabel Pikle's correction.'

'Maybe he has another reason, a good and sufficient reason that no one else knows, see you, why he should be so strong in the defence of a woman he's never even been *seen* talking with.'

'Shut your filthy mouth,' I cried, whirling on the little Welshman. 'Go on, get up, take yourself out of this house, you pollute it.' He rose from his seat and began to make for the door. 'Hurry,' I shouted, 'unless you want help from behind.'

Eli and Pikle rose too. Eli had the temerity to lay a hand

on my shoulder and speak as though I were a restive horse. 'Steady,' he said, 'steady.' I flung the hand off.

Pikle, most nearly concerned of us all, now spoke for the first time. 'Mr. Ollenshaw, I've come to take my ... the woman back to the Mill. If Mr. Thomas feel that exposure in the stocks tomorrow will at once help her to atone and be a warning to others I and my family must bear the shame. Thou heard'st just now from his lips only what everyone will be saying if thou persist with thy mistaken notion of kindness. . . .'

'You have to have a filthy mind to think things like that, and Zion hasn't so many of *them*, thank God. And your daughter stays here, for ever if she wants to. Understand that. If you use force to get her I shall resist with force. Good night.'

By this time we were all outside the door and I shouted to Andy to bring round Mr. Pikle's horse. Eli looked at me with puzzled resentment and walked away through the trees.

'That was a dirty swipe,' said Andy loudly, jerking a thumb at Mr. Thomas as he mounted Pikle's conveyance.

'How do you know?'

'We was all in the hall, listening at the crack of the door.'

'You're a lot of miserable eavesdroppers then,' I said harshly.

'Well, Mahitabel was there first, and she began to cry again so Judy went to her, and then we all joined on because it sounded good. Then we was afraid you'd hear the girl crying so Judy took her upstairs again.'

'Might have had sense enough for that in the first place. That talk wasn't for her ears of all others.'

I went into the kitchen where Judith was making supper. She gave a glance to the ceiling to indicate Mahitabel in the room above and said, 'She's settled down nicely now I've told her you mean her to stay here.'

So suspecting nothing we sat down to supper and afterwards smoked our pipes and talked things over and decided that even Mr. Thomas' strange spite against the girl couldn't last for ever and that it would all blow over in time.

At last I knocked out my pipe and asked Judith to make a bowl of bread and milk thinking that I would take it up to her myself and reassure her about her welcome to stay.

I told Judith to put the food in the best blue bowl and myself got out one of Nathaniel's silver spoons with an apostle on the handle. Women notice such things.

I limped upstairs and tapped at the door. There was no answer and just to assure myself that she was sleeping in peace I opened the door a crack and peeped in. A candle was burning, low and smokily, but it gave enough light for me to see that the bed was tumbled and empty. I called sharply, 'Mahitabel. Mahitabel.' There was no answer until Judith asked from the stairs, 'Did you call me?'

'She's gone,' I said.

We searched the house thoroughly, but without hope, then we lighted lanterns and set out, waving them and calling her by name. We went as far as the Mill House and within the night's course knocked up everyone in the village with the question, 'Have you seen anything of Mahitabel Pikle?' No one had. As soon as it was light Ralph and Mike went back along the river to the Mill and this time they found her, drowned in the mill pool.

They brought her home, limp and dripping with weed in her hair and green slime across her face. Judith washed and laid her out, sacrificing one of her clean summer gowns for the purpose.

I sent word to the Gap and to Mr. Thomas and to Eli, but no word came. On the second day I sent to the minister and said, 'What about the funeral?'

He made it quite clear to me that so far as he was concerned there was going to be no funeral. 'Suicide is a mortal sin,' he said.

So Andy and I made her a coffin and when we had laid her in it with a little shavings-stuffed pillow beneath her head I could see quite well what Simon, the swarthy, robust fellow had seen in her. She had a pallor and a frailty that was appealing and in death the marks of tears had gone from her face leaving it serene below the limp fair hair that Judith had combed out so carefully.

We had dug a grave for her beneath the trees on my side of the river and I again said what I could remember of the old burial service as we lowered her into it. We patted the mound smooth and as I turned away I said, 'I shall never set foot in the meeting place as long as Mr. Thomas holds office.' Mike replaced his battered old hat and said, 'Well, that's something to be thankful for.' As we turned away a sound on the other side of the little clearing arrested me and turning I saw Linda, out of breath from running. She had a tiny bunch of rosemary and lavender and two frostbitten little rosebuds in her hand.

I turned back, Mike and the others disappeared among the trees and Linda and I were alone. She went forward and laid the pitiable little offering on the grave and as she stooped I saw two tears fall from her eyes and lose themselves in the raw moist soil.

There was a scent of upturned earth on the air, and now, mingling with it the clean fragrance of rosemary, a combination that I shall remember till I die. Linda slowly drew out her handkerchief and wiped her eyes.

'If Eli knows that you came, and brought the flowers ...' I began in a voice that wasn't quite steady.

'*If* he knows,' she said in a voice of iron, so unlike her own that it might have been the voice of a stranger. 'He doesn't have to know everything. And thanks to you the flowers are my own.' She looked at the grave again and then said sadly, 'I wish I'd known her, well enough for her to have told me about it. I could have stopped her.'

'If she'd told us,' I said, with my eyes on the line where the black hair met the white brow, 'we'd all have stopped her.'

'Oh you would, I know, Philip, you're so kind. But some of the others wouldn't. They'd have held her under. But I didn't mean that. I could have stopped the *reason*. Nobody need have a baby if she doesn't want to. Oh, I know I have the twins and I'm quite fond of them now but when I first knew I was appalled. But I was at sea you know, and nothing grows there. But I haven't had any more, have I? And I shan't. But that isn't Eli's fault. He'd like twelve, like Jacob or whoever he was. Sometimes he wonders. I can see him. But that's another thing I keep to myself, or have until now. You're dangerously easy to talk to, Philip. You've got the one heart left in Zion. All the others have just got stones, with the ten commandments graved on them.'

'Oh, far more than ten,' I said, 'there's nothing about not smoking, or drinking, or staying away from meeting in the original lot. Still, I do believe in a way that these people do right as they see it. And I do admit that they are a moral community, truthful and honest and industrious which is saying a lot. The only one I really intensely dislike is . . .'

'Eli?' asked Linda, cutting into my sentence.

'Oh no. I disagree with him, over, I suppose, every matter under the sun, but I don't dislike him. No, it's that slimy Mr. Thomas. He was intensely rude to me on Sunday and I shan't forget it in a hurry.'

'You know, he went against Eli over Keziah's affair and I really thought, I did quite hope that Eli would fall out with him over it. But he simply said, "Thomas acted as it seemed right to him", and they were on good terms next day.'

'That's because Eli trusts him, because he thinks he's godly. He wouldn't suspect him of spite or a purposely wrong judgement. If it had been me now . . .'

'He's just as tolerant of you actually, Philip. Perhaps you should know that. He came home on Sunday and said that you were very much misguided but sincere and that your wrong ideas were due to faulty upbringing.'

'Well, thank you, Linda, for bringing me such good news. I shall sleep better o' nights after that! Tolerance of that kind is damnably patronising don't you think?'

Her face hardened again, exactly as it had on the night when I had criticised my father to her. Strange to see this older, altered face set in those same lines.

'No, I don't, Philip. It isn't *in* him to be patronising. He's extremely narrow and fanatically religious, I see that now. And he's hard as a stone over a great many things. But he wouldn't understand spite or that kind of spiritual pride. Or would he? I don't know. I suppose I'm biased. You see, when all that awful time was and I realised that what you had told me about your father was true, and more, Eli seemed, well, I daresay it sounds silly, but he did seem like God to me. All my life since I was about twelve I'd had a mad old man on one side of me and a lot of rogues on the other. Men in our lodgings, men we owed money to, men in the streets. Then there was your father, he seemed so different, so good and kind to us and he was worst of all I think. After that, Eli, who gravely explained that he ought to marry me because he'd seen me in a torn bed-gown—well he just seemed like something from another world altogether. It was like being washed, Philip, when you're very dirty. Can you understand that?'

'Cleansed with hyssop? I always thought that sounded an unpleasant process! Especially when it condemns you to spend your whole life, dreadfully clean, in company with the hyssop.'

She puckered her brow and looked at me, puzzled for a moment. Then she said,

'Oh, with Eli, you mean. Well, you know, he's strict but he's just and he doesn't come home in a bad temper when things have gone wrong with him. And in a place like this—he fits, doesn't he? He's big and strong and not afraid of anything. Of course I'm not good enough. I deceive him and he says I spoil the children and I still have a worldly mind.'

'For which God be thanked. I think we must meet a little more often and give our worldly minds exercise.'

'I'll come and see you next time Keziah calls. She won't forgive Eli and always comes when he's not in the house, but she adores the babies, especially the naughty one, James, so although she hates me she can't keep away from them. But she'll be wanting to go now. Good-bye, Philip.'

She smiled at me and settled the cloak primly on her shoulders. In the few steps that it took her to pass the grave again and cross the little clearing I could recognise the old swallow-like swooping grace of movement. It had returned because she was not walking beside Eli.

As soon as she had disappeared I sat down on a stump, got my pipe going and thought over what she had said. It was plain enough that she and Eli were ill-matched, not of one mind; but she had made it equally plain that Eli's personality had a powerful hold upon her still. And even more plain, more horribly obvious, was the fact that she had not the slightest idea of my feelings towards her. That straight direct gaze, the frankness of our conversation left no slightest doubt of that. Why, I wondered, did she never guess, never hear behind my casual or testy words the hot avowals, never see the heart hammering at my throat, the ill-concealed hunger of my gaze. Ah well, thank God that she didn't. It was easier this way. One ill-advised word, one misplaced step and the friendliness which was all that I had of her might be spoiled for ever. I spent a little while reflecting upon the deadliness of friendship between man and woman. Judith, now, was never my friend. She could be the remotely efficient ruler of my kitchen, she could flash out at me in temper, stab me with a mocking glance or word, but somehow the remoteness, the temper and mockery were far less dividing than a phrase such as, 'You're dangerously easy to talk to.'

I could feel depression settling down on me, not just an intangible mental gloom but a physical state that slowed the pulses and made the stomach hollow, the hands and feet cold. I swore, knocked out my pipe and stood up. Before I left the place I looked once more at the little posy upon Mahitabel's grave. I remembered Linda's little hands, chilblained and rough and scored by dozens of little cracks that could not be cleaned properly. The pang that the memory sent through me showed me only too well that nothing, no disappointment, no friendliness, no proof of Eli's power could ever shake or change me. I loved her.

At my swiftest and most rocking pace I hurried back to my house. There I found Judith Whistlecraft carefully laying out the household supply of salt in an enormous cross on the newly scribbled floor of the spare chamber where Mahitabel's corpse had lain. I stared at the salt already spread and watched her as she dipped her hand into the stone jar, brought out another handful and scattered it. Salt was so valuable, so niggardly hoarded, so carefully outdoled that I could hardly believe my own sight.

'What on earth is the idea of this?' I asked, when I had reassured myself that it was salt and that the dampness of the floor was beginning to work upon it. She straightened her back and pushed away the tawny hair that had fallen into her eyes.

'You don't want her ghost walking here, do you?' she asked roughly.

'Do you think that would stop it?'

'I'm sure it will.'

'What nonsense,' I exclaimed. 'Stop wasting that salt. Do

you hear me? We've none too much as it is. Why should she trouble us, even if she could. We did what we could for her, poor girl.'

Unheeding she put a last handful upon one of the arms of the cross and replaced the lid on the jar.

'I don't know any whys or wherefores,' she said, with an air of dismissing the subject. 'But I do know that she killed herself. And I do know that we're put here for just so long and that if we're cut off violently, we pace out our time.'

For some reason unknown to me those last five words rang in my mind with a doom like note. Perhaps it was their supreme simplicity, or the word 'pace' so unusually employed. 'We pace out our time.' It was like a law being laid down.

I forgot the waste of the salt and the calm way in which she had gone on spreading it after I had told her to stop. My eyes went to the open window and the bright winter sunset beyond. I saw suddenly the world spread out like an enormous map, and over it, tentlike, the sky stretched. And on the earth, beneath the sky I saw men, like ants, going about their business. I saw one group separate themselves, cross the sea and toil over land until they reached a resting place. Of that group three detached themselves, little ant Eli, little ant Philip and little ant Linda. I thought how strange it was that out of all the wide earth, out of all living people, out of all ages of time, these three little atoms of life should have collided, should have learned one another's names, spoken and touched.

Was it all planned out? All arranged? And if so, by whom? Some remote being perhaps, who bored by omnipotence and omniscience, having nothing to wonder or to be curious about, knowing that the tide would wash in and out and that the acorn would inevitably become an oaktree, had tried to enliven the tedium of timelessness by staging a puppet show. Perhaps this urgent pressing life that we, the puppets, found so engrossing and important, was nothing more than an hour's entertainment for the gods.

Then my mind lurched suddenly and I saw the world, the sky and the little people with all their hopes and labours, their ambitions, troubles and loves spinning away down the slopes of eternity, of no more importance or permanence

212

than the leaves which fell from the trees into the stream and were gone.

What matter then that I loved Linda, or that she was married to Eli? Nothing, nothing on earth mattered at all.

Judith's voice with a note of terror in it broke in on me.

'Oh, master, what can you see?'

'Nothing,' I said. 'Nothing at all.' Then, recovering myself with an effort I said, firmly, 'What should I see, you foolish girl? Mahitabel's body is lying at peace under the trees by the river and her ghost, that is her spirit, has returned to God, who gave it,' I added, quoting the words that I had spoken how many aeons earlier. 'Shut the window and come away.'

But in the abyss into which I had unwillingly been gazing, there was neither God nor spirit. There was only the sorry, vulnerable, transient flesh, under whose cover we pace out our time.

Going downstairs, with Judith's eyes still following me fearfully, I thought, even despite ourselves we must hang on to the idea of God because without the thought, the belief of an idea, a plan, a controlling Hand behind it all the whole thing is too horrible to be contemplated. But I thought, clumping off the lowest step, it need not be Eli's stern Jehovah. There have been many before Him, and there will be others after, and each man must find his own.

'One dish of salt on the table in future, and that not too full,' I said over my shoulder.

'Yes, master,' said Judith, and there was no mockery this time.

The year turned and the Spring came on, outwardly a season of sowing and strenuous labour, inwardly a time of unrest, of unleaping desire. There were moments when love decked every tree with the buds of promise and called in the voice of every singing bird.

Early in January Hannah Wright had borne her child, the poor posthumous Harry Jacob who had lost, not only his father but his embryo wits in that morning's tragedy and was destined to grow up into the dreaded, though harmless village idiot. As soon as she was about again Hannah announced her intention of going back to the Mill and carrying on Harry's trade. The double tragedy of the gloomy place had no terrors for this grave woman, aged before her time.

'There's good stuff in that wench, for all she's so whey-faced,' said Ralph admiringly. Very soon, as the evenings grew lighter, he took to gobbling his supper hastily and rushing out on some errand of his own. One day he admitted, half shamefacedly, that he was helping up at the Mill. It was more than a woman could manage alone.

The rest of us smiled knowingly and awaited developments. February came with green evening skies and the wild geese going Northwards with a whirr of wings. The black-faced ewes dropped their second lot of long-legged woolly lambs. Nor were they the only additions, both Lucy Steggles and Mary Carter had babies. And the Spring or something worked in Judith's rejected Jake Crane and he married Edith Lomax who blossomed in one day, it seemed, from a frigid, pallid rather soured girl into a rosy happy young wife.

In all this time I had kept my vow and not set foot in the meeting house. My household, only too happy to have a good reason, stayed away too. Ralph used to go up to the Mill early on Sundays and mind young Harry Jacob while Hannah went to meeting. His way of minding the baby was to settle him comfortably on a pile of sacks and get the Mill working. He used to come home, dusty and tired but singing happily late in the evenings. One evening Mike asked him flatly when he intended to marry her.

'I don't intend at all,' he said shortly.

'Does she know that?'

'I dunno. She said once that her heart was in Harry's grave and I've never made an effort to get it out.'

'You'll get her talked about,' said Mike. He spoke so seriously that knowing that he was more in touch with the life and opinions of Zion than any of us, owing to his trade and his visits to various houses, I asked,

'Does that mean they're talking already?'

'Oh no. At least, not to my knowledge,' said Mike off-handedly. But after Ralph had gone, yawning and stretching to bed, he said,

'That was a lie I told you just this minute. You'll have noticed that there's been no rain this month. Well, you'll be sorry to hear that that is because evil is creeping into this holy community. There's one whole household that I needn't mention by name which profanes the Sabbath every week. There's a young unmarried man, who shall likewise be nameless who spends far too much time with a young woman whose husband has not been long dead. And there are other nameless ones who get far too much satisfaction out of a pipe and a glass. All this has got to be altered. In token of which, Mr. Councillor Ollenshaw and myself are ordered to attend a meeting tomorrow night.'

'Who told you all this?'

'The reverend Mr. Thomas stopped me this evening when I was coming from Mrs. Steggles'. She isn't getting on as she should and the youngster is not yet christened. He was going down there to fuss about it and I warned him that if he did anything to upset my patient he'd have me to reckon with. Did he like it? He did not. And I'll bet he slunk back there as soon as I was out of the way. I can't understand Steggles.'

Next evening Mike and I cleaned ourselves after a heavy day. It was true that there had been no rain for weeks and the soil in the fields was dusty, the thin green corn far less lively than the weeds that we warred upon. The dust was in our hair, our eyes and our nostrils and worked into cakes between our sweaty toes.

The day's work, the wash and change of clothing and the good hot supper that Judith had ready had cast me into a peaceful mood. The twilight seemed to linger lovingly as we made our way to the meeting house where the women's old sleeping place had been furnished with seven stools, a rough wooden table and a supply of candles.

I was in the state of mind where I found it easiest to think that they must run the place as they liked. I could be an active minority no more. I didn't intend to go to meeting whatever they said, I should still smoke my pipe and occasionally join Mike in his drinking. As for Ralph he must either bow to their censure and stay away from the Mill, or marry Hannah, or ignore what was said. Mahitabel's case had proved to me that these men were implacable and indifferent to argument: and perhaps if I hadn't interfered she might have sat in the stocks and felt purged of sin and have been alive today.

Mr. Thomas took his place by the middle stool, fell on his knees and started to pray aloud. He prayed for guidance, for patience, for blessing in our work and for a single good mind among those who had the welfare of the people in their hands. Then he settled his fat behind on the too-narrow seat of the stool and the meeting began.

'Seventeen months have passed away since first our thankful eyes lighted upon this blessed spot. We have been, like Martha, busy about many things, but now the time has come when we must, like Mary, seek the better part....' The monotonous sing-song of his voice droned over the carefully prepared phrases and though I did not listen to every word the meaning of the speech reached me well enough. Zion was to be tightened, cleansed, dedicated, purged. He used all those words.

He made several things clear through the wordiness. Every able-bodied person was to be compelled to attend the meeting every Sunday. Fines were to be instituted for swearing, drinking fermented liquor, smoking tobacco, absence from meeting. Every householder, according to his means was to offer to Mr. Thomas a contribution from his yard or his fields because Mr. Thomas found that his spiritual duties prevented him from engaging efficiently in husbandry. Loose behaviour such as that which had recently given rise to scandal in the village was to be stopped. And Mr. Thomas still thought that the erection of stocks and the threat of using them would be a good deterrent.

They were the chief points. He ended poetically, 'if we are of one mind in these things nothing can withstand us and we can make of this favoured spot a little Eden, a second garden where God may walk at eventide surveying His work and seeing that it is good.'

There was a suitable silence. Then Mike shuffled his stool and I realised that everyone was looking at me. It was as though I alone had been guilty of all the misbehaviour and must answer for it now.

'About the meeting...' I began at last, able to bear the

eyes and the silence no longer.

'I stopped coming.'

'We know.'

'And you know why, too, don't you? Because I found that the people who were foremost at meeting were cold and hard and cruel and spiteful where ordinary humanity was concerned. On the day, Mr. Thomas, that I was compelled to bury Mahitabel Pikle in unhallowed ground and without the benefit of your office I swore never to attend another meeting where you officiated. And it will have to be a very powerful argument that will move me from that decision.'

Forgetting that instead of my solid chair I had only a three-legged stool beneath me, I tried to lean back with impressive nonchalance and the stool tottered and I had to clutch Mike's shoulder to recover my balance. They waited until I was steady again. Then Crane said, unexpectedly reasonable, 'Thou must see, Mr. Ollenshaw, that every community must have some laws to guide it. In the sad case of friend Pikle's erring daughter we acted according to our convictions. And though thou sawest fit, most lamentably to thwart its course nevertheless the law is right when it tries to punish sin.'

'And who makes a thing a sin. A lot of men getting together like this and passing laws. If you have your way tonight when we go from here every man who is fond of his glass or his pipe will be a sinner. Any man who refuses to give a portion of his hard-earned goods to Mr. Thomas will be a sinner. I'm fond of my pipe and occasionally I drink. Mike here is fond of his glass and occasionally smokes. I completely fail to see why Mr. Thomas shouldn't till his soil for himself. And for these actions and beliefs although at this moment I am not a sinner tomorrow morning I shall be.'

'You have mounted the wrong horse there,' said Mr. Thomas. 'These things that we have named are displeasing to God. In a loose community they continue, heedlessly to displease Him. Here we mean to root them out.'

'If the majority of us here tonight decide to lay down rules against these things then disobedience to them is wrong.' That was Eli. I twisted round on my stool.

'Eli Makers,' I said flatly, 'in the place from which we took quite a lot of trouble to free ourselves, the majority of men were quite willing to go to church, to look at candles and crosses and a railed-in altar and to sing their responses. In fact the law ordered that they should. By your present reasoning being in the majority made them right. But I seem to remember your thinking quite otherwise in Shad's forge.'

But tonight I couldn't rouse Eli. He looked at me quite sternly but his eyes were benevolent, not flashing. Also he began by calling me 'Mr Philip' which was always his address to me when cajoling.

'Mr. Philip, you've an advantage over the rest of us. You've a quick mind, you've book-learning. You had your spell in London where no doubt you sharpened your wits on better brains than we can boast. Mr. Gore thought highly of you. Now we are all simple men' (here Mr. Thomas began to frown and bridle, but Eli didn't even see him) 'but sometimes the wise are confounded and the way is made clear to the simple. We're not making rules for the sake of making them, as you seem to think. We believe that smoking and drinking and loose living and staying from meeting are bad things and that by not taking action before this we have displeased God.'

'But, Eli, why do you think you have? In what way is He displeased?'

'He has withheld rain—and other things,' said Eli gravely.

My mind gave a leap and despite my best efforts I felt a smile widen my lips. I put up my hand to hide it. No other person there knew but *I* knew that Eli believed that because Zion was not strict enough Linda was having no other children! It was so funny and at the same time so appallingly primitive that I could have roared with laughter and shouted with rage at the same time. In order to distract my own attention I hurriedly selected the other point with which I wanted to deal and said,

'And about this loose living. I don't see any myself, but I've heard a whisper that people are talking about Mrs. Wright and Ralph Whistlecraft. And I wish the tongues that wag round that subject could rot and drop out. I happen to know that Ralph goes up there on the purest charity. And he goes in the evenings because there is no time during the day. If that is loose living it's a pity there isn't more of it.'

Mr. Thomas wetted his lips.

'Wasting our time we are,' he said. 'When the said Ralph Whistlecraft returned from Salem he brought me a letter from the Reverend Alfred Bradstreet in which he begged and exhorted me to do what I could to put this community upon a sound footing. And that we must do. We have had before us the shining example of Salem and we shall be lacking in our duty if we allow mere exchanges of words, however clever, to deflect us from our course.'

'There's just this to add,' said Eli, 'if you can't bring yourself to see eye to eye with us, or at least to act with us, Mr. Philip, the only fair and just thing is for you to resign.'

I thought that over. Then I said slowly, 'I wish I could. In order to explain why I can't I must tell you something that I have never mentioned before. The fact that we are here today, that you, Eli, are not fretting away your life and your talents on a hired acre or two, that you, Crane and Pikle, are not outcast and persecuted in Salem, that you, Mr. Thomas, have any kind of a ministry at all is due entirely to one man, Nathaniel Gore. Unfortunately for all of us he died before he could set his seal upon his work. His last words to me were a reminder of something he had said much earlier to me in criticism of the Salem that Mr. Thomas so much admires: and after his death I found a letter addressed to me in which he commended to my care what he called his dream of a land made for men's enjoyment. I haven't got it here but anyone is at liberty to read it at my house and anyone who does so will find in it these words, "I don't like Salem. I couldn't have been happy there. I am not looking forward to the stay that we must make in Alfred Bradstreet's holy land. (The letter you should know, was written at sea.) There must be some mean between licentiousness and dreariness, between the worship of vice and the tyranny of virtue." The letter ended with an exhortation to me to find it if I could. And that is why I do not intend to resign and why I shall always be against anything that smacks to me of interference with individual liberty.'

There was another long uncomfortable silence. Mr.

Thomas broke it. 'Mr. Gore was a good man, but he was not God.'

'No,' I said, 'but he was as near as any man I have known. And for his sake I will compromise with you. I will return to meeting myself and I will persuade my household to come with me. I'll agree to a fine for swearing in a public place and for drunkenness outside a man's own home. If there ever is any evidence of what you call loose living I'll discuss it with you again. And I think that contributions for Mr. Thomas' upkeep should be voluntary.'

'You've expressed my views exactly,' said Mike. 'I kinda feel that I'm the drunkard you've all got in mind and I'll be very careful not to come outside when I have drink in me even if someone calls me to a deathbed. And now if you'll excuse me I have a visit to make to Mrs. Steggles.'

'I'll walk with you,' I said, glad of an excuse to get away.

When we were outside I said, 'If you're in a hurry, Mike, I won't come with you. I just wanted to get away.'

'I'm in no hurry,' he said, suiting his step to mine. 'I'm just taking the poor woman something to make her sleep.' He shook his coat pocket and I heard the rattle of the pills in the little birch-bark box which Mike, from some lingering sense of professional pride, took pains to fashion for each patient.

'You missed your vocation, you know,' he said presently, 'you should have taken to the law. It's a fine tongue you have.'

'Oh no, Mike. I'm not cool enough. I get angry. But then, wouldn't it make you angry to hear how Ralph's action, for instance, is criticised?'

'They recollect poor Mahitabel and Simon I fancy. And it's possible that in any place a couple, young as they are, who spent every evening together like that would get talked about. But all this other humbug, you know, we must make Zion strict because otherwise God won't let it rain, well really that is as bad as the old African medicine men. Sometimes I think mankind doesn't move forward at all, that we just go in a circle and that this age's religion is just another name for yesterday's superstition.'

Just as we turned off the main path to go up to Steggles' place Pikle and Crane passed us on their way back to the

Gap. With their long thin legs they were rapid walkers and the fact that they had not passed us before led me to think that an indignation meeting had followed the formal one.

One window of the tiny wooden house showed a steady candle-light, the other the flicker of a fire.

'I'll wait out here, it's quite warm and there's a stump to sit on. Steggles won't want company just now.' We could hear the feeble steady wailing of the new baby though we were still some yards from the door when I halted.

'I shan't be long,' said Mike.

I folded my coat tails into a pad against the roughness left by Joseph's axe, sat down and got my pipe going. With my tired ironed leg crossed over the other I was soon comfortable and almost drowsy. I didn't even think about the meeting but was in a kind of dream in which I saw the Zion of several years ahead, with a proper road to the Gap and pack-horses making regular journeys to the sea, and a street where shops could hang out their signs.

The baby had stopped wailing soon after Mike's entrance and the silence was intense. Suddenly, far away it was broken and I raised my head to listen. Soon I could identify the noise of more than one horse's hoofs and wondered whether Pikle or Crane had reached home to find something that brought him hotfoot back to the village, or whether some of their horses had broken out and were stampeding.

It was very dark and I could see nothing, but I got up and drew back into Joseph's gateway. As it drew level with me however the thudding changed to a slithering and a voice, quite strange to me, cried, 'It was true, thank God. Here's a house.' I could at this distance just see three horses, each with a rider, one of whom had a body slung like a sack across his saddle.

I stepped forward and said, 'You're in a place called Zion. Where do you come from?'

'Does this house belong to you? Can we enter? I'm afraid I have a dying man here. Edward, help me with him, you too, sir, if you please. Zillah stay where you are and mind the horses.'

The voice that rattled out the orders was quick and arrogant.

221

'Wait a minute,' I said. 'I don't know whether you can be accommodated here. It's only a two roomed shack and there's a sick woman and two small babies. You'd better come down to my house. It isn't far. And I could borrow a lantern.'

'Is there by any chance a doctor in this place?'

'He's inside there now.'

I went to the door and pressed down the latch. Mike was replacing his coat and talking soothingly to Joseph. '... as right as rain now. You'll have to get the baby fed for a day or two as well as you can. Mrs. Carter might help, she's got plenty of milk.'

'I'm sorry,' I said, 'but we've more trouble outside here.'

'Keep it out then, for God's sake,' said Mike, 'she's just dozing off. Fetch a lantern will you, Joseph?'

We went outside and Mike closed the door firmly behind him.

By this time the man with the arrogant voice and the other one were carrying the wounded man towards the house.

'Accident?' asked Mike laconically.

'Shot in the breast, badly. I've done what I could, but we were riding for our lives. Is it really necessary to go any further?'

'I might plug him up here, if you'll keep quiet. There's a very sick woman inside. All right, Joseph, I'll have a look. Clear the table will you?'

Joseph Steggles, moving with clumsy stealth, cleared the table and held the lantern high. They laid the wounded man on the table and as his head fell backwards the man with the voice motioned to the boy to go outside again and himself stepped round and supported the head in his hands. I went outside as well.

'Where do you come from?' I asked the boy.

'Dixonville,' he said. 'I say, do you mind if I go and stand with my sister? She's rather nervous and she's had enough to make her.'

'Where's Dixonville?' I asked as we went towards the horses.

'North of here. From Salem you come almost to Burnt Hills, but you don't cross, you go North instead.'

'Well,' I said, 'and what has been happening there?' He stopped walking and gave a little shaky laugh,

'Isn't that funny, one always leaves out the main thing. We've had the most *awful* Indian raid. Nobody got out except us, and we shouldn't if it hadn't been for Geoffrey. He's the one in there. He's a kind of cousin of ours. Hullo, Zillah, are you all right?'

'Yes, but I'm so tired,' said the girl in a flat sweet little voice. 'Can't they take us in?'

'Not here,' I said. 'You're coming home with me. I'll go and see how long they'll be. Maybe we could go ahead.'

But when I re-entered the kitchen Mike was drawing the bloody shirt back over the breast of the unconscious man.

'He'll do,' he said, 'it's missed his heart and clotted over nicely. I can't do any more till we get down to the house where my tools are. I'll take out the bullet and dress it properly then. What happened to you all anyway?'

For the tall man had a bloody clout round his head and moved stiff-leggedly.

'Indians. Have you had any trouble yet?'

'We lost one man and a few beasts last year. Nothing so far yet.'

'You will,' he said succinctly. 'Is that wagon nearly ready? I wish we had some brandy for him.' His manner was fidgety and impatient.

'Best without. Start him bleeding again most likely. And here's the wagon now.'

Joseph had thoughtfully forked straw over the wagon floor and we lifted the wounded man in carefully. I took the reins and Mike climbed up beside me. The two youngsters, hustled by the energetic young man, mounted and we trundled away through the darkness to my house.

At the sound of hoofs and wheels the house door flew open showing Andy and Judith outlined against the light in the kitchen.

'What's wrong?' asked Andy sharply. 'Master, are you all right?'

'Quite,' I said, starting to descend. 'Come and give a hand with the horses, Andy. Judith, we want hot water, beds and food. Where's Ralph?'

'Not back yet from the Mill.'

For the next hour or so the house was in a tumult. Mike, with the exquisite skill which lay awaiting the call beneath his casual manner extracted the bullet, washed and plugged and bound the wound.

'He'd better have Ralph's bed, Mike,' I said, 'then you can keep an eye on him in the night. Ralph can come in with me, that'll save making up any other bed. Judith will share with the young lady and the other two can go in the guest room.'

They carried the man up and laid him in the bed.

'Now some brandy to bring him round,' said Mike, 'and after that some good strong broth. He's lost a lot of blood and I should judge he's older than he looks.'

'He's seventy,' said the young man.

While the operation was going forward in the kitchen the girl and boy had been eating in the parlour and as soon as they had finished they went thankfully to bed.

'Now,' said Mike, 'let's look at that head of yours.'

The young man untied the granny knot at the back of his head and removed the bandage, grimacing with pain as he did so, and I gave a cry of dismay as a great flap of his scalp tumbled forward, obscuring his eye.

'It's only a flesh wound,' he said, looking at me with the other eye. Mike began calmly to thread a needle.

I couldn't watch the performance. The mere idea of the needle at work upon that raw and bloody flesh turned my stomach into a churning well of nausea. Hastily I thrust a pipkin of Mike's brandy into the man's hand and made for the door, muttering that I must see whether Andy had bedded down the horses properly. He had, so I re-entered the house by the front door, went upstairs, clumsily made the bed in the guest chamber and replenished the fire. When I judged that the operation would be over I went into the kitchen again.

'... skull like a black's, that's what you've got,' Andy was saying as he washed his hands.

'God be thanked for that. One moment's unconsciousness would have been the end of all four of us.' Then, as he became aware of my presence he set down the brandy and rising made me a little formal bow.

'Sir, I am greatly in your debt. And I have not yet introduced myself. I am Geoffrey Montpelier, at your service. The young folk are my cousins, Edward and Zillah Cambody. The wounded man is none other than Dixon.'

He brought out the name with a kind of reverence and as he spoke I had an answer to the question that had been nagging at my mind ever since the boy had mentioned Dixonville.

'Sir,' I said, 'it is meet and proper that we should give him aid. We are Nathaniel Gore's men.'

'Well, of all strange things. And where is Mr. Gore?'

'Dead. He died at Fort Outpost on the journey. He often mentioned Dixon and his plans for settling. I believe it was his admiration for those plans that made him wish to found a similar settlement. But I did not even know whereabouts the place lay, or I would have made some effort to visit it.'

'We will hope,' said the young man gravely, 'that Mr. Gore's foundation will have better fortune than his friend's. They were burning the last house as we made our escape.'

'I must hear all about that,' I said. 'Will you come and take some refreshment and tell me the story. By the way, my name is Ollenshaw, Philip Ollenshaw.'

We went into the parlour where I threw another log on to the fire and lighted new candles. With so much hurry and business I had not found an opportunity of looking at him properly and I was now surprised to see that he was much younger than I had expected. I had never seen a face made up of so many planes. There was nothing curved or rounded about it. Everything was squared and flattened as though it had been cut from some malleable yet resilient material with a knife. Even the tip of his slightly tilted nose and the sockets of his eyes were squarish and his black smooth hair went back from a squarish forehead and then, on the unbandaged side fell back again like a fold of cloth. His eyes, at the moment sunken and over-bright were the vivid deep blue of cornflowers and he had long, thin humorous lips and small ears that stood out from his narrow skull.

'You have a nice establishment here, Mr. Ollenshaw,' he said, looking around him. The panelling by this time was finished and well beeswaxed, and although it was largely

225

the work of my own hands and therefore for some strange reason should not have been admired by me, I did like it. The whole room, though it was plain and only half furnished, had a solidity and a proportion that was pleasing at least to my eye.

We talked casually about building, timber and brick making until he had finished his supper. Then I offered him a pipe and we sat down on either side of the fire.

'Tell me about the Indians,' I said then.

'I don't want to alarm you,' he said with a sudden smile that made all the planes of his face shift and catch the light in different places. 'But I think it would be as well if you were prepared for a visit. We had no trouble at all until the end of last Summer. I suppose you heard all about King Philip's War. That was just ending when I landed and all the way to Dixonville I heard the same story, the Indian menace was over, they were finished, wiped out. I daresay you heard the same.' I nodded. 'We had a family or two at Dixonville who were more or less civilised, they'd do a little work now and then and act as guides when we wanted to go hunting. They owed a certain allegiance to a sort of petty chief whom we called Billico, a decent little fellow who came into the place once or twice and seemed friendly. We never had any trouble with them except when they'd been given stuff to do a job and then hadn't done it. But about at the end of the Summer we started losing things. Several horses went, one or two at a time, and then guns would be missing or somebody would find powder and shot gone. Dixon rounded them up and threatened to turn them out of the place if it went on. He was very good with them as a rule and I suppose it was because of that that Billico came in soon after and asked to see him. He told them that they were preparing for a great war with a tribe that had got guns from the French up by the Lakes. It seems, and mind this is only a story, that there was a chief born some years ago in the eclipse of the moon. And a wise woman foretold that he should have two meals, one of red meat and one of white and then he should rule all the land between the Lakes and the sea. He is called Troubled Moon and is a warrior of some skill and courage.

'Well, Dixon listened to all this and then, thinking he

knew Billico's crafty little ways, told him that the story was very interesting and that we would like our horses back. In the end Billico promised that they should be returned and took himself off. Next day there wasn't an Indian in Dixonville. I'd had a load of Dutch bulbs brought up from Salem and was waiting for the fellow who did a bit of garden work for me to come and put them in. He didn't come and at last I got sick of waiting and planted them myself. I was rather fond of my garden and meant to have daffodils and tulips in plenty this year. Then a couple of our men went out fishing and passed Billico's village and saw that it was all burned. Still the fools went on fishing and didn't come straight back as they might have to warn us. And the day after they did get back Troubled Moon and his braves arrived. Of course we were practically helpless. They'd got several guns and quite a lot of them were mounted and the rest had bows and arrows or bloody great tomahawks. It was a tomahawk did this.' He pointed to his wounded head. 'You see we weren't ready. We weren't even in one place. The houses at the West end were blazing before the rest of us knew about it. We got together then and tried to fortify Dixon's house which was the biggest and the one to which people naturally fled.' He stopped and shuddered. 'It was pretty awful, Mr. Ollenshaw. They have a way of fixing torches to arrows and shooting them at a building until it catches light. In the end when almost everyone was killed or wounded and the place was burning I grabbed Dixon and the Cambody children and made a dash for the horses that were in the yard. How we got through I shall never be able to tell you. But we did, and you may be grateful for that. How many men are you, all told?'

'Nineteen. One is fairly useless and two are elderly.' He threw out his hands in a gesture of resignation.

'That's horrible hearing. It's suicidal. What *was* Gore thinking of? Why, in Dixonville, even after the first houses were fired we were forty, fighting strength. And we were on open ground. Ah, well, if they come on here I have, like the nursery rhyme, lived to fight another day.' He knocked out his pipe in a gesture of finality. 'I think, if you don't mind, I'll get to bed. It seems a long time since I had my clothes off. And tomorrow there'll be a great deal to do.'

I led him up to the room where Edward Cambody was already sleeping the deep sleep of exhaustion, his fair young face rosy against the pillow.

'Did they lose anyone?' I asked.

'No. Fortunately they're both orphans. They have no one in the world except me.'

When I had bidden him good night I went as quietly as I could to the room that Andy and Mike were sharing with Dixon. It was a low long room and the candle by Mike's bed gave no light to the doorway. I picked it up and looked at the old man who seemed to be sleeping peacefully.

'He's asleep now,' whispered Mike, 'but while he was awake awhile since he talked fit to give us a nightmare. I only hope half of it was delirium.'

Not knowing what the old man had said I comforted him by saying, 'Maybe it was.' But as I made my way to my own room fear ran over me as water might from a bucket emptied over my head. There were forty men in Dixonville and three and a girl had come out alive. There were nineteen men in Zion!

As I undressed I thought of Harry Wright's body as we had found it in the wood. I remembered that Hannah had said that he had taken his gun. We had never found it. It might be one of those ranged against us. A pleasant last thought for the day.

Then, when I reached my room where I expected to find Ralph, for it was very late, I thought of other things beside Indians. My bed was smooth and empty. So he hadn't come home. For the others would have sent him along here if he had. Still, I reflected, as I climbed into bed and stretched out my weary body, it was no use worrying about both things. If the Indians came Ralph's behaviour would be forgotten in the general massacre. If they didn't I should be so much relieved that I could gladly deal with him. So shuffling off both considerations I resolutely composed myself for sleep.

In the morning Dixon was conscious and able to take the breakfast of broth which Mike tenderly spooned out to him. The Cambody brother and sister slept on, but Geoffrey Montpelier was early astir, and joined us at breakfast.

'We must do something about making at least one place in the settlement fireproof. That was where they had us. When a house is burning the stoutest defence is wasted. Even if you never see an Indian from now till Doomsday it would be a good thing to have one place fireproofed and well stocked with food and water.'

'There's the meeting house,' I suggested. 'We all lived there before we had our houses built. We could plaster it well with river clay. If they came straight from Dixonville here how long would it take?'

'Oh, but they won't. You see Troubled Moon believes that he can never have any luck except when the moon is on the wane. So he'll do nothing until after full moon. Billico told Dixon that and we realise now that poor little Billico wasn't just spinning a yarn. Also, and this is important, there was a good grog shop in Dixonville and that was the one place they didn't fire. The fellow who kept it had got tired of getting thimblefuls of stuff up from Salem so he'd made a still of his own and by some special process he could turn ordinary raw barley into as good a brew as you ever tasted. And the place was well stocked. I don't pretend to know a lot about Indians, Dixon is the man to ask about that, but I fancy they won't do a great deal about this march to the sea until the contents of that shop are almost exhausted. And quite apart from these theories, we rode quite hard for twenty-four hours and they're not all mounted by any means. You've got at least a week. Oh more, because I do believe that story about the moon.'

'I'll go and see Eli directly after breakfast,' I said, and at that moment Ralph walked in.

I introduced our guest and gave him the brief outline of the night's happenings and news. He was almost childishly relieved to find a counter interest in the house. But when he had finished breakfast I beckoned him outside.

'Well,' he began, before I could say anything at all, 'it happened, just as I always knew it would. She blundered down carrying a sack of flour and I picked her up and kissed her and there we were. But the pig-headed mawther still can't get in a mind to marry me.'

'She must,' I said flatly. 'I can't stop now to tell you all about the meeting last night, because I've got to see the

229

council about this Indian business. But I had to stick up for you, tooth and nail, and we simply can't have any more bother from your family. I mean, it'd simply make me look ridiculous. You go straight back, Ralph, and tell her that you've made all arrangements to marry her tomorrow. With this business hanging over our heads we can't afford to lose a day; and when the meeting is held to talk about defence I'll slip the word to Mr. Thomas.'

'But I'm not plumb sure that I want to marry her,' he protested, changing his ground immediately.

'Rubbish,' I said impatiently. 'What took you up there in the first place? What else would make a man work all day on Sunday? You won't admit you're in love with her because she's rather plain and serious and she won't admit that she loves you because you're a bit uncertain. Women aren't all fools you know. Off you go and ask her properly, as though you meant it. And don't come back here until she's said yes,' I shouted.

He turned meekly towards the Mill and I went on to Eli's reflecting that I could manage everyone's business better than my own.

I found Eli most curiously engaged. The two horses that I had given him were already harnessed to the wagon and he was loading it with miscellaneous gear. Two pigs with their feet tied were lying by the tail-board and at the moment he was lifting some hens into a netted space while others, from a safe distance squawked derisively. The cow seemed to recognise me and turned her tethered head from the side of the wagon and looked with what might have been pride at the calf tethered beside her.

'You needn't have bothered,' said Eli, lifting his head, 'I was coming over to your place as soon as I was sorted out.'

I blinked at him.

'Why, have you heard? How?'

'I've heard nothing, but naturally I guessed. 'Tisn't reasonable that I should have the use of your gear and profit by your beasts and then go against you as I have been doing.'

'Oh good God, Eli,' I said, 'that's all forgotten. Here, let those poor beasts run and then come and listen to me.

We've got something more than difference of opinion to bother about. I've got a lot of serious news.'

With big gentle hands Eli freed the pigs and the hens. Then I perched myself on his sawyer's block and told him everything that had happened last night and everything that Geoffrey Montpelier had told me.

'I've sent for the rest of the council,' I ended, 'and when they come we must get all the men together and see about fortifying the meeting house. Meanwhile the less said to the women the better.'

Eli stroked his beautiful golden beard. 'So it has come,' he said. 'Where are the others meeting?'

'Down at the meeting house.'

'We'll go then, shall we?'

As we turned out of the yard Linda came to the window with a child on either arm and looked out inquiringly. I waved to her, and at her order each of the babies waved a fat wrinkled fist at me.

'All the same, lad, you should take back your gear. In my mind I likened you to your father.'

'So should I you to yours very likely, if I'd known anything about him.'

'Did you never hear?' asked Eli, staring straight before him. 'He was a Mersea man my father. One night he fell down in a drunken stupor and was drowned in a little runnel of water not six inches deep. He was a fine man too, when he was sober. And he left ten children, all sons.'

'I suppose that is what makes you so set in your mind against liquor,' I said, putting a simple, human construction on Eli's mania.

'Not at all,' he said frowning, 'man is made in God's own image and a drunken man is a disgrace to it. I'd feel the same if I'd never had a father.'

For myself I doubted it. But I was not out to argue with Eli this morning.

Mr. Thomas had brought his newly written list of rules with him and was busily and innocently tacking it to the meeting house door when we arrived. I thought of the reason for which we had gathered and gave a half hysterical cackle of laughter as I watched his little hammer rise and fall, and saw the bunch of cobbler's tacks held inexpertly in the corner of his puffy mouth.

The council was frightened into approving of the plans for fortifying the meeting house and during the ensuing week while the moon waxed stronger and stronger the whole village worked like slaves, plastering the wooden walls and the roof with dripping clay dredged up from the river and then pressing sand and small stones into the surface of it. We dug a well, and fenced in, partly with clay-plastered timber, partly with stone, a stockade large enough to take a considerable number of the animals.

And all the time we worked I went on feeling the cold fear pouring over me. I could picture the terror and the confusion that there would be if ever this place were used for the purpose for which we were preparing it. Sometimes I could feel the tomahawk slicing into my skull as it had into Geoffrey Montpelier's and at such times his high spirits and gay good humour astonished me. Didn't one go on and on feeling the severed nerves.

He was popular in the settlement from the first morning when, with the clean bandage very white about his head and the blue coat still bearing the marks of blood, he strolled down to lend what strength remained in him to the work of fortification.

In part this popularity was due to the idea that he had come to warn us. In a way he had, but only because, riding hard and hoping that the rumour he had heard of a new settlement west of Fort Outpost might be true, he had come, inadvertently upon us. But in part, and that the greater, it was due to his own personality. He had, more than any man I have ever seen, the quality of being all things to all men. By that I do not mean that he was a humbug, far from it, but he did seem to have the knack of lighting on the very word that interested and pleased the person he was talking to. And also he had, for them perhaps as for me, the powerful attraction that goes with a person who comes from afar. Everything about him was strange. His manner of speaking, of flicking a speck of dust off the dirty coat, of laughing, of pushing back the square flap of hair, even his very bandage, set him apart.

Also, and this was remarkable in that community, the fact that he was, unmistakably, a gentleman made him

232

popular. Without boasting I can state the simple fact that I was, by birth the person who could most nearly lay claim to that state in Zion. But I had forfeited my claim because I had wrought with my hands, hacked timber, welded iron, shoed horses and worked in the fields. Geoffrey Montpelier merely rapped out orders and the meekness with which they were obeyed astonished me. Slowly but very surely I came to the conclusion that so long as the overlord is pleasant and benevolent and has the common man's good at heart—or seems to—the common man enjoys being told what to do. And I realised that what Zion had long lacked was the master's hand. Nathaniel had died and I had not adequately filled his place.

But I did realise too that Geoffrey Montpelier had charm as well as lordliness. When they asked him, half frightened, whether the Indians who sacked Dixonville were like those that they had seen tamely walking about in Salem he said, 'Oh no. Much dirtier. They can never steal up on the windward side of you. They stink like skunks.' And somehow that made the terror of them less. And that was what we needed. When a danger is so actual that you are driven to set guards as we did at night at the Gap and the Mill and to the East of Eli's farm, it is a help if that danger does not have the added terror of being vague and unknown.

'Indian war paint.' Consider that phrase, simple enough, but one which, if you consider for what reason it is put on and think that you are likely at any moment to meet it, is not simply a collection of harmless letters.

'They're easy enough to pot,' said Geoffrey Montpelier, 'because they've most thoughtfully drawn a damn great target in yellow ochre right in the middle of their foreheads.' Oh, cheering twist of thought, not something to dread, something to aim at. I believe even Eli forgave him for that *damn*.

A week passed without incident. The meeting house was provisioned and every household was ready to make for it at the first sign of trouble. The clay that we had plastered hardened. Dixon was able to be propped up in bed and then to sit out for short spells in the rocking chair that we heaved upstairs. Mr. Thomas made his rounds warning people about being absent from meeting and the rain came on the very Monday that followed the praying for it by the full assembly.

Ralph after two more assaults upon Hannah's determination not to marry him, returned on the Wednesday after the rain had started, triumphant at last. Mr. Thomas, informed of the impending marriage, though he took it as proof that his worst suspicions were well-founded was delighted with the sinner's repentance and the gloom that had been gathering over Ralph was dispelled as though by magic. He was quite frankly delighted to marry Hannah and I judged that she was not as whey-faced as he had thought.

Next day, Thursday, and the following Monday was to be the full moon. Geoffrey's impatience came to a head.

'I'm going to have a little scout around,' he announced. 'Once the moon is on the wane Troubled Moon will move and I should like to know whether he's aware of this place's existence. Would Judith pack me some food?'

'How much?' asked Judith, who alone of the household seemed to be impervious to his charm.

'Oh, enough for two days, maybe three,' he said carelessly. 'By the way, Zillah, my sweet, where were you last evening?'

Zillah reddened to the edge of her curly hair.

'Mark Pikle—you know him, Geoffrey, from the Gap, asked me to go there to see the calves. Edward came too, didn't you, Edward?'

The boy reddened in his turn.

'And was one of the calves named Mary, and did'st thou admire that one adequately?' asked Geoffrey mockingly. Edward's clear blush of embarrassment darkened to the brick red of fury.

'It's nothing to do with you. And if anybody's whereabouts are to be questioned where were you yourself?'

Geoffrey ignored the thrust.

'Oh yes it is, my child. Don't forget that I'm your legal guardian. Well, be good and confine your attention to young calves, until I come back. Mr. Ollenshaw I commend them to your charge.'

'I'll look after them,' I said, ignoring Edward's surly glance. 'And above all look after yourself and be sure to come back.'

'Could I fail?' he asked with one of his darting glances at Judith. She merely said, 'Here's your food. Eat the pie first. The rest will keep.'

'Which way shall you ride?' I asked as I stood beside him while he fixed the food to his saddle.

'Oh, up and down like Satan. Don't look so concerned, man. I shall return to trouble you again. Have you any message for Makers or his missus? I shall stop there to say good-bye to them.'

'No,' I said, 'I don't think I have.'

He mounted, as graceful and beautiful a man as I had ever seen. Lassie the mare, glossy coated and full of spirits after a week's rest and good feeding, set off, stepping high, tossing her head and girding at the rein. Her rider had discarded his bandage for the first time and the fall of black hair almost covered the rough puckered edges of Mike's needlework. Together they made a romantic picture and they were going on a romantic errand.

Judith stood by the kitchen door with her arms folded. She was watching him out of sight too. Suddenly I wondered.... Perhaps the mockery on his part and the shortness on hers covered something that they wanted for a while to remain secret. It was, the more I thought of it, a most probable thing. The gypsy girl was, in everything but status—and when has love tarried for that?—a fitting match for him. I remembered the question which Edward had asked and which had remained unanswered. Yes, Judith had been out too last evening. I remembered because I had been sitting with Dixon and had gone down to get him his broth and it had been left on the hob covered with a plate.

Well, if this Indian menace could pass over without catastrophe we should be able to give our attention to homely things again and this romance would be one of them.

Just before midday Linda hurried into the field where I was working. She seemed rather distressed and out of breath and as soon as she had given me a hasty greeting she said, 'Is Mike about?'

'He's in the yard somewhere. Why, Linda, what's the matter? Nothing wrong with the twins I hope? Look, I'm just going to stop. I'll come back with you.'

'Nothing really wrong. I wondered whether Mike had any of that green salve, you know, the stuff for burns. I haven't any left and that wretched James burnt himself last night. Eli went up to the Gap after supper to see some calves Pikle wants to sell and as both the children were asleep I slipped out for a little walk and some air and James woke and started his favourite trick, poking sticks into the fire. I've told him a thousand times and smacked him for it but he will do it. Last night of course he burnt his hand and dropped the stick on the rug, the fur one you gave me and I arrived back to find pandemonium. I'd just got it cleared up when Eli came home, and if I can I want to keep it from him.'

There was a kind of hasty uneasiness about the explanation, out of all proportion to its seriousness.

'Why?' I asked. 'It wasn't your fault.'

'No I suppose not. Even if I'd been there he might have done it. But you see Eli thinks I'm not strict enough with them. And James is really a very naughty little boy. He's precocious too. And if Eli sees the burn and asks me why I let him do it the little monkey is quite capable of piping, "Mummy out". So I thought I'd get some of that green salve which heals a burn in no time. . . .'

It wasn't the story, or the fact that she had left the twins alone, though that was a rare thing for her to do, it was the flurried way she told the story that first struck a shaft of suspicion through my mind. It wasn't really a very strong suspicion and it was dissipated at once when she added,

'I ran up to Lucy Steggles just to see how she was and whether there was anything I could do for her. But she's getting better. She's feeding the baby now.'

By this time we were in the yard and Mike was there. He went indoors to get the ointment.

'Where are your brats now?' I asked.

'Leashed up like dogs to a couple of staples in the wall. It's the only way. Eli's gone to Mill with the wagon and I shall just get back ahead of him if I hurry. Oh, thank you, Mike. I'm deeply obliged. Good-bye. Good-bye, Philip.'

She set off at a run.

Going into the house I thought, if Eli has taken a load to

236

the Mill and is expected back so soon he must have started out early. So it was to Linda that Geoffrey made his farewell. And Linda saw him set off, as I had done, a blue-eyed, blue-coated figure on a fine bay mare. And she, I thought, is so simple, so vulnerable that she could see all chivalry in my father's heavy-handed patronage, all goodness in Eli's Puritan strictness. Could she fail to see all romance in that handsome adventurer?

During the next two days I saw quite a lot of Dixon, for at last he was able to creep downstairs and sit by the open window of the sunny parlour. He was interesting, though not very cheerful company. The raid on Dixonville had been the end of his life's work. All the dead had been known to him, respected and in many cases loved. And he was not able, as were the other, younger, refugees, to shake off the melancholy that the catastrophe had brought upon him.

'If I were younger,' he said once, with a far-away look in his milky old eyes, 'I should have faith in the future. This Troubled Moon as they call him, will eventually go the way of King Philip and Mighty Thunder. He *must*. The day of the Indian chief is done. And when he and his braves are finished the land will still be there, and the lake and everything that made Dixonville what it was. But I shall be too old to start again. I'd just got the school going nicely too. There wasn't going to be a person in the place who couldn't read and write. And there were sewing meetings and tea meetings where the women could get together and enjoy themselves, a kind of club where the men could smoke a pipe and take a glass in peace after their work was done. All wiped clean off the face of the earth by a set of savages ruled by a devil with a crazy ambition that he can never realise.'

'The land was theirs you know, to start with,' I said for the mere sake of argument.

'And what did they do with it? Did they till it to the best advantage? Did they make civilised townships? No. Stinking lodges full of bones and hides and indescribable filth. Their women mere beasts of burden and their children bloodstained little savages. Possession cannot be allowed to stand in the way of progress. The earth belongs to those

237

who can make the best use of it. We ended King Philip's War too soon. They shouldn't have left one yellow hide between the lakes and the sea. It's no good beating the sword into a ploughshare unless you're certain of peace in which to plough, you know.'

'I expect you're right. It's only that sometimes I think of one Indian who was shot in this very yard. I looked at him. He was very thin and rather small and his dead face had a very peaceful look. He made me feel sorry for the whole lot of them. They didn't *ask* us to come.'

'That is an argument, of course. But after all, Mr. Ollenshaw, you're an educated man and will understand what I mean when I speak of the relentlessness of civilisation. It is a force that can't be denied. And there's a shape about it too. Think. Every invasion has been from the East to Westwards. The Tartars moved Westwards, so did the Goths and the Romans. Forces like Mahommedanism and Christianity moved Westwards. It seems to be part of the world plan. And in accordance with it the white man will move West across this continent. There'll be other Troubled Moons, other Dixonvilles, but they'll no more stay the movement than Hereward the Wake stayed the Normans. There'll be other old men like me, too, I'm afraid, with nothing left but the memory of their labours.'

To change from a painful subject I said, 'I wonder what Geoffrey has found and whether he's all right.'

'What is to be found, he will find. And what safety is possible will be his. He has a lucky star.'

'Do you believe in that kind of thing?' I asked in astonishment. The old man seemed so practical and so little given to fancy.

'Where he is concerned I must believe it. He's only just twenty-four and his adventures already would fill a book. His father was a Frenchman, you know, and he was born in France and held a commission in the army at seventeen. There was some kind of bother with a senior officer's wife and he decided to go to India. The ship was wrecked but he was picked up, lucky star again you see, and instead of arriving in Chandernagore he was taken to the British settlement. He'd had an English mother, and entertained a certain affection for the English so he settled there and had

238

a job in one of their factories for a time. In connection with this he was sent to London and by accident there met a man named Billings; I daresay you've heard mention of him from Mr. Gore. Billings was just about to leave for Dixonville and Geoffrey had just taken charge of the Cambody children, relatives of his mother, orphans and practically friendless. He couldn't take them back to India with him so he made up his mind there and then to join Billings. And his life hasn't been just a placid pasture with us, I can assure you. But in defence of what I said just now, notice that the two cousins who kept close beside him, and I whom he picked up more or less in passing, are the only people who escaped from the recent holocaust. I wonder will he stay here now. You're pretty strict aren't you?'

'I, personally, am not. But I don't think your ideas of a club would be very acceptable here.'

'Oh, I shouldn't be in a position to start anything. If I stay here I shall have all my work cut out to earn my bread. I was thinking about him. We were far from strict at Dixonville, but he had one or two brushes with the authorities there.'

'What about?'

'Pretty faces,' said Dixon shortly. 'He simply cannot resist them. It doesn't mean anything but of course other people find that difficult to understand. He's had several angry fathers and savage husbands after him with shotguns. Literally. That very same Billings, the man who brought him over, shot him through the calf as he climbed out of Felicity Billings' room one night. You notice when he comes back. He's got hardly any calf to one leg at all.'

'Is he married?'

For the first time in almost a fortnight Dixon laughed.

'Not to my knowledge and I should say not at all. Shotguns can be dodged more or less but an angry wife at home would even stop his gallop a bit.'

What a life it sounded! So different from mine. A gallop compared with a sober jog-trot. Even his slight lameness was picturesque, now that one knew its reason.

More than ever I was irked by a desire to know whether Judith or Linda were his present quarry. I had no real reason for thinking that either of them was. And yet I kept on thinking about it. Why had Edward asked that question? Why hadn't Geoffrey said, 'You saucy little brute I was doing so and so'? And I had it from Linda's lips that she had been out and I knew from the evidence of my own eyes that Judith had as well.

I tried to dismiss the whole subject by telling myself that I was neither angry father nor savage husband, but it nagged on and after supper, finding myself along with Judith in the kitchen for a moment I dragged the talk round to a place which I could shoot my question.

'Oh, Judith,' I said, giving my whole attention to the quill I was fashioning, 'I suppose you didn't happen to call in at Lucy Steggles' last night?'

'No. Why?'

'I just wondered how she was. I don't think Mike has been there this week.'

'Mrs. Makers could have told you this morning. She was there last night.'

'Oh, you saw her, did you?'

'Yes.' The word came out like a snap but I was so much relieved at the information that I did not mind the manner of its imparting. But as though to compensate for its shortness she added after a moment, 'I went up to the Beetons' place. Ralph brought me a length of muslin when he went to Salem and Christina is making it into a dress for me.'

Now I was able to look up. If Linda had gone to Lucy's and Judith to Christina's, neither of them could have had much time to spare for Geoffrey Montpelier.

So I looked up and said, 'It'll soon be weather for muslins. What colour is it?'

'White with a red spot and there are cherry-coloured ribbons to go on it.'

'All the elders will disapprove of you. But you'll look lovely I'm sure.'

A look of complete pleasure shone nakedly on her face for a moment and I rather regretted the words.

Next day was Sunday and we all went down to the transformed meeting house. The end of the room was stacked with provisions, sacks of flour and meal, smoke blackened hams, stone jars of honey and pickled meat. The sight of them reminded us of the danger which was still imminent, and the evidence of our eyes was reinforced by that of our ears for Mr. Thomas preached about the terror by night and the arrow that flieth by day. And I thought of all the psalms, which I well knew, having read them very often since I first spelled them out with Shad, all the good heartening psalms that there were from which he could have found a text applicable to our situation. My dislike of the miserable little fellow increased.

As usual I had taken a seat where I could sit and watch Linda. Eli solemnly held one twin, she had the other. Their funny little faces, so absurdly alike, shone with health and thorough washing with strong soap. Their bright yellow curls caught the light of the sun and seemed to throw it out again magnified.

Linda looked just the same, a subdued, brought-to-earth version of her bright vivid self. But all the same there was something that marked her off from the other woman sitting there meekly and stolidly clutching their children in their laps. There was still a sheen on such of her hair as could be seen and there was the curiously graceful way in which her head was set on the long slim neck and the neck on the straight little shoulders. She was captured and repressed and tamed, but not yet quite subdued, not bowed down like the others by marriage or maternity. Even Zillah Cambody in the full bloom of her youth did not sit so gracefully, so poised.

It was soon easy to see which was the naughty twin. Until the new rule was made Linda had seldom taken them to a meeting, a fact that had made my vow much easier to keep. The naughty twin, with a loud crow reached out a fat hand across Linda's arm and made a dart at Eli's beard. Linda edged a little farther along the seat and Eli repulsed the hand firmly. But James must have been the embodiment of the untamed part of Linda. He reached out more determinedly, standing up to do it and bracing his feet against Linda's thighs. He managed to get his fingers in the golden stuff and immediately chuckled with delight. Eli signed to Linda and passed John, the quiet twin, to her, seized James and with a good shake set him down hard on his knees.

That's settled him I thought. Eli thought so too. He eased

his grip a little and fixed his eyes on Mr. Thomas who was hissing on about punishment that inevitably overtook back-sliders. From where I sat I could see James, with a look of intense concentration busy with his own foot. Then suddenly up in the air, over the heads of the startled people flew James' little lambskin shoe its laces dangling.

Even Mr. Thomas could not be unaware of this interruption. I wondered whether he regretted his insistence upon everyone attending meeting. Eli rose and tiptoed to the door and one or two people tittered a little. Smack, smack, smack, came the sound of Eli's hand. Linda looked round once, anxious and embarrassed at the same time. Loud bellows which even my inexperienced ears could hear contained as much rage as pain, greeted the punishment. They stopped as suddenly as they had begun. Mr. Thomas resumed his discourse and presently Eli tiptoed in again with the twin held like a sack under one arm and took a seat just inside the door.

Outside it was brightly sunny and even warm for the time of year. People gathered in little groups. Even if the men met during the week often the women didn't, so they enjoyed the weekly gossip. There was quite a crowd around Ralph and Hannah, the newly-engaged couple and another around Lucy Steggles out today for the first time. Linda and Eli set down their burdens and let them totter about in the sun.

'Now what do you think of my naughty baby?' asked Linda. 'Isn't it queer. They're so much alike that even I can hardly tell them apart and yet one is a little angel and the other has demoniac possession. Oh, get that other shoe, Eli, will you? They take me ages to sew. I don't want to lose one.'

Eli stepped back into the meeting room and Linda said, 'He never noticed his hand and it's getting well quickly.'

The glance with which she accompanied the words somehow put us both in the conspiracy against Eli and my heart warmed.

'He's a very naughty little boy,' said Eli, returning and taking up the conversation where it had been left. 'He'll have to be punished. I noticed when I slapped him just now what looks like a burn on one of his hands. I suppose he's

242

been playing with the fire again.'

'Which is which?' I asked quickly.

'This is John,' said Linda, indicating the one who had dropped on his haunches and was busy picking the few early daisies. 'And that is naughty James. I can tell straight off because of their clothes this morning.'

As if to prove that she was right James waddled straight up to little Betsy Steggles who stood on the edge of the group admiring the new baby and caught hold of her plentiful tow-coloured hair. Taking a good grip he lifted his feet from the ground and swung his whole weight on it. Betsy gave a shrill piercing scream and James, like a tiny ape, came scuffling back and took shelter behind Linda's skirts.

'You see,' she said helplessly, 'he does *know*. He's really a terrible child.'

'And he's going to have a terrible smacking when he gets home,' said Eli, picking him up and giving him another shake. 'Now say you're sorry to Betsy.'

'You're sorry to Betsy,' said James in a loud clear voice.

Everyone laughed and Eli said, 'This is making him worse. He thinks far too well of himself as it is. Let's be getting along.'

From his father's shoulder the subject of demoniac possession smiled cheerfully down on the company as he was borne away. I looked at John whom Linda carried on her hip and then back at James. There was something almost eerie about the latter's precocity and assurance. He didn't seem like John's twin at all, infinitely older, infinitely wiser he might have been. And I thought of the old stories of fairy children substituted for real ones. Some cases like this must have given rise to such stories. I could almost believe that some spiteful fairy had fashioned James purposely for serious Eli's discomfort and smuggled him into the wide double cradle.

It was one of those bright mornings of Spring whose beauty is never matched again, even by the summer of which they seem to be forerunners. Everyone seemed more than usually leisurely and good-tempered. Even Keziah! For presently Zillah Cambody came hurrying after us and asked me in her pretty diffident way,

'Have Edward and I your permission to go to Mrs. Pikle's for dinner?'

Edward, who had resented what his cousin had said about having them in my charge, hung back, sullen and yet awaiting my answer with obvious anxiety.

'Of course,' I said. 'Enjoy yourselves.' Though how anyone could do so in Keziah's vicinity puzzled me.

Eli spoke the only light words, I think, that I have ever heard from his lips,

'Keziah must have something just on the turn, or a pie so stale no Pikle'll face it,' he said dryly.

Zillah climbed up beside Mary and Edward and Moses hurried along behind, making pretence at trying to catch up, puffing and blowing and laughing, while the girls rocked with merriment and clung to one another. So young, I thought. The gloomy meeting house, the terror-inspiring sermon, the dampening presence of their elders, all forgotten because the sun was shining, the year was young and so were they.

The sun shone on Linda, too, lighting the depths of her greeny brown eyes and showing up the soft down on the oval curve of her cheek.

Andy and Mike soon joined us, took a child each and pretended to be horses, racing. Even solemn John came to life then and the pair chuckled and shouted and waved their fat legs while their hands clutched the heads of their steeds. Eli watched the performance with half tolerant, half impatient, scorn.

'They'll make them wild as hawks,' he said.

'Never mind,' said Linda comfortably, 'they'll go to sleep as soon as they get home.'

As though to divert Eli's attention she asked, 'Has anything been heard of Mr. Montpelier?'

'No. And this is the fourth day. He should be back soon.'

'I hope nothing unfortunate has happened to him.'

'So do I.'

At the bridge we parted. Andy and Mike lowered their riders and having handed them over stood for a moment waving to them and re-gaining their breath.

'That James is a splendid little chap,' said Mike. 'I could do with one like him. I hope Eli won't make a life's work of

244

crushing all the spirit out of him.'

'He'd have a job,' said Andy. 'It's t'other one as'll get the crushing.'

We entered the yard to find Geoffrey Montpelier grooming his horse.

'Dear, dear,' was his greeting. 'What a good thing it is that Indians don't understand the workings of the Christian faith. *What* a place this would be to sack on a bright Sabbath morning.'

'I never thought of that,' I said stricken.

'Nobody ever does, until afterwards. But never mind. They haven't sacked you yet, and they shan't. Andy, finish her off, there's a jewel. I want her again presently. Come on, Philip, I've a lot to tell you.'

We went into the parlour, so warm in the sun that I flung the window wide. Geoffrey had his coat off already, now he struggled out of his riding boots and curled up on the settle like a cat. His fingers and mouth were occupied for a little while in getting his stubborn pipe going. At last a great billow of smoke went up towards the ceiling. He took his pipe out of his mouth, smiled at it and then at me, and began.

'What is that lovely outlandish word of Andy's ... I know, mastrous. He says he's mastrous hot, or mastrous busy. Well, I've been mastrous lucky. I've found the arch villain's camp, and I've found out all about his plans.' He drew heavily on his pipe. 'That Indian Alexander I told you about is called Troubled Moon, because of being born in the eclipse. Isn't that a lovely name—Troubled Moon—why don't we have names like that?'

'Civilisation I suppose,' I ventured. 'I should be Hop-on-an-Iron, or something equally hateful.'

'Well,' he went on quickly. 'Troubled Moon has been informed about this place. It is a place where many men live, so many that some stay awake all night to watch the pigs. In fact he has an altogether false and exaggerated idea of your strength, which is good. What isn't so good is that on Tuesday or Wednesday of next week he is going to make an attack on it. You see, working out his destiny, wiping out every settlement between the lakes and the sea. Dixonville, Zion, and then on to Fort Outpost. He hopes to get

245

many horses here. But he never moves when the moon is full and it is full on Monday night. So he has camped about thirty miles away and is waiting for the camp followers, old men, untried youths and squaws to come up to him, which they will do on either Monday or Tuesday. As soon as the moon is troubled—that is on the wane—he will move. Until then he is having a glorious time, celebrating the Dixonville victory with much meat and much fire-water. There was a decent little tavern in Dixonville, with its own still and all and Troubled Moon didn't overlook it.' The pipe was out again and he drew at it impatiently.

'Just a minute,' I said, 'did Troubled Moon give you all this esoteric information? If not how. . .?'

'. . . did I get it? Ah, that was where I was mastrous lucky. Just above the camp there's a little copse and a stream. Troubled Moon of course camps in the open. I stayed under cover, naturally, to the leeward side and watched, trying to reckon how many braves there were. I should reckon about two hundred. I thought something might happen, and something better than I had even hoped for, did. On Friday afternoon there was a great to-do in the camp. Shouting and wailing and such going to and fro that I thought for the moment that Troubled Moon had burst himself or something. Then out came a party of them, some distance from the camp, with a man all tied up with raw-hide rope. They hammered four great posts into the ground and strung him up, one post to each hand and foot. He was face downwards. Then they lighted a slow fire underneath him and danced round the affair leaping and throwing up their spears. I was afraid they'd stay there till he was all burned, or unconscious, but it came on dark and was suppertime and they went back into camp. As soon as they were gone and it was properly dusk I slipped down and untied him—cut him down rather, for their knots in raw-hide defy mere fingers, and dragged him up into the cop-pice. He was a frightful sight, but those fellows are tough and though his chest and his stomach made me sick to look at them, poor devil, after a shot or two of rum he could *speak*. And this was where the most mastrous luck was. He was one of Billico's men from Dixonville. He'd escaped from the massacre when Troubled Moon set about them,

246

and he talked in a kind of English I could understand. One of Troubled Moon's women had been sheltering him and he'd been trying to pass himself off as one of them, but they'd sniffed him out. They'd dealt with the woman in a rather worse way the day before.'

'And what did you do with him?'

'I pointed to something and said, "Look there," and then clubbed him on the head. I daren't shoot, naturally. I was sorry for the poor devil but he'd only have starved if the burns didn't kill him. Then when it was quite night I went back and chucked him on the fire. They wouldn't inspect him very closely I should think. I hope not, anyway.'

I thought for a moment, inconsequently, there's a whole story here. The man escaping and masquerading as one of the conquerors when really he was one of the defeated, and the woman who sheltered him and the end of them both. And I had to suppress a shudder of horror at the thought of the callousness, ruthlessness and barbarity of the people themselves. There were forty men at Dixonville, I thought again. And then a kind of anger rose hotly through the chill of my fear. What could Troubled Moon do with the country even if he conquered it. Even if he did rule between the lakes and the sea. In his hands it would just go back to barbarism. Whereas in ours . . .

Geoffrey had got his pipe going again while I was thinking, and leaning forward he said,

'Now this is what I propose. Troubled Moon is expecting to attack, not to be attacked. Tomorrow is the night of the full moon, he'll do nothing then, it wouldn't be lucky for him AND IT WON'T, because we are going to ride down and attack his camp in the middle of the night. It'll be light enough for shooting and they'll all be sleepy or drunk. What do you think of that?'

I looked at him, hatchet-faced and eager with his blue eyes, wide with weariness but glowing with enthusiasm.

'Do you think that is the best thing?'

'The best thing! My God! The only alternative is to sit like trapped rats in that gospel hall of yours and wait until two hundred braves come yelling up, all thirsting for blood. Ask yourself, my good man.'

He snorted at me, rapped out the unsatisfactory pipe on

the grate, shook back the square fall of hair that tumbled forward as he stooped, and then, filling the pipe with care said, more slowly : 'Of course nineteen is a pitiable number. It's an odd thing that a danger is more to be feared when it's on the wane than when it's at its peak. Fifty or sixty years ago people came here *prepared* for Indian trouble. Nobody in his senses would have planted nineteen men in so remote a spot then. Now with all this false assurance more people are going to be in danger than they were when every bush was suspected. Still, that's neither here nor there. Out in the open we shall have room to move, we shall be united and above all we shall take them by surprise. In fact we shall be giving our small force every advantage possible. At Dixonville, you see, we were literally trapped. That mustn't happen here. Well, shall we gather the city fathers and put the plan to them?'

'I think they should have their Sunday dinner—they'll have started it anyway.'

'Lord yes,' he said, uncurling himself and reaching out for his boots. 'I had forgotten that solemn institution. I'd even forgotten to be hungry myself. That must have been a peculiarly substantial sort of pie that wench put in my nose-bag.'

Over the meal—at which I was puzzled and interested to notice that Judith always presented Geoffrey with the least choice of the food, the blackest of the potatoes, the dried-off end of the joint—we talked over the plan with Mike and Andy. Andy received the information as he received everything, calmly and stolidly. If we rode to attack, then he would go with us and if we stayed at home then he too would stay, why waste words when food was on the table and his insatiable appetite was to be stilled? Mike said dryly, 'I told you, didn't I, that I'd seen this country before? On that occasion I said, "That's pretty country, looks fertile too." And the fellow I was with said, "It crawls with Indians, won't be safe for fifty years". Wish I'd took more notice of him. I shouldn't have listened to your blarney then.'

'You'll get lots of chances to practise your plain sewing,' I said with a lightness I was far from feeling.

We gathered the council members and Geoffrey put the case to them exactly as he had done to me. Pikle and Crane gave me the surprise of my lifetime by rising immediately and declaring that they had no intention of attacking anyone. If they were attacked they would fight back in self-defence but they would never strike the first blow.

'But it isn't,' cried Geoffrey hotly, 'they struck at Dixonville and it's merely a matter of time before they strike here.'

'If thou goest backward through time questioning of first blows thou wilt arrive at the one which Cain dealt Abel,' said Crane, gravely. 'That Dixonville was attacked, and thou lost thy house and thy friends we all regret. But that does not justify us in aggression.'

I remembered the way he had blenched at the mention of throat evil outside Fort Outpost, and yet had presented himself beside us as we went down the hillside. The man was not a coward. He had principles and though they might be illogical and dangerous they must be respected.

Geoffrey gave vent, half under his breath, to an expression never heard before at a council meeting, but he quickly controlled his tongue and said quietly,

'And what about your sons?'

'They are of age, they must speak for themselves,' said Pikle, equally quietly.

'Thank God for that.'

Mr. Thomas lifted up his sing-song voice to say,

'After all somebody must stay with the women and the little ones. That shall be my place, with Mr. Pikle and Mr. Crane. I am also a man of peace, not of war.'

He was the colour of suet, and, badly frightened as I was myself, I had little toleration for him.

'All right,' said Geoffrey, brusquely, 'wait but wait without me and mine. I have no wish to be caught again. Where they are now, idle, unsuspecting, dazed with liquor, we could make hay of them and then sleep in peace. If you prefer one more week of uneasy quietude have it by all means.'

Eli suddenly spoke out, rounding upon Mr. Thomas for, I think, the first time in their acquaintance.

'I never read,' he said, in that mellow roar of his, 'that the

249

Lord God of Hosts advised waiting. Do you not remember how He sent Gideon out? His army was small to start with, but first the faint-hearted were sent home, and then the careless were weeded out. And the little, stout-hearted band that was left put to flight the hosts of Midian. His hand is no weaker now. I'm with you, Philip's with you, Mike's with you. Come, Lomax, you're silent. Where do you stand?'

'Need you ask?' said Oliver Lomax with his cold, peculiar smile. 'Harry Wright is on my mind and my good dog Adam.'

'Then let's get all the men together and make ready to start,' said Geoffrey. 'I'll go to the Gap.'

I knew that he meant to put his case to the young Quakers before they could realise that any principle was involved.

For the rest of that pleasant Sunday, with the afternoon that seemed to linger on, reluctant to give way to the twilight, we were going hither and thither, rounding up Mark Pikle where he walked the hills with his fingers shyly seeking Zillah Cambody's; disturbing Edward who was making more rapid headway with his love-making to Mary. Ralph clattered in from the Mill, bringing Hannah and a bundle of clothes and all her livestock with him.

There was a general feeling that the women and children would feel safer if they were all together in the meeting house than if they were scattered about in the lonely houses. But even as we helped to move them in the futility of the action mocked our labours. We were going to throw ourselves like pebbles into the rising tide; if we failed to stem this pitiable fortress would be a shambles. There was no help to come from anywhere. Our nearest neighbour, Fort Outpost, was far away and the people in it would never even know our fate, though they might conceivably share it.

I had to put these thoughts away, for besides my share in the moving, I had a few personal matters to attend to. I wanted to write a letter to Linda in case the men of Zion should win the battle and the village be saved yet I myself be killed. I yearned, in that moment of tension and emotion to blurt out on paper all that I felt about her, had felt so long and should feel until the moment that death took me.

250

But although I drafted one letter along these lines I tore it into shreds. When she read the letter I should be dead and there would be no point in letting my secret survive me. One day, if I lived, and Zion went on, and the miracle happened, then I would tell her myself. Otherwise, let it end with me. So I wrote,

'Dear Linda, I want you to have my house and all that I have for your very own. You might like to live in the house. Please be kind to Andy, and if he wants to, let him go on doing the work here for you. Mike has a job that will always assure him of friends and a livelihood, but if Bluey comes out all right I'd like him to have her. I would also like Judith to stay here as she needs a home. When she marries let her have a cow or a couple of calves or my best bed so that she doesn't go quite empty-handed.' A thought struck me and I added, 'Let her have the bed in any case and something else. I hope that you will have a long life and a great deal of happiness.'

I had seldom written and never read a more stilted collection of words, but that is what happens when everything that one wants to write is forbidden. So, knowing I could make it no better, and might do a great deal worse I signed it, 'Your sincere friend, Philip Ollenshaw,' and folded it up.

Then I went to find Dixon, who, despite his protests, was to be left behind. It was absurd of him to even imagine otherwise. He had never ventured out of our yard yet, and the hole in his chest discharged still. He took the paper when I had told him what it was and for whom and said, 'But of course. And I hope you'll be asking me for it yourself when you come back safe and sound.' I said, very heartily, 'So do I.' That done with I went up to the cupboard in my room where I kept my powder and found there with it a couple of pistols that had belonged to Nathaniel and which, with my passion for systematic arrangement I had put in that cupboard and forgotten. His guns I had long ago given to Andy and Mike. I now took out the pistols, looked them over, tested and reloaded them. I then changed out of my Sunday clothes into the patches and faded garments that I worked in. Good stuff was

251

precious and not too easily come by. If I lived I should need the things again, if I died it would be a pity to have wasted them so entirely. I hung them in the cupboard and closed the door.

By this time the darkness was thinning out. We were to start at dawn. I looked round the bare room and saw the window greyish against the solid darkness of the wall. My good wooden bedstead with the woollen mattress and coarse white sheets which Judith bleached every wash day stood there, the cover smooth and unwrinkled, the pillow unmarked by my head. I suddenly savoured in my mind the pleasure of getting into it and laying my cheek on the cool pillow and letting sleep blow over me 'her drowsy gale'. I hadn't had a very exciting or prosperous or useful life, but it had been full of little pleasures. Going to sleep was one of them. It was strange to think that I might never go to sleep again. And then, still looking at the bed—for all these thoughts took but a moment to pass through my mind—I thought of something else, remembered one night when I had gone to that bed and not to sleep. I had locked that memory away with the other things better forgotten, Shad's hanging and the stink of that stricken village. It seemed so long ago now that I did remember. And suddenly I thought, I despised that night, despised Judith because she wasn't Linda, yet she was sweet and kind and patient with my clumsiness. And now that may be as near to life as I shall ever come. . . .

I went down into the kitchen where Judith had brewed hot coffee and made flat cakes smeared with honey. Geoffrey and Andy and Mike and Ralph were standing round the table eating and drinking, laughing at some of Geoffrey's nonsense no doubt. I had another pang of that old inferior feeling, but this time it was not concerning my foot. They were all, grizzled Mike, bow-legged Andy, careless laughing Geoffrey so much braver, so much less selfish than I was. While I was skulking round preparing for death, almost kissing life farewell, they were stuffing their bellies and stretching their lungs. And any one of them might be going to die too! Hoping that I did not look so green and gloomy as I felt I went to the table and accepted coffee and biscuit from Judith's hand. 'Slip outside a moment and wait for me,' I said out of the corner of my mouth as she lifted the honey towards me. Presently she opened the back door, and Geoffrey said, 'Look, it's getting light. We must be off. Some of those horses move at little more than plough speed you know.'

I set down my cup and went to the door, looked out and then followed Judith. 'Look,' I said, holding out the old pistols. 'If ... if the worst should happen ... you could shoot yourself. And give one to Mrs. Makers will you and tell her the same.'

Her eyes, always so queerly pale in her dark face shone like clear water in the dim light.

'I'll shoot her for you, if you like, if it comes to that. She'd probably think about her brats and botch the lot.' Her voice was rough for all it was no more than a whisper.

'Thank you,' I said. 'Our fingers touched as the weapons changed hands and hers seemed burning hot to my icy ones. She held the muzzles between the three first fingers of her left hand, letting the butts swing groundward.

'Be careful,' I said, 'they're loaded.'

She gave her hand a little toss and twist and there they were, lying athwart her palm. And all the time she was looking at me, sideways, speculatively.

'Well, good-bye,' I said after a moment's awkward pause.

'Good-bye, Philip!' she said, in a warm firm voice. 'Good-bye, Philip.' Her right arm shot out and circled my neck, pulling me towards her. She gave me a long, fierce kiss.

'God keep you,' she said.

I mumbled, 'And you, Judith,' just as the rest of them tumbled through the door.

'Was she at you to let her come along?' asked Ralph as we mounted.

'Why no,' I said, 'no. Why, did she want to come?'

'She's almost pestered my life out. That's the worst of women like her. They can do so many things that they can't realise that there are some things women aren't fit for.' He brooded for a moment. 'Wonder why she didn't ask you.'

'I can't think. I'd possibly have let her. Is she any good with a gun?'

'Excellent,' he said briefly. 'She may need to be yet.'

253

Aha, I thought, here's somebody else who isn't so sure of victory, and a big brown full-blooded man at that. And though the thought in itself was discomforting I took comfort in it. I'd hated being the only doubting Thomas.

But there was one man in the company who was not doubtful, and that was Geoffrey. For the first half of that day he was like somebody very young out on a jaunt. Even his horse was different, picking up its feet, tucking in its chin and prancing about, not in the least like a beast that had covered this same road this morning ... no yesterday morning, this was Monday now. 'Let's sing,' he said. 'We can sing till about two o'clock, then we'll begin to go warily.' And it was really a morning for singing, if you could forget the errand that brought us out of our sheltered valley.

A little to my surprise the invitation to sing was taken up by Eli who filled his lungs and started,

> *Thy will our law, Thy love our light;*
> *The cloud by day, the flame by night.*
> *Lead on Thy people.*
>
> *Our only guidance Thy command;*
> *Our strength and shelter in Thy hand.*
> *Lead on Thy people.*
>
> *Against all weakness and all sin;*
> *Against the foes without, within.*
> *Lead on Thy people.*
>
> *Lead on, oh chariots of the Lord;*
> *Lead on Thou everlasting word.*
> *Lead on Thy people.'*

It had been a favourite all the way from Salem to Zion, and I admit that there was something about it. It had a good marching tune to it, and I always thought that there was a flash of poetry in the first lines, as though whoever wrote it had just thought of those few apt words and wasn't content to leave it at that but must go on and make a hymn of it, in length at least.

Geoffrey, riding at the moment beside me, raised up his voice with,

> *'Now in the pleasant month of May,*
> *If you would go a-wooing. . . .'*

and Ralph, just behind, joined in,

> *'The maid will hardly say you nay . . .'*

and I said quickly, 'Ralph! Not that!' And to Geoffrey, who had stopped in astonishment, I added, 'They'll turn back if you sing such things.' He laughed, hummed for a moment or two and then started off, loud and clear, with no intention of being silenced a second time,

> *'There is a lady, sweet and kind,*
> *Was never face so pleased my mind.*
> *I did but see her passing by,*
> *And yet I love her—till I die.'*

He paused on a most haunting note. 'Go on,' I said, 'go on.'

> *Her gesture motion and her smiles*
> *Her wit, her voice my heart beguiles,*
> *Beguiles my heart, I know not why,*
> *And yet I love her—till I die.'*

He paused again, still on that haunting note and laughed. 'More?' he asked, as one speaks to a baby. I nodded.

> *'Cupid is winged and doth range,*
> *Her country, so my love doth change.*
> *But change she earth or change she sky*
> *Yet I will love her—till I die.'*

'Did you make it?' I asked, breathless with the beauty and the aptness of it. Had he seen Linda walking in a wood and lost his heart forthwith?

'Lord no. It's quite a well known one. In a song book. There's another too, that I like.'

He pulled the prancing Lassie in beside my soberer steed and sang.

> *'Forget not yet the tried intent*
> *Of such a love as I have meant*
> *My great travail so gladly spent*
> *Forget not yet.'*

I listened entranced. Never had my feelings been put so adequately and beautifully into words. If I live, I thought, I will go home and destroy my little blundering book, since nothing can be said perfectly but once.

> *'Forget not! Oh forget not this!*
> *How long ago hath been, and is,*
> *The mind that never meant amiss—*
> *Forget not yet.*

> *Forget not yet thine own approved,*
> *The which so long hath thee so loved,*
> *Whose steadfast faith yet never moved:*
> *Forget not this.'*

'Perfect,' I said, when he had, at my request, sung it a second time, so that the words were mine for ever. 'Perfect.'

'Lord, Philip, you are enthusiastic! Does he ring the right bell for you—old Wyatt I mean? Are you poet—or lover?'

A sideways, searching glance showed me no mockery in his face.

'As either I am the most complete failure. It was with me exactly as the song says. I saw her once and I was finished.'

'Whose steadfast faith yet never moved, eh?' he asked, pushing back the flap of black hair. 'What's wrong? Won't she look at you?'

I gave a noncommittal grunt.

'I envy you, I envy you, I envy you,' he said rapidly. 'At least it *means* something to you. If you *could* suddenly find yourself hopping into bed with the amorous fair one you would *feel* something wouldn't you?'

'Wouldn't you?'

'Some slight physical symptoms—yes.' He turned out his palms on either side of Lassie's neck in an expressive gesture. 'Quickly roused, quickly doused. Maybe it's my French blood—my father was French, did I tell you and the mongrels are always despised for some reason—maybe it's that. Like mules or something. But my mind is never engaged with it. I lie and make comparisons. Would you believe that? Can you *imagine* the handicap? Still there's always hope and I believe, I believe, I believe,' he tapped out each 'believe' on Lassie's neck with his fingers. 'I *believe* that I have at last lost my heart as well as ... wait a minute ...' He left my side suddenly and rode on swiftly, scouting ahead. I saw him hold his fingers in his mouth and then test the wind on them. 'I thought so. The wind has changed. We must ride around, get to leeward of the bastards. They've got noses like dogs.'

The air was heady with Spring and the sun warm on our backs. On every tree the knotted boughs were sprinkled with tufts of green or spattered with blossom. From the edge of a coppice a pink wild currant bush leaned out, shook its clustered flowers and loosened a sharp fragrance on the air.

I looked round on my company, clumsily mounted on the horses not meant for riding, with sacks or rugs thrown over in place of saddles. I had a keen eye for the nervous gesture that betrayed, beneath the outer calm, the same bowel-loosening excitement as discomforted me.

I thought, I might have been in some comfortable lodging in London, writing poetry, writing plays, my slippered feet on the fender and the coffee house, with its congenial company, waiting around the corner. Oh, Linda, it is on your account that I am riding out to do battle with savages, just as it is on your account that a love song batters at my brain as I ride.

The detour that must be made on account of the changing wind took a long time, and it was twilight by the time we reached the edge of a wood and could look down upon the cluster of tents in the glow of sunset that seemed to redden the plain. The smoke of woodfires went up into the quiet evening sky and dark figures moved between the tents and the stream. The wind blew our way and Geoffrey sniffed at it. 'They're cooking,' he said gladly, 'they'll eat heavily and sleep the sounder.' He was no longer the singer,

257

the lover, the regretful philanderer of the morning's ride, but a man of action, full of plans and assurance.

We fed our horses and then stood or sat about cramming food into our mouths with our hands. To me what I ate was completely tasteless, like chaff, and like chaff it was dry in my throat. I gave up after a couple of mouthfuls. The whole of my body was full of water, alternately icy cold and boiling hot and I had to make several errands behind a great tree-trunk, to rid myself of some of it.

Eli came up to me, a chunk of bread in one hand and a lump of cheese in the other.

'If anything should happen to me,' he said, casually, between bites, 'have an eye to my wife, lad will you? James especially will need a man's hand.'

'I'll see to it,' I said in a thready voice. And at the mere notion my heart gave a great leap so that it seemed at one moment to be in my throat and my belly; and I looked at Eli, steadily munching his victuals and thought, perhaps in the next hour you will be dead and my way clear to Linda. But hard on its heels recantment came, that great live sturdy body, that vigorous golden beard with a crumb or two in it, those steady brown hands and the mellow voice. Oh, Eli Makers, why must you marry Linda and convert me into your secret enemy, with my mind always working against you, even though my body makes no betraying sign. And suddenly I was praying, 'Not that way, oh God, not that way'. But my reason asked, 'How then? How else can you ever have her?' There was no answer.

Twilight deepened and through the gathering gloom we could see the fires pricking the plain before us.

'They're having a grand time,' said Geoffrey, pausing by me and looking ahead into the night. 'I hope they've got something that'll lie in their bellies like lead, the bloody-minded ——s.' Eli heard him.

'Mr. Montpelier. God is with him. Affront Him not.'

'Sorry, Makers, but that's what they are.'

'What they are concerns us little. They will be food for the fowls of the air.'

'Well spoken,' said Geoffrey, and laughed.

And now, by imperceptible but steady steps the moon

climbs the sky, beating down the darkness as she climbs, whitening the land, making our hands and faces float suddenly ghostly out of the night.

Eli, like Cromwell, makes a prayer before battle. 'Oh Lord God, who wast in days of old a sword and buckler to such as trusted in Thee, protect in this hour that handful of Thy servants who go to do battle in a righteous cause. Few are we and unskilled in war and should the victory be ours to Thee will we ascribe the power and the glory and the honour from this day henceforth and for evermore.'

Brief and to the point, and if it sustains and comforts you, Eli, it is a good thing. I envy you the steady voice in which you raised your petition. My whole face shakes upon its bones. I can't shoot at all well, and I cannot run well either. True, I have shot a bear, but that was threatening Eli. Yes, but these Indians will be threatening me as soon as they are awake. Geoffrey says that they don't come round after drinking as white men do. But how does he know that? Also, if a tomahawk is what I think it is and anyone comes at me with one, I shall think of that flap of flesh which fell forward when Geoffrey took off his bandage and I shall either fall down in a faint with fear, or turn and get the back of my head cut off.

I listen to the last directions, but the words are mere sound and mean nothing.

'Shoot when you can, but don't depend on your guns too much. Try to keep in pairs so you get half a chance to reload.'

'There are only six tents. Eli, Carter, Mark Pikle, Mike, Oliver Lomax and myself will take one each. We shall have no time to reload. Shoot the first and axe the others.'

'Aim low when you shoot. Axe between head and shoulder, you can't miss there as you may a head.'

'For the love of God move stealthily at first, our lives depend upon surprising them.'

We steal down, out of the shelter of the friendly trees into the moon-whitened plain. It seems to me that my heart is beating as loud an alarum as any drum that ever went before an army. At every other step, almost, my iron strikes upon a little stone and the clink rings loud in the silence.

Nearer and nearer. Will they wake? Will one wake and turn to his fellow, 'I smell danger in the night?' Even like this they might have stolen upon Zion, in any dark night. God bless Geoffrey Montpelier. If we live he shall have what land he wants in Zion, and we will all build him a house and he shall be chief councillor of all.

Now we can all smell the lingering scent of the meat that they cooked for supper, and after that, as we draw nearer still, the mingled odour of a camp where men have dwelt for some days, odour of breathing humanity, unwashed bodies, greasy clothing, hides and bones. Now we can see the six little tents, and around them, beside the ash-smothered remains of the wood fires, the recumbent bodies wrapped in slumber. Unaware, defenceless, how dare they lie like that under the open sky? Doubtless Geoffrey was right when he remembered the liquor shop at Dixonville. Surely if this affray resolves itself into a victory for us even Eli will recognise that out of evil good may come.

'Kill quietly until the camp is roused,' was one order. And now at last here we are, Andy and I, and at our feet lie six men sleeping, their moccasined feet turned in towards the fire, their faces towards the ground, the moonlight white on the shoulders hunched in sleep. We have our guns, but we must not use them yet. We have, newly-ground, the axes that have reached the heart of many a stout tree. We have our knives with their bright sharp blades. Andy chooses his knife. I see with a shrinking eye that he tries it, from habit, on his thumb before he stoops, and like an avenging ghost silently plunges it home. I choose my axe, I imagine that I shall feel less the terrible thrill of the impact with the living flesh. 'As though it were a tree,' I think wildly: and 'between shoulder and head.' I swing it and it crashes home.

We kill three of the six. But the fourth, as I axe him lets out a scream and at the same time another man yells from the other side of the camp where similar stealthy work has been afoot. Instantly all is pandemonium. The two men by our fire spring up. I thrust my axe between the upper part of my arm and my body, and raise my gun. It is the first shot of the battle and it reaches its mark. Andy shoots at a distance of less than a yard and that is six accounted for. We pass on. If the others have been as lucky as we the odds are greatly reduced.

But now they are awake and desperate. The night is loud with cries of pain and wrath, with musket fire, with the impact of blows. A man, he seems enormous, escapes from one of the tents evading Eli by the opening and comes straight at me. I try to fend him off, but he hits me heavily in the face and I go over backwards and he plants a heavy foot in my stomach as he passes.

I struggle up with blood pouring into my gaping mouth and now I am no longer human. No more do I dread the impact of the blow. I court it. When I have time to reload I shoot, I use my gun as a club, I swing my axe like a maniac, at close quarters I make sharp stabbing thrusts with my knife. Never in my life have I moved so easily. I can run, I dodge and turn. I snuffle through the blood that pours from my broken nose. An Indian, flat on the ground, reached out and takes me by the ankle and we fight like cats. He has a knife in his right hand and without thinking I seize it by the blade in my left hand and feel no pain at all, only a mad exultation as my own knife goes into his throat. He gurgles and is still. I cannot tug my own knife out again so I take his, struggle to my feet and go on, plunging into the swirling madness, the grotesque and crazy dance of death.

Within, I suppose twenty minutes, the whole thing was over and the Indians were lying where they had fallen and Geoffrey and Eli were stooping over the ones who still groaned or struggled and cutting their throats.

The air reeked of warm blood. The moon, high aloft and narrow now, looked down unmoved and upon the shambles around the one tent that remained upright.

Something stirred in my stomach as though an enormous snake were there uncoiling himself. Just at that moment I put my hand to my face, and felt the bloody mash that had been my nose. And at that the snake rose to his full length and struck. Falling to my hands and knees I was deathly sick.

I kept on being sick. It was worse than the crossing on the *Westering Wing*. I was aware of Mike's voice.

'Ain't hurt inside are you?' There was a flattering anxiety in it, but I could say nothing. I just went on being sick. He thrust me back so that I lay on my back, staring at the reeling sky. I smelt the rum before I heard the grit of the flask on my teeth, my mashed lips were incapable of any sensation except pain that was almost numbing in its intensity.

'Go on. Swallow it. *I* know what's best for you.'

I swallowed, rolled sideways on my face and was sick again as I lay.

'That's right,' said Mike, undisturbed, 'now try again.'

I tried to say, moving only my tongue and not my mouth, 'Go away, Mike. Leave me in peace.' But the words were all blurred and he took no notice, simply dragged me over on to my back again and poured the spirit into my mouth so that I must either swallow or choke. I swallowed; and the snake melted. Warm comfort flowed where the cold coils had lain.

'I'll leave you now. Plenty need me,' said Mike. He went away and after a few moments of lying there, almost blissfully relaxed I raised my head, then my body and clambered to my feet.

Slowly and deliberately I counted the figures standing up. Andy, Mike, Ralph, Eli, Oliver Lomax, Isaac Carter, Jake Crane, Amos Beeton, the three Pikle brothers. I counted them twice. William Lomax, Joe Steggles, Thomas Crane and Tim Dendy were not upon their feet at least.

Geoffrey Montpelier came near me. 'All right, Philip?' he asked. I said 'Yes,' and then, 'Are you?' speaking with difficulty.

'Would you believe it? All Mike's sewing to do again!'

He had been struck in the very same place as before and the same horrible flap of flesh was hanging loose.

'The others?' I asked.

'Will Lomax and Thomas Crane dead I'm sorry to say. Joe Steggles is in a poor way, and Tim Dendy hasn't come round yet. There's nothing much to show. Cracked skull probably.'

'Oh dear,' I said, thinking of their folks.

'Damned lucky to get off so lightly. Do you realise that we've wiped out two hundred? Two hundred.' His voice cracked.

'Thanks to you,' I mumbled.

'Thanks to little old Jones' liquor shop. Why half of them never knew they were hit.'

We dragged ourselves, our wounded and our dead a little way out of the shambles and waited for morning. It came at last, not such a dawn as yesterday's had been, just a grey light that began in the East and widened until it embraced the earth.

Now we could see the cost of the victory. Every one of us was wounded in some way or another, though I could see no face quite so marred as mine. My nose and my mouth were so swollen that I could not see my chest. I had a snout just like a pig. Mike produced his needle and thread and replaced his stitches in Geoffrey's head and after he had washed his face in the stream he looked quite presentable. Both Eli's hands were in the same state as my left. Oliver Lomax had a gashed cheek and a cut in his calf about six inches long. Mike sewed them too. Isaac Carter had one eye closed and a slashed wrist. Amos Beeton had a stab in the ribs. Mark Pikle's right arm was burned where he had fallen into the ashes of one of the fires and his brothers had minor wounds. Not one of us had escaped scot-free.

'Well,' said Geoffrey, 'the camp followers and the youths will be here at any time now and we're not in shape to try conclusions even with them. Besides, even if we were it would be better for them to find the camp just ruined as though a multitude had struck at it. We'd best get back to the horses.'

'What about the dead?'

'We'll bury them up here under the trees. It's a pleasanter spot and the ground is softer.'

So with great difficulty and toil those of us who were least wounded carried the four bodies, the two dead and the two seriously wounded up to the little grove where we had left the horses.

I saw Geoffrey carefully collecting strips of rawhide down in the camp, but I was too tired to be curious.

When we reached the horses an unpleasant surprise awaited us, six of them had broken their tethers and made off. For home, doubtless, as Eli said, but even that knowledge was little comfort to wounded men faced with the long tramp back to Zion. My Bluey stood there, and Geoffrey's Lassie, both whinnying with pleasure at our return.

Lacking shovels we hollowed out shallow graves for Will Lomax and Tom Crane with our axe-heads and our hands. Eli made a prayer over the graves and at his request I murmured, through the over-stuffed sausages that were my lips, what I remembered of the burial service. It was coming more fluently now. In a sense it was my third burial service. As we turned away I saw Geoffrey Montpelier at the foot of the mounds muttering something that I did not catch. He saw me watching him, crossed himself, and said, 'I'm a Catholic, didn't you know?'

'No,' I said. 'I'm afraid that's going to make it awkward.'

'Make what awkward?'

'Tell you when my mouth is better.'

Next we had to think of the living. 'We'll make litters,' said Geoffrey, drawing out the rawhide ropes that he had salvaged. 'Anybody with whole hands, cut down four decent saplings will you?'

We took turns. Even I, with my sound right hand, made a few wild strokes. Growing momentarily more and more pale until his colour was deathly, Geoffrey Montpelier worked until the two rough litters were completed. Each had the sides of the saplings, lashed across the rawhide, fir boughs and coats laid across the two strips of rawhide making a V shape that was attached to the saddles of two steady horses. Andy, Edward Cambody, Moses Pikle and Jake Crane, being smaller and lighter than the others rode the four horses that carried the litters, the rest of us divided off as best we might, the most severely wounded riding, the others walking beside.

And as usual Eli fell to my share. I rode Bluey and he hooked his arm through the bridle. For some reason we fell to the rear of the procession. Oliver Lomax and Geoffrey shared his Lassie and occasionally when Geoffrey was riding he pushed on ahead to see how the litters were faring. When Oliver rode he did so heavily, with a stricken face and I realised that he was fonder of his brother than one might have suspected.

Just before noon Lassie stumbled and went lame. Oliver Lomax who was riding her at the time while Geoffrey walked beside me, talking, dismounted and stood helpless.

'Oh, for God's sake,' Geoffrey said savagely, 'that's what

comes of lending your horse to a fool! Couldn't you *see* where you were going. Bloody great hole. What's a rider for?'

He went over her fetlock carefully, the stiff blood-soaked lock of hair falling forward and his white face whiter than ever.

'Get out of my sight, numbskull,' he said, 'go share Beeton's cart horse and tell him from me not to let go the bridle while you're astride it.'

Poor Lomax, looking even more stricken, hurried ahead to be out of the range of Geoffrey's tongue and Geoffrey himself fell back beside us, leading Lassie and trying to urge her forward with caresses and gently coaxing talk. She tried to take a few steps, the injured leg dangled suspiciously and she looked at him with a piteous expression in her liquid dark eyes.

I pulled Bluey to a standstill and looked back. I saw Geoffrey's blue eyes under his discoloured, battered forehead fill with tears and my own throat thickened. Oliver had lost his brother—naturally he wasn't looking too shrewdly where he was going : but the mare was Geoffrey's darling. I thought of how gaily and with what spirit she had come this way only yesterday.

He fondled her nose, leaned his head against her velvet forehead.

'Just try, darling. Hop on three legs, my precious. I can't leave you here, the Indians would get you.'

Lassie turned her head from side to side in the gesture of a dumb beast in pain. He bore on the bridle. 'Come on, darling. I'll help you. I'd carry you if I could.'

She hobbled forward about a yard and stopped again. He stooped over the leg. When he raised his head he was, literally, weeping.

'Go on!' he shouted to Eli and me. 'Go on, get out of sight.'

'Come on,' I said to Eli, 'there's nothing we can do.'

'Her leg's broken,' said Eli.

We moved forward a little way until a bend in the trail hid from us the pathetic spectacle of Geoffrey bestowing a last caress and then unslinging his gun. After a few moments a shot rang out. And after a moment or two more he passed us, running as though the devil were after him and joined the main procession.

'Ride now, Eli,' I said presently. 'A walk will do me good.'

He looked up at me with one of his rare and lovely smiles. 'I'm all right, lad. If we drop behind a bit it doesn't matter, does it?'

'Not to me,' I said. 'But you ought to take your turn. The others do, that's why they're leaving us behind.'

He plodded on beside me and I fell into a kind of doze. The open plain ended and the way back to Zion began to wind through trees again. In my dreamy state I smelt the currant bloom. It woke me.

'Now, Eli,' I said, 'you either ride Bluey for a bit, or you go on ahead and share with someone else.'

'I'd hardly catch them,' he said.

'Never mind that. Unless you ride I shall just hurry on and stop one of them. You can't walk all the way. Even if only your hands are injured you've lost a lot of blood.'

'Well, just for a piece,' he said grudgingly, helped me down and swung himself heavily into my saddle.

With me on foot we made worse pace than ever and when I had hobbled for about half a mile Eli reined in.

'Come on, get back on your mare, every one of those jarring steps of yours goes through my limbs.'

He lifted me back, laid hold of the bridle and stepped forward more briskly.

I went back into my pleasant doze.

A sudden jerk and a noise that I couldn't at first identify brought me back to consciousness with a start.

'What was that?' I asked sharply.

'A horse,' said Eli. 'It's been following for some time. Just now it whinnied. I believe it's mine.'

'But yours is up there with one of the litters,' I said, thinking of the horse Eli had ridden yesterday and which had been taken for the litter because it was steady.

'Ah, not that one. Meggie.'

'Meggie?'

'The roan I shipped at Plymouth and lost last year. You know, the one Keziah claimed. There were two, but Meggie was the best. I think I'll just step back and see.'

266

We had entered another of the little groves of trees. A thin gentle rain was beginning to fall and the birds in the thickets were greeting it with bursts of shrill song. No horse was in sight, but as Eli hurried back along the track he stretched out his hand and his voice was coaxing, 'Meggie,' he called, 'good girl, Meggie.' He disappeared where the trees ended, but in ten minutes he came back with a look of intense exasperation on his tired face.

'It's her,' he said, reaching for Bluey's rein. 'She seemed to know me. Let me get quite close and then sidled off as if she couldn't quite trust even me. And small wonder: she's been ill-used by the look of her.' He fiddled with the rein.

'Take me down,' I said, answering his unspoken plea. 'If you ride back a bit she may come to the other horse and give you a chance to grab her.'

He lifted me down, quickly, but with care and I could see that his face had lightened. 'I won't go far,' he said, getting into the saddle and turning the horse's head.

'Good hunting,' I called after him and settled myself on some dead fern with my back to the smooth bole of a tree, glad that the bud-smothered boughs offered a slight protection from the thin rain.

I dozed again and lost count of time. When I roused myself it was because of the rain which had suddenly increased in volume and was spattering on the young leaves and dashing off the branches in little water spouts. I turned up my collar and rose to my feet. I thought, I'll walk a little, at least that will keep me warm, and I actually walked about fifty yards up the trail towards Zion. Then the idea struck me that if Eli returned and didn't find me there he might waste a minute or two looking for me, so I turned and retraced my steps.

I walked back as far as where the trees began. In the open, without the scanty protection of the boughs the rain drove full in my face like arrows as I looked straight ahead, then to the left, then to the right, searching for the sight of Eli coming towards me on Bluey I hoped that he would have caught Meggie, then we could both ride and make up for lost time.

Through the shimmering grey downpour I saw him, riding hell-for-leather towards the trees. The roan, with tail and mane streaming backward raced beside him—but that wasn't all. Right on his heels, like a pack of hounds after a stag, leaped and ran about ten Indians, their hair and their fringes borne backwards on the wind of their own motion.

One outdistanced the others, leaped forward, level with Eli and laid a hand on his foot. Eli jabbed out with his axe and the man loosened his hold, stumbled, recovered himself and came on again. Bluey, not fresh to begin with, and never remarkable for staying power, slackened pace visibly. I saw Eli smite her on the hindquarters with the hat he snatched from his head. The action frightened the roan and she sheered off, careering away to the left. In doing so she crossed the path of the Indians and gave Eli just a second's respite.

In it he saw me, shifted his axe to his left hand, dropping the hat as he did so, roared, 'Get ready to jump!' and bending down low in the saddle stretched out his right arm to catch me to him. I tensed my body, drawing it into a compact mass, ready to cling to him with hands and feet and teeth. Even now we might do it—just.

But the Indian who had been jabbed in the face paused, poised his knife in his hand, took careful aim and flung it. It struck Bluey in a hind quarter and she reared up beating the air with her fore feet. Eli, poised to catch me and unprepared was unseated and fell to the ground, rolling over until he was almost at my feet. The next instant we were surrounded. Yelling with delight they closed in on us; the foul breath from their open mouths tainted the air.

'I'm main sorry, lad,' said Eli. 'I've brought your death on you.'

I tried to speak but no words came.

After those first glad yells the Indians fell strangely silent. Occasionally a word meaningless to us, would fall and be answered by a grunt. But they turned, and holding us by the elbows in a merciless grip, dragged us with them. The fact that we were not killed outright was disquieting to an indescribable degree. Memories of Harry's mutilated body battered at my mind.

The rain fell fiercely. Through it we made about a mile back along the way to the camp of Troubled Moon, then broke off suddenly towards the South. By the time that we had covered the second mile of the new path I was no longer making even a pretence at walking. I was being dragged like a sack between the two silent, soft-footed Indians whose grip on my arms was like the grip of Death itself.

The rain-darkened afternoon narrowed into the grey light of approaching dusk. We reached a belt of trees, and here, without, it seemed, any warning to one another, by common impulse the party stopped. Eli, who had been marching along, very upright, put his hands together, turned his shut-eyed face towards the sky and prayed. I saw the upright jerk of the great golden beard. I, too, ought to prepare for death, but my flesh was crawling in such a deadly apprehension of terror that I could neither think nor pray. What manner of death awaited us? My eyes, like those of a trapped rat, hunted about for signs. Could they get a fire going in all this rain?

A few more single words, a few more grunts, too few and disconnected to be called a consultation, and our fate was decided. They cast us down flat on our backs. Merciless hands held us down by head and wrist and ankle. Out came the knives.

All my life I had dreaded and avoided physical pain. Never willingly had I inflicted it upon any living thing. Last night, it is true, I had shot and clubbed and killed several men suddenly roused from drunken slumber—but that was in war and the war was not of my seeking. Dog-fighting, cock-throwing, bear-baiting, all becoming popular again in the England of my youth, I had rigorously avoided. I could not understand how men, themselves made up of blood and flesh and vulnerable nerves, could find any pleasure in the presence of so much pain. I had hated the popular way of killing a calf by cutting its throat and letting it run into the meadow, bleeding to death while the veal whitened. No calf of mine had ever been killed that way.

And now, I, to whom agony was the final evil, the shuddering and dreadful contradiction of the goodness of God, was doomed to be the prey of its bloody gloating ministers.

They tore off our coats and shirts. Then with their long sharp knives, they made four slits in each of our chests; two on the right, two on the left, prising loose the flesh between each pair so that for a space of six or seven inches over

269

each nipple we wore, as it were, braces of our own skin and muscle. They knew their dreadful business well. No vital part was severed. Less blood was spilled than Andy lost when his chisel slipped in the yard at the back of Beadle's.

Then they bent down young trees and stripped off the twigs and the small tufts of leaves and speared the braces with the supple boughs and when they let them go we went up with them, and so hung, each suspended by his own flesh between two trees.

The whole operation was conducted in silence, save when I yelled and Eli groaned. When they had finished and the bent trees were creaking back into place they sat around, still quiet, gloating, immobile upon their haunches, until the dusk made our writhings, the sweat and the blood of our torture invisible to them. Then they rose in the same silence and trotted away, their vengeance complete, darker shadows on the dusk of evening. Eli and I were left alone to hang there until agony or thirst should make an end of us.

The darkness deepened, but for us there was no time. Minutes and hours so neatly docketed, four o'clock, five o'clock, breakfast time, suppertime, bedtime, those little distinctions are for the whole, the same. Swung there between heaven and earth with severed nerves crying and the rough boughs biting like saws into the raw flesh we knew that time is fluid and changeable. A minute there was an endless agony.

Once I thought, quite coherently and clearly of the cool moist ground where we had laid our dead that morning. I had pitied them then. Now with a dreadful bitter envy I envied them. Death, the old enemy whose very name is so threatening that no man will willingly wear it, had in one short hour become desirable above all things.

Others have praised him.

'Oh eloquent, just and mighty Death, whom none could advise thou hast persuaded . . .'

From what locked storehouse of the brain have those words come?

Suddenly I became aware of other words, not remembered, not imagined. Real words, spoken by a human voice. Eli's.

'We must keep a hold on ourselves, lad. If we weaken we shall hang here until we die.' Oh, but Eli, already you

270

are weakening. Your voice tells me that. And why fight against death? Let it come swiftly.

'We've got to think of some way of getting down from here while we've still strength to do it. Think, Philip. The pain is less when you think.'

I think. The silver birch is of all the trees of the wood the most lovely. Graceful and beautiful at all times of the year. Only this morning I admired the buds on the trees and was so glad that I was still alive to see them.

I never thought that the crown of a cool and lovely tree could be bent and twisted into an instrument of torture. But I might have known, because there was a tree on Calvary. That was in the Spring, too, Eastertide. And there a gladly budding tree was shorn and warped for the torment of shrinking flesh. Oh, how lightly we had taken that story, inuring even the ears of children to the sound of nails, thorns and spears. Three hours *He* had hung. Then the spear had ended it, and the felons' legs were broken. But for us there was no release. God if that is blasphemy You must forgive me, I am no longer the master of my mind.

Now at least I know what lies at the bottom of the pit of pain from which I have ever shrunk away. All blows and stripes, the pangs of women in labour, the agony of the beast snared in the depths of the wood, the galled coach horse who every morning faces another day in the collar. I shall never again suffer these things in imagination. I shall *know*.

But that, of course is foolishness. I shall soon know nothing. Soon I shall hang here a grotesque and senseless lump, an insult to the morning. A thing which was called Philip Ollenshaw, that has eaten and drunk and slept and will do so no more.

Drunk. Cool, cool water, bubbling from the clear spring, spurting obediently from the tapped cask, running brightly over the stones.

Without water men go mad.

'Philip, feel in your breeches' pocket. Did they take your knife?'

'They took everything.'

'Mine too.'

Ages more of pain; but now the mind is growing a little dimmer. I am sinking now and there are spaces when I forget where and who I am, merciful little spaces when I even forget what has happened to me. This is what Eli says we must fight, but why? Better to sink and sink, release the cord of consciousness, unhitch the scarred mind and sink into a swoon, and from the swoon into the arms of death.

'Philip. The moon is rising.'

'What of it?'

'Listen. On the right side my strip is only about two inches wide. On the left it is three. What about yours?'

Why ask? Why bother to look when every movement is an increase of pain that tilts the brain upon the reeling edge of madness? Yet I look.

'Both three inches.'

'Then mine is frailest. I'm going to break through on the right side with God's help and soon we shall be free.' I hear the creaking of the trees as he throws himself from side to side. Then as the moon brightens I watch, against my will and with an increase of nervous pain that I should have thought impossible as Eli frets away the two-inch strap of flesh that binds him to the tree. He tears it with his hands. He groans now and then and calls upon his God, but he does not falter. I can hear the slow drip of new blood. It is a performance as horrible as it is heroic and it goes on for ever.

At last however, with a scream like a wounded stallion's he ceases his labours, and slowly both his trees right themselves. The one on the left is free and the other is no longer bowed towards the other, it merely holds Eli speared on it, four feet from the top where the outcrop of boughs keeps him suspended.

'Are you all right?' I whisper.

'Aye,' he gasps and stays there for a long time breathing hard. Then, slowly but steadily, using his arms and his feet he heaves himself to the top of the smooth shaven trunk. After two efforts that fall short he unhooks himself with a convulsive upward thrust. Then he falls to the ground and is still.

I called, but no answer came and I thought, Eli is dead. Even at the end his God was mindful on him and gave him a speedy release. For him there will be no longering madness, no more timeless drawing out of pain.

Ages passed. Then suddenly the low hoarse voice called

me back from the distant place where I was wandering, hurt and weeping.

'Keep a stout heart, lad. I'll have you down in a trice now.'

But it was more than a trice. It was an immeasurable time before he freed me. For as he heaved me up the relief of the weight made my trees spring apart in a way that almost tore my body asunder and made me scream to Eli to leave me to hang. I could hear his vague exhortations to patience and courage and from shame, remembering how he had dealt with himself, I tried to be silent, but there was nothing left in me except a desire to avoid more pain.

Finally, still spitted, I fainted and when I came to I was down on the ground with my head lying across Eli's knees as he sat leaning back against the tree-trunk.

'That's better,' he said, as I stirred and sighed. He put his head back against the tree and rested for a while, as he might rest after a long day at the plough's tail.

At last he spoke, 'Well, we'd better be moving. They're bound to come back and look for us and we're a long way off the trail. We must get back to the place where I first heard Meggie.'

'Damned horse,' I said weakly. 'We'd be safe in Zion but for her.'

'Don't curse her,' said Eli, gently. 'She was trying to get home, poor thing. And she's back in their hands now.' Weakly, staggering like men far gone in liquor, we took the way back. At every step it seemed as though I lifted my feet yards into the air, and yet I knew I was dragging them because anything a hump in the ground or a little twig was enough to make me stumble.

'It was a mercy of providence that they missed the iron on your foot,' said Eli. 'They're hogs for iron Mr. Montpelier says.'

The strip of flesh that he had broken through hung down towards his waist like a piece of strap, bloody and flapping. Every time I caught sight of it a special sharp pang went through my own throbbing gashes. He held my hand as though I were a child and steadied me when I stumbled. And all the time he went on plodding steadily.

At last, with infinite pain and dole we had covered, Eli reckoned, about a mile and were half way back towards the place where they had turned off our trail. I knew by that time that I should never reach the little grove of trees. The solid ground was rocking and tossing more violently than ever the *Westering Wing* had done. Even Eli's hand was unstable, one moment it seemed large as a stack, the next it had dwindled to the size of a pebble.

I gathered up my last fragment of sense and implored him to leave me. I fell forward on to my knees and said,

'Let me rest, Eli, please. You go on. I shall be all right.' And it was not from any self-sacrificing motive, it was simply from a desire to lie down and die in peace. I had a certainty of feeling now that I had only to stop making an effort and I should die quite easily.

Eli dropped my hand and took me by the shoulders, gently shaking me.

'Look at me, lad, if you lie down now you *will* die. And we haven't done all this in order to die. Look at me and listen. YOU MUST GO ON TRYING! Come on, I'll help you.'

I saw his eyes the size of a crown piece staring at me, willing and willing me to walk on. His voice came from a great way off and was muffled by the roaring in my ears. I did make an effort and took two more steps, right, left. Then the darkness through which I had been struggling rose breast high, closed over my head.

When it receded I was being carried along on Eli's back. He was bending over and breathing like a broken-winded nag; but he was moving along, one step and then another. I was overwhelmed with shame. 'Put me down, Eli, please. I'll walk.'

He straightened his back a little and my feet slipped to the ground. We stood still for a moment while he got his breath again. Then, 'Look,' he gasped, 'it's—getting—light.' Taking my hand again he began plodding forward.

With steps as slow as ours, but far more certain, the dawn came on and soon we could see one another. There was little comfort in the sight. Ghastly, blood-smeared, mutilated. We crept on for another quarter of a mile and then I stopped again.

'Eli,' I mumbled, 'I cannot take another step. And I forbid you to carry me. Go on by yourself. If you meet them in time you can come back for me. If you drag me along you'll be too late.' My tongue was so dry that it rasped in my mouth and the words tumbled out, unformed, almost unintelligible. Eli looked at me with bloodshot eyes and slowly shook his head.

'It can't be far now,' he said. 'We must bear up and go on together.'

Another painful furlong and then our path was crossed by a stream of water. A busy little stream, gushing along over small brown pebbles. We threw ourselves down and drank like dogs and it was not until we had drunk our fill that I said, 'We crossed no stream yesterday. We're lost.'

'God sent it,' said Eli simply. 'Like the manna.'

'But it means that we're lost,' I repeated.

'Not by much. They walked us West, then South. Today we go North, then East. The sun is on our right now. We can't be far wrong.'

'Let us sleep a little then,' I begged. 'We slept last on Saturday night. Sunday get ready. Monday fight. Tuesday in the trees. Eli, this is Wednesday. Let us sleep here then we drink when we wake.'

'Our one hope is to get on to the track. If they miss us where we broke off we may never be found. Or found by Indians and finished off so. Come on.'

We dragged ourselves through the shallow water and made perhaps another mile. By that time it was noon. I kept trying to think where the sun should now be if we were keeping to our course. But when I looked at it, it swung about and grew large and then small so that I knew I was in a high fever. We spoke no more. We had no strength left to speak with. Eli let go my hand and shifted his grip to the belt of my breeches, feebly trying to heave me along. My left leg was now a useless lump and I had to move it along with my hands.

All at once Eli's grip, instead of being helpful was a drag on me. He stopped, said something that I didn't understand and pitched forward on his face. I thought he would breathe better if I turned him over, but he was too heavy. I turned his face a little and scratched a hollow beside his nose to give him air. I wished we had not left the stream. And wishing that I lay down beside him and pain and weariness were swallowed in merciful sleep.

'Don't shake me,' I said, 'I'm not all in one piece any longer. If you shake me I shall fall apart and all the king's horses and all the king's men couldn't ... oh, don't shake me!'

That's not my voice. It's a woman's voice. Poor woman, Shad's being hanged today, and although nobody knows it she has been in love with Shad for many years. Almost as long as I have been in love with Linda. So she screams. Yes but that is because my father has suddenly shown himself in his true colours. You see, Mr. Seabrook, he isn't really a generous man. He only had you here because Mr. Gore mentioned that your daughter was beautiful. And she *is* beautiful. I've never told her so. Go, lovely Rose, tell her that wastes her time and me that now she knows. But knowing, will she care? I carried the roses from Fort Outpost to Zion. I set them in the ground for her, but it meant nothing.

Eli, you don't realise what you have done. Even now as we stumble over the red-hot floor of hell you don't understand. You married the one woman that I have loved, the one woman with her head put on so cunningly, the voice of honey, the mouth like a June rose. But you don't appreciate these things because you're mad. You said we were walking through manna, when all the time it was the ashes of hell. And if we can't walk we must crawl. Can't you see, Eli that I *cannot* crawl, when I put weight on my bad knee the whole thing goes dead. And you can't carry me either. You've got twins, the sons of Boanerges: that's enough for any man. You've got Linda, too. I love Linda. I've loved her ever since she wore a mulberry-coloured gown. It was all tied up in a bundle.

She doesn't love me, and she doesn't love you, Eli. How do I know? Oh, that's simple. I've seen her in love. Once she was in love with my father. And now she is in love again. I guessed it, that is my secret. My love makes me wise. Aha, I shan't betray her. The Indians tried to lay bare my heart to discover the secret, but I kept it well. I might tell you, my friend, because it concerns you. Here, bend down, promise not to breathe a word. Linda loves Geoffrey Montpelier. And can you wonder? He's young too, and beautiful and brave. And *merry*, Eli, a thing neither of us is.

Eli, please put me down now. I've told you all I know. It's no use shaking me. After all it's much worse for me than it

is for you because I love her, and you don't. You're better off
too, because you're going to heaven. I must stay in Hell.
Why do you stay with me, Eli Makers? You know my
secret now. And you don't owe me anything. I lent you the
gear for Linda's sake, not yours. And when I shot that bear I
did it despite myself because I didn't want your ghost between me and Linda. Please leave me to lie down and sleep.

I walk a few steps. I try to crawl. I talk very earnestly
to Eli who never understands a word I say. When he shakes
me, or tries to carry me I cry and cry, like a beaten child.
The whole earth tilts. I struggle up the incline and fall over
the edge into dark and bottomless space. Yet I find Eli there
and go on imploring him. At last I say, 'You've got strong
hands, Eli, kill me please.' And he does, for the next black
fall has no bottom : I am absorbed in its void.

When next I reached a conscious thought I felt as though
I were a piece of flotsam, washing in to shore on a strong
tide. I reached out my arms and seized something on which
to float, and found to my amazement that I was clutching a
cool soft pillow. I put my cheek against it. The tide, receded
suddenly, and there I was, blissfully at ease, cushioned from
all evil on my pillow.

Then Judith's face, all ruined with tears, looked down on
me from a great distance.

'Don't you know me?' she asked.

'I should if you weren't crying,' I said, 'What are you
doing here. Be careful. If the Indians get you ... it'll be
worse for you than it was for us.'

'You're home, here in your own bed, look,' she said. She
put her hand behind my head and raised me just an inch so
that I could look round. And there was the room and the
cupboard and the press for my clothes which I had looked
at in such a sad grey light one morning very long ago.

'Well,' I said. 'I never thought I'd see this again. Or you,
Judith.'

'And I began to think I should never hear you say a
sensible word again.'

She fussed around, smoothing the covers and plumping
the pillows.

'Would you like to eat some food now?' She gave one of
the little unsteady laughs with which women often follow

tears. 'Feeding you has been so funny. You would *talk* all
the time we were pushing sloppy things into your mouth.
You wouldn't swallow, often. You could have something to
bite on now, if you like.'

'Then I'll have bacon and egg,' I said.

She went out of the room swiftly, and I lay flat on my
back, savouring every evidence of returned sanity. The flat,
steady bed beneath me, the warmth of the coverings, the
sun pouring in through the window and making golden
pools on my good oak floor, growing every day more shiny
with the beeswax rubbed into it by Judith. I was safe. I was
home. For a moment or two I rejoiced in the mere realisa-
tion of the two facts. Then curiosity stirred. I could remember lying down beside the fallen Eli. That was clear
and vivid in my memory, but after that everything was
shattered, like an image in a broken mirror. Vague recollec-
tions of being shaken, being dragged, being carried, of
crawling up steep slopes of pain and tumbling into darkness
on the other side. I found myself awaiting Judith's return
with impatience. Who had found us? How was Eli? I had
so many things to ask.

My fingers strayed up to the gashes. They were gashes no
longer, but long-ridged scars, sensitive, but not agonising to
the touch of my careful fingers. I felt my nose. It was its
normal size again though the bruised bone ached when I
pressed it. I must have been in this bed for some time.

Judith returned bringing a tray. I could smell the coffee
and the appetising scent of fried bacon.

She lifted me carefully and doubled the pillows behind my
head.

'Tell me,' I began, 'how long have I been here? How is
Eli? Who found us? Has there been any more trouble? Tell
me everything.'

'There you go,' she said. 'It's been like that all the time, the
moment I brought food into the room off you went, jabber
clack, jabber clack. Now you take the food as I give it to
you, and use your mouth for eating and I'll tell you everything.'

'Eli brought you in, ten days ago. You were both as mad
as Bedlam. How he did it nobody can understand. He says it
was the guiding hand of God, but I want to know why, in
that case the guiding hand didn't bring you straight back,

278

not let you wander about for a week. All the same it was a miracle. You'd had nothing but water, I should think, judging from the bags of bone that you both were, and Eli was right down on his hands and knees with you on his back. He came crawling through the woods just by the Mill. He fell down at Ralph's feet and said, 'I have kept the faith; I have finished the course.'

'And by God, he had,' I said, not stopping to empty my mouth before I spoke. 'He's a man in a million, Judith. If you had seen . . .' The picture of Eli plucking himself free from the bond of his own flesh came before me, and I shuddered. 'How is he?'

'A better man than you are,' said Judith, 'he was back in his right mind in twenty-four hours and up and sitting in the sun within a week. Really, I shouldn't think any of the miracles in the Bible made more excitement. They'd been searching and searching for you, you know. And then they found poor Bluey with an Indian knife still in her spine. She'd run until she dropped and was miles from where you'd last been seen. We gave you up then and your names were mentioned at the service along with the other dead. You'd be surprised to know how well Mr. Thomas spoke of you.'

'I'm sure I should.'

With my head at an awkward angle I drained the coffee cup and handed it back to her.

'You should sleep now,' she said, lowering the pillows and speaking like a mother to a child.

'I've slept long enough. I want to see everybody. I *must* see Eli. If he can't come to me I must go to him. And Mr. Montpelier, and Andy. I must see them all.'

'I'll fetch Andy. I know where he is. He'll be pleased as a dog, poor little devil, to know you're back in your senses. He used to come in and look at you and you used to say the most terrible things to him—and to me—at times. We'd got almost used to the idea that we would be tending a lunatic for the rest of our lives.'

She made this confession of faith and loyalty as she loaded up the tray, casually, as though she had no idea of its implication. Suddenly there came a thin shrill cry from the depths of the house kitchenward and she snatched the last plate and poised it unsteadily and carelessly on top of the cup and made for the door.

'What was that?' I asked.

She pretended not to have heard me and went out without answering, closing the door meticulously behind her. After a time there was a step outside, and a whisper. Andy said, 'I'll say nought. What do you take me for?' and then came in. He stood by the bed in which I had roused myself to look in as good shape as possible and took one of my hands in both his hard horny ones. His little grey eyes were moist and he was obliged to take away one hand in order to smear it across his face, giving a little cough to distract attention. 'Well, Andy old man, I'm glad to see you. How's your shoulder?'

'Right well again, master. How's yourself?'

'Doing fine now.'

There was a little silence while we stared at one another. Dear, familiar, homely face.

'If I ever get athin reach of one of them devils I'll givem hell. I'll flayem alive,' said Andy.

'If it ever comes to a scrap again I shall go to it in a more vicious mind myself I will admit. Tell me Andy, what was it that you were to say nought about?'

'Nothing,' said Andy, lying valiantly.

'There's a baby in the house, isn't there?'

'I seen none.'

'Don't lie to me, Andy. What baby is it? One of yours by any chance?'

He grinned and said more confidently now that he could be truthful, 'I haven't got a baby in all the time I've been here, master.'

'Too bad,' I said. 'That must be attended to. Whose is the one in the kitchen?'

'Somebody called to inquire about you, I guess.'

'Oh, I see.' He had had time to invent a plausible answer. But that didn't explain Judith's haste, or the whisper outside the door.

'Where's Mike?'

'Over to the Gap. Poor Mrs. Crane took her boy's death very hard. She bin ailing, don't sleep a nights. Mike git over there most days with a little something soothing. She wouldn't half carry on do she knew her sleeping medicine come half outa Mike's rum cask, would she?'

280

I laughed as I was expected to. Then I said, 'I sent for you, Andy because I want to get up. I didn't fancy Judith helping me into my breeches.'

'She wouldn't mind,' said Andy. 'But I dassent help you.'

'Watch me then,' I said, throwing back the covers.

'I dassent do that either, master. Judith'd bawl the head off me.'

'Then get out and know nought. You're good at knowing nought, aren't you Andy? Don't be a fool, man. I'm of age, I'm in my right mind. You can't treat me like a child. What is it I mustn't be told? It's about Eli, isn't it? You've both lied to me, he's dead. Of course he's dead. I might have known. No man could have done what he did and live.'

I sat for a moment swaying on the edge of my bed, then, hopping, crossed the space between the bedside and the press. It was on the opposite side from Andy and he had to round the foot in order to put his hand on my arm.

'All right, I'll get what you want. You take it calm now.'

But I couldn't be calm. If anything had happened to Eli—and even in that moment I thought, 'God forbid,' I must get to Linda. 'My shoes, Andy,' I snapped. 'My shoes. They're the most important.'

'Eli ain't dead. Lively as a colt he is,' he said, diving under the press and rising again with the freshly polished shoes in his hands. 'Little did I think when I shone 'em that you'd ever ask for 'em again,' he added thoughtfully.

'Then what the hell is this mystery?'

'It's Mrs. Makers.'

'Not dead?' I asked in so sharp a voice that I startled myself.

'Aw no. Not dead. You know I reckon you shouldn't be outa bed yit. You sit down nice and comfortable and let me explain like.' So I sat down on the bedside and was glad to for my heart was bounding about all over my body and my newly resurrected mind was recoiling from this fresh blow.

'There now. Well it seems like Mr. Montpelier was very struck with Mrs. Makers, the first time he seen her. He used to meet her down in the wood by the river. Nobody knew but Judith. You know what women are, always know when another is up to some trick. She seen 'em several times, but she didn't say nothing. Well, on the Sunday afternoon afore we rode out, you remember, they was there again, and Judith also, listening for all she was worth. She heard them arranging that if all went well and he come back Mrs. Makers'd leave Eli and go away alonga him. See? But Judith didn't tell about that neither till we come back athout you and athout Eli. 'Twas well known that Mr. Montpelier had seen you last. Then Judith up like a crazy thing and accused him of killing Eli so's he could hev his missus athout a lotta bother and killing you too because you was there, see? Excuse me, master, but whether you know it or not, that girl is main fond of you. Right wrapped up as they say. Maybe you know?' He cocked his head on one side and looked at me questioningly.

'Get on with the story,' I shouted, 'and don't ask fool questions.'

'Well, a crazy woman shrieking these things all over the place had to be took some notice of and people started remembering. Mr. Montpelier did stop ahind alonger you two for a bit and we had all heard a shot. We'd halted too, not knowing what it might be. Then he come a-running up saying as he'd shot his poor mare and acting very upset.

'Nobody had any doubt at the time. But when Judith come out with her accusal nobody could remember seeing Eli or you after the shot. She made sich a uproar that Mr. Thomas and Mr. Crane put Mr. Montpelier under arrest on suspicion and as soon's it was light a Wednesday out we went a-searching. I went along, sleep or no sleep, shoulder or no shoulder. Judith came too, with a nasty-looking pistol in her hand what you give her she say, and if we find evidence against Mr. Montpelier she confides to me she's a-going to shoot him and Mrs. Makers and all. And I shouldn't have stopped her.

'Well we found Mr. Montpelier's mare with the bullet clean through her brain and that shook the story a bit and then days arter we found poor old Bluey with the Indian knife in her backbone. But neither fur nor feather of you two did we find.

'So back we come and Mr. Montpelier laughed and said, "A jealous girl and the story of Uriah the Hittite give me the narrowest escape I ever had," and went off and made Mrs. Makers a proper proposal which she took. Next day Eli walked, or ruther crawled in with you on his back. But the show wasn't over, oh, not by no means.

'Crazy as coots the both of you were and Mike sue you up and we got you to bed and in a day's time Eli was sensible agin.

'Mr. Thomas called on him then and told him he'd got sumpin wholly peculiar to tell him. You see the pair was planning to get married next week and though everybody thought that was rather soon there wasn't any real reason agin it. Eli shut him up quick. "I know it," he said, "so you cin hold your peace. The voice of the Lord told me all about my wife and Mr. Montpelier what time I wrestled in the wilderness." Ain't that a mastrous amazing thing? "If he want her he can have her," said Eli. "Never shall she cross my threshold or tend my sons agin."

'Arter that nobody in all Zion'd have either one of 'em in. But, to make matters wuss, if that was possible, on the day we found Bluey Mr. Dixon handed Mrs. Makers a letter that was supposed to come from you in the event of anything happening to you. On account of what you writ in that Mrs. Makers come up here and said you was her only friend and couldn't she and Mr. Montpelier come here and wait till his head was better and they'd reckoned out what to do. Mrs. Makers said that if you was dead it'd all be hers, see, and you wouldn't want her turned away from the door. But Judith was like a tiger cat.

' "He never knew you for what you are," she said. "I do. And even if he die you come in here over my dead body." There was a mastrous proper upset I can tell you. And to add to it, there was you up here, every time anybody come in, a-bellowing and a-bawling about ladies sweet and kind and Eli going to Heaven and so on. Do you still want your shoes?'

'Tell me one thing more. Where are Mrs. Makers and Mr. Montpelier now?'

'Half way to Salem if they've had ordinary luck. There was nobody'd takem in see? So they stopped down at the meeting house till he could get some horses. Fifteen gold guineas apiece he give too. And then they set off. Mind you, I think they're wrapped up in each other right enough. They went off looking happy as kings, she wearing a kind of purple dress I never seen afore under her cloak and her hair all curled and showing.'

'All right, Andy. That's all. You can go now.'

'And I ain't upset you like Judith said I would if I told you.'

'I'm not a bit upset Andy. Thank you for telling me so nicely. And now go. Go quickly before I burst into tears before your eyes. Before I scream and beat my pillow with my fists. Before I . . .'

'I'll go and meet Mike and tell him you're yourself agin. It'll be the best news he ever had,' said Andy happily and shambled away.

I went on sitting on the edge of the bed; but I had hardly begun to think before Judith opened the door and peeped into the room. Her face was a study in mingled concern and relief.

'Andy says he's told you.'

'And why not indeed?'

'Don't take it too hard,' she said. The softly comforting, almost caressing tone of her voice grated on my nerves.

'Why should I?' I asked savagely. 'So you've got Eli's twins downstairs?'

'Well somebody had to have them. He was in a fix, being ill himself. And though Keziah offered to take them he wouldn't let them go to the Gap. And though I never liked him, nor he me, I was grateful to him for bringing you in.'

'What's going to happen to them now?'

'Mrs. Will Lomax is going to move in. She and Edith never got on so well after Edith married. Some of the men are putting up another room at Eli's now.'

Her eyes travelled to my feet, dangling over the bedside.

'Come on,' she said. 'You get back into the warm and I'll tuck you in comfortably.'

I submitted meekly, partly because of weakness, partly to get her out of the room. But when she had gone and the warmth of the bed was soaking into me, soothing and relaxing, I knew that I couldn't stay supine there another minute.

Some strange compulsion was on me. If I gave in now I was ruined, finished, done for. I might even lie there and go quite mad.

I flung off the covers again, reached down and found my shoes, thrust my bare feet into them and stood up. My bones were all jelly and my ears roared, but I went on, supporting myself by the bedpost, the corner of the press,

284

the handle of the cupboard door until I had collected all the clothes I needed. I chose a clean shirt and the good clothes that I had laid away on the night before the battle.

For a little while the business of dressing, of arranging the clothes carefully and unhurtingly over my scars demanded all my concentration, but at last it was finished and I sat down in the chair by the window and gave myself up to my thoughts.

The trees in the valley were all in leaf, a green veil of beauty spread out in the sun. From across the river I could hear the sound of hammering, the extra room going up in the house where Eli was rebuilding the life that Linda's defection had only shaken for a moment. And over there was the Gap and through it Linda and Geoffrey were riding down to Salem and a new life together.

'Happy as kings.' Well, I must be glad of that. They would be happy too, both beautiful, young and lighthearted. From him Linda would have all the adoration, the pretty speeches, the consideration that I had longed to give and which Eli had denied her. I thought of the conversation that Geoffrey and I had held as we made our way to Troubled Moon's camp. I could not have chosen better for her had the choice been mine to make. He had the poet's eye and heart: he had come to anchor after long dalliance: he had a lucky star. What more could even I ask, even for Linda?

Step by step, from that first meeting in Hunter's Wood, from Marshalsea to London, from London to Salem, from Salem to Zion I traced the course that my love had led me. Sadly I reflected that I had been in the pest house when Linda turned to Eli, and when she was begging at my door for shelter I was wandering in the land of a demented mind. I had loved her, followed her, tried in small ways to serve her, but I had failed her every time. It looked as though it had all been wasted, the effort, the sweat and the blood; one with the million acorns, only one of which can hope to grow; the million spawning fish of whom the majority merely make food for the others.

But there was more in it than that. Sitting there by my open window, looking out across the blossoming valley I was forced to admit that my love, though benefiting the recipient little, had infinitely enriched me, the giver. To me

Linda had been incentive and inspiration. For her I had shouldered a burden that I might have shirked for ever, a man's place in the world. Because of her I had broken away from my ancestral home, from my father's rule, from the limits of my own physical disability. I now had a place that had been made by Philip Ollenshaw, not by some other Ollenshaw away in the past. I had my acres, mine because I had sweated over, not inherited them. I had my friends, faithful Mike, Andy, Ralph and Eli, who were my friends because I had won them and they had won me, not because we had been to school together or because our estates marched alongside one another.

And there was Judith too. Back at Marshalsea I should have thrown her an odd coin and bidden someone look closely to the hens and the linen spread to bleach while she was about. Here at least there was no artificial barrier of that kind. Here she had ministering hands, a loyal heart that even lunacy or death could not alienate.

Yes, I had benefited by my love. Linda had given me more than she knew, not only the poetry, the call of the spring, the moonlight, the stars and the flowers, but the humble prose of life, independence, a place, the good sweet bread in my bin. And now I must set her free. Eli had let her go and I in another case and from another cause must be as generous. All the hooks of desire, the nets of imagination must be loosed now. Into the intimacy of Linda and the man she had chosen even my mind must never pry. From now on the account between us was settled and it must be as though Linda had never been.

Around me the life in Zion would go on, deepening and strengthening and multiplying. With gun and plough we should go forward, as Eli had gone forward, beaten to the ground by pain, madness and exhaustion, yet sharing the last beat of his brain and his blood with me. The thought of Eli reminded me that I had still Nathaniel's charge to keep....

Linda had gone out of my life as he had entered it, beauty in a mulberry coloured gown. But even without her life remained. For a little while the wound would ache, but it would heal, it would heal, and then I should marry Judith. There would be children. And of them, if not of us, the solitary places would be glad. For them, if not for us, the wilderness would blossom like the rose.